THE MUSTEE;

OR,

LOVE AND LIBERTY.

By B. F. PRESBURY.

To hold you fast doth still my heart implore me,
  Still bid me clutch the charm that lures and flies:
Ye crowd around; come, then, hold empire o'er me,
  As from the mist and haze of thought ye rise.

FAUST, *Brooks's Translation.*

BOSTON:
SHEPARD, CLARK & BROWN.
1859.

ELECTROTYPED AT THE
BOSTON STEREOTYPE FOUNDRY.

PREFATORY.

In fleeting tide among these silent leaves,
The mystic current of my dreaming flows,
And, gliding onward, in my soul there glows
The hope that o'er its deepest murmurs breathes
A tone which will not tremble to its close,
E'en when the cloud that dims my country's stars
Shall vanish in the holy light it bars.
Whence are the thoughts that like the morning soar?
Thrown up like pearls are they along our shore
By the deep waves from some diviner sphere?
I know not how within my heart appear
The rays now joining the auroral gleam;
There seems a spell upon me while I dream,
And in weird whispers come — "You but transmit the beam."

Taunton, Oct. 23, 1858.

THE MUSTEE;

OR,

LOVE AND LIBERTY.

CHAPTER I.

We do not make our thoughts; they grow in us
Like grain in wood. FESTUS.

"ARE you still feeding on law-calf and sheep?" inquired Anthony Featherstone, as he entered the office of Brian Park, on returning from a somewhat protracted pleasure excursion.

"Even so," was the reply of the student.

"But you are trying the dust of Lyttleton and the bones of Coke once more!" said Featherstone, with surprise; "I thought you had studied law, and been called to enter upon its practice."

"I have so far prepared myself as to be permitted to commence the practice," replied Park, laying down his book; "but to have thoroughly mastered the voluminous and profound science, only those who have grown old and continued lovingly constant can lay claim to have done."

"That may be," said Featherstone; "yet I do not intend to bend over it as I have hitherto; for when I was admitted to the bar, I considered that the world was laid open to me far wider than it had been; and I intend, as I may be able, to look in upon its shows, and taste its various vintage, as well as to climb the steep where laurels grow."

"You think so, I have no doubt; and it may be even as you imagine," replied Park. "Still you may behold, also, in the same magic glass, whose rosy pictures fill you with such hope, the shadows of the dangers which follow the votaries. You can see, if you will, how the merest trifle may prevent you from enjoying the one, ill health, which lies in wait there, deprive another of all its charms, while a single misstep, taken within its tempting precincts, shall put the last beyond your aspiring grasp."

"But to acquire the means for pleasure has been my chief spur throughout all the fagging toil of preparation," urged Featherstone. "Would you have me now, when she begins to appear before and beckon to me, and whisper of reward, pass her by unrecognized? Do you see any weakness in me, or want of power, that raises this ghost of failure to flit before your eyes?"

"Not want of power, certainly," Park replied; "but economy of strength, singleness of purpose, a sleepless devotion to one aim, making continual and untiring shots at one mark, until you have trained every faculty to sight on that centre. Such competitors there are on every shining path; hence he who desires to ascend must arm himself to meet them; and, so armed, lie down with his weapon chained to his wrist, and rise up to give it edge, or to acquire new dexterity in its use. Lord Mansfield declined marriage even, that he might reign supremest of chancellors."

"If I occasionally visit a way-side bower," explained Featherstone, "it will be only for refreshment or repose; they cannot bind or enervate; on the word, I shall go forth, nor cast a single lingering glance behind. I do not intend to avoid exertion or struggle even; yet I must and will have some change, as constancy appears to me stupid and monotonous."

"I think that I understand you," replied Park; "and the better, because what you say of yourself accords with my own observation. But these fair-seeming pleasures take time, and that is the least of what they take — their fires consume either strength or heart, goods which none of us can well spare. You smile, as though you thought yourself invulnerable; and I am aware that your bodily health and constitutional vigor are remarkable; yet I know, also, the tastes and appetites that must be laid, like weeds, in order that something nobler may spring there — something worthy of the gift of life. If you did not like the study of the law, you should not have vowed yourself to it; for *it*, also, can only be conquered by love; and when one loves, he cannot be easily enticed away."

"If I had wealth," said Featherstone, "I would not open another law book. Indeed, I never pretended to like the study for itself, but only for what it promised to give. I labored for future reward; and I supposed that you were doing the same; though I think I see now where you stand, because I perceive there is a striking agreement between your preaching and practice. Yet we are unlike; so much so, that we have never come in contact, and therein may be found the reason why we have gone on so smoothly. I look back now and see that you carried off some of the honors of the classes, not because yours was the strongest arm, but by the cunning use of your weapons: and yet, after all, the dexterity was natural to you; hence it was easily developed, so that you took the appropriate rewards without the toil of many who failed; and you may continue to take, without exciting either envy or emulation in me, for the world has richer prizes.

But you will give me leave to say that it is the fault of men of your cast of mind to see no other course than your own for any man. Yet the most promising rarely walk the path you prescribe."

"It may be so, and is so frequently," replied Park; "and observation of it is not without a lesson of wisdom; for if they, the gifted,

'The primrose path of dalliance tread,'

their fire will grow dim. What has become of the young men who were the bright particular stars when we first went to the university? Where is A., the wit? paragraphing for the newspapers. Where is C., the poet? dead of his excesses. Where is P., the brilliant debater? ascended to a desk, in a room with twenty others, at the Custom House! Now, I do not name these men to jeer at them, but to seriously ask why so much promise was obscured or quenched. Is not the answer obvious? namely, because they believed in the sufficiency of their genius — which fact flings a doubt on the possession. For what is Genius? certainly not a patent to exempt from application; but rather to do that with love which all others must bend to as a task: it is to have a predisposition, by nature, to something great and glorious, so that we can cheerfully pour time and strength, and even life itself, as libations for its approving smile. And if we turn to the wine cup, or the bower of Calypso, of what avail will be the radiant gift, except to make those whom we may meet there the more charmed, and consequently the more persuasive to detain? Indeed, who that does not soar on its pinion can hear the voices which lure one down? You will not suspect me of merely playing the preacher in these remarks; on the contrary, you may believe I am seriously aiming to lay open life so that I may realize it unto myself; for I have entered the lists with an unblazoned shield, and see before me the pennons of the brave and the arms of the mighty."

"I know that you are ambitious," said Featherstone, "and, if you live long enough, will be likely to accomplish your purpose, whatever it be; and you may think it your pursuit of happiness. But do not wrecks lie all along that path also? Even most of the successful few, who, cutting through every obstacle, at length reach the height, all covered with scars, find only a 'barren sceptre in their grasp.' Yet, after all, this knowledge does not deter the brave — and it is something to have so aspired — only the finest of the Alpine peasants become the hunters of the chamois."

"It is discipline and practice that make their daring successful," replied Park. "I have many times admired the vigor of your arm for a single blow, and have seen the luckless debater stagger before it; yet you could not follow up and demolish him; for, relying on native strength, you had neglected the science of offence and defence. Indeed, the wild forces of the mind seldom bear conviction with their exhibition; while the trained thinker can forge a chain of reasons which shall bind you to the remotest thing. You may struggle against it, but you will only rattle your fetters until a more able mind severs them link from link, and redeems you from the bondage. And, by way of illustration, I have been reading this morning an opinion of our Supreme Court, overruling a decision of twenty years' standing. During that period persuasive advocates have assaulted, flaming declaimers have stormed it, in vain; while now it goes down before the scientific approaches of a cold and acute reasoner. Looking upon this, and kindred triumphs, I regard reasoning as a fine art, and one in which it is very difficult to win the highest success, requiring, as it does, that patience and persistency of thought which only an iron will can enforce.

"The ablest reasoner of our time, and not surpassed in any, on the facts of a case and the principles of law that could be made to apply to it, came with a poet's gifts from the hand of Nature. Yet he devoted himself with all patience to the art of discipline, until not only the drill was complete, but even the uniform made sober! In the course of a long life he went down to many great fields, and, although he has given them to the memory of the ages, no man ever saw him call all his reserve into action. Calmly and warily he surveyed the hostile lines, until he had searched out the weak place; then, on it, he columned up, and bore down, and clove deep, always to fame's wreath, if not to the victor's crown. Yet, throughout all, though endowed with an imagination the most soaring, he seldom took wing whenever he felt the earth firm beneath his feet. Only here and there some high-flaming bannered thought outrolled to 'the sun in the heavens' as he broke through his opponent's defences, and swept over the disputed ground.

"Though destined to such meridian splendor, dark clouds beset his rising; and even far up the morning only faint gleams of light laced their folds. Still he bore on. And if there were times when he sought for repose in some obscure place, he yet pressed forward when the breath of friendship or the fire of genius rekindled hope — so with alternate heat and cold the blades of Damascus were tempered."

"No one admires the display of such powers more than I do," said Featherstone; "but, if they are only to be brought out and subdued to use by such long and laborious training, I shall not aspire to their perfect mastery. Others might enjoy it, I could not: he may be an example for you, but not for me. You may continue to pour water on your napkin, and bind it around your forehead to drive away sleep in the still night, while you bend over the pages of your Coke on Lyttleton, but I shall look for my pleasure elsewhere; and, when I find it, help myself at once, for it aggravates me to see any one leave to the chances of to-morrow that which might be tasted to-day."

"As you have led the conversation back to yourself," said Park, "permit me to say that you appear to have no fixed principle; at least, your words import that you mean to be governed chiefly by impulse. Now, much of it may be good, I grant; but some of it will be likely to be wrong, and all of it must be reckless."

"Well, perhaps it may be so," replied Featherstone; "and I know you are a different being; but does it follow that you are a better? You speak as though you thought your plan proceeded from principle! Yet I understand it to be nothing more than a system spun from expediency. You may fortify your path with reasons; but those, too often, can only justify it to yourself. Simply because you have determined to take no step in life without calculating its consequences, must I infer that yours will be a worthier course than mine?"

"Safer, perhaps," said Park, smiling.

"For the time, it may be," said Featherstone; "yet in the long run — well, we shall see. But, by the way, and to change the subject, — for I am tired of this, — I met your cousin, Mrs. Fardel, at one of the watering places a few days since, though I presume she has returned to the city, as I have received her card for next Wednesday evening; and may I inquire if you think of wasting an hour in such a way-side bower?"

"That is my intention now," replied Park, smiling; "although, generally, I take no great pleasure in large parties. Yet it is a part of my system, as it pleases you to call it; for one makes the acquaintance of men of business in such places who may be shaped into clients by a grave and taciturn demeanor, — which you know is natural to me, — with careful and concise remark when you can agree with them in opinion. I look upon this as fair ground, and on it I intend to neglect no opportunity of seed time, however remote may be the prospect of harvest. I suppose, as a matter of course, I shall meet you there."

"Not in *that* part of the field," said Featherstone; "but in the neighborhood you may — or at least I have so answered. Yet, your motives have so changed its aspect, I fear I shall not find the pastime and entertainment for which, it seems to me, such displays are intended. I had thought chiefly of dancing and feeding, together with some lively and interesting chat with youth and beauty, under circumstances so favorable to the display of their charms. But when I think, as your view has made me think, that success in my profession must be won before I can enter to compete for the prizes which are advertised there, (for we are about sure to be told what each one is marked at!) it appears to me it would be only an aggravation to look into the market."

"Yes; every thing is bought, though the noblest can only be paid for in kind," replied Park. "And your reflection brings up our starting point, namely, that business must come before pleasure to those who have to strive for themselves; or else they must so choose that their business shall be their pleasure. Happy is he who has found this last, and all honor wait on him who patiently follows the first."

"I admit your facts," said Featherstone, "and accept your inferences, and think I see through them as plainly as another; but I do not intend to be a martyr, and may sometimes turn aside for recreation, when I believe it will not seriously interfere with the march."

"I may have my dream, also," replied Park; "but I shall not attempt to awaken to its realization until the shadows of the night are passed, and a clear and steadily ascending sun assures me of the day."

CHAPTER II.

"Blood tells."

THE foregoing interview and conversation occurred in the city of New York, some few years since — the precise time being of little consequence now, as it will be made sufficiently apparent before the speakers vanish altogether from our view.

It is not to sketch the peculiar features of any singular and extraordinary crisis, that I take up the pencil and unroll the canvas: they might have appeared any time within fifty years; they may have been seen yesterday, they arrest the gaze of the thoughtful to-day; for the laws which reveal them are still strong in the will and high in the sanction of the makers; still rejoiced in by thousands who gather ease, luxury, and indulgence from their partial action. Consequently the elements from which my story evolves have no secret, mystic charm; for the nation and the world know them by heart! Yet, from the ocean-like vastness of the subject, there is still many an inlet unvisited, where the explorer may find room and food for meditation, the constructor here and there a relic from which he can reproduce the life long since shrouded in silence.

It is said that, amid the imperial splendors of her reception by Napoleon III., the Queen of England suggested the enlargement of the liberties of his people; perceiving, no doubt, that there must be less antagonism in the ruling of their realms, in order to give their alliance vigor and continuance; feeling that there was something disingenuous in their attitude, which would shake the faith of their subjects; knowing, also, that professions of liberty will not be accepted by mankind — for whose opinion it has come to be wise for princes to have a decent regard — when any who arm in its cause are inclined to absolute rule. If this be a truth of history, as it is of eternal logic, it should make us blush for our country, in its present unmistakable tendencies. For these states are not united for the single purpose of a war, but for all the unfolding, continuing influences of peace, and that, too, in the name of Liberty. Consequently, with an emphasis that no tongue can give, a single statute in a single state which is in conflict with this lofty ideal, calls for the most earnest and unceasing fraternal exertions of every disciple of the fathers, of every soldier of freedom, and of every lover of the enduring glory of the Union, until it be erased from the record.

Such a law far oversweeps its prescribed bounds. If it repel some, it may attract others, thus influencing the opinion and shaping the life of the remotest American. Indeed, one of the young men whose ideas and aims have been laid before you, will not escape its quicksands, although born and nurtured in a free state. But I anticipate.

Park and Featherstone were both reared east of the Hudson. They had been classmates in college, with the exception of one term that Park passed with the hunters on the prairies, on a plea of health, which he found in the bosom of Nature, our true nurse and teacher. They had also been fellow-students at law during a portion of their reading, and had opened office in the course of the same year in the great mart of our commerce. Sprung of thrifty and forehanded families, yet of an entirely different strain, — that of Featherstone being of traders, while Park's was from farmers, — their circumstances were made easy during their student-days; but the time had arrived when they were expected to take care of themselves. Indeed, they had already so far entered upon the difficult and doubtful struggle, that hope began to venture forth, and catch glimpses of a fair prospect. They were not better educated or deeper read, perhaps, than thousands of others who start in the great cities, and pass on with the crowd; but they had that intuitive knowledge of men, however it differed in degree and kind, from which the most adroit find it difficult to escape, and in which the mass of mankind place confidence. They both possessed personal attractions also; yet in these they differed as widely as in their mental constitutions.

Anthony Featherstone was a little under the medium height, well made, though perhaps a trifle too full for elegance; and if, to the close and critical observer, his extremities partook of the same fault, he was aware of it, and studied to make them appear comely; and, to the common eye, he quite accomplished it. In truth, he was particularly careful of the outward man; favoring bright colors, it might be, too much for the severest taste, although the world's passing glance was a commendation. This he saw, and it sufficed, for it was his aim; but we have raised him into view for a more searching scrutiny.

The face of this "fine-looking man"—so the multitude called him—was nearer round than oval, with a certain harmony of features; yet no single one seeming as if Nature had lingered over it with her cunningly-forming hand. His forehead was ample, though not commanding, and around it flowed hair, black, glossy, and curling. His eyes were of the same dark hue and bright lustre, yet prone rather to enforce than to win. Altogether, he looked resolute and determined, without any striking marks of serene courage or soaring thought. He was free and social, sometimes boisterous, even, laughing easily, though not deeply, yet disclosing such fine teeth in the act as to grace the emotion. If the tone of his voice gave the nice ear a more favorable impression of his lungs than of his heart, it was not without its attractions to many a listener; for, within certain limits, he was quick to perceive, and ready to reply, sometimes with wit, and never without force or meaning. He was sensitive to any thing that looked like a question of his power, for he estimated himself at his full worth; and if he saw but a shadow of impertinence, it opened in him a vein of irony which was hard to parry and difficult to answer. He had other traits also that keep one from being the pet of a coterie, or the plaything of the idle. Full of vigor, though of a carnal type, as if formed for labor, even muscular exertion, you could not look upon him without being persuaded that he had the capabilities for a man's work, and would do it, if circumstances so favored as to draw him away from the shoals of appetite and the rocks of passion.

Brian Park, whom the multitude thought plain, was of a different make and manifestation. He was much taller than Featherstone, with a smaller frame, and not so robust of muscle; paler, also, and with a less roving glance, he passed unmeasured by any, and unhonored by those who ornament the pavement. Yet closer viewed, his form, though light, was well proportioned and straight as an arrow; and if, beside some, he seemed like that winged shaft, his port gave you an idea that, however pliantly he might yield to grace and kindness, it would be difficult for force to move him. His face was long rather than oval, his jaw strong, his chin and lips firm and finished, with hair so brown and soft and long as to subdue the severe and mysterious brow even to gentleness. His eyes were gray, full and prominent, taking silent note of all things, yet without lustre, except when some strong emotion took wing and came flashing up to the light, to disappear on the instant, or to come forth in the felicitous phrase of a master. His smile was pleasing, even warm and winning, although it rarely overswept all the lines of his thoughtful features. Altogether, he seemed formed for repose in a world of agitation, appearing as if action were the exception of his nature, and gaining purity and power in long periods of musing. Not over-fond of solitude, he yet coveted silence, much preferring it to those cheaply minted words which form the chief currency of the hours; and, occasionally, there was something in his expression that showed how little he valued such intercourse. This caused him to be thought cold and unsympathizing by the many; for

"Your smilers guess not how
Beats the strong heart, though less the lips avow."

He was not a talker, in general society, however much the subject under discussion might interest him, although he sometimes uttered a pointed and vigorous remark that opened a new view to the discerning. He could also help a good converser, or confound a babbler, by the significance of his manner of listening; so that Pretension feared him, and even Gayety was shy, although he did not always decline her invitations, for she knew his silken hand to be sinewed with steel, and his mind set on something which she saw not nor desired to see, feeling that it was unsuited to her mirth. Still, his heart was full of kindness to the kind; and if it occasionally led him to join in their light laugh, out of a desire to please, he found it an unnatural or an unaccustomed exercise, making his face ache in the effort, while it rang false to his ear; hence it soon had an end. But if he found a thoughtful person in that region, he possessed the power to take her into a more charming circle, leading her down "through Deva's winding vales, or by the shores of old Romance."

These two young men had long kept up a kind of companionship, and were friendly — not *friends*, certainly, in any high sense of the word, for circumstances threw them together, as circumstances, but above all, development of character, will cause their courses to diverge. They were too unlike, or, more strictly speaking, too unequal, ever to have any fulness of communication. Featherstone's view of life, and his opinion of human nature, tended to make him wary; for he was gaining faith in the idea that "men are what they name not to themselves, and trust not to each other." But Park was so constituted as to keep his own counsel, until he should find in a wife a comprehension and a depth of love such as we sketch in musing, and color in dreams — sacred pictures, that fill the heart with yearnings, and strengthen belief in the divine intimations of our being. They were both men of good habits, as the world gathers the evidence and gives its opinion. Yet the one could see but little in his own heart to restrain appetite or ambition; while the other, in the earnestness with which he pressed forward, may have lost much wayside beauty, passing by many a bower of pleasure, with his eye fixed on some shining height, or dreaming of some distant Eden.

They had already become so much known that business began to seek them; their days of rehearsal were passing away, and the drama of their lives was opening into action. Its every shifting scene was of vital importance to them, and some of the more striking parts may not be without significance to us; yet they are only types of a host who are continually passing from shadow to shadow. The temptations which beset them were not singular, for they have been organized into law, sanctioned by custom, or excused by passion, and are as likely to catch us, or ours, in their toils as either of those whose trail we are about to take.

CHAPTER III.

She spoke, and turned her sumptuous head with eyes
Of shining expectation fixt on mine. TENNYSON.

ON one of those up-town avenues, which are now filled with blocks of brown stone dwellings shaped into beauty and decorated with magnificence by the hand of Labor, and inhabited by those who have the cunning art of appropriating the greater share of the proceeds of labor, stood the home that Park and Featherstone had been invited to enter.

It was a large, square mansion, having a door in the centre, with a piazza and colonnade running along the front and down the sides; and, sloping away from thence, there was a strip of velvet lawn fringed with flowers. The house was but two stories high, and for that reason it had a look of comfort, seeming to stoop to the passenger in friendly greeting; and especially so on the evening of the revel, when it was flung open, and every apartment and passage were bright with hospitable light. This illumination, together with the unclouded rays of the full-orbed moon, so defined the features of the surrounding space, that the birds talked of it in the shrubbery.

As the favored guests passed into the enclosure, they involuntarily drew a long breath, feeling that there was room for it, or because they had more confidence in the air; and some of the gentlemen lingered a few moments ere they entered, in homage to that crowning grace of the temperate climes, a luxuriant turf. Not often can cities show it, for the dust of traffic is hostile to its beauty. But when it does look out, green and fresh, how the children press their glad faces against the bars which protect it! how old men pause upon their canes to contemplate it! These last, indeed, had hurried by it for half a century; but as their vigor abated, and their feet grew weary, their greeting or their gaze became more frequent and friendly; for they mused and meditated that, when art, and wealth, and affection could do no more to arrest their declining steps, Nature, taking them to her bosom, would lay over their forms this her final mantle, renewing it with the tears of each succeeding spring time, and tenderly caressing it into beautiful unfolding through all her loving summers.

But the repose and pensiveness of the scene were changing. The fashionable hour of reception had fully arrived, and carriages were drawing up before the gates in rapid succession, and muffled forms were rustling past, so that, in the space of half an hour, most of the guests had entered.

The announcement and the consequent ceremony over, they turned away to give place to others, joining some group of their particular "circle," where they were soon talking of the beauty of the night, the lovely ride of the morning, the opera and the "divine" performers, and the gayety of the season, or on some of the less prominent topics which help to charm the hours. If there were a few who were too much embarrassed, or too diffident, for even that line of conversation, there was a table quite loaded with engravings, to which they could turn, and find in them an excuse for silence, or a theme for remark when they should calm their agitation: many of these were the most attractive, as their emotion sprang from the freshness of their presence in the gorgeous arena, and the supposed superiority of steady eyes and disciplined hearts.

The ladies of maturer years sought out comfortable seats, and those who had son or daughter present — though without seeming to do so — were approvingly, or, it might be, anxiously observing them.

The elderly gentlemen, some of them thin and yellow with application, disappointment, or dyspepsia, and others full and rosy from contentment, dulness, or digestion, having white locks and moist brows, were grouped together, and gravely discussing the success of old projects and the feasibility of new ones — this man's gains and that one's losses; in fact, taking up the conversation at the point where they left it, at the bank or the insurance office, when they separated to dine.

Young men shunned that group; and young ladies only approached it to vainly try to persuade their fathers to mingle in their pleasures; wondering in their light hearts, as they turned away disappointed, how any one could come to be so indifferent to that which to them was a crown of rejoicing, — little dreaming that the attractions of Plutus charm longer than those of Circe, and the seeming cold monosyllables of their fathers' speech were the murmurs of their deepest love.

Featherstone entered amid the press, and moved on with the current to receive and give the same greeting as they; for ceremony should be faithful to form, in word and smile, that all may feel an equal welcome. Yet, as he was a particular acquaintance of the entertainers, he remained near, and took occasion, when the tide ceased to flow in, to give and receive the words of friendship also, in their appropriate moments. Mrs. Fardel, indeed, liked Featherstone for the zest with which he entered into every thing, even the lightest amusements, and for a confidence that was seldom abashed.

On leaving her, he passed down the bright and imposing circles, touching at the various groups, and addressing his acquaintance in a lively manner and with an assured air, which would have made dull men envious had he not been politic enough to draw them out in passing; thus giving an impetus which kept them talking for a few moments after he had left, and for which they took credit, fancying it the offspring of their own minds! as if a windmill could move its arms without a breeze, or yield that which could nourish, from the motion, unless some grain be poured into the hopper.

Still farther on in the evening, the last of the guests, came Park; for he had adopted the rule of Mr. Pitt, with regard to parties; namely, to go late and leave early. He entered with that natural ease which makes so apparent the over-coloring of art, and passed on, amid the gay and glancing groups, without recognizing any one, took his cousin's extended hand, and retained it for a moment, while she looked up to him archly, rallied him on the lateness of the hour, and chided him for being a recluse.

"Not so much so but your kind invitation gave me pleasure," said he.

"Well, your eyes can kindle yet," she replied. "But you must not pore over those dingy books so unremittingly: they will change you to parchment. It is the amusements of life that keep us young."

"Keep us smiling, you mean. Yet I have seen smiles which were only the witnesses of a weary and worn-out nature. I will remain in my closet, and plough my face deep, ere such weeds shall flourish and fade there."

"Ah! I cannot permit you to moralize now. I require gayety! In the midst of such waves you must be light as the foam."

"Then you wish me to be a bubble of the moment?"

"Yes; that is the finest accomplishment of the hour, and one of the most difficult of attainment; for, like those airy nothings, you must instantly reflect every light and color, and be as brilliant and changing."

"But suppose you are before those who have no light or color which it would please them to see reflected?"

"What a supposition! But, in that case, you may float on to a fairer presence. And now I wish to introduce you to some friends."

The ladies to whom she presented Park were visitors in the house from a distant city, and had that tact, vivacity, and graceful ease, which society cherishes and honors: and gliding into conversation with them, he was borne like a feather onward, until he wearied of the flash and play, and felt the limits to be oppressive; for the tendency of his mind, however lightly moved, was to sow truth, as the thistle-down, while seeming to wanton with the air, is bearing a seed across the continent.

From this, however, he was soon relieved by the presentation of other persons. As he turned away, Mrs. Fardel took his arm, and, speaking low, said, "I wish you would always be as interesting: you really charmed me. And you must come and dine with us on Sunday, for one of my friends is an heiress, and I think she will just suit you; I am certain that it would be a capital match. So, if you see a very beautiful young lady here, you must remember that you are engaged." And meeting her husband at the moment, she added, "Love, here is cousin Brian; and, as he has recently come in, I wish you to see that he does not immediately disappear."

The dapper little man expressed his pleasure at seeing Park in his house once more, and said, "How singular! I was thinking of you when we met, as I wish to introduce you to one of our city beauties."

"You are very kind. Yet I think that I must be excused, as I am shy of extraordinary beauty; for, unless there goes to it an intellectual strength great enough to perceive that a glittering casket must shrine a glorious gem, it can bring me nothing but disappointment, not to say disgust; as, after all, Nature is so economical in her giving, that, where I see the exquisite fashioning of her hand, I doubt the inspiration of the soul."

"How odd!" said the host. "But I do not think she can long escape your keen eye; and, if you happen to change your mind, I will forgive and present you."

Park moved on among the bright assemblage, bowing to the persons of his acquaintance, and giving his hand to two or three whom in his heart he honored; yet saying only the conventional commonplaces of the hour, as he shrank from disclosing any depth of tenderness to the worldling's smile or sneer.

At length he joined the gray and faithful votaries of Mammon; and entering slowly and carefully into the examination of the projects which they brought forward, the gleam of his intelligence lighted up whatever it touched, disclosing sterling worth or hollow pretension at will. As soon, however, as he saw that he had made the desired impression, and, by it, fully accomplished what he called "the opportune and necessary business of the occasion," he felt at liberty to look around him.

Moving from point to point, now pausing at the centres of attraction, and now gliding from the circle of the waltzers, he came near a group who were examining a copy of a Madonna, which had caught some faint rays of the original glory of the master's canvas.

The knot was formed of four or five young men and a lady. Among them Park noticed Featherstone; the others were not of his acquaintance, being of that exquisite class whose vanity leads them to flutter around beauty, and chatter of the Rhine voyage or of Italian sunsets, yet have no eye for the Hudson, or for the bannered pomp which follows the dying day over our western hills. But, in this presence, they entered not into his thoughts; they were lost in the radiance of beauty; for, there before him, was one who "once seen becomes a part of sight."

He had viewed many a vaunted beauty, and dreamed of Eastern bowers and houris' charms: but this surpassed his ideal. Rising above the common height, with every line gracefully curved and rounded, and her most fair complexion touched with that luscious mellowness of bloom, which only a peach in its summer ripeness and selectest perfection could approach, she dazzled the eyes and arrested the steps of Park. She was so formed, you might not say this or that was beautiful, for

> "Each feature into others flowed,
> As neck and bosom blended."

To keep the harmony, even the wealth of her dark hair was not displayed, but lay shapely to her perfect head, and coiled in a Grecian knot behind. Her robes were of the purest white, and as she stood with one foot advanced so as to disclose its shape even to the springing arch of the instep, he felt that she wanted nothing but the jewelled sandal to make her the ideal of Athenian perfection. And crowning all her queenly charms, and inspiring her loveliness, her ripe lips were crested with thought, and her eyes were a-flame with meaning, as if a Grace and a Muse were melted and moulded into one.

As Park came up, Featherstone was lamenting the scarcity of good paintings in America, and concluded by saying, "Yet, after all, it may be well, for it induces men to travel, which may liberalize even more than Art herself. Still, her galleries are among the chief attractions from over the sea; indeed, who is there who does not hope, some day, to see and enjoy the riches of the European collections?"

"I have had such dreams and such desires," she replied; "but when I stand beside a picture like this, I am reminded of what one of our profoundest thinkers and most original poets has said —

'Why need I galleries, when a pupil's draught
After the master's sketch fills and o'er-fills
My apprehension?'"

"That may be true, and it probably is the record of a certain mood of the mind," said Featherstone. "Yet there are a multitude of pictures among the vast number which the centuries have sanctioned that one wishes to look upon; and I hope, at some future time, to try all the charms of their variety."

"I have no doubt that it might be a pleasing pastime to rove like the bee from flower to flower, seeking for beauties as they search for sweets," she replied. "Yet the long-continued earnestness and devotion of the great artists lead me to hope for some revelation of a deep unity; it is that, rather than their variety, which would draw me to visit and study their canvas."

This remark seemed likely, by the way it was received, to change or terminate the conversation, as one or two were turning away, and there was an unmeaning smile on the faces of the others. Yet her eyes had met Park's in the midst of her last reply, as it were appealing from their inapprehension, and appearing to take cheerful confidence from his assenting glance, he turned to seek his entertainer.

Finding him in a moment, he said, "I have come to claim your promised introduction."

"Ah, indeed! Well, I shall be most happy; but you must permit me to find the fair lady first," replied the smiling and assiduous host, as he arose tiptoe and looked around.

On which motion, Park, slipping his hand within the arm

of the searcher, said, "Let me conduct you to her presence."

So, threading the groups, they crossed to the Madonna, before which they found her standing quite alone. Drawing near, their entertainer said, "Aurelia, (for he was one of those who like to take their acquaintance by their Christian names,) may I be permitted to disturb your devotions?" And as she turned upon him with a smile, he continued, "Allow me the pleasure, Miss Vernon, of introducing to you my friend, Mr. Park. And, as the refreshment room will be flung open in a few moments, let me persuade you to walk in that direction; and as you know the way to reach it, Brian, you will excuse me, and do the honors."

So, with rather an abundance of manner, he took leave, when Park gave his arm to Miss Vernon, and, soon after, they were partaking of ices and the delicious fruits of the mellow autumn.

They were not long, however, in finding their way back to the vacant parlors, and into the sphere of the Madonna's attraction.

Looking on the painting with pleasure, and remarking upon it with discrimination, Park at length said, "When I first saw you, Miss Vernon, you were near this picture, and gave utterance to an idea which so chimed with my own fancy that I made haste to know you."

"I think I observed you," said she; "was it not that suggestion about the unity of art, which closed the conversation, and dissolved the circle?"

"Yes, that was the thought," Park replied; "and it was well and appropriately said in this presence, for the Madonnas are a striking illustration of the truth of the idea, painted, as they have been, by so many limners, and in such different eras, yet all having a family likeness."

"There is yet a higher unity in the Christs," said Miss Vernon; "for the artists have frequently ventured to copy 'Mary Mother' from actual life, but rarely the Saviour; therefore his features and expression are more uniform, because more purely ideal."

"It is indeed true of all that I have seen, even to the form and softness of the meekly-flowing hair," replied Park. "In the lone vigils of the great masters, so far sundered both by time and space, there arose upon their vision the same sorrow-exalted soul. Yes, mighty ideas mould the features of men. The stern leaders of the commonwealth of England had a certain resemblance; and our Pilgrim Fathers as well. They literally set their faces to a great work, so that it entered into their very gait, and modulated all their steps. No artist can ever make us conscious of their indomitable purpose and unflinching aim, unless he traces their thought among fortified features and beneath corrugated brows."

"It is a pleasure to feel that even the hardest features will change in the fires of the mind and heart, and how all deep things tend to unity," said she. "In brightest hours I sometimes indulge the dream that I may yet walk those distant halls, which were hallowed by the victories of the pencil — for color is life — when there was a unity of faith that gave the inspiration."

"Do you like the studied forms and stately ceremonial of the Roman religion?" Park inquired.

"I confess they charm me sometimes, at least away from denunciation," she replied, "particularly when I call to mind through how long and fiercely destructive a period she nursed and fostered and gave shrine to art."

"Yes, she has done well in some things," said Park, "and must still continue to do, else how could she survive for a single year? Only the manifestation of a fonder love and a fuller liberty can cast her out from the hearts of men. Yet, with the deep-blue sky of Rome above me, I should be gazing upward, and would not hesitate to set my foot on the mitre, if I could hope thereby to descry her ancient eagles — types of that freedom which, to me, is more desirable than all art, and more vital than any mere form of worship."

"I believe that these loftiest of human emotions will yet arise above conflict," said she; "for when I think how august Liberty is, it appears to me that she must have a soul touched with the spirit of adoration."

"I feel your remark to be true, although the histories of the dead and dying sects do not give it confirmation," he replied. "Indeed, so far otherwise is it, that I see Liberty constantly withdrawing from the old forms, and leaping, with a joyous pulse, into the new. Yet, source of doubt and sorrow as this is to many, I observe how the pinions of Hope have expanded, and with what faith she soars, and take heart for the future."

The company, at that time, beginning to flow from the refreshment room into the parlors, and many drawing near, their conversation closed. Yet still standing together, while the young and gay were forming to music and gliding around, Park led her to the dance. This finished, having fulfilled her engagements, she declined further invitations, and soon after they moved out through the open casement on to the piazza, and into the soft evening air, — it might be to make room for the waltzers, perhaps for other reasons, — and walked down the path of flowers, bathing in the mystic, deep-flowing river of their perfume. There the night and the distance-mellowed music gave them tender, pensive thoughts and fond emotions, which, on many a succeeding day in each of our own sad histories, we have smiled or sighed away, as if they were only vapor, while, in reality, they were the celestial dews which sought to nourish and unfold the heart's holiest blossoms.

"What a change," said Park; "and that, too, by a single step into the presence of Night!"

"It is indeed a star-bright evening, and one that suggests thoughts far different from 'On with the dance.' It was a feeling that the serene silence was not in unison with his levity, which made Festus say —

> 'O Heaven, let down thy cloudy lids,
> And close thy thousand eyes.'

What a personification! As if the veiling of an eyelash could quench the sidereal fire!"

"It is a comprehensive image," replied Park. "And how he tosses the systems asunder in these lines on the final destruction! —

> 'He shook
> The stars from heaven like rain-drops from a bough;
> Like tears they poured adown creation's face.'"

"It does agitate them; they seem to tremble on their thrones," said she. "What a picture, and in what lightning-like vividness it appears!"

"Yes, in similitude he has no superior, either in excellence or affluence," Park replied. "The pages of 'Festus' are strown with gorgeous poetry; yet as a poem it did not greatly impress me. It is not well constructed; we are not drawn to its conclusions. I see the vision, but not the faculty divine. With all its sparkling spray and sky-ward soaring, it is but a fountain, while Tennyson's 'Princess' is a river; and though winding amid tropic bloom, and whirling with Orient passion, its deep and onward current is as resistless as the finest strains of the song."

"I like 'Festus,'" said Aurelia; "and though it does not strike as a whole, many of the pictures have imperishable beauty, like the evening which is passing. How fresh the air is, and what a charming place, seeming as if life, in such a home, might flow on fair and bright, as in some happy dream. What a treasure is a little garden ground in the midst of a great city! Are you fond of flowers?"

"Where they are strown so profusely as here, I soon tire of them. Yet when I turn a page of Nature's volume, by running water, or in some gorge of the hills, I see that they are the last touches of the Maker's hand, the perfection of his style. I feel a strange and pleasing surprise whenever I come upon the coy beauties in sequestered places, for there one appreciates their worth, and no true admirer can pluck them, seeing how it would devastate the landscape. If they be severed from the stalk, how quickly they droop, and fold themselves up, as if shrinking from the touch! Yes, I may well say that I like flowers, for I have looked upon and reclined among them in wild places, beyond the pioneer's cabin, and passed on my way leaving no soil upon their leaves. But garden blooms do not so affect me; they appear more familiar, and will touch your hand, as you pass near, caressingly."

"I have had but little opportunity to be a companion of nature," Aurelia replied; "yet I can fancy how the floral color might throw a fascinating smile over the stern and rugged features of the wilderness; and I shall never walk among field-flowers without thinking of their modest grace. But are you not unjust to the pansy in its lowly bed?" When stooping, she picked two or three that were near, and, placing them amid some of the lanceolate leaves of the sweet-scented verbena, presented them to Park, saying, "Those will fill a whole house with fragrance, while the wild appeal only to the eye."

Park received them from her hand with a thrill of pleasure; and, as they walked on, he selected a rose—not one that leaned near, but carefully chosen, and gave it to Aurelia, saying, "It is the queen of flowers, the first in beauty as in wealth of odor; and may I venture the hope that it will be as lasting, as a memento, as it is true as an emblem?"

Aurelia accepted the flower, and the words which flung a perfume on it, in a silence that was audible with sweet accord. It was one of those moments around which, in long after and perhaps lonely years, sad memory turns to linger and to mourn; or a happier fate leads fond recollection there to muse over the sweet dawning of a lovely day. They were so moved that both sought to veil their thoughts. Hence, when they resumed conversation, it was of passing things, and, returning to the house, they parted on the piazza, to join the gay and glittering crowd unobserved.

It was but a few moments, however, before Park departed, and soon the company took leave. And what a change! The rooms became silent, the lights burned dim, and then retreated to distant chambers, to at length vanish away just as maternal Night was withdrawing her stars from the warm glances of Morning.

At that still and most secret hour, Aurelia, in the privacy of her chamber, took the rose from her bosom, and unclasped her snowy robes, which, like fleecy clouds, obscured the heaven, with mingled, if not conflicting emotions, and sighing, said, "O, would to God that there were but we two in the world! then I might venture to dream of Eden. Yet I must not, I dare not, without wider search. O that such part should be allotted to me! but I shall try to enact it, or *her* frown will visit, and her despair haunt and moan, even among the leaves of the myrtle."

CHAPTER IV.

Disguise e'en tenderness, if thou art wise;
Brisk confidence still best with woman copes;
Pique her and soothe in turn, soon passion crowns thy hopes.
BYRON.

AWAKING early, Park gave the cool hour of the morning to reflection upon the scenes of the night, for the fascinations of congenial thought, made transcendent by the tender glance and queenly grace of beauty, had taken possession of his spirit, and borne it into that aerial realm where Imagination lays out the paradise and rears the palace, in which we dream of that supremest society — a single chosen soul. But all its "cloud-capped towers" toppled and fell before the glance of Day; and the host of mankind, resuming their march, broke and trampled on buttress and foundation, and Park turned away from the ruin to think of the enchantress.

So came the questions, "Who is she? Has she drawn near me for an evening's pastime, to return and forget? Yet even if she fondly remember the hour, there are barriers between us, there may be lofty ones, which I shall be years in bearing down; and will she cheer me, while I advance to the onset? On the course, what thrilling music her voice would be, what reward her smile! To feel that, by some invisible and celestial union, another lives in our life, is an inspiring emotion; under its influence, what might I not accomplish! Love, indeed, is the ultimate aim of us all; but I will not idly dream of that which, when we meet again, a glance may determine."

The house in which Park and Featherstone boarded was

presided over by a lady of the name of Summers, a young widow who wore her weeds so coquettishly and lightly, that well nigh the wooing summer air, certainly a sigh from almost any manly heart, could stir the dusky veil, and half reveal the lily and the rose; for the coy May time and the fresh June had passed, and July suns are magical in their unfolding influences. Indeed, she had quickly recovered from her connubial bereavement, for she was elastic in form and spirit. There was a deal of wisdom in her smile when things were mentioned concerning which she knew little, but desired to know more, and a corresponding look of unrecognition for those with which she was familiar, yet thought it wise to ignore. In short, she was good-natured and cunning, petite and pretty, talkative and sly, liking to hear much and willing to communicate something.

She was born in the city, in a family of that numerous class who claim to have seen better days, and had been taken from a milliner's shop by a middle-aged gentleman of dilapidated constitution and estate, for her skill in fascination. Stimulated by her charms, and urged on by his failing physical and pecuniary means, he sent her a few terms to a finishing school, married her in her twenty-first year, and at twenty-seven she was a widow. Soon after she became so, she consented to take a few friends into her family; only a "limited number," however, for the reason that her house was small. Yet on this account it was a desirable place, and still more that the rooms were large, one suit of which she reserved for the married, feeling more secure if there was a man of that class near her; while a lady, thus connected, was in a way of knowledge which is always interesting; and so, occasionally unburdening herself, she could exchange commodities to advantage. The other chambers of her house were occupied by, or reserved for, single gentlemen — ostensibly for the reason that they were better suited to their wants than to those of single ladies, but really, on account of their being able to pay higher prices, and passing less time in the house.

Mrs. Summers was wont to say of her way of life, whenever she thought it worth while to speak of it, "I was induced to take a few friends to board with me because I felt lonely after the death of my husband, not from any other motive, as I owned the place, and might have lived on the income, had I chosen to rent it: and I continue the practice, partly from habit, but chiefly from having learned that an active life is the most cheerful."

The truth, however, did not entirely come out in her statement, as there was a mortgage on the estate, and she had taken this way to lift it, and not without some prospect of success. She had no children, and made up her mind in the outset to take none as boarders. Referring to them, she would say, "They are all over the house, and forever into something, and damage furniture and waste food much more than their parents can believe, or for which they would be willing to pay." Consequently, when the suit of rooms became vacant, as they did by removal, or death, or some other act of nature, she Italicized in her notice, "None but those without children need apply."

The etiquette of her table was very carefully arranged, like many of the class, it being an attempt to make the restraint of the feeble appear like the repose of the great, every thing being reduced to the form and precision of a military drill — every thing except the conversation; and even that, for the most part, was so constrained from its natural life and motion, as to be a manufacture, an imitation, a poor counterfeit; yet few are so inane as to mistake the spurious metal. Still, *form* has this virtue, that it tends to impose silence, which Mrs. Summers perceiving, she closely adhered to it among the many, and gave way all the more freely to her pent-up spirits when with the few.

Our two friends did not appear to be particular favorites of their fellow-boarders, as they had but little to say to them; for Featherstone was usually busy at table, and Park was naturally silent, — a gift with which few people sympathize, — and neither of these characteristics were gratifying to the widow. Yet she wished them to remain, for she saw that they were men of more mark than the others of her household, and sought particularly to please them. On this account, they felt grateful to her, and, after a few months, began to indulge her in conversation, on the departure of the others from table, though not always in her vein; and seeing that she did not quite understand them, it soon became Featherstone's pleasure to mystify her more deeply whenever he saw opportunity.

In speaking of them to the married lady, when conferring together, Mrs. Summers would say, "I dread Mr. Park's glance sometimes when I am talking, for it confuses and puts me out, and then he will not say any thing himself. And Mr. Featherstone I do not quite understand, only that he is certainly hearty, and appears as though he might be *enterprising*," emphasizing the concluding word with a smile, as if it had taken on a meaning like that of "occupy," in the days of Dame Quickly; in which remarks, particularly that on Featherstone, touching his appetite, there was much truth; notwithstanding which he generally eked out his day's rations with a goodly number of oysters in some "saloon."

On the morning following the party, as Park sat waiting for Featherstone to finish his breakfast, the others having withdrawn, there was unusual animation on the countenance of the widow, while she inquired, "How did you like the party last evening, Mr. Featherstone?"

"I relished some portion of it," he replied.

"Did you not enjoy it all?" inquired she. "I fancied it would be a delightful reunion; and I hope you will be so kind as to give me, who have withdrawn from the gay world, the pleasure of hearing what particularly impressed you."

"I should like to give you pleasure," replied Featherstone; "but in the case to which you refer, as it made no especially delightful impression on me, I am at a loss to know how I can convey such to another; and you, of course, would not wish me to criticise or disparage that which was so freely given."

"You do not mean to say, Mr. Featherstone, that you did not enjoy yourself there! I heard that it was to be a very elegant entertainment."

"O, as to the table, that was various and magnificent," he replied.

"Indeed!" she emphasized; yet quickly added, in a softer tone, "but you certainly can tell me who appeared to be the belle of the evening?"

"That is dangerous ground," said Featherstone; "as, by so doing, I might offend many others; and then, at our next meeting, I should have a cold shoulder served up to me, to the injury of my appetite."

"That would really be a misfortune!" retorted she, with a wider meaning in her glance than he had intended to give to his remark. Whereupon she added, "Yet I do not see why you need fear it, unless you suppose that I would repeat your conversation."

"I have no apprehension of that," he replied. "And were we alone, I should take pleasure in gratifying your desire; but Park's judgment is so much superior to mine, that I defer to it. You must ask him."

"If I wished for a *legal* opinion I think I should," she quickly returned; "but in fashion and pleasure I thought you more likely to give me information."

"It is unfortunate to be so misunderstood; and I have no doubt but that he would be pleased to undeceive you in regard to his tastes; for he kneels at the shrine, while I only venture into the vestibule."

Perceiving at what Featherstone was aiming, Park immediately said, —

"I fancy something must have gone wrong last evening with Mr. Featherstone; and it may be that I can give the information which he seems to evade, rather for his own amusement than yours." And, thinking over the matter rapidly, it occurred to him that it was a favorable opportunity to sound the widow for any knowledge she might have of the family of the person in whom he had become so suddenly and so deeply interested — and not without hope of acquisition, as Mrs. Summers was one of that class who know a little about a multitude of people. With such end in view, he only made this general remark: "The party was a brilliant one; so much so, indeed, that it was all that the receiver, or even the giver, could desire." Thereupon, as he perceived that Featherstone supposed he would evade or defer the point to which he had turned the inquiry, he immediately added, "And among the beautiful, although I may not have seen all, I venture to say that a Miss Vernon was conspicuous. And to this Mr. Featherstone I think, will assent, as I saw him lingering around the 'vestibule.'"

"I only observed her a moment, as I found that she was a transcendentalist," Featherstone replied.

"What is that, pray?" inquired Mrs. Summers.

"Something which I do not understand, neither am I desirous to," said Featherstone; "as it is mystery beyond flesh and blood, and I am not yet ready to part from those."

"Vernon?" said the widow, turning to Park. "I once knew a family of that name; and the old gentleman used to look into our window frequently. They had a daughter Aurelia. Is that the name of your beauty?"

"I think I heard her so called," replied Park; "yet I may have misunderstood."

"Aurelia Vernon!" said the widow. "Well, I should not be surprised, as she must be twenty years of age now, and she had a bright face then. If it is that family, I remember them. Indeed, I knew much of them formerly, as we lived on the same street. They once had wealth, and consequent station, but lost them without losing their pride; and if their daughter has beauty, hope clings to it, and is leading it to the market. Poor girl! she has got a difficult part to play. Pray, how was she dressed?"

"Very perfectly," replied Park.

"But I mean," said the widow, "what did she wear?"

"White," he answered.

"It is her style of dressing," cried the widow, laughing, "that I wish to know. How perverse you are!"

"If you desire me to descend to particulars," replied Park, "I must say that my observation did not extend so far; besides, it seems to me that people are well dressed only when particulars are not noticeable, as in a perfect face we do not find peculiar features."

"You certainly observed whether she wore short sleeves or long, high or low neck!" said she; "and what jewels — but those she would not be likely to wear, for, if they have any, they are too old-fashioned now to be displayed with any pleasure."

"I cannot call to mind the particular cut of her dress," replied Park; "yet your suggestions may help me out, as I have a lingering recollection of very charming flesh; and, if I saw none, where did I get the impression? And concerning gems, I think that she favored them; but they were of a subdued character, and did not mar the harmony of her toilet — a ring wrought up to a perfect hand, clasping a single pearl, and a bracelet of those 'tears of the Orient,' set with the same pleasing art, were put to shame upon her arm and finger."

"Then I venture to say they were borrowed for the occasion!" said she.

"Is that a common custom among ladies?" questioned Park.

"Ay," she replied, ("as Mr. Forrest says in the play,) it is common."

"Did Mr. Vernon amass property, and then have the misfortune to lose it?" Park inquired.

"O, no," she explained; "had that been the case, he would have returned to business, and tried to rise again, instead of lying idle, or sauntering listlessly along the busy streets. His fortune came by inheritance. Mr. Vernon's father left him a large estate; but some ten or twelve years since — for it was in my school days — it was talked of as quite gone. Their horses and carriages disappeared, and, although the house was in some way secured to Mrs. Vernon, their manner of living was entirely changed. Their name was removed from the door, the blinds were closed, and the dust was allowed to gather on them just as if no one dwelt there; so that it seemed a gloomy place even in the daytime, and in the night it was really dismal. And their daughter, when she returned from school or church, always passed down an arch, and entered into a low door away in the rear. So it is very plain to be seen that it is a condition to which they have never become reconciled; and you may be sure that hope broods over the beauty of Aurelia, — for she is an only child, — and dreams that it may yet restore the faded splendor."

"Are you acquainted with Mrs. Vernon?" inquired Park.

"I used to see her occasionally," the widow answered; "but she is one of those dark, mysterious, unbending women who silently carry their point, regardless of tears or entreaty. Is it not strange that a mother should think more of money than a father does, as a motive to the marriage of a daughter?"

"If we examine their different situations," replied Park, (quite willing, now, to draw the conversation from personal to general,) "and reason from them, it does not appear particularly surprising, for man has many resources. His mind gathers vigor as it stretches out to measure the return of voyages, or bends to comprehend the result of speculations, although he have no object but money: while woman is well nigh restricted to spending it; and, if supplied in profusion, it is apt to lead into fashionable frivolity, which wastes the substance of the mind and perverts the judgment. When a family of this kind fall by mercantile disaster, or sink down through foolish expenditure and display, the husband and father sees before him a wide field for activity, with increasing motive to enter it; while the wife and mother has but little employment save to mourn over the ruins — as neither hand nor mind has been trained to the arts of reconstruction. It is this inability to create wealth which makes her over-estimate its consequence, and display so little wisdom in its use. And if she be one of those ladies whose faith and hope are exclusively in 'ton,' — a prevailing religion! — she sighs, and ponders, and looks back. Weak in all things but pride and mortification, such persons have no resource save to dream of the vanished show and the departed pleasure — unless they have a child that they can lead to the altar and sacrifice for their restoration. For this reason, if for no other, they should have a more rational education, and a wider arena for their faculties."

"Woman's rights!" cried Featherstone. "Yet the day of any material change in their condition is far distant, as the world is not a yielding mass for every dreamer to mould to what fantastic shape he pleases, but keeps its form with tough determination. And, as at present constituted, it will continue to play the game of life as it has done, with a very delectable talk, no doubt, of making hearts trumps! yet always turning up a diamond whenever it be possible, not hesitating to take it from the bottom of the pack, even. How long have you been an advocate of woman's rights, Park?"

"Ever since I saw and reflected upon the inevitable tendencies of the system of her education; not in schools alone, but in almost every home, where lessons are more deeply impressed," he replied. "And if those so educated at length come to think and intelligently examine, the most startling revelation of all will be, how entirely dependent they have been taught to live. Whereas all education is but enforced weakness, which does not place in the power of the pupil the means of becoming more independent — its long catalogue of accomplishments is only for a lure and a snare. When a worthy development shall be the aim in her training, a wider sphere must come also; and not only the form and the mind, but every fibre of the affections, will gain strength and grace thereby."

"Would you have them crowd around the ballot box," asked Featherstone, "and fight for their favorite condidates?"

"Do not slander woman by suggesting that she would act like man!" said Park. "On the contrary, it is my conviction that, if she were to vote, it would so humanize and elevate the electors and the elected, as to arrest the downward tendencies of the nation. If you will but look around, you can see that the associations from which she is excluded do not keep the purity and elevation incident to her presence. And, sneer at it as we may, she is the last hope of freedom; a mighty force not yet called into complete action; a power full of heavenly beneficence. Such is her nature that she takes no part in destruction — if she follow, it is to mitigate the woe. Behold her amid the carnage and cries of battle, or where the fever and pestilence more silently slay, and ask, Who among men equals her in self-sacrifice? Who so resolutely follows the monitions of conscience? Who so calmly takes the path of duty and eternal right, and in a spirit so gentle and devoted, so meek and unwearying?"

"I scarcely meant to be serious in what I said," Featherstone replied; "and there may be something in your idea: it certainly sounds very well, like all new theories; yet I should be a little afraid to set it in operation. However, there is no immediate danger; as the ladies themselves, for the most part, oppose the movement — preferring, I have no doubt, to have some one to look up to and lean upon."

"Yes, indeed, I am sure they do!" said the widow; "and, after all, it seems to me to be their natural sphere."

CHAPTER V.

What are our hopes?
Like garlands on Affliction's forehead worn,
Kissed in the morning, and at evening torn.
DAVENPORT.

RISING from the breakfast table, they left the widow better pleased with them than she had ever been before, and half regretting the sharp replies she had given Featherstone, as she thought of his fresh and rosy face and warm expression, and particularly of the sadly reproachful glance which he gave her at the moment of leaving. But neither Park's conversation nor his person interested her enough to be recalled; his pale and expressive face was beyond her range.

Turning down Broadway, Park and Featherstone called at the post office, found letters, and passing on to the building in which they had rooms, each retired to his own, to see if any memorandum claimed attention, to learn of the porter if there had been any calls, to peruse their correspondence and the morning papers. Although they found nothing pressing, the day did not pass without business—which was received with a thrill of pleasure by them; for first clients excite the legal aspirant as much as it does the country boy to entrap his first rabbit; and we might run the parallel still farther, when we reflect how likely both are to be skinned, were it not quite too obvious to require more than a passing allusion.

In the course of the morning, Park had a call from a gentleman by the name of McRae, who lived in Greenville, and laid claim to a large estate in that town, of which others were in possession — a case where the evidence relied upon, although appearing of record, was in language so ambiguous as to require the most careful analysis of a complicated act of conveyance, to be followed by long and laborious investigation of favoring and opposing judicial reasoning and decision.

Featherstone received a visit from parties who desired him to draw up an agreement, into which they proposed to enter.

When the occupation of the day was over, and the hour of dining had nearly arrived, Featherstone called at Park's office, that he might have his company in walking to their boarding house. As he entered, he inquired, "How is business this morning?"

"It comes slowly round this way, as Coleridge said of spring," replied Park. "I have passed the day in the examination of a claim, which I think is promising, quite promising. But what have *you* found which makes you look so conscious of success? You carry that slender cane as though it were a sceptre!"

"Me!" said Featherstone; "I have only drawn an agreement. It is rather an important one, however, and I think it very likely that I have drawn it wrong, as my thoughts were elsewhere: if I have, I hope you will make two or three thousand dollars assaulting or defending it, some day."

"One would suppose that you were about to retire from the profession," said Park, "if he might judge from your tone and style of remark!"

"Have you any rich relations?" inquired Featherstone.

"I am not aware of any such connection," said Park; "or at least none who would be willing to enhance my income so much that I should be likely to find trouble in spending it. Have you found such a one?"

"I cannot say precisely what I have found," replied Featherstone; "for it lacks the confirmation of death or title deed;

therefore you perceive it can be now only a good intention; but it looks well, and, as you just said of your case in chancery, is promising, quite promising. It makes its appearance in black on white, also, being in the form of a letter from the Crescent City. So I think it good for a pleasant journey and a gay winter, if not more."

Upon which, taking a seat, he drew out the letter, and, handing it to Park, continued, "If you will oblige me, I should like to have your opinion on the prospect."

Park took the proffered document, and read, —

"NEW ORLEANS, *September* 20, 184—.

"Dear Sir: Since my return from the north, I have been revolving in my mind the idea of withdrawing from active business; and I should like to have you leave your profession, if you are not greatly attached to it, and enter our house, with a view to the succession. I hope, at least, that you will so far entertain the proposition as to come out and pass the winter, and see if the place and the occupation be agreeable to you. If they should not prove so, you can return at your pleasure; and, whichever you may choose, you will find in me a friend.

"With expectations of soon meeting you here, I remain

"Truly yours,

"RUFUS MERTON.

"Anthony Featherstone, Esq., New York."

"Short, but certainly very promising," said Park, as he returned the letter. "And I advise you to comply with the terms, which, I have no doubt, you made up your mind to do on the first reading; merely asking advice, as most men will of their friends, to see how it agrees with their own determination! But who is this Mr. Merton? He writes as though he was not only an acquaintance, but a connection."

5

"He was born in New England," replied Featherstone. "He used to come to my father's house, occasionally, during my boyhood; he also called upon me once while I was in college, and I dined with him, at the Astor, this past summer. He was second cousin to my mother, and I believe was partial to her in their early days. But he went south before coming of age, where, engaging in business, he devoted himself to its many cares until he had acquired what he thought a competent income for marriage, when he came north to find my mother a bride. Whether she felt any regret for the irretrievable step which she had taken, I never knew. She, however, always welcomed Mr. Merton with sad sweetness; and I can look back now and see that he was very tender. Indeed, he must have felt that he had no cause to blame her, as they had parted making no declaration; while he was absent long enough, without writing, for her to have obtained a legal separation, had she been his wife. Still, I can see it was on that youthful attachment, more than in any consanguinity, that the favor and kindness flourished, strengthened as it was by occasional visits, and kept in thought by semi-annual correspondence. And, although she sleeps in the village cemetery, it seems that the sentiment survives, and now he solicits me to become its recipient. So, the testimony being all in, what do you think of the case?"

"It appears to me to be a good one," replied Park. "Hence I believe that you will give it your most careful and skilful attention until you have won it. When do you leave us?"

"In a few days."

"That will not only surprise but disappoint Mrs. Summers."

"Why so?" inquired Featherstone, slightly coloring.

"Because she has designs upon your heart which absence

will frustrate: if you continued near the vestibule, I think you would be drawn to the shrine."

"Very fair! Yet not true; for she replies to me too sharply."

"With the tongue, but not with the eye! That sharpness is the principal evidence on which I base my opinion, as she is one of those whose emotions quicken their wits. And a little disguise pleases her, as a petted dove pecks at the hand by which it would be caressed."

In a few moments thereafter, the two lawyers were out and walking up Broadway together.

The bracing air and the bright sun of the early October, and, above all, the throng of "ladies clad in colors bright," made that broad pavement very attractive; while the dawning fortunes of Featherstone showed it to him finer than ever, inspiring him to feel as might an ancient Roman, who had just been initiated into that "order" whose talisman was the secret name of the Eternal City. Under this new influence, beauty appeared more beautiful; the long lines of imposing palaces more accessible; the high-mettled horses, with all their costly caparison and flashing equipage, more desirable; and even the armorial bearings and blazonry more significant! for, hitherto, he had felt compelled to resist, and, sometimes, defame their charms; but, in that hour, his blood was beating high with the vision and the hope of possession. So, feeling the secret ties of union and ultimate fellowship, he was ready to defend the order.

If Featherstone had been long in training for an Olympic game, it was to enter the arena where strength and skill alone avail; and if he had dreamed of a victor's wreath, the day of the crowning was far on in time. But now, and swiftly, —

"As from the stroke of the enchanter's wand," —

he beheld a princely charioteer stoop from his triumphal car, to present to his hand the reins of steeds formed for success and foaming for the course. As he thus stood upon the the brink of fruition, there opened a gorgeous prospect — making the air more vital and his step more elastic; while the silent, immeasurable, wide-arching sapphire put on a more friendly aspect, and bent over him as though he had grown precious in nature, or was more worthy of protection; for we ourselves contain and call forth the colors, sweet as the palpitations of divinest music, or sombre and sad as the shades with which imagination has touched the woe of eternal gloom. Look where we may, we can see little save the hues of our own spirits. The magical perspectives of the various landscape, night's infinite hosts, with their far-flashing crests, fail never to visit the eye; but unless some strong emotion flings wide our brazen gates, they pass, and paint no pictures.

Park, also, had his dream — a dream that closed his eyes to all this material splendor. For a spirit hand was playing, where none but he might hearken, the enchanting prelude to the highest harmony of which the heart is capable. There, to its witch-notes, as rose the walls of Thebes to the tones of the lyre of Orpheus, a temple was shaping itself either for a shrine or a sepulchre. And to it a form was drawing near, before which the incense of life will be burned, unless found unworthy or unresponsive. If it be so, however fair the enchantress, true strength can lead her forth, and wave her from the sacred place; while time and aspiration will yield a dearer dweller or a noble recompense — one of these, whoso has faith and continuance shall surely win. But full often is the temple closed on the first disappointment, and a house built beside it for the daily life too low for Love to enter. Can there be any wreck so disastrous? Yet behold the coast!

Well may we study the one for whom we rear this structure; as the riches of our nature must go to form its walls, and Hope may fold her wings within the dome, while, in all meditative hours, Thought will lead us down its sunny, or silent, or gloomy aisles, to cheer, to sadden, or to petrify.

But these introspections and forebodings were not of their mood — are not woven among the golden threads of their dreaming. To them it was a high and a lordly hour; full likely none more charming will they ever behold — for they saw not all which we see, who are gazing when

"Young Harry Percy's spur was cold."

At length they came out of their musing; but it was only to speak of trite and fleeting circumstance, for neither thought of bringing forth the treasures of his meditations.

Having entered the house, they found that their long consultation at the office had detained them beyond the dining hour; consequently they had only Mrs. Summers for company, who smilingly chided them for being late, saying, "Pray, what has happened? Were it Mr. Park alone, it would not much surprise me. But it is quite new for you, Mr. Featherstone; so much so that I thought you dining elsewhere."

"It is an offence, madam," replied he, gravely, "that I shall not be likely to commit again under this roof."

"I hope you do not think of leaving us, Mr. Featherstone."

"Such is my intention now."

"You really astonish me! And certainly I hope you are not going on account of any thing which was said this morning, for I was just beginning to like you."

"It is not strictly that, but rather in consequence of something I learned this morning, I have thought it safest and best soon to change place."

"Why so? I am sure I have spoken only in your praise, and if any other in this house has done so, I despise the act and the doer of it. Is Mr. Park intending to leave also?" continued she, looking up to that individual.

"I have not come to a conclusion," replied he, rather oracularly.

"Well, certainly, if I ever spoke truth in my life, I do now, when I say I had rather they would all go than you and Mr. Featherstone. Truly, I hope you will not mind what I said, or be influenced by the idle or envious remarks of others."

Featherstone, having eaten but a trifle for him, drew back his chair, which the widow observing, said, "I hope, at the least, you will dine with me to-day, Mr. Featherstone."

"I have dined," he replied.

"Then it is something more serious than I had feared. Pray tell me what has happened; is it any thing that I have done?"

On this, Featherstone arose from the table, and moving towards her, inquired, "Will you give me your hand?"

She mechanically extended it, and the tears stood in her eyes as she did so. When taking it, he placed some bank bills in the warm and dewy hollow, slightly pressed, and parted with the treasure.

Observing the money, she said, "Pray, what is all this for? You owe me but a trifle, and I have no desire to receive that now."

"I have eaten so light a dinner, — and I observed Park did also, — that we shall be hungry by ten o'clock, and I wish you to get up a very choice supper, about that hour, for us three, at which time I may inform you why I think it due to myself to leave your house."

"Will you, sure?" inquired she; when, seeing his face soften a little, she continued, "do take back this money, and let me provide for you; now do. It shall be just as nice, and I shall feel so much better. Yes, do; will you?"

"In the evening, I may have an opportunity for explanation, and, having heard me, if you say that I ought to receive back the money, I will do so. I cannot take it now."

"Really, I think you are cruel to keep me waiting until that time before you tell me what has given you offence; why cannot you communicate it at once? I long to know——. Now do give me some hint of it, if it be only a very little."

Park having stepped into the hall, Featherstone said, "I suppose I might speak it low."

And drawing near on the word, she rose up to meet him, when, placing his hand lightly on her shoulder, he leaned towards her ear, but succeeded in getting no farther than her lips! She saw the direction of his glance as he approached, and, if surprised an instant, she sweetly yielded; so that one would have thought, from her appearance when they separated, that the mystery had been explained to her entire and perfect satisfaction — although no word had been spoken or whispered.

In a few moments after the explanation, the young lawyers left the house, and walked down the street; and for a time Featherstone's thoughts lingered warmly around the affectionate widow. But soon, too soon, the opening prospect of fortune fixed his gaze, and took possession of his heart, bearing it away from the sunny but fluctuating sea of passion in whose foam Aphrodite was forming; for he knew so little of the regal soul of Love, that he desired, above all, those golden treasures with which he thought every thing besides could be purchased.

As they proceeded on, they came opposite to a window bright and warlike with swords and sashes; and Park, drawing Featherstone into the store, requested to see some dirks.

The attendant having laid them before him, he selected the most beautiful of the collection, on the blade of which was blazoned, "I protect." This he presented to Featherstone, saying, "As you are going among a chivalrous people, it is necessary that you be prepared to respond to their courtesy." On receiving it, Featherstone replied, "It is generous and acceptable, and it may be useful; for a show of it, even, will sometimes make insolence skulk to its kennel."

Resuming their walk, they soon entered their respective offices, where Park proceeded in the examination of his land case, and Featherstone wrote a letter of thanks and acceptance to Mr. Merton, and then went out to walk, as he was too much elated with the thought of the pleasing change that awaited him for quiet study or calm reflection. When, however, the hour of ten came round, they entered their boarding house together. The widow met them in the hall, and conducted them into the library, where she had spread the table, and made a fire, for the evening air was chilly. After closing the door, she said, as she rang the bell, "Now, isn't this cosy?"

Truly it was bright and cheerful. While the well-turned figure of Mrs. Summers was arrayed with particular care — indeed, every thing was so neat, and fitting, and graceful, that even her delicate little slipper was an influence! There was just the slightest touch of cunning in her smile, seeming, somehow, as if she had thought of some sweet way of reconciliation, though still fearing and hoping for its success.

"It is not only a pleasing, but a warm reception," said Park, in reply to her question, (for a bright fire was to him one of the most agreeable of things,) "and I think that I shall live with you so long as you will take care of me."

"What can I say to express my appreciation of your kindness?" said Featherstone.

"Say that you will remain here as long as Mr. Park does, and you shall have every thing to please you."

"I have placed that out of my power, having gone too far

to recede. Yet I must say that I never felt the attractions so strong as at this time."

"Then why not yield to them? For I cannot think that you have made it impossible; I will not believe that you could have been so hasty. Did you expect to find a more congenial place?"

But before Featherstone could reply, the servant entered with the supper. And when it was all arranged, even to the removing of the wires from the wine, she said, "I will excuse you from further service, John; the table may remain as we leave it until morning." John having left the room, she continued, "Take seats at the table, gentlemen; I ought not to have kept you waiting a moment, as you scarcely tasted any thing at dinner."

Featherstone smiled incredulously on the widow at this idea, and, catching his meaning, she colored, and slyly repaid his glance, while Park, seeing all, appeared not to see. So, taking a seat, he removed the covers, and helped them to brown and reeking reed-birds — the choicest delicacy of the autumnal year.

But observing that the widow did not eat, Featherstone said, "I shall not soon forget this place and its pleasures, and my chief regret in leaving the city is, that I must part from some in this house."

"Then it is not *us*, in particular, but the town, that you are about to depart from! Well, I do feel relieved. At first, I feared that I had offended in some way; and then I thought that some one else had — you appeared so serious and sensitive."

"Not offended, by any means; you must have misinterpreted my sad and ill-suppressed emotions. Indeed, I feared so at dinner; and I thought of explaining myself more fully but I was too much agitated for utterance. Let me help you to a warm bird."

"If you please."

"May I have the pleasure of a glass of wine?"

"I thank you," said she, and her eyes beamed it more warmly than her words, as she pressed the glass to her lips. "But pray tell me where you are going, and why you must go."

"I have been invited to New Orleans, to pass the winter, perhaps to find a home there for some years. I have a relative in that place, who seems to be desirous to help me to a fortune, and I am bent on examining the prospect, thinking, if it be good, I may grasp the extended hand, and suffer it to lead me."

"We shall see you in the summer then, unless you intend to quite forsake and forget us."

"I know so little what my situation will be, that it is difficult to say how soon I can visit you; but

'Do the birds that fly south still remember their nest?'"

"I think that these will not; so let me help you to another," said Park. "But what do you intend to do with your office?"

"I have concluded to give notice on the door that Brian Park, Esq. (office No. 9, next floor below) will take charge of the business during the absence of the subscriber, then lock it, and leave the key with you. In all which laborious duties I shall hold the said Park accountable for faithful and diligent performance. And, Mrs. Summers, I call on you to witness that he so promises, and accepts the trust."

"I shall not forget it; and, if you must go, I engage that he will attend to it nearly as well as you would."

"It may be so; but when I come on, if I find any thing wrong, I shall look to you for satisfaction."

"I think that I may venture to promise so much," said she, laughing, "if it can be settled as agreeably as was our last misunderstanding."

Supper being quite over, Park arose, saying, "I am sorry to separate from such pleasant company, but as I have some preparation to make in a matter which is to be heard to-morrow, you will be kind enough to excuse me."

To this there was remonstrance, and then a parting glass, when kindly wishes mingled with the wine. In a few moments, warm smiles lighted him out, and grew more expressive as he turned away; knowing which, the sympathizing reader will be pleased to learn that Park closed the door after him, although it must necessarily close the chapter.

CHAPTER VI.

Ill-fated race! the softening arts of peace,
Whate'er the humanizing Muses teach,
The godlike wisdom of the tempered breast,
Investigation calm, whose silent powers
Command the world — these are not theirs.
THOMSON.

RUFUS MERTON went to New Orleans, and became a resident there, soon after Louisiana was ceded to the United States. He sprang from a family of consideration and wealth in one of the interior New England towns, where, at an early age, (his father being dead,) he found himself the heir of so much estate as was needful to facilitate his entry into business; and in the course of years, by skilful management and good fortune, he had become rich. He was endowed by nature with a gentle and kind disposition, and assiduously cultivating friendship, he had also kept his heart open to all the voices of distress, giving relief to many a want-stricken family. If disaster lowered around any one of his acquaintance, he came at once to avert the dangers of the storm, or, if that exceeded his power, to save him from sinking amid the wreck; and if he occasionally suffered loss by so doing, it did not throw distrust over all the future, or harden his soul into selfishness.

He had left the north (as Featherstone has said) with a feeling towards his cousin, which, had his nature been more bluff and prosaic, would have declared its love ere he departed. But, through the rich coloring of his deeply-adoring heart, she appeared so pure and priceless, that he felt too poor to ask such high acceptance, and went away to live on the hope of one day returning more worthy of her love. They parted tenderly; yet neither revealed what most they felt; and if vivid recollection did frequently call forth the scene upon a summer's eve, she began to fear that it was a vanishing dream of fond and fleeting youth — the one picture on which we turn to gaze and muse while Memory can hold her lamp to illuminate the scroll. She, indeed, had leisure to recur to it, and did, even when doubt had dimmed its brightness, and hope found no sweet perspective. But his was an active life, and in it he was apparently absorbed, seeming as if something more substantial than a maiden's charms had fixed his gaze and filled his aspirations. Yet he hoped and believed in a coming and an appropriate hour, dreaming that, if she loved as he did, she was as cheerfully and hopefully waiting, never once considering that she had not the same sustaining motives, such as winning home and station, with daily drinking at the stimulating fountains of success.

During all this time, he did not dare to write to her, feeling that he could give no adequate expression to his emotions. Neither did he venture to name her in his letters to his sister; it was too tender a subject even for such exposure.

So she came to believe that she had faded out of mind, had been forgotten by the long absent and silent lover, and at length yielded to the suit and siege of another.

About that time Merton, having attained to a degree of independence which gave him confidence to declare his love, turned his face homeward, and entered into all the familiar and softening scenes of his boyhood to find his cousin a bride.

She had been married only a few months to a sharp and thrifty shopkeeper, who — so the gossips said — was a good match for any body, looking at it, of course, in the ordinary light of trade. So Merton found her wedded and to all appearance she was happy; consequently he kept his secret, and no one dreamed that the cause which occasioned the visit was other than such as turns us all, at times, to the place of our birth. The valuable articles which he had purchased to present to her, he gave with words which outweighed the gifts, if they were lighter and calmer than they would have been had he found her fondly awaiting his coming. He saw that he had no cause to reproach any one but himself for his loss, and he did not lament it the less when he learned that she parted from the hope of his love with a reluctant heart; hence he became her true and most tender friend.

During the summer, Merton met her frequently, and saw her husband also; and although he found nothing in him to like, he strove to treat him with kindness for her sake. He planned and executed many a little party of pleasure; now a picnic in some grove, now a drive to points of attraction in the vicinity, and now berrying among the hills: these made the days bright, and winged the hours. So the husband came to feel — as Merton paid all attendant expenses — that he had not only married a fair and useful wife, but won a rich and liberal relative besides.

In this manner the warm and genial season fled away; and, in the early autumn days, Merton bade her farewell, saying, " Dear cousin, if any trouble come near you, I desire that you will let me share it, or prevent it, if it be in my power. I pray that this confidence and this privilege may be mine — I should grieve were you to prefer another. May I hope that you will so far remember me ? "

There were tears in her eyes as she falteringly thanked him, and he released her hand — tears that I dare not analyze ; for the deepest emotions of her bosom were apparent as he entered his carriage and departed.

Returning to his adopted city, Merton once more engaged in business with all his former assiduity, and more than his early fellow-feeling; thus seeking to soothe the disappointment which had so disarranged his scheme of life and destroyed his youthful hope. Still he could not quite forget it; consequently, clouds of sadness canopied all the hours of his rest, and even his days grew dreary, as time began to reveal the desolation of his heart and fill the void with pain. He had been at home but a few months, when one day, passing through a mart where slaves were sold at public auction, he saw among them a pale quadroon, apparently about twenty years of age, with comely features, shapely person, and modest expression, yet withal a look so woful that it arrested his steps as with a spell. But when she observed him thus standing and gazing, as he could not but do, compassionately upon her, her face shone with some faint ray of hope. Thereupon he approached her, and inquired, "Is there any thing that I can do for you?"

"If you will only take me from this dreadful place!" cried she; and then the tears gushed, and her frame was shaken like a tree that the tempest tosses.

On this Merton drew near to her, and, when she had composed herself somewhat, inquired, "Do you wish to return to your friends?"

"I have no friends!"

"I mean to the place you came from. Where were you born?"

"In Virginia."

"Is it not your hope to go back there?"

"No, never! For my mother is dead, and my relatives have cast me out."

"I understand. They are white, I suppose."

"Yes," said she, after another moment of deep agitation.

"Have you had any useful teaching and instruction?"

"I have learned needlework, and know how to keep house."

"Have you ever kept house?"

"I have not; but my mother did, and she taught me."

"Can you read and write?"

"Yes; my fa——, my master taught me to write, and instructed me in the English and French languages."

Merton, not knowing at the moment what further to say, hesitated, and thought of turning away, but at length inquired, "How can I relieve you?"

"If you will only have mercy and buy me."

Seeing that she faltered, he tenderly inquired, "Why do you wish me to become your purchaser?"

"Because I believe that you will be kind; and in that lies my only hope — there is nothing more now for me to cling to." Again agitated beyond utterance, she at length continued, "If you will only buy me, I will do any thing: it would be easier to die for you than to live with some who have questioned me to-day. O, when I think how either one may purchase, and so acquire the power to possess me, I feel it to be hell! and I see no escape, I know no refuge, but to implore you to save me. O, do not think me too bold; but see only how I am crushed down and cast out utterly from all protection, with no hope remaining, save the pity of some generous heart."

Merton had seen the slave markets many times, and observed the goods which were exposed there; yet he had passed on without giving the subject much attention, as he wished to avoid it. If feeling thrilled over the abyss for a moment, he drew back with instinctive dread. Beyond this he had not ventured; as the beings whom he had seen in such places previously, were, for the most part, dark, uncouth, and silent; perhaps he may have thought that, in the blending series of creation, they were an inferior race, requiring protection: what kind of protection that was which he daily saw, strange to say, he had never analyzed.

But now, when he beheld the outrage by the light of maiden beauty, clothed too with a natural grace and heightened by surrounding woe, revealing the sad story in tears and the pathos of the English tongue, it struck home and deeply moved him; so, if suffering plead, it is truly of the first consequence, to most of us, in what form it comes, as well as what boon it craves. If, at that hour of our national consciousness, she had besought Merton to give her freedom, he would have turned away, — sorrowing, it might be, like the young man that came to Jesus by night and was seen no more, — as his mind was not prepared for such a stride. But, as she only declared preference, her imploring words found a way to his heart, while they aroused him to action; for the pressure of the inexorable law was imminent, and only to be met by purchase. This being the case, it will be seen that compliance with her wish might put off a weight of woe which would be hard to bear, even in the memory of one who had observed only to pass by on the other side. How could he leave her so utterly helpless and despairing, caught, as she was, in the strong net of power, and crying to him through its terrible meshes? He found her trembling and moaning, like some poor helpless bird that sees a loathsome serpent coiling to the nest of her callow brood, and saw that the hour of her rescue or her doom had come. Thus it was displayed to him. And when he at length came out from a flood of anxious and contending thoughts and feelings, and said, "Do not weep more; I will see that something be done for you," hers was not the only heart that rejoiced. With this view he turned to speak with the person who kept the place; yet his face flushed when he thought how the act would be interpreted by him. He had met the man often — indeed, was quite well acquainted with him in the way of business. So, as he came near, the keeper (who had been observing him) said, "Well, Merton, what do you think of her?"

"I think that she is to be pitied," he replied.

"How much? fifteen or eighteen hundred dollars worth? But without joking, Merton, if you want her I won't bid against you."

"What part of the country is she from?"

"The Old Dominion, the mother of States; and very probably she is the daughter of statesmen. But here is the bill that came with her; we indorse what is there set forth; and for any thing further, you can examine and trust to your own judgment. I must say I fanced the 'piece' when I first saw her, and talked with her about it; but she told me flatly that she did not want me to buy her. However, there have been a number of others to examine her, for she is a desirable article, young, handsome, and all that; yet, as near as I can find out, she has answered them all pretty much in the same fashion."

Merton looked over the bill, and seeing that, as far as it went, it entirely corresponded with her own account, he returned it into the hand of the vendor, with a sum of money, saying, "I wish you to purchase the girl; and, if the price be reasonable, you may expect something more when I cash the bill."

When Merton went back to the quadroon, and told her to be comforted, for he had made arrangements with the keeper to become her purchaser, and then passed away to avoid the gaze of the curious, her rigid features melted, her hot eyes overflowed with sweeter waters, and long and refreshingly fell the tearful rain on that heart which was well nigh parched to a desert.

All that day, in the intervals of business, Merton listened to his better feelings, and was filled with "the low, sad music of humanity," making the walls of exclusion tremble to their fall, as did those of Jericho to the trumpets of Joshua; so that, in the evening, when he went to the place where he had directed the girl to be conveyed, he was nerved with the conscious strength of one who had resolved to break shackles and clothe a slave with freedom. Feeling that this was her right, he rejoiced that he had the power to give her back the treasure. A swift seeming change! yet not strange; for one gust of free thought can dissipate a cloud like this as easily as the westerly wind rolls off the mist from our Atlantic coast. Seeing him enter, she met him as her deliverer; and, when she had thanked him again and again for his pitying kindness, and had calmed her glad weeping, he opened the high purpose of his heart.

But her beaming face dipped down into sad shadow as she said, "My home seemed so secure, until recently, that I never realized such a want as freedom; and although it may be a rock of refuge, it appears like a desolate place. If you give me liberty, where shall I go? I cannot go home; I have no home! Spurned from the house in which I was born by my kindred, would you send me back to their scorning?"

"Not to them, but into one of the free states, where you will find friends; and I will see that you do not want for any thing; while you are so nearly white that the people may receive you without prejudice; you at least will be secure there, and may be happy."

But she began to weep; for she shrank like a child from all the lofty struggles of life. And how could she else, as the peculiar machinery of law and custom by which she was manufactured, enervates what should be made strong, and develops that which requires control? Liberty may, indeed, be so utterly trampled out of the mind by the fierce footsteps of oppression, that we shall not only no longer sigh for it, but, through the weakness which such wrong induces, it will cease to be desirable. Yet not so with the affections, for they are the fire and motion of the soul — throbbing with the last pulse of the heart, and going out with the last light of the eye.

The slave, who had thus been cast forth upon a "sea of troubles," saw amid the billows this outstretched hand; and, having succeeded in grasping it, who can reproach her for desiring to hold it fast? or measure the distress which made her say, "All that I desire is to be your servant; and then you may sell me if I do wrong; but that I can never do, for my only hope is to be yours. To sell me now, or to send me north, seem to me so alike in their dreary prospect, that I have no wish to choose between them. I may not venture to say how the master feels, but the slave has only one thing to seek in life, which is, to find a kind heart; so that we come to search and study faces for that single trait. O, how many did I gaze on to-day, without hope, until you came! and I looked upon no one after you had gone, and I shall never wish to more."

Thus she spoke, with her bowed head upon her folded arms, and ended sobbing — seeming like a beauteous temple shaken to its deep foundations and stripped of all its sacred ornaments; its pinnacles and heaven-pointing spires all broken; yet still making a mute appeal to be saved from utter ruin and desecration.

If Merton gave her room in his heart, when thus invoked, who will severely censure him? for the wrongs which had so crushed and devastated her, touch the act with the color of virtue — an act which may not receive our full approbation, or pass judgment in the final accounting of conscience; yet it is of the kind that the heart will forever seek to palliate.

But that was long ago. For, at the period when this story opens, they were living in one of the quiet parts of the city, in a pleasant and spacious house, with many servants at their call. They also had a daughter, eighteen years of age, and formed by nature to be a blessing in any home; yet appearing there under circumstances which excluded her nearly as much from society, in that proud community, as it would from the most correct circle of Christian New England. For, to say truth, they were not so entirely isolated there as they would be here, as Merton took his friends home frequently to dine; and Madam (that being the name by which she was known) always presided at the table, and with the ease and elegance which is rarely, if ever, acquired in a single generation. "Blood tells!" is a phrase which was frequently on the lips of Randolph of Roanoke; and they who, like him, would trace the current to its parent lake, could see that this quadroon was the daughter of culture, although her limbs were marked with manacles. Never did more graceful attentions, or more gentle voices, make music in any home, than those which charmed the life of Merton. The kindly question and the fond reply, anticipated wants, and meeting eyes beaming with love light, drew him there like a bird to his nest, making it so downy soft and warm that neither heart nor hope ever dreamed of aught beyond.

CHAPTER VII.

How poor a thing is pride! when all, as slaves,
Differ but in their fetters, not their graves.
DANIEL.

TURNING another page, we shall see that Merton was not without his troubles. The form of his domestic life furnished a theme for censure precisely in proportion to the value of the qualities which marked and illustrated his course in every other particular. If he did a generous or a noble thing, and it was praised in the presence of the mean, they straightway pointed to the darker spot; and as he gave them frequent opportunity, so it was often spoken of. If his name was mentioned in connection with any public office, — and no man in the state would have filled one more acceptably, — some wily demagogue, who was ready to beg, implore, or basely procure a place, would suggest that there might be a reason why the people could not vote for Merton.

Even when the church asked him to give of his abundance to the building of a temple, they never invited him to bring his family there to worship — they shrank from such fearful contamination. Merton, no doubt, saw all this; saw it as no man else could see it; yet it did not sour his spirit or stint his charity.

Neither were these, and their multiform offspring, all. His sister, who had always exercised great influence over him from her superior mental force and persistence, had married a merchant of the city, and, becoming aware of the connection, set her face against it like a flint. Yet, for a time, she made her protest only in coldness of manner and studied reserve. Merton saw the change, but made no comment, although he visited her less frequently. This gave her an opportunity to reproach him for neglect, and allude to its cause; and so reaching the subject, she did not leave it without expressing a decisive opinion on its merits.

At first Merton made no reply; he even smiled amid the storm. This, however, did not dishearten Mrs. Steel. She knew that the judgment of the enlightened world was with her, and that continual dropping wears the rock; so she continued her laudable efforts for her brother's reformation. She misstated that he might correct; she so spoke against his course as to lead him to defend or palliate it, for she felt that in the court of reason she could convict him of wrong. She even sought to tempt him with what she thought "metal more attractive," for she had been educated to loathe "people of color." "Now," said she on one occasion, "if you would only arouse yourself from this hallucination you might marry the lady whose denunciation is the deepest and most frequent. There is Miss E., who always speaks of it as a terrible thing! and the widow V., who lets no opportunity for allusion pass by unimproved, calling it horrid and low! yet, although they are of fashionable families, and have a most surprising estimate of their own worth, either of them will go with you to the altar to-morrow, if you would only say — this thing is over."

When Merton smiled, — as he could not but do at his sister's enthusiasm, so calculated to fill him with vain hope, — she continued, with more emphasis, "I feel sure that, if you will only do as I have said, you may choose between those delicate and exemplary ladies."

"But my *child*," interposed Merton; "what shall I do with *her?*"

"Is it not a slave's child?" inquired she. "Were you not fully aware that the laws had fixed her place? — laws which were made on mature deliberation of all the facts and circumstances, by our wisest men, for the well-being of the state."

"Do you think that course possible to me, even though *you* recommend it?"

"I only indicated the way prescribed by statesmen."

"Thank God," said Merton, rising from his seat, "that even our law-makers dared not wholly prevent the action of feeling when it possesses the power of wealth! They left a narrow path where the sunlight may fall; they did not venture to completely overshadow the land with the Upas they cherish. Had they so done, the poisonous tree would, long ago, have been torn up by the roots! And if it has struck down and found nourishment, and gained strength, and spread wide, the heart deplores it, and every strong thought tosses and cracks its branches. They may prop them up by enactments, and grow lethargic in the sickly shade; yet, though it be very bitter for the bondmen, it drugs only the cup of the masters, who are slowly, but surely, failing through its enervating influence. But this is ground that I tread reluctantly, and from which I shrink when I behold its vast sweep and multiform obstructions. Still, did I only observe how the system closes up your heart, I should know it to be pernicious. Indeed, any and all laws that seek to stifle whatsoever is generous in our natures, have never yet had the seal of the eternal Lawgiver; nor can they, for any length of time, meet with human acceptance. Great interests may shape statutes, and banded strength enforce them, to the detriment and sorrow of the weak; but silently, surely, and dreadfully it is heaping up wrath against the day of wrath! And some future historian, glancing back on our broken or completed course, will write, as all his predecessors have written, amid the wreck of empire, 'Only that which is just can partake of the life of God.' Looking at the deed to which you so often urge me — this separation, this desertion — by such a light, how can I feel that it would be right? Will it not increase human suffering? bring woe, not only to me, — for that I would try to bear, — but to those who so entirely trust in me? Mary, whenever I take up this subject, — and you may believe that I give it frequent and anxious consideration, — I start with the clearest convictions of duty; but soon I hear such lamenting voices that I close the painful contemplation all weakness and irresolution."

Desiring to lead him to still further confession, she softened her tone, and said, "Dear brother, I would not have believed, from any other lips, that you were so infirm of purpose. Has it come to this, that you think you have so hopelessly entangled the thread of life that it can run smooth no more? If so, what a sad mischance that you should have seen her!"

"There lies the doubt!" replied Merton. "That is the problem which I cannot solve; as I know it was pure kindness and compassion which led me to her, and detained me to listen to her story, and seek to wave back the furies from her heart. Having so done, I offered her freedom and competence; but, the sense of their value being lost or buried deep under accumulated wrong, she chose rather to cling to me; for she loved me, and was capable of inspiring love — did inspire it; and has kept it glowing and growing; and God knows it."

"You shock me, Rufus. Love, pure love, springs only in the bosom of virtue — a virtue that can lay its reverent hand on the altar, and raise an untroubled eye to the throne of the Infinite for a blessing on her virgin vows. The law of marriage I know is right; it has survived, and shall! for it is the keystone of the social arch; and whoever builds on any other foundation can rear no sightly structure in which his children shall rejoice."

"Do you wish me to marry *her*?"

"For Heaven's sake, no! I desire to erase the blot, not to make it indelible. I would save my daughters from suffering by it; and you should remember them, too, Rufus."

"How sensitive you are, Mary! Do you believe if I loved a woman whose uncle, or brother, or father even, was living as I have done, that it would cause me to change?"

"No; yet it might deter you from approaching her at all. If friends forbear to point to this, the censorious, perhaps envious, world will, sooner or later, make us feel the stigma. If you furnish a quiver of arrows, be sure there will be no lack of expert hands to launch them from their 'long bows,' though probably not until they have been dipped in the archer's poison."

"It may be so. I am aware that there is a large class of persons in every community who, like ink-fish, befoul the waters that they themselves may the more securely escape observation."

"Do you propose to take advantage of the turbidness of the current? Is not that a sufficient reason for leaving it?"

"I admit that you are right in this matter, Mary, when viewed in the abstract. Yet how little are the feelings disposed to admit that frost is virtue, if it does appear to preserve! Who can make his heart heed such teaching, when reason is but a barrier of ice on which affection breathes, and it is gone?"

Time continued to pass without working any material change in Merton. At length, having had a fit of sickness which left him weak in mind as well as body, and seemed in a measure to have impaired his faculties, he became more vulnerable. Seeing the opportunity, Mrs. Steel took up her task with renewed hope, and, approaching him on the side which his condition suggested, said, "I hope your suffering has been for your good; that it has aroused you to a sense of your sin, and made you resolve to change your course."

"It is too late — too near the close of the voyage, I fear."

"It is never too late to do well, Rufus."

"That which you complain of, Mary, will soon be terminated by the common course of nature. Yet I have resolved that, while I live, I will do all the good I can; and even after I am gone I shall continue to be kind towards *them*, if a will in their favor may be so considered."

"Can you think of such an unblushing exposure as that? Will you so perpetuate the disgrace? Thus circumstanced, they will not only claim the connection, but substantiate it — the very thing I wish most to avoid. That course would be weakness rather than benevolence; for of what value, I pray you, can property or liberty be to them, when it is not in the power of man to remove the tinge of servitude from their skin? I hope that you are not so infatuated as to be deceived by names! If not, you will perceive that the change which you propose can only take them from labor to consign them to vice. By so doing, you repair no ill that now is, but, on the contrary, are arming temptation with a power superior to that which drew you down; for there is something in the delicate hand of leisure which can take captive and lead wherever it desires. Does this class of persons ever marry? You know that they rarely do; and they cannot, except with the coarse, the rude, or the sordid. Seeing to what a life your fancied kindness, but real weakness, would conduct them, I ask you to pause and reflect before you so act."

"Would you have me leave them exposed to the rigors of the law?"

"Were their case so singular as to be entirely unknown to

the law, it might plead for some special privilege. But the singularity is entirely in your way of viewing it. The law which points out their place, and prescribes their sphere, is not a peculiar oppression; and to relieve them from its action will awaken hope in the bosoms of many of their class only to end in disappointment, and so you would actually increase suffering. Hence, considered in all its bearings, it is an error of judgment to free a slave; for in removing one from bondage, you awake reflection and excite hopes that may put the lives of many masters in peril. Partial exceptions are dangerous to the public peace, and the legislature should withdraw from the citizen the power of making them. If there is to be any amelioration it should fall equally on all — that is the way of wisdom; only he who moves in that direction is entitled to the name of friend to humanity, or even to the slave."

"You may be right, Mary; but to make *them* free and comfortable is all the reparation that lies in my power, and conscience will be satisfied with no less."

"Conscience! *that* is disease, Rufus! The very first movement of conscience would be to warn you from the error of your way."

Merton had become singularly open to this mode of attack, and Mrs. Steel pursued him with every pitiless weapon with which she was acquainted.

At length he so far yielded to her importunity, or his own apprehensions, as to say that he would try to separate from them.

"Dear brother," replied the proud and correct Mrs. Steel, "it is a noble resolution, and Heaven will help you to keep it; so, in a little while, we shall see you restored to true happiness, and accepted by virtuous society."

"No, I can never see happiness more! When this tie is severed I shall drift down the dark current alone."

"Alone, Rufus! Have I not often urged you to come to me? and, if you will, you shall find as fair a home as ever was formed by a sister's love. In granting me this boon, you have given me all that I can ever ask at your hands; indeed it fills my desire."

Mrs. Steel artfully assumed that her brother had consented to her utmost wish, knowing that he religiously respected the faintest semblance of a promise; and Merton made no remonstrance against the assumption, as he had no inclination to open the painful subject afresh, to discuss it further, but silently reviewed his concessions and fixed his position.

CHAPTER VIII.

Men make resolves, and pass into decrees
The motions of the mind. With how much ease,
In such resolves, doth passion make a flaw,
And bring to nothing what was raised to law!
CHURCHILL.

How few can visit the panorama of their past lives with pleasure! They see too many sad vistas; too many graves of the gifted and the loved; too many gloomy spots where bright hopes and high resolves fainted and fell; and too many long tracts lying bleak and desolate, with here and there a haggard ruin, haunted with upbraiding voices.

If Merton's last interview with his sister made him sad and sleepless, it spurred him to action. Desiring, first of all, to provide for those who were dependent on him, he called at the office of William Rutledge, Esq., a member of the bar, who, although a much younger man than himself, was yet his long-tried and intimate friend — a counsellor in trouble, a companion in leisure, and conspicuous for excellence in both.

To a man like Merton, who felt the need of continual sympathy, Rutledge was a treasure, as he could trust him with his open heart — indeed, secrets constantly flowed to him, drawn by the spell of his power. It may be that the Indian blood in his veins had marked his mind to receive confidence, and to keep it with that sacredness which was a characteristic of the noblest of the aborigines; for the strain was high, whether you traced the Saxon or the savage current. Almost feminine in the delicacy of his make and the gentleness of his manner, he yet had the falcon cast of countenance, with wing and spirit for the loftiest game, if such darkened along the sky to fling a shadow on his path. Graceful, powerful, and commanding as these traits made him, still it was his large heart, above all, which gave him to be the legal adviser and daily associate of the generous merchant.

On entering the office, Merton took his accustomed seat, — for he was in the habit of spending some time there every day, — and inquired, "Are you at leisure this morning, Mr. Rutledge?"

"If pleasure be in your mind, such as a ride down to the plantation," replied he, smiling, "I must say no: if business, it is possible I might say yes; for you look serious enough to be thinking of your last will and testament."

"It has been the subject of my thoughts, Rutledge, and it is their restlessness which made me seek you so early this morning."

"I hope you find yourself quite relieved from your late attack, my friend," said Rutledge, laying the smallest hand that ever man had upon the broad shoulder of Merton.

"Yes, I think I am; and that, you know, is an important fact to establish, when the testator has distributed his estate in an uncommon and perhaps distasteful form. I know that it is the custom of men who have lived as I do to leave little trace of it on record. Yet, although on some accounts it would be very agreeable to me if I could escape it, I see no way now that it can be done, and carry out what I believe to be my duty. How different is the life we look back upon from the one we looked forward to! How many things there are, to which we cling, that we would not like to confess on the corners of the streets! Still, I may say to *you*, it tinges my cheek when I imagine that some one, who may take my name and bear it on, will come to examine the disposing record, and, feeling the stain, blush for me with my blood! when none can tell the circumstances which might help to excuse me."

"I am aware how tender you are on that subject; but the view which the feeling leads you to take is not quite the true one. I, indeed, look upon it with far different emotions; for the propensities of our nature will not change, neither will humanity be a reproach. And if there ever come those who can regard a token of reparation in the light you speak of, why may we not fling forward the scorn which would greet them if they breathed it now? When such persons take your name they will be unworthy to wear it; though they should mortify their flesh, never so severely, with scourge and fasting. No; you may cherish a more cheerful hope, and do the deed, believing that generosity and kindness will increase with freedom; or, at least, that they may continue to characterize great souls when the curtain of green turf shall veil the stage and the actors from our eyes."

"It may be so; certainly your words cheer me, and incline me to do in the matter what I believe to be the best that can be done."

"Your plan has my warm approval," said Rutledge, taking up his pen; "and I am ready for item first."

On which, thinking a moment, Merton said, "I give to Anthony Featherstone, Esq., of New York city, attorney at law, on account of the affection I bore his deceased mother, and the esteem in which I hold him, the sum of fifty thousand dollars, to be paid by my executor herein after named.

"I give to my housekeeper, Madam, and also to her daughter, Flora, their freedom; and I hereby direct my executor, hereinafter named, to take the necessary legal steps to manumit them as soon as may be after my decease. I also give them, or the survivor of them, the house where they now live, together with the furniture, appurtenances, and provisions in the said house at the period of my decease, to their sole use and benefit. I further give each of them ten thousand dollars, or the survivor of them twenty thousand dollars, to be paid by my executor, hereinafter named, from my city stocks at their par value — the interest or income of which, I hope, may be found sufficient for their comfortable support and maintenance.

"I give all the rest and residue of my estate, of whatsoever name or nature, to be equally divided, after all just demands against said estate have been paid, between the children of my sister, Mary Merton Steel, wife of Ward Steel, and the aforesaid Featherstone — meaning that each child of my sister Mary shall take equally with the said Featherstone.

"I hereby name and appoint William Rutledge, Esq., of New Orleans, attorney at law, to be the sole executor of this my last will and testament."

"I should think," said Rutledge, "that this matter had been shaping itself in your mind for some time, by the fluency of your speech and the forms which your thoughts have taken."

"You can say nothing more true than that!" Merton replied. "It has pressed upon me by night and by day; and when I have executed the instrument, a weight will be removed which has become painful."

"In any event I am glad that you have proceeded to action, partly for the reason which you assign, but chiefly because I believe you have done right; and I will add that I think it nobly done towards those who can look to you alone for care and comfort, or even protection. Your estate is so ample that your nephews and nieces will scarcely perceive that their legacies have been diminished; and, besides, their home expectations are large; while this Mr. Featherstone will find himself wealthy — and, by the way, I think that I have heard of his mother."

"Yes," replied Merton, sadly smiling, "I believe that you are acquainted with her story; such things crowd around an instrument like this, and I am not inclined to resist their influence, although it may seem a weakness."

"Not to me," said Rutledge. "Although most wills are mere skeletons, I like to see them with some traces of flesh and blood. And with regard to the executor of this instrument, if he ever come to act as such, he will be found to understand how to take his share of the estate; yet he may well fear that he shall not get more than he is now receiving in two or three sumptuous dinners every week, with other constant friendly attentions and recollections."

"I shall take care that you do not desire a change then," replied Merton. "Still I hardly have faith to believe that I give as much pleasure as I receive when you dine with us; if so, I should persuade quite often where now I only invite."

"How many times have I entered without invitation?" inquired Rutledge, archly.

"Never, to my knowledge. Indeed, how could you — seeing that you have been requested to come at your liking or your leisure?"

"I yield — to the truth as to the temptation."

"Yield still further, then," urged Merton, "so as to favor us by dining there to-day. And take that instrument along when you come, and, if we are free from other company, read it to one or two who are mentioned therein."

"I have some engagements, yet I think I can find time to draw out the document; so that you may count on me at half past three o'clock; for the favor you ask is as agreeable to my feelings as to my taste. And in the course of the evening some of our friends may call, whom we can take for witnesses, and so complete the business, if that course will suit you."

"I see no objection to it, if, as I believe, there be no necessity for those who sign in such capacity to know the contents of the paper."

"It is not at all necessary, and not usual; their signatures are evidence only of your declaration, signing, and sealing."

"If that be the case, it will be agreeable to me; as, by so doing, it may be the sooner dismissed from my mind."

So they separated; after which Rutledge completed the form of the will, and when the hour of dining came round he entered the house of his friend.

The cloth having been removed, and the ladies being about to withdraw, Merton said, "I wish you to remain a few moments, as Mr. Rutledge has something to read to us."

After some playful remarks upon the nature of the story, Rutledge drew out a paper, and read the last will of Rufus Merton, to which they listened with feelings of happiness and sadness strangely intermingled. Is it singular that their eyes were wet, when they had to pass by the grave of one so well beloved ere they could have a view of what lay beyond? Yet it did break and scatter the thick darkness which is wont to settle over that solemn mound for such as *they* — revealing a secure path, if it could not bring consolation. They hoped, indeed, in their fond hearts, that the fatal day might be far away, for his life was immeasurably more to them than his estate, as his love had always included it. Still their faces beamed thanks, seeing that he had so generously reached forward to shield and sustain them, when he could no more raise his protecting hand.

In the evening friends called, when the instrument was executed, and passed into the hands of the devisor.

But we have seen that, after all, it was something which Merton felt to be a duty rather than a pleasure; for it made the wrong that he had done, when he had thus accomplished all the reparation in his power, to stand out irreparable in its great features; and privately perusing and meditating over the instrument, noble as it was, it seemed to him only a solemn acknowledgment of that sad truth. So he looked at it frequently, deeply, sorrowfully, and learned how impossible it was to purchase up the consequences of his acts. Too feeble and self-accusing to look calmly into the future, he communed with the shadows of the past, and tinged them with a gloom not their own. In truth, his mind had become so disordered that he could see nothing of his doing but what appeared to be evil. Even the long charm of his life was "fluttering, faint, and low."

Madam became alarmed at his depression, and, perceiving that she could do little to alleviate it, she besought him to take a journey. To this he at length gave ear, as the initiatory step in carrying out the promise which his sister had extorted from him; and, it being the first of June, he made his arrangements to travel north, and pass the summer. On leaving, Merton placed in the hands of Madam ample means to supply every thing which they might desire during a much longer period than his contemplated absence, for he had persuaded himself that he should take up his abode at the St. Charles on his return. This, however, he kept secret, out of kindness towards them rather than from any suspicion of the failure of his own resolution.

It was in the course of this journey that Merton invited Featherstone to dine with him, and found that he was agreeable, vigorous, and capable. Yet he met him but once while away, as he was in constant motion, visiting all the places of fashion, and all the points of interest to a traveller — not because he found pleasure in them, but only hoping that they might help him to forget. In this art he did not make progress; for, in consequence of activity, his health was returning, with a feeling of the life that now is; and although he set his will against the sway of his affections, they continued to gain dominion over him day by day.

It is sad seeking in the gayety of the crowd, the serenity of art, or the grandeur of nature, when we seek to veil the faces of those who are dear to us, especially when the show is expected to take the place of those we love! The heart retires from all such chaffering for its gems, and soon grows weary of all outward attraction.

It was in this mood that Merton turned from the throng to enter the quiet village on the edge of which his youthful love lay buried. As he bent before the headstone of the grave, and read her sculptured name, he was drawn back to early scenes, to meditate on the mysterious frustration of our schemes; on how rarely we reach that which we seek; on how different from our plot Fate draws out the tragedy of life.

So he left the sad place, more perplexed than ever, and aching for sympathy, yet struggling against thoughts of home. As his health had become quite reëstablished, go where he would, he found the needle of his soul still pointing painfully southward, swerving, it might be, for a few moments, to some other point, yet finding no rest there. Thus being made to feel, day by day and hour by hour, that, although a voluntary wanderer, he was no less an unhappy exile, the early September found him on the way to New Orleans.

When he arrived out, he seemed to be oblivious of the charms of the St. Charles! and as the shades of evening fell, he entered into that house over the threshold of which, three short months before, he had persuaded himself that he could refrain from passing. So the custom of a lifetime smiles at the impotence of sickly resolution, knowing that it can succeed to power, over far mightier obstacles, well nigh when it pleases. So he felt its summons, and so he yielded.

Yes; Merton had come to confession! and what are they who do not know enough of themselves to follow him with pity? Truly, the heart of man is a great deep; and over all its warm and rich latitudes trade winds sigh, and suffer no change of direction; only the colder and more barren regions are swept by variable and uncertain gales.

Yet, after a time, the memory of his defeat would steal in to trouble his spirit, and that of his broken promise to reproach him. That these recollections disturbed his repose is sufficiently apparent from the way in which he sought to divert his thoughts into other channels. His letter of invitation to Featherstone, written almost immediately after his arrival home, is an indication of the unrest of his mind. By this light we can see how the dove of his soul was seeking, in outward activity, far-reaching kindness, and apparent benefit, some peak above the flood to rest upon; and no doubt it may at length return, on weary wing, with something like the olive of peace; but it can be only a torn branch, that may never take root beside his door to cast its protecting shade around his hearth.

CHAPTER IX.

> Sweet, good night!
> This bud of love, by summer's ripening breath,
> May prove a beauteous flower when next we meet.
>
> SHAKSPEARE.

A FEW mornings after Merton had received the letter of Featherstone, accepting his invitation, he called into the St. Charles, as was his daily custom; when, seeing his young relative's name on the register, he made inquiry, and, learning that he had arrived late in the night, walked into the reading room to look over the news of the day while awaiting his appearance.

In a short time, however, Featherstone came in from the breakfast hall, and very cordial and mutually pleasing was their meeting.

The congratulations being over, Merton remarked, "You must be somewhat wearied, or disturbed at least, by your long journey, and you should take a few days for rest and recreation. Our city has some attractions; and you will find a pleasant drive down to the Battle-ground, or out to Carrolton, or over the shell road to the Lake."

"I do not feel the need of repose or pastime," replied Featherstone, "as every stage of the travel has been agreeable, and without fatigue; and, if it still be your desire, I prefer to enter immediately into business — taking views of the town and its environs as occasional hours of leisure, in the intervals of employment, may afford me opportunity."

"That shall be as you please. And when you are ready, I

will introduce you to my associates in business. They know my views, and are expecting you."

So, without more ceremony, he entered into the commission house; where, with a mind naturally keen and comprehensive for trade and commerce, and with fine health and firm resolution, he soon mastered all the forms, and became familiar with the details, so that, in a comparatively short time, he began to look forward and calculate the prospects and suggest operations which were received with approbation and sealed with success. If he was skilful to please the members of the "firm," and taught them to feel, in many ways, that he was an acquisition, he was yet sensitive to his own independence, and careful not to defer too pliantly to any, not even to Merton himself; but met him with reasons, and won his respect by making him feel that he also was a man. It is possible he discovered that such a course would best please him; yet it is extremely doubtful if he would have taken any other, even had it appeared more useful at the moment, for he was shrewd, and observation might have taught him that it was next to impossible to play a part every hour in the day, wherein, if he failed but once, he would be looked upon with distrust. Such disguise is a portion of the daily dress of very many. Yet no man was ever so uncouth of manner, or dogmatic in opinion, but his natural habit was the best for special occasions, as well as for common wear — being not only more easy, but more becoming even. Certainly, a simpering make-believe is game quite too worthless for the poor arrows of ridicule.

From the first, Featherstone rendered himself very acceptable; and, while he was unfolding his business talents under the keen and approving observation of the merchants, Merton felt a degree of satisfaction which led him away from looking too curiously into his own condition. In opening a path to affluence for the son of his cousin, he had intended a kind action; and now he believed it to be a wise one as well: this sent a current of peace to his troubled heart. In fine, judging simply from his appearance, a man of the world might say that he was taking a more healthy view of things; yet, perhaps, a higher point of observation would have disclosed a different prospect. Be that as it may, he certainly was more reconciled to his way of life, as he could again trust himself to speak of it. Taking Featherstone to ride one day, — as he did frequently after business was over, — he said, "It is a great satisfaction to me to see that you are making friends here; and you have shown such talents for business that we hope you will come to the conclusion to remain with us."

"I like the place and the employment," replied Featherstone; "and, if it be for me to decide, the decision is already made."

"Such being your pleasure, I will take care that it is for your interest also," said Merton. "But let me caution you against applying yourself so closely as you have done; for much of the year our climate will not sanction it. You should give more hours to rest, and take more frequent recreation. There is little necessity of your returning to the store after dinner, and never so soon as you do. The time which is socially and temperately passed at table is not only the brightest of the day, but is richly repaid in health and length of life. And, speaking of this, I should like to have you dine with me at my house; but I have hitherto refrained from asking the favor because that, you being from the north, I feared my way of living might hurt your sense of propriety; therefore I feel bound to give you an idea of it before I go further. You are aware that I am not married; yet a woman of mixed blood keeps my house, and has for many years, and takes her place at my table, whoever may be the guests — in truth, she and her daughter are my family."

"I see nothing in the picture to deter me from taking the chair you offer; on the contrary, I should like to look upon it."

"If it be every way acceptable, it will be gratifying to me to receive you," said the patron. "So come to-morrow — three o'clock will be in time."

Entering the city by the canal, he drove through a street, with shade trees in the centre, and pointed out to Featherstone the place of his residence; which he looked upon with eager curiosity as they passed by, for he had been fully informed, by more than one, of the elegance and luxury of the abode.

If rumor had exaggerated his conception so that he saw nothing remarkable in the mere exterior, his mind turned all the more readily to what might be within — and especially on the beauty and seclusion of the daughter.

When, at length, the night had passed, and so much of the day that the time appointed for dining had arrived, punctual to the moment he presented himself at the door and touched the bell, which was answered by Pomp, in full official costume, — black, with white vest, — who, on learning his name, conducted him into the parlor.

There Merton soon met him, and leading the way to the dining room and the sideboard, proffered every variety of refreshment which that choice piece of furniture could display in the day of its social preëminence. After a few minutes, however, they returned to the parlor, when Madam came down. Calm and self-possessed, she glided easily into the ordinary topics of conversation; fluent, graceful, and so kindly withal, as to make the guest feel that he was welcome. Every thing was touched with the fairest propriety; so much so, that, when the slave placed the tureen upon the table, and Pomp threw wide the doors, and turned to his accustomed place without a word, and drew back her chair, while Featherstone led her to the seat, and was invited to take one by her side, —

if he had come with the expectation of seeing any thing singular, he did not find it, except in unusual deference and friendliness. The entertainment itself was of the first order. In richness, variety, and art, the courses surpassed all that he had seen, and were heightened to their utmost zest by the ministering spirits of the world's vintage, some fresh and sparkling, others sedate with age, and sunned to perfection; while all the attendant circumstances flowed on with the ease and harmony of a daily custom.

Agreeable as was every part of the feast to Featherstone's inclination and increasing habit, he yet felt disappointment in not meeting the daughter; but thought it not wise to inquire the reason, still hoping to see her before the evening had passed away.

As the dinner drew to a close, and he found leisure to contemplate the scene, he felt that he was not only in gentle and cultivated presence, but that every word and glance were tokens of affection. Of that glowing temperament for which her color is celebrated, Madam could be said to have, at that period of her life, only traces of beauty; and perhaps it was never so remarkable as in many of quadroon blood; yet her sweet soft voice and yielding grace made it easy to perceive, that, if fascinated by the first notes, you would fain linger for the last strain of the song. And chafed and tossed by the fierce surges of commerce, as Merton must have been in his long career, one could see that *there* he ever found a placid and sunny haven.

At the usual hour the horses were drawn up before the door, and, dinner being over, the gentlemen took seats in the carriage for Lake Pontchartrain, — one of the most charming of drives, — where the soft south wind whispered to the trees, fanned the savanna, and just agitated the susceptible surface of the refreshing water, from the shore of which they gazed on the glory of the departing sun, as he bent over the wave with a lambent glance, and gave its sweet bosom a parting kiss ere he sank to rest.

It was a clear and serene evening in which they loitered home, while the pale shadows began to flit along the landscape as the full moon came forth to queen the night, and unfold a world of beauty that fills with adoration those who own fealty to her throne.

When, at length, they drew rein before the eastern entrance to the house, where, the door standing open, the level moonbeams had glided in to play with the shadows and turn every thing to picture, and amid which Madam appeared like a fresco, smiling and breathing welcome,—Merton felt the night to be his friend; and Featherstone thought of what he had heard, and read, and dreamed of sunny climes and secluded bowers.

As they entered, Madam said to Merton, "Some gentlemen wait for you in the dining room."

On which announcement he passed in, while Featherstone paused to speak with the quadroon. But seeing another lady at that moment quite near him, though in shadow, it arrested his remark, which Madam observing, she said, "Mr. Featherstone, permit me to introduce you to my daughter Flora."

Being thus called forth, she arose and advanced a step into the moonlight, which flashed from her dark locks, and seemed, to Featherstone's excited imagination, to flow and nestle over all her form, like bees on the fairest and sweetest flower of

> "The gardens of Gul in her bloom."

Featherstone also advanced, and taking her hand, said, "It gives me pleasure to meet you; indeed, I hoped to see you at dinner; and I should like to hear what excuse you can offer for being absent."

"The time is not suited to my studies," she replied, smiling; "for at that hour I take a lesson in French from one of the Sisters of Charity."

"Your mother might readily save you the trouble of going from the house for that learning, or at least occasionally; for I observe that she speaks the language with ease."

"O, no," said Madam; "I should be a poor teacher, for I am not always certain of my accent when I pass out of the common phrases of conversation. And Sister Henrietta is a native of Paris, and knows the best usage; and besides this, which makes her so desirable an instructress, the money that she thus acquires finds its way, like rays from heaven, into the darkest paths of distress."

"They are a singular class of women," Featherstone remarked; "and I have read something of the charities of her order; yet I confess to little interest in their faith, and less in their persons."

"But Sister Henrietta is a charming person!" interrupted Flora.

"There may be exceptions," Featherstone explained. "I hope she has not quite persuaded you into adopting her way of life."

"She has deeply interested me in herself," Flora replied. "Indeed, I like her so much that I have no wish to close my lessons. There is something so gentle in her ways, so touching in her accents, and so pensive in her expression, that I linger near her when I should leave, wishing to hear her story, yet fearing to ask the favor. And yet she makes me sad — seeming as if when she spoke, it would be of the loved and the lost; for she appears as though she awaited some one who is long in coming."

"Has she youth and beauty?" inquired Featherstone.

"I have never thought of them, she is so lovely," replied

Flora, "and has such courage amid the fever — such feeling for those who suffer."

"Then she is, probably, trying to escape from disappointment in devotion; or in some desperate hour has been lured to the taking irrevocable vows, which appoint her to a mission beyond teaching French and ministering to the sick — being an instrument of that Power, which, seeking for universal dominion, enters every avenue of distress, penetrates every passage to the heart, carrying comforts rather than the crucifix to the dying parent; hoping thereby to gain the child that it may enervate the conscience so as to stamp the mind with its opinions; thus slowly but surely leading back the generations to the Roman fold. What work are you reading with her now?"

"We finished Corinne to-day, and it made me very melancholy; while Sister Henrietta's eyes filled with tears over many passages, so that I was ready to believe, had it been possible, in point of time, that she was Corinne herself, only that the sister was more resigned to her fate."

Madam here asked to be excused, saying that she had engagements for a short time.

When she had gone, Flora and Featherstone walked to the door, as if simultaneously drawn by the moonlight, which was softly leaving the hall as the orb ascended.

Standing near, they were silent for a few moments, when Featherstone said, in his softest and most subdued tone, "You must not so wrong me as to be absent when I dine here again."

"Is not a night like this more lovely than the day to meet in?" she inquired, as she looked out on shadow and tree, with the leaves just kissed by the breeze, and saw, bending above them, the sky from which the stars seemed to have withdrawn while Diana walked the heavens and mused of love and lonely fate.

"It is truly a most charming evening," replied he; "and to remain in the house is almost wronging the hour; do you enjoy walking at such times?"

"I rarely step out after dark; yet the calm and brooding beauty of the scene seems to whisper, 'Come!'"

"Then I hope you will kindly listen and permit me to go with you."

On this, with a sweet assenting smile, she disappeared. But, in a few moments, the rustle that had died away in some chamber rose again, and with a folded shawl on her arm and bonnet in hand, she joined Featherstone at the door. He took the garment, and, while she was tying her bonnet, wrapped it gracefully and tenderly around her form, and, taking her hand, drew her arm gently within his as they turned down the quiet street.

Touched with new and thrilling emotion — for he still retained her hand — she walked in silence. He, too, felt the power of the spell, and at length said, in a tone accordant therewith, "Your teacher must be a charming person to have so won your heart as she seems to have done."

"She is gentle and — affectionate," said Flora, trembling with the weight of the word.

"Have you ever loved any other so tenderly?"

"Yes; Oswald lured me from her for a time, until I found that he had married another and left Corinne to mourn," she replied, with ingenuous ardor. "Yet I felt so sad for his loss, seeing how it came, that I could not hate, I could only pity him!"

"How deeply you sympathize, to find in books this pulsing life! Yet only such should look into *that* mirror, so full of the reflection of the writer's heart, ever yearning for deeper and still deeper experiences of love — as though fortune's height was cold, fame's wreath repulsive, if one chosen eye did not smile on and adore the achiever of them."

"I know that it is what they call fiction; yet it seems to me so true! Do you not think it natural?"

"Yes, it is nature, heightened by art and glowing with poetry, such as we hope to find her invested with, such as we will dream we may."

So concluding, (they having reached the door on their return,) he pressed her hand to his lips; for he was one of those who win through selfish audacity what the generous cannot take even when it seems to be offered; and whispering adieu, passed out and away, full of the wild emotion which anticipation yields to such natures in such hours.

If he had some doubts how his attentions to the daughter would be received by her parents, they were dissipated when Merton, in the course of the morning meeting him in the counting room alone, said, "Now that you have learned the way to my house, Mr. Featherstone, I hope you will take your dinner there often. I should like to have you come without further ceremony whenever you are so inclined; and you will find ample room and a friendly welcome. When you cannot make it convenient to dine with us, call up in the evening; we shall always be glad to see you."

The friendliness and scope of the invitation were so unexpected to Featherstone that it gave him some embarrassment; which was certainly a new vein in him, as he expressed his acknowledgments, and spoke of the pleasure of the visit. He, in truth, was thinking more of the opportunity for continuing his attentions to the daughter than of the words of his reply. Cautious at first, he gradually availed himself of Merton's invitation to the full extent; particularly for the evenings, wherein he took a lively interest in all that gave Flora pleasure or employment.

So he approached her; so through the winter he pressed on, assiduously unfolding her affections and gaining her confidence with all the appliances known to that kind of conquest under the most favorable circumstances.

But why tell the often-repeated tale that another all-trusting heart had listened to the summons, believing it to be love, when it had no deeper meaning than passion, and yielded the treasure of her affections to one who not only gave no bond, but would be full likely to squander it or toss it among his companions in arms when he marched on!

Yet *she* loved, and, having but little hope besides, she listened. Let us not censure, but ask if the fault be not partly ours. Let us remember that the circumstances of her birth, with the inhuman laws and prejudices which beset her race, had not only dimmed all brighter prospect in that direction, but had left yawning at her feet a fiery gulf, which made this seem a heaven.

CHAPTER X.

Ye who have known what 'tis to dote upon
A few dear objects, will in sadness feel
Such partings break the heart they fondly hope to heal.
BYRON.

As the spring advanced, the fact intimated at the close of the last chapter became known to Merton. At first he was filled with astonishment, and burned as with fire. Then he doubted its possibility; for he had thought of his daughter only as a child. This roused indignation against Featherstone. But, when the first lacerating emotions had subsided, he began to see, in the way which they had taken, so strong a likeness to his own indefensible course, that all thought of it recoiled upon himself with the deepest condemnation. So applying the moral, he grew more lenient than ever towards others, and took home to the silence of his own bosom more than he could bear. This unceasing pressure bore down his health, and at length shattered his mind. He walked, as it were, in a cloud which dimmed the light of home, and repelled him from the public places of the city. Even the smile of his acquaintance hurt him; and if they passed with a serious face, it wounded still deeper.

His friends saw the effect, and thought his constitution was breaking up. His physician advised a change of air; to which proposition Merton acceded as he would have accepted medicine from his hand. If thence came the motion, it was business that gave direction to his steps. In truth, its far-stretching threads seemed to draw him away; as some time during the year a correspondent of their house, who lived in one of the southern cities of Europe, had become insolvent; and in distributing his assets a valuable real estate had been decreed to them, making it necessary that one of the "firm" should visit the place in order to come into legal possession.

Towards this Merton came to look, not hopefully, but as the fairest prospect which lay open. When he had settled on his course and made some preliminary arrangements, he invited Featherstone to a private interview.

That gentleman trembled as the hour of meeting approached; and at one moment, such were his apprehensions, he thought of avoiding it altogether by flight. But having so much at stake, he quickly banished that idea; and while trying to nerve himself for the emergency Merton entered. Yet he came in so humbly that Featherstone saw, at once, there were no reproaches to fear. Indeed, he seemed like a suppliant; for he was thinking how completely the happiness of Flora was in his keeping. Hence he had determined to treat him gently and generously, so that he might not only retain kind recollections of him, but have it in his power to make the path of those easy whom he found it necessary to trust so absolutely to his care.

Hastening to speak, — for he saw that it would be a relief to Featherstone, — he said, "I have some thoughts of going abroad soon."

"I saw by your despatches that such a journey had become necessary," said Featherstone, with something of his usual confidence of tone.

"At my time of life," resumed Merton, "so long and adventurous a journey ought to be prefaced with all the forms which one would think it necessary to use if he knew that he should never return. Feeling this to be my true course, I find it incumbent on me to dissolve my connection with the house of Merton & Co. That, however, will require but little examination, as it is my intention to transfer my entire interest there to you; also the house where I live and all it contains, together with the horses, carriages, and stable. And, as you are a lawyer, I wish you to draw up the titles in the way that will most effectually secure the estate and appurtenances to your sole use and benefit. You can do it without making much stir, which is what I desire most particularly to avoid. Having still other property of value in the city, if, in my communication inviting you here, I awoke expectations which these gifts do not fully realize, I wish you to say so, and you shall have more, as my near relatives have no need of it; and what I do not give you now, or at some future time, I shall leave for the law to divide."

"It is ample! You have most profusely given! so that my expectations, as my skill in thanks, are far surpassed. But these titles, of which you speak, contemplate my immediate possession; would it not be much better for yourself to make a will in my favor?"

"O, no! no! I desire to avoid that instrument altogether," Merton replied, with increased energy.

"Excuse me if I seem to advise," interposed Featherstone; "but are you not pruning so deep that you may regret it when you return?"

"I think not. And that which I give you I feel to be still my own, with the assurance that it will go on increasing."

Understanding him too literally, Featherstone inquired, "Do you wish me to give you a bond to that effect?"

"I see no occasion for it; for there is a satisfaction in trusting, as well as in giving, which I desire to take. Were this property passing into the keeping of any other, I should have much to say about the final disposition of certain persons, in case I should not return; but I now yield up that responsibility, leaving it to rest entirely with you. My feelings with relation to them you surely know, for they must find a voice in your own bosom." The tears stood in his eyes as he finished this sentence, and his lips so quivered that there was silence. But in a moment he resumed, saying, "I wish you, also, to take charge of the estate which I reserve, receiving the rents and dividends during my absence, and place the money — after my family expenses are paid — to my credit in account with my bankers."

"I will attend to that, and whatever else you desire me to do."

"Be careful of my family. Use the means in your hands for their comfort. Such is my will, and in nothing do I need a more faithful executor. For the money that it may please them to spend, as well as the property which goes to you, it gives me true pleasure to bestow. The thoughts which such acts form I grow covetous of gathering, hoping that they will help to warm and cheer me, when I sit in the chill shadows of the evening of my days."

In accordance with the views which Merton had expressed, the deeds and bills were drawn and sanctioned, while he made ready for departure.

Most of his friends, on hearing of his intention, congratulated him — thinking he would find it an agreeable change, and wished they could see their own way clear. Some few, however, who had viewed enough of the world to know the value of home, said, "That which the traveller deepest learns is the strength of ties long since formed."

After the interview with Featherstone, Merton called on his sister, and, making her acquainted with his intention ot visiting Europe, asked her to accompany him, qualifying the invitation, however, by adding, "if you will be ready to leave in the course of the week, as I wish to depart at the earliest moment."

"Are you really in earnest? Have you truly so decided?"

"Yes, Mary; my preparations are well nigh completed."

"Well, I am delighted. With your tastes, and situated as you are, I could not have so long resisted the attraction. Do you really desire me to go with you, or is it only a compliment?"

"Can you think that utter loneliness would be so agreeable to me as to make you doubt my sincerity, Mary?"

"No, indeed, Rufus. And I should like to go with you, as Europe has long been to me a fond expectancy. Yet I cannot now; that would be to desert my post in the hour of engagement; my daughters need my watchful care more than ever. When I get them well settled in life I shall feel myself entitled to a furlough; and then I hope to have it in my power to see that society which gives tone and fashion to the world. But pray tell me what sends you away in such haste that you can wait for me only one little week?"

This question touched him so deeply that for a moment he was unable to reply; but at length, with constrained accent, he said, "Business calls me. One of our debtors has failed. The presence of one of us is required."

"I hope it may prove a fortunate loss!" said she, with a vivacity which sprang from a determination not to notice his depression. "Truly, I wish the failure had occurred long since, if it could then have influenced you to so desirable a step as this. How long do you intend to be absent?"

"A year; perhaps more, if I find any thing to take my attention."

"How can it be otherwise, among so many attractions! You have cultivated a taste for the beautiful, and possess the means to purchase. Hence you will not only enjoy the various charms of the works which have become famous, but may search out to hearten the struggle and foster the promise of to-day."

"Art is serene," Merton replied, "and invites only the calm in spirit to her contemplation. The cares of business and the deep entanglements of life are not the best schools for preparation to enter her presence."

"Why will you look sadly on that in which all the world hope to find exceeding pleasure, and which many, when they return, harp upon as if it had exalted to something almost supernatural? It is really sorrowful, and will make me anxious whenever I think of you. But you have come to tell me what you have done, or intend to do, with that sad business of which we have so many times spoken?"

Merton's cheek blanched and quivered, yet he said, "It will soon be over. That which you desired has come, and I am alone."

"Alone! Is that kind? Yet I will not reproach you when you bring me such good news. Is it entirely ended, so that I have nothing to fear?"

"I trust so. Desiring to veil it from the public gaze, I have made such disposition of it as, for a long time, will keep it in obscurity."

"Ah, that limit! I hope you have not made a will to come forth, like a ghost from a grave, and 'frighten us from our propriety'!"

"Mary, I have listened to you in this matter as much as lay in my power. I wear that *here* which prays you to be tender while we remain together, and which ought to make you think kindly of me when I am gone."

Seeing that there was no more to be gained in the direction in which she had so long pressed him, Mrs. Steel immediately changed her tone, and said, "Dear brother, do you imagine that I can do otherwise, when I remember what you have sacrificed for me and mine, and when I can see that it was the fulness of your heart which betrayed you? O Rufus! would to God that it was as it might have been! Had you mated yourself worthily, what sweet intercourse we should have had in the many years we have been so near each other! But *that* dreadful shadow would always enter along with you and make it cold. Yet I loved to see you come, notwithstanding, for your noble nature made me believe in a day of redemption."

Yielding to the impulse which she had designed to give, and to which his sorrow was so inclined, tears filled his eyes, and hers overflowed at will, for she had power to restrain or command them.

So softened, when they resumed conversation, they went down to childhood's recollections, to early affection, and together, in imagination, visited the home which ancestral energy had reared, and a mother's heart had warmed, to talk there of all the treasured past, the while the sister's pride appeared to be vanquished, and the brother's erring love to be cast out, by the presence of these purer spirits. So arises a summer tempest, cooling and purifying the atmosphere for a time; but the heart, like the sky, soon assumes its wonted aspect, and to-morrow will find Merton and his sister much the same as yesterday. She may, indeed, appear, and perhaps be, less sensitive; still it will proceed from the fact that the cause of irritation has been removed, while he will change his place, but not the current of his affections; therefore it is all an outward seeming.

Beyond mere business arrangements and an occasional pang, Merton kept his own counsel; for Rutledge, to whom alone he could have unbosomed all, was away on his northern farm; he had left town some weeks before the thought of separation entered the mind of his friend.

On the day of Merton's departure he clasped a chain of gold — from which was suspended a glittering diamond cross, with rubies to mark the prints of the bloody nails — around the neck of Flora, and placing his hand on her brow, silently invoked God to bless her; when, kissing, they turned away in tears.

So came the hour for another parting, upon which I do not choose to lift the curtain. That it was full of sad and fearful foreboding, may well be imagined. If he tried to soothe Madam with the hope of soon returning, she feared it was delusive; for she knew that he was stricken, and felt that, like the wounded deer, he was turning aside to die.

Thus Merton left the city of his adoption, in which he had made — so the world said — a brilliant fortune. In due time he arrived in New York, melancholy in manner and sad at heart — so much so that his travelling companions observed in his conversation an occasional inconsequence, or mental misstep, followed by a wandering on a way in which he seemed lost. And although after a little rest he appeared rational again, as if the aberration was but the weakness or weariness of the moment, still it gave sign that there was some singular, and, at times, overwhelming pressure on his mind.

CHAPTER XI.

O, seek not destined evils to divine,
Found out at last too soon! cease here the search;
I will impart far better; will impart
What makes, when Winter comes, the Sun to rest
So soon on Ocean's bed his paler brow,
And Night to tarry so at Spring's return.
LANDOR.

THE house in which the Vernons lived had once been a proud mansion. Its broad foundations were laid when there was many a green lawn in the quarter of the city in which it was situated, affording it room to spread out like a pasture oak, so that it bore but little resemblance to the crowded habitations of the present day, which appear, like trees in a forest, to be stretching up as if to find a purer air and a crown of sunbeams. Although its youth had long passed, and its melancholy days were come, yet it still stood firm, and wore a venerable aspect; and the wide, deep arch of the door-way indicated the generous nature or the private sumptuousness of him who reared the structure for his abode, and bequeathed it to his daughter, an only child and the mother of Aurelia.

Seen at the period of which Mrs. Summers spoke, the sketch she gave of the habitation did not overshade its gloom. But at this time it had softened somewhat, as one of the upper blinds was quite open, and even the window upraised, for it was a warm and bright afternoon in May. And making it brighter still, within, there appeared a lady seemingly before a mirror for the purpose of imparting the final grace to her apparel (by the way in which she turned, and touched fold and ribbon) ere she passed out to give her wealth of beauty to the public eye, and diffuse a charm which makes the frequented promenades of a city forever attractive.

But while she was adjusting her bonnet, the door opened, and Mrs. Vernon entered. Instantly observing her daughter's neat, yet simple, toilet, she rather imperiously inquired, "Why do you not wear a silk? The people whom you are intending to visit make dress a subject of thought and conversation. Why do you persist in doing what you know I do not wish you to do?"

"Do you think that I have no better reason for my choice than simply to oppose you, mother?"

"I am sure I don't know what other motive you can have."

"I am a creature of moods, mother, not mode, only in so far as it pleases me. Besides, I have a particular fancy for this dress to-day, and thought I might venture to indulge it."

"I cannot approve of your taste, for, considering the friends you are to visit, it is very unwise. People in our condition should be careful, on such occasions, to dress as richly as possible — a muslin is too suggestive of our state. But where are your pearls?"

"Since you told me that it could not be long before I should be obliged to part with the gems, for something more necessary, I cannot wear them."

"That is silly. *I* should wear them the oftener. You cannot hurt them."

"If you did not desire their disuse, you should not have mentioned the fact, for you know that I scorn deception."

"How singular you are! The ornaments are still ours, and we may never have to part with them; at least I shall struggle to keep my father's wedding gift."

Perceiving that her mother was about to enter upon a subject which she had frequently lectured upon of late, — more, she thought, than was necessary for instruction, — Aurelia chose, half playfully, half satirically, to adhere to one more hackneyed, inasmuch as it was less annoying. Hence she said, "Mother, I value the ornaments quite as highly as you; though it be now only for their exquisite settings, and the fancies that flit around when I muse on their antiquity — found, as they were, with the remains of the wearer, in the lava-tomb of Pompeii."

This being a favorite reminiscence of Mrs. Vernon, as it recalled the affluence in which she was reared, she replied, with an eager glance at the jewels, "Yes, your grandfather and I were in a newly-excavated palace of that long-buried city, when a soldier followed us apart, and timidly showing them, named a price which was quickly paid. Time, indeed, had dimmed and corroded the gems, and they were replaced with the choicest that could be procured from the orient. Yet, valuable as they are, my father always prized their perfect mounting far above the pearls. And when he gave them to me, he said, 'Let them pass down with our blood' — and it would be one of the sorrows of my life to part with them."

"I am pleased that my grandfather so regarded the jewels. I like to trace to him my passion for art; and fancy it stronger for the lineal current. But may they not have taken some baleful charm from the skeleton on which they were found?"

"How childish! I hope you will not encourage such superstitious fancies."

"Do not ships bring diseases from the Indies, mother? And when I call to mind what the Pompeians were, may I not be shy of their trinkets? Yet they are worthy of the best days of Grecian cunning," she continued, taking up the ring. "Observe the indentation of the palm, the vigorous grasp of the veined and manly hand, so life-like in every part, and finished to a nail, as Horace said of Augustus. How many have had joy, in putting it on, which did not last! I sometimes fancy that Dido might have worn it when she stood,

> 'With a willow in her hand,
> Upon the wild sea banks, and waved her love
> To come again to Carthage.'"

"I wish you could think of something else besides love, Aurelia."

"Of what would you prefer that I should think, mother?"

"Of that without which it is not respectable, and cannot subsist, if you will make me explain."

"Mother, I have listened to this lesson many times in deferential silence, hoping that, when you saw it was understood, you would cease. But, seeing no such prospect, I feel impelled to say, that any further iteration will be more likely to make me wilful than wise."

"Indeed, Miss Vernon! But what if I feel it to be my duty to teach until I see that you heed my teaching?"

"Do you believe it right, mother, to be continually directing my attention to the mere money prizes in this lottery, when you know how much the whole current of glittering life inclines us to overvalue them?"

"Are you expecting to meet Mr. Park at Mrs. Fardel's this evening?"

"I have no reason for such expectation; yet, to be frank with you, — believing you to be my friend, mother, — I certainly hope to meet him there."

"Do you think it dutiful, or becoming, to disregard my most serious admonitions, and seek the society of a person, who, although he may be every thing which you fancy him, has not the means to make you comfortable in a respectable boarding house even?"

"Well, mother, he has not invited me to that kind of entertainment; and, if he do, I pledge myself to consult you before I accept the offer."

"My child, you may some time learn that this is not a light matter, or an ignoble aim, to which I point, although it pleases you to treat it so now; yet if you live out half your days you will come to think as much of wealth and respectability as she whose advice — given solely for your good — you so strangely disregard."

"I fear it, mother — from my soul I do; for I frequently find myself wishing that Mr. Park could add wealth to his gifts and accomplishments; and I sometimes weigh them even; yes, put gold over against a glorious nature, coolly trying to estimate the joys of each! and there are moments when I incline to the gilded side. Is it not a sad confession?"

"I hope it may be a true one. If you do not wish to continue to descend the dark way in which we are now walking, you must beware how you get your heart entangled with any thing that may prevent you from leaving it; and remember, that it is as clear as noonday that your fortune is in your own hands," (this was an allusion to a middle-aged gentleman, of large estate, who evidently desired to purchase her,) "and if you do not take advantage of it you will certainly come to repentance. In this I give you the lesson of experience as well as of observation; for I have seen youth, and known love, and feel the shadow, and have felt the sun, which you have not; yet you have it in your power to make it shine once more on our house, if you but resolve on it."

"Mother, I have said that there are times when I am prone to put my trust in riches; and I have a taste for luxury in its most voluptuous forms; for the taint is in our blood — and do you think that it requires precept on precept to develop it?"

"Do you mean to reproach your parents? What an ungrateful child you are for all our sacrifices that you might learn wisdom and secure your happiness in life!"

On this, Aurelia, turning towards the door, said, "I think that it is quite time for me to go; and on the way I will try to meditate on the happiness which you desire for me."

As the door closed Mrs. Vernon said, "How few children prove blessings to their parents, or will be guided by their counsels!"

If Aurelia, in talking with her mother, had exaggerated, she had truly disclosed, her inclinations, and foreshadowed the future. She was essentially the child of her parents. Of the ruling trait of her mother's mind she had deeply partaken, though veiled and graced by an amenity of manner that came from the paternal line, as well as her more ardent and impassioned temperament. In her tastes she vibrated to extremes; now musing of the simple and secluded life of the heart, and now dreaming of the gorgeousness of a queen, and the sceptre of dominion.

Had she fallen on a time when some Pericles swayed people and state by the authentic supremacy of genius, she would have been drawn to him as was the gifted Aspasia; and, like her, cared little for the mere "forms and ceremonies" where there was no fear of an imperfect union. So impressible was she, that, in the midst of the art and society which such masters gather or create, she would have studied simplicity, and kept their elevation; and, for the same reason, should circumstances lead her to a barbarian court, she would be likely to sink to their tone, and become ambitious of their gauds and gold.

Aurelia met three or four other persons of her acquaintance to take tea; soon after which they sat down to a *lively* game of whist; for it was full of conversation, or question and exclamation, such as—"What is the trump?" "Whose lead is it?" "Let me look at the last trick." "I'm sure I've forgotten what suits are out — wasn't that your lead?" "There, you've trumped the best card!" "That's a thirteener!" "Honors are easy." "Excuse me, but I played three" — all of which was mingled with considerable by-play and consequent merriment; so that a game of skill — and one of the most intricate in its highest combinations, and requiring the best diplomacy, also, as every glance or motion of your opponents may be weighed — in their hands sank nearly down to the blind chance of the die. Evidently whist was the nominal, not the real object for which they had gathered around the table. Late in the evening Park came in, and, of course, was chided by his cousin for delay. The other persons expressed their pleasure at meeting, with the exception of Aurelia, who was nearly silent, —

> "But when in turn she gave her hand, I ween
> Their tender glances met and kissed between."

Park did not fail to notice her simple attire; and, with his view of life it was a source of pure enjoyment, for it seemed to him a good omen. So he thought, "Our tastes are alike in this, also; or she has adopted it to please me!" which, for the moment, was the sweeter hope.

Under such influence, he entered with spirit into their conversation, and heightened it with wit, and point, and piquancy, until it moved on a higher plane, to which the company were borne so easily that they were not aware of the change before it began to subside after he had gone.

As Park and Aurelia walked down the street together, he said, "It has given me pleasure to meet you at my cousin's, and, although she is somewhat frivolous, I am grateful for her kindness, as I just told her."

"She may be rather busy with trifles, yet she has ready

sympathy on all occasions, and is very friendly to me. But what a funny little thing her husband is! He seems to be her spaniel; and I fancy that she keeps a ball, and trains him to 'fetch' when they are alone. For he appears to be forever on the watch, and wags round as though he were anxious for you to drop something, so that the play might begin; and I have indulged him in a handkerchief and a glove two or three times, to his great satisfaction and my amusement. Is it not singular that she should have married such a person?"

"It does not much surprise me, when I consider how often the mistake is made by those who have but little discernment, or who close their eyes to consequences; and my cousin must fall into one or the other of those classes. Yet she had a face which pleased me in my boyish days; for she had aspirations, but they have long since gone. Still I have no doubt she had a hope, or rather a hallucination, that marriage with this man would foster her ideal; as it would bring books, and pictures, and leisure; yet, instead of fulfilling, it has dissipated the dream."

"I should think it quite equal to that," said Aurelia; "indeed, a desert with the Memnon, musical only to the morning, or even the dull Sphinx, would yield more desirable sustenance and companionship."

"Yes, the wigwam of some Osceola, it seems to me, would be a stronger temptation! For truly, a simple life is the most cheerful; and to have but few wants is wisdom. Pictures are but poor and imperfect copies of that nature which lies open to every seeing eye; and books, even, are but *reflections* of our own spirits, more or less dwarfed, deformed, or exaggerated by the reflectors; while men are great and original in proportion as they explore the depths without these aids. And that leisure, also, which we so desire, soon becomes a dreary vacuity to those whose minds are not the royal instruments on which some Muse lays her inspiring hand."

"I know that use rarely follows possession; yet the world is striving for these goods, or something less worthy; and I confess that they have charms for me, thinking they help to unfold and sustain."

"It is true that such is our hope and expectation; yet they will be found to have little value, save as means to an end. I see adequate life only where there is an aim which imparts something of nobility to the countenance. Tried by this test, how many of the proud would be brought low, how many of the humble exalted!"

"On so rugged a march, would you shun the things that grace existence, even to the passing by society and friendship?"

"I would give but little time and less thought to one, but to the other my heart runs as the rivers to the sea. An equal friend is the true mirror; and he who finds the treasure has reached the height of fortune, has gained the one human solace, has entered the one earthly haven. When the great, like Greville, find it, all their after seeking is only for offerings worthy to be laid on its shrine; and he ceased not at death, even, but made his own epitaph in the praise, and sweet with the name, of Sidney."

They had reached the end of their walk, and were pausing on the steps of the house, when Park finished the last sentence; to which Aurelia made no audible reply, yet he felt that she deeply sympathized and approved.

So they parted, as they had done on similar occasions; for Park declined invitations to enter, except when calling for that purpose.

As her form grew dim in the shadow and then vanished, while the door closed, Park turned away on his homeward walk, and mused of love, and beauty, and high-mated souls; and said, in his secret spirit, "She is a perfect creature, in mind as in mould! Ah, had I the fortune and the power, now, which in five years I will wring from the world's reluctant heart, I would lay them at her feet, and make her relations proud of the alliance. But as it is, what would my offering seem, other than a supplication? Therefore I must strive to lay these sweet sad visions, and learn to labor and to wait."

CHAPTER XII.

What is the worst of woes that wait on age?
What stamps the wrinkle deeper on the brow?
To view each loved one blotted from life's page,
And be alone on earth, as I am now.
Before the Chastener humbly let me bow,
O'er hearts divided and o'er hopes destroyed.
BYRON.

WHEN Merton had embarked for England, his near relatives felt relieved; yet, fearing the future, they inquired how they might honorably prolong his absence. Having this chiefly in view, — as a new administration had just succeeded to the places of power and favor with which he sympathized, — his friends applied to the president to appoint him consul of that city whither business of a more private nature was directing his steps. For this important purpose they appeared with such names and such weight of political reasons, that he bore off the prize from the contending host; so that, when, after a leisurely journey, he arrived at his place of destination, he found a stately packet awaiting him, closed with the broad seal of his country.

Reflecting upon this honor, which he supposed came unsolicited, he indulged a hope that the chief magistrate was not yet wholly subject to the multitude of office-seekers who beset the steps and besiege the abode of a newly-inaugurated president.

Having examined and deeply pondered the important matter, he was, on the whole, pleased with the appointment; for he saw that it might afford some little occupation, and lead persons to call on him whose information might be acceptable, if their society was not such as he would have thought desirable at home. Indeed, when we are far from home, one whom we knew only by sight, and passed with indifference in those accustomed walks, comes to us clothed with deep and strange fascination.

If Merton suspected, from the appearance of the port, that the emoluments of his office would not be large, it was some satisfaction to know that they would come in the form of fees; therefore he should receive for the actual labor just what the great statesmen of his country had estimated it to be worth. And, on the whole, he felt proud of the freedom of the government, when he realized how completely they had left him at liberty to entertain all those "fellow-citizens" who might call upon him, without any mercenary taint on the motive; for the love of giving was deep in his heart — so deep, that he received some satisfaction in administering from his own treasury to those national wants which lie beyond the ken of the eagle.

There, like a valiant man, as he was, he held the post for more than three long years, against all comers. Yet, in that time, it had grown to be exceedingly irksome; for his spirits had died out, and his flesh had wasted away, making him to appear as though some invisible and sleepless foe had laid siege to the man, and, while sapping and mining all the towers of his strength, was slowly consuming him with famine. The malady of his mind also, was becoming more and more observable, so that, at length, he yielded; but not until there came over him the conviction that it was too late.

The resignation of his office, however, gave but little relief; and, feeling that his life was drawing to a close, he journeyed slowly from place to place, — finding still some strength for that, as perpetual change had come to be his most soothing potion.

Moving on, he passed the beautiful and ever-varying landscape with a listless eye, though he would rouse up and take notice when he caught a glimpse of some bright arm of the Mediterranean. Yet human happiness pleased him more, so that he could not pass, but would order a rest, when, as the sun declined, he saw the healthy and gleeful rustics dancing in the shade. At such times, the children venturing near, the vetturino would take some of the fair and bright, and place them in the carriage, that Merton might kiss and send them away pleased with many a coin — to wonder, perhaps for some years, why he prized their lips so highly; but if they are living now, it is no longer a mystery; and it may be that this very hour they would give those, and more, for some young peasant's smile.

So, at length, he reached Naples in the most delightful season for that gay city. Taking lodgings in one of the frequented and picturesque parts of the town, he said no more about departing, but from a pleasant balcony, day after day, he watched the passing crowd, "in pleasing colors dight," and seemed to have become as a little child. His landlord thought him eccentric, and seeing that he was so weak as to need more than a servant's care and attention, he made inquiry into his condition; and finding his letters of credit ample, he gave him into the especial charge of his daughter, a graceful brunette of twenty years. He thought her particularly qualified for the office, as she had made quite an acquaintance with the English tongue, in her intercourse with the many visitors to his house from the nations to whom that language is native. Perhaps he had other reasons, which are apt to give alacrity to motion and assiduity to service.

When she first entered his apartment — for he had then been there some days — he was gazing, not only intently, but anxiously, into the passing crowd. On hearing her light step near him he looked up, and, seeing the maiden, slowly extended his thin, worn hand, and said, "I have grown weary in watching for you; I feared that I had been forgotten. But you did not come alone; where is Madam?"

"The mother you speak, say?" jumbled the girl, though in a tender tone.

"Yes, I wish her to come to me now, for I have waited very long, and I must go soon. There, it grows dark! I dare not wait longer, if they do whisper that I promised. I cannot mind it more; no, never again, never!"

On this the maiden went out, and, finding her mother, related something of the sick gentleman's conversation and his request. Soon after she entered the chamber, with the daughter, where he still sat by the window, leaning earnestly forth as if to see if any one entered the house. But, on hearing their approach, he turned his face slowly towards them, and, looking on one and on the other with a glance which came nearly to the point of sanity, though the rays soon diverged again, inquired, "Do you wish to shun me, while I am trying so hard to get to you? Did you fear that I had changed, that I had no desire to see you more? If any one has told you so he is my enemy; and if I said it I was false! O, more than in all beside. Look at these poor hands, and see how they have pined for yours; and feel how wasted I am because I could think only of you, yet you came not. Did they say that it would hurt your good name? but I will not ask the reason of your long delay, now that you have so kindly come. Let us eat; bring meat, bring wine, for now I can grow strong again, hoping to be happy if divided no more." Understanding something of what he desired, the daughter, procuring it, drew up a small table, and placed it before him. But he looked on the food listlessly, and at length put it away, saying, "I must have dined before you came, and you need not wait, for you have travelled far; and I will rest a while." Turning away, he closed his eyes a few moments, and leaned as if sleeping; yet soon aroused, and, with a faint smile, said, "I was glad to see that you enjoyed your dinner," although they had not tasted. And, continuing, he said, "Ring, and have what remains taken out. How cold it is! let Pomp make a fire, for Rutledge, and S——, and P—— will call in this evening, and we shall want our punch warm. I had begun to think that they would never come again; no, never!"

So pausing, he appeared to fall asleep; when they glided softly away, leaving him alone. But, soon after they had gone, he roused up and fell to examining the passing people with the same careful scrutiny, though apparently more feeble than before; and the tears trickled over his worn cheeks as he said, "Ah, it was only a dream! yet dearer than all waking and waiting years; for I dreamed that I had found them, and that they still loved and believed in me; but it is all dark, cold, cold; they will come to me no more, never again; O, never!"

The landlord learned, through his wife, that the sick guest was growing more unwell and weak, and put away nourishment as though he had forgotten its use, or had lost all inclination to taste it. Indeed, Merton was fading away; wandering down toward the silent realm, the seeming rest, the ever-agitating mystery, where belief shrinks and faith trembles; yet hope, the eye of the soul, looks beyond and sees a guiding star.

On hearing how Mr. Merton appeared, the host was reminded of the priest, and kindly sent for him.

Yearning for peace, and seeing the serene repose of a *united* church, Merton had, a few months before, entered its fold under the guidance of one of those gentle shepherds, who, in seeking to assuage sorrow, still follow the Master's divinest steps.

The father whom the landlord summoned was of a different

stamp. Yet he quickly came with the implements of his profession; and — after a short interview with the publican — entering into the presence of the dying man, he found him still sitting in the bay of the window, where, although the evening was somewhat advanced and the street nearly deserted, he continued to gaze into the darkness with the same touching anxiety. But being aroused by the confident approach of the burly priest, Merton looked up, and seeing his sharp eyes and rosy face, — for his stop below was to congratulate the landlord in a bottle of his best, which became an item in his (meaning the landlord's) final account, before he ascended to shrive the dying, — a bewildered and painful expression flowed out faintly over his wan features while he said, "I thought that I had resigned; I intended to. Yet, if I am still consul, dinner will be served soon, and I am glad to see some one who looks as though he might enjoy it. Do you prefer crawfish soup? I see your face is the color of their shells." A faint smile touched his features, but, in a moment, tears obliterated it, and he continued, "I thought I was going home, and should soon see Madam and Flora. Will they prevent me? has my kind sister persuaded the president not to allow me to resign?"

The priest, who spoke the English tongue, — in truth he was born in Ireland, — replied, "It is my holy office to teach you to be resigned to the will of Heaven; and, leading you from the vanities of this life, lay open to your soul the prospect and the assurance of paradise."

Merton heeded not his words; yet, seeing the signs of his calling lying on the stand beside him, he reached out for the rosary, and, fumbling over it long as with a babe's untutored hand, at length he grasped it; though not to "patter prayer," but to shake the beads gleefully, as with an infant's comprehension. Then, fixing his gaze on the ivory crucifix a moment, he let the rosary fall, and clutched at the cross in the same painful manner. When, after much effort, he had got possession of it, he turned it over and around; and, having viewed it on all sides, he shook it with seeming dissatisfaction, and putting it away would not notice it more, but closed his eyes and leaned his head against the pillows, as though he was very weary and would fain rest.

Thus he remained while the high appointed official of Holy Mother Church went through the saving ceremony for the dying, in the faith that he was opening the gates of eternal bliss to this departing spirit! Having finished the mystic rites, he gathered up his emblems, and went down to deepen the purple of his cheek, and kindly help the host to a little more profit, ere the account of the dying guest was closed.

Yet when morning came, and the tide of life once more flowed in full and flashing current beneath and around, Merton looked out upon it with something like hope resting on his features; as if he thought that where so many were coming, those he so loved would surely come also. So, through some days, he continued; for

> "The hull drives on though mast and sails are gone;
> And thus the heart will break, yet brokenly live on."

The leeches — priest and doctor — came frequently to look upon the case; it was nothing but a case, for the generous soul of Merton was already inurned and awaiting the touch of Him who is the resurrection and the life — came rather for their profit than his, as they imbibed more than they imparted. If, while they were present, he uttered the names Madam and Flora — which seemed to be all that he now remembered — they would inquire, "Madam who? what madam do you desire to see?" Yet they were never the wiser; for these learned men did not call to mind that slaves and kings are known only by their Christian names.

But this could not last; and so, at length, as a tender child puts its little arm over the mother's neck when it has drunk its fill and desires to sleep, he turned away from the crowd, and drew his arm around the pillow which supported him, and nestling his cheek into its yielding substance, as though it were a fond, protecting bosom, breathed out his life and his love together.

When the "maimed rites" of the funeral were concluded, the body consigned to its resting place, and the bills swollen to their utmost limit, the kind and attentive disciple of the apostolic church wrote the following epistle to Featherstone:—

"City of Naples, ——

"Dear Sir: The painful duty has devolved on me of communicating to you — as I learn from your consul at this capital that you are the person whom he desired might be informed if any thing important should happen to him — the decease of your relative, Rufus Merton. I hope it will be some consolation in the midst of your distress to hear that he died without pain, and in the full communion of our Holy Church. He took the sacred symbols with child-like trust, yet, being very weak, we could not have that assurance of his immediate acceptance by St. Peter, the blessed, in whose hand are the keys eternally, which we most devoutly desire. Therefore we beseech you, for his sake, that means be supplied to say masses, so he may have that intercession which can appease and elevate to peace and bliss forevermore.

"Learning that he was a man highly honored, he having been clothed with office and intrusted with a portion of the power of your great republic, we did not bear his body to one of the city pits, but purchased a place for his burial, so that his weeping country may gather his ashes when they build his monument.

"If you should have any directions to give, or desire any further information, please address the writer, and your request shall command me.

"Yours, with the salutations of Holy Church,

"FATHER BONIFACE.

"Anthony Featherstone, Esq.,

"City of New Orleans, U. S. A."

Thus did the living seek to take profit from the dying! So passed the sorrow and penance of Merton's spirit; so found he his rest.

If, on some future memorial stone, his country chisel his epitaph, it may well read, "Faithful and devoted." If it be done by blood connections, it must be, "Generous and self-sacrificing." If Love be permitted to engrave the letters, it will appear, "Tender and true." But if some correct and spotless nature should stoop to write a word of warning, humanity could not heed it, and our kind mother Earth would lead her gentle seasons there, to weave over it a veil of perennial mosses.

CHAPTER XIII.

If trouble come, O, lie not down in tears;
Be like the mountain pine, whose soaring spears
Ne'er vanquished were by Winter's icy arms,
But fill the tempest with Eolian charms.
ANON.

DURING the four years that had passed since Rufus Merton went forth a sorrowing yet uncomplaining exile, but little change was apparent in those in whom he was chiefly interested, except what might happen in many families without particular comment, even from those who take most careful notice of the lives of their neighbors. If Featherstone no longer dined at the house, as formerly, he could plead that, Merton having withdrawn from the partnership, the larger amount of business which necessarily devolved on him made so long a walk impracticable at such an hour.

If he came in late at night, as he frequently did, he at first excused himself by explaining the custom of entertaining business friends who visit the city — a custom which had come to be considered important to success in trade; and, no doubt, the manœuvre overpays the outlay.

On such occasions — and they were frequent — he always found Flora watching, with a book for her amusement or her excuse, which she laid down in the earlier days when she heard his step, and rose up with a trembling heart and a tearful smile to meet him.

If he remonstrated, as he often did, against this course, she replied fondly or evasively, according to the mood of her questioner. Coming in later than usual, yet feeling something of his early kindness, which, being a fever of the blood, had begun to intermit, he said, "I wish that I knew how to cure you of waiting and watching for me."

"If I desire to see you as soon as you come, you will not say that you do not approve of it, for you know that I am fond of reading; and works of imagination, which you sometimes chide me for liking so well, are only felt in their fulness in night's brooding hours."

"It sounds very well, my dear; but I am thinking the book does not get your entire attention, for you wear an anxious face, which I do not wish to see; it will spoil your beauty some time."

"May I not think of you when I hear footsteps, and pause and listen even to learn if they be yours?"

"Can you distinguish my step from another's on the street, or must it touch the doorstone first?"

"I think I know its measure; for I am not often deceived, unless I have been hoping long."

"I doubt whether there is any thing more than the gradual abating of the gait, as I draw near the end of the walk, to guide you; if so, how do my steps differ from others? what is the peculiarity?"

"It refuses to be described. Yet you know there are many things from which we take intelligence, that no words can convey; for it is not in our faces alone, or our forms, or our voices, that our individuality appears, but it glances from every motion, and there is a susceptibility which notes a peculiarity in each person's atmosphere."

"That is a region which gathers no statistics, only the striking coincidence is remembered. But you would never have made my steps a study, if you were not too nervously awaiting their coming; and that, in time, will steal the color from these sweet lips," he concluded, pressing them to his.

Twining his black locks around her fingers, Flora pleaded, "Now don't you say any thing more against my sitting up until you come; for if I retire I cannot sleep, and the pillow muffles my ear so that I cannot hear; and then, if I chance to drowse a moment, I awaken with a start, like one who falls asleep in church."

"If I were you I would dismiss the thoughts that so trouble the night. Yet I suppose you will continue in the way which you have chosen; and I may try to prevent you from watching by coming earlier hereafter."

Flora did not trust herself to reply, but kissed him again and again, and clung to him as though from the deep of her heart the mists of fear were climbing up the sky of hope.

Indeed, Featherstone was not what he had once appeared to her to be; and, as time moved on, there were not wanting other indications of change — for such truth gets various confirmation — which came to trouble "the spirit of her dream." They had no true social relation. The circumstances of their connection tended to prevent them from entering into conversation on the themes which agitate and elevate the human mind. If they continued together for any length of time during the day, he appeared moody, and his tone became hard and his accent unkindly, so that Flora would take refuge in silence; this made the Sabbath as long as childhood finds it in the house of the grave and formal. Only for moments did he caress; in truth, what else might be expected of him, when his attachment penetrated no deeper than the passions? It is doubtful whether a nature like his can ever soar to those heights of love where no cloud of selfishness obscures the ineffable heaven; certainly, on the path which he had taken there was little hope, for how could he be made to see that her way was noblest, and strive humbly to walk therein? What could curb such a nature into showing any respect for one who was subject to him? No such emotion could reach Featherstone over the wall of circumstance which divided them, for his was not one of those hearts that feel sad when they can give no more; but, under the most favorable circumstances, it seemed to him enough if he attained to what may be termed delicacy of appetite. Let it not be supposed by this that he is to be classed with the grosser crowd, "the mob of gentlemen who live at ease." On the contrary, he almost nightly declined the invitations of the "elegants," with whom he associated, to descend to their pleasures; so that they thought him squeamish, and marked him as peculiar.

Flora saw, also, that he was ambitious, that he had not yet reached his aim; and consequently she felt that sooner or later he was capable of casting off every weight which he thought might retard his rising. And, notwithstanding his usual playfulness and occasional tenderness, she was aware that in no hour of calm and thoughtful joy did he think of her as an attainment, or, when storms lowered, did he turn to her bosom as a haven of rest. Being almost secluded, and having trusted so deeply, she studied her lover in every light in which he presented himself. As they grew intimate, and glimpses of his character more and more frequently came up to view, which threw doubt on the tenure, she fell to examining her security, as a miser might pore over a disputed title to his whole estate. So, at length, she saw all; and having been endowed by nature with a fortitude of soul which could meet fate, be that fate what it might, she slowly and sadly admitted into her mind the possibility of change. It was from this discovery that, painfully yet perseveringly, she began to build up in her heart a separate existence, and in time came to enter it with composure, and pray for its continuance. It gave her strength and elevation to go down and muse there; so that Featherstone saw — when she came out as from some mysterious place, like Numa from the Egerian grotto, to greet his coming — that she had a soul which could dwell apart; an apparition that chastened his manners and imposed a more thoughtful course on his conversation. Strange to say, this did not please him; for, however he might have valued it in another, here he had looked only for dalliance; indeed, he had never thought of his mode of life as any thing permanent, but only as an arrangement for a time.

So viewing the connection, the birth of a son, in the autumn after Merton's departure, did not help to bind their union, but set him to harden himself against all its natural influences. He would not permit it to take his Christian name, although the then fond girl and doting mother implored him with tears. He would not caress it or smile upon it, but turned away as though he loathed the sight, yea, dreaded that sweet bud of life, that heavenly flower, with capacity of infinite unfolding, which nature had committed to his care.

This was too chill a blast for even her affection; and sorrowing over it long, at length every tear turned to stone, to form a dividing wall, and shape into a habitation separate from that which Featherstone had promised her; for she felt the need of a sanctuary whereto she could take her son, making it not only a holy but a happy place.

In this way the child came to be the hope of Flora, as he was the solace of Madam, giving her almost constant employment during Merton's long absence, and that too of such a charming nature, it saved her from many lonely, sad, and desolate thoughts.

To appearance, Madam had not greatly changed since Merton's departure. Something of her flesh, it may be, had gone; yet, though she saw many silent hours, and often wore an introverted eye, she still had health and heart. Her chief struggle had been in the parting hour; for she saw in it a conviction that he would never more return; and she felt nearly all that she might have done had she closed his eyes for the grave. Yet there was that in the cause of their separation — as she understood it — which awoke a resolution to bear. She could not see, as he did, the calamity which had so crushed him; hence she thought that he had gone forth, partly for his health, partly on account of business, and something of dissatisfaction with his mode of life — no more; for Merton had kept his sister's torture, and the spectral perturbers of his spirit, veiled from her eyes.

All communication, too, had closed with his departure. She could not write, because he had made no such request; and if she long cherished a hope of receiving a letter from him, it came not, nor any token of remembrance ever reached her from his hand. If Featherstone had knowledge of him, — which he rarely received, and then only in relation to business; for Merton's affections, as in his youth, were still sacred to their object, — it was his humor to withhold it from her; and, situated as she was, she could not persuade herself to make inquiry in that quarter — his bearing towards his child having filled her with distrust and dread. In truth, she did not often see him; his footsteps being a warning for the withdrawal of his son, and she always went with him.

To this the child was not averse, it being in the nature of the mother, as it was her office, to guide and correct, while his grandmother was his companion and playmate — one instructed, the other amused; consequently, it is easy to perceive with which he preferred to pass the hours.

Frederick, or Fred, as they always called him, was a bright and high-spirited boy, quick to learn and strong to retain; and well he might be, if what Tennyson sings be true, that the mother makes us most. He could already question curiously, and sometimes deeply; while his most careful and considerate mother, in this particular certainly, never wearied of answering, but sought lovingly to bring every thing, towards which his young mind was struggling, down to his comprehension. In this, how few affectionately consider, and so are truly wise! Yet to those who heed and kindly help these strange inquirers, it will be no surprising intelligence when I say that this child led Flora into new fields of thought, which could not but give strength to her mind, and frequently filled her with the purest pleasure.

Such moments the curious child was sure to mark; and, not feeling the happiness which he saw that she was enjoying, he would inquire, "What do mother see? Tell Fred what it be, mother."

But she could not answer; for she felt that she had ranged into a realm as yet incommunicable to him; so she kissed him, and pressed down the lids of his unfathomable eyes, which seemed to be straining for comprehension; drew him to her bosom, called him her darling, her treasure, her precious trust; sighed, and smiled, and wept, as she was swayed by varying and all-blissful emotion.

O, a child is a divine gift, a sweet and long-unfolding mystery; and she who has one that she can love, and, for the glory of his promise, admire, and beholds a free field spread out before him in which to expand and contend, with a final tribunal that will consent to crown only the most worthy, has but little left to sigh for, and can nerve herself to step firmly among the burning ploughshares.

At length Featherstone began to perceive that he was not the all in all which he once had been; and having no affection for Fred, he naturally grew jealous of him, because he saw that he was the light of Flora's eyes. In this form did his offspring visit his spirit, until he received and entertained the thought — and came to look calmly upon it, yea, gloat over it

— that it was in his power to sell the boy whenever he pleased! He even had it on his tongue's end, two or three times, for utterance, when Flora did not meet him with warmth, although he himself was cold; yet he suppressed it; not that he relented through returning tenderness, but because he feared the malediction of Merton.

Along such a gulf had Featherstone mused and contemplated the prospect — for he was naturally exacting and overbearing; while his uniform success, in all his undertakings, had helped to harden his heart. If fortune had favored him with reverses, and, for a season, made him feel some sadness and brokenness of spirit, he might have turned to her who would have been quick to perceive, and skilful to pour wine and oil into, his wounds; the recollection of which would have made him less harsh and ungentle, and touched him, at times, with tender and grateful thoughts. But, as it was, he could talk about his "arrangement" (so he called it) with his associates, and laugh over it, as though it were merely a spring blossom, which would fall to the earth, or wanton with the winds, whenever something more desirable should naturally put forth to flourish in its place.

It was in such a mood that he received the letter of Father Boniface, communicating the decease of Merton. And if, for a moment, he was startled by the sudden unveiling of the spectre that flits from the grave to visit the guilty, he soon shook it off, as there arose, over all, the thought that the bolts of power had at length descended to his quiver, arming him to crush what he could not win — for it was in him to prefer to subdue or even to devastate a heart, rather than so attract as to be joyfully invited to its throne.

It was not in Featherstone to perceive that Love is the only true, the only absolute ruler — the smile beaming from her sacred lips being the noblest guerdon of devoted service.

He was not aware how every other power curses the possessor, in proportion as he sways it to his own gain, hardening all upon whom it falls, and rousing up resistance irresistible; while Love melts and moulds, and gives form, and life, and joy to the universe. Love, indeed, is that magic word which welcomes the true possessor to all that heart desires, and all which young-eyed Hope can descry from her mount of vision.

CHAPTER XIV.

Let us swear an oath, and keep it with an equal mind,
In the hollow Lotos land, to live and lie reclined
On the hills like gods together, careless of mankind.
TENNYSON.

SOON after Featherstone received the letter of the priest, he enclosed it, with the following note, to the sister of Merton:—

"Dear Madam: I hasten to convey to you the mournful intelligence, which I have just received, of the decease of your brother and my friend; trusting that you will find, in the attendant priest's account of the concluding scene, some consolation for the bereavement.

"I received another favor at the same time from the same place, relating strictly to business, which, whenever it be your desire to hear, your request will receive my attention.

"Your obedient servant,
"A. FEATHERSTONE.

"Mrs. Mary Merton Steel,
"Canal Street, No. ——."

It was on Friday morning when this event was communicated; and in the church of their faith, on the following Sabbath, the mourners listened to the forms provided for consolation in such sorrow, and were something calmed, if not healed thereby; for on Monday, Featherstone received a line requesting his presence in the evening. Complying with the terms of the note, he called at the house, and, being ushered into the parlor, in a few minutes Mrs. Steel made her appearance.

They had never met before; but the slave having taken his name to his mistress, she advanced to where he remained standing, and said, "I am pleased to see you in my house, Mr. Featherstone;" when, giving him her hand, she added, "and you have our thanks for your delicate attentions."

"I am obliged for your kind expressions; and permit me to hope that the excitement and distress of the hour, in which I received the intelligence, will excuse me for any want of formality in the way I have presented myself to you."

"You need have no doubt of your action; indeed, I esteem it a particular favor; and, besides, I believe we are related, and ought to have been acquainted before — your mother was very dear to me."

"I have heard her speak warmly of you; and I should like much to hear you talk of her at some convenient time, as one is always curious to know how his parents appeared and acted in their young days."

"Your mother was a sweet girl and my friend; and, although your general resemblance is not striking, inclining to your father most, I think, your hair is precisely like hers, when, in our wild and frolicsome days, we used to race down the hills together, for then it would float in rings on the wind — but she too has gone!" —

Such thoughts and recollections, mingling with her recent grief, clouded her spirit and came down in tears, — for Mrs. Steel, though a woman of firmness, had feeling, and indulged emotion when it would not clash with her purpose, — but she gave them way without losing self-possession; so they soon ceased.

Thereupon Featherstone said, "Shall I read you the letter to which I alluded?"

"If you please, as it is something about which I have been not a little anxious; so much so that I shall find some repose in certainty, whatever the tidings may be."

Mrs. Steel had supposed that the letter was from her dying brother, and contained his last directions. But it was simply a statement from the American consul at Naples, giving the information that there were some thousands of dollars remaining in the hands of the bankers of the deceased, which sum was subject to the order of his administrator; and that his other effects had been sealed up, and would be forwarded by the first ship.

Having finished the note, Mrs. Steel remarked, "I am sorry to say that it does not give the information I seek, which was not so much concerning property, as of the singular distribution of it. If this be all, I am inclined to the opinion that my brother made a will; indeed it was so rumored. You, however, Mr. Featherstone, I have no doubt, are aware if such be the fact, as I believe he confided in you almost exclusively, during the last few months of his remaining with us."

"I think I may fairly infer from the tenor of Mr. Merton's conversation on that point, and from certain dispositions of property which he made before departing, that, if he had ever signed, he did not leave such an instrument, unless he saw fit to do so after sailing for Europe. Was it recently that you heard he had made a will?"

"O, no; it was some time ago; it was before you came south."

"If that be the case I think it will never appear."

"You mentioned the disposition of property; did my brother actually dispose of any of his estate previous to going abroad?"

"Some portion of it passed from his hands. He gave me his interest in the commission house and the house where he lived. I remember, also, that he spoke of the remainder of his estate, — the rents, interest, and income of which are some fifteen thousand dollars per year, — and said it was his intention to leave that for the law to divide."

"You give me great relief; as we were afraid that he had made a will, in which there might appear some strange directions and bequests, for my brother was a very singular man. Are you aware what course he finally adopted with regard to manumitting certain persons?"

"Do you mean those at the house where he lived?"

"My allusion was more particularly to them."

"He made no such intimation at the time, and could not do any thing afterwards, as every appurtenance of the establishment passed to me when the titles which he approved were signed."

"I am rejoiced to hear it, for I believe it safe. Truly, I feel as though it was the finger of Providence which directed his eyes to you, as one worthy to receive benefit at his hands. We feared that he might do something shameful, for he appeared weak; but it seems now that he was more considerate than we imagined. He certainly, however, at one period had thoughts of setting them free, and of making the connection conspicuous by giving them property, at which time I pointed out to him not only the folly, but the wickedness, of such a course; and as he could not meet my objections then, so he appears to have been unable to come to the conclusion, when viewed in all its complex and painful bearings, that such a procedure would be just."

"I did not suspect such folly in him," chimed in the obsequious listener.

"Mr. Featherstone, I like charity. I respect philanthropy, if it keep within limits; yet when it trespasses on disputed ground, and proposes not to change the laws, but to create a class upon which they necessarily frown, and one which, from the nature of their situation, must sink below the slave in moral degradation, I confess that I can see in it nothing but a 'flattering unction' for human weakness."

"It gives me pleasure to say to you that I entirely coincide with your ideas. But, even if I did not, I should be the last person to disturb a law or an approved custom in a state where I have found such friends and fortune. And I will add, also, that I am averse to change — a disease which seems to be in the walls of legislative halls, and which only serves to show our statute books to be the mere wrigglings of small politicians, like the tracks of snails upon the shore, and with as little intelligence or continuance. In truth, the laws of a state, like the shrouds of a ship, should not be displaced until they have become unsafe; and even then it should be attempted only in times of calm and security."

"Mr. Featherstone, had my brother only possessed your natural firmness, or your conservative views, I believe that he might still have been living among us, honored and beloved. It was not that he turned aside, in the thoughtless hours of his youth, into a doubtful path; *that* I could forgive; but that he would continue to walk therein, and at length think of laying it open to the eye of day, was what filled me with astonishment and dread. Yet it seems he has kindly forborne the stroke, and I pray, as I hope and believe, that our family may find in you a trusty guardian of their honor."

"If I do not forget how much I owe them, or swerve from my own inclination, I think you can venture to depend upon me."

"I believe I may; and I do it with a degree of satisfaction that is difficult of expression. Yet I cannot refrain from saying that the wealth which my brother conveyed to you I see to be worthily bestowed; so much more worthily than I fear it would have been had you not come among us, that you cannot rejoice in the direction it has taken more than I do. Indeed, I think that when you know me, — and I hope to see you often in my house, — you will concede that it was not the desire for his estate which haunted my sleep and clung like a shadow to my thoughts, but the fear that it would become a blot on our name. That was my trouble; and although it be the hand of affliction which has laid it in its final rest, it appears to me like mockery to express sorrow at the event. Not that I did not love my brother; you will not think for a moment that I had not a deep affection for Rufus. All loved him; for

> 'His heart had a look southwards, and was open
> To the whole noon of nature.'

Yet, if I had the power, I could not reanimate his form, so much do I dread the change which might come. You will forgive me, Mr. Featherstone, for expressing myself so freely to you; but these are my thoughts and feelings, and they would have utterance."

"You certainly have no cause to crave excuse; rather is there need of thanks from me, for your ideas and views are lights which help to show me the way; and thus confirmed and sustained, I shall walk it with celerity and confidence. It is true that, before, I felt free to act, seeing what Mr. Merton gave he gave without conditions; yet you have supplied motives that I had not hitherto considered, and which, I now confess, seem to me quite sufficient for any emergency incident to the case. Still, I think that I may well claim to have long looked upon this matter in a more reasonable and practical way than very many among whom I was bred are accustomed to do. Abstractly, perhaps, they believe in the right of the people of a state to rule, but deny or decry the practice when it does not coincide with their notions."

Much elated with the assurance that her long trouble was over, she grew liberal, and replied, "Let us be just to those who hold different views from our own, for I do not think you give them quite fairly. I suppose they would contend that the slaves themselves must have a vote — a horrible thought — before they would admit that the voice of the people had been heard. Mr. Featherstone, I may say to you, in this connection, what I truly believe — that slavery cannot be successfully defended on principle; consequently, principles should never be appealed to by us; and when they are by others, we must point to the vastness and complexity of the structure, and the ruin which waits on its overthrow, and lament its introduction, as I do most sincerely. Yet it appears to me inexplicable, as principles are unchanging and eternal, that the universal conscience should have been blind to this wrong in its inception, which certainly was the most propitious time to arrest and the only time to prevent it, if such a course were desirable. Does it not seem as if Providence had some great design, some far prospective end, some infinite good, slowly and mysteriously developing? for as his ways are not our ways, who can search his counsels! Surely I have sought to measure it, and slavery appears to me to be here like necessity, having the force of a decree of fate; to question it now would be to doubt the wisdom of the divine Ruler, as much as though you denounced the tempest's crash, the sea's wrath, or the earthquake's shock. Kindness, most certainly, we should feel towards every one; but to think of radically changing the condition of a whole race of men, and that too by the stroke of a pen, seems to be a most delusive dream! As I stand face to face with this more than Grecian Sphinx, I mark its capacity to devour, yet learn no satisfactory solution of its dread mystery. I, indeed, hear a distant cry of 'Abolition!' but I see no lovely flower on that stalk only after long ages of culture."

"That is a shriek of the wildest fanaticism!" interposed Featherstone.

"I may be deceived," she resumed, "but I believe my servants are deeply attached to me, so much so that I doubt if any one of them has ever wished for freedom; and if I should come to imagine such an act necessary to *my* happiness, — that being generally the spur to manumission, — I confess I do not know one among all the number whom I could reasonably hope to be the gainer by the change! That there are such, I do not doubt; for I have seen two or three who exalted their chains into glorious ornaments. There is one of that class, now a steward on a river steamboat, who might stand in any presence and compete for the highest favors. And when I was last at the north I saw and heard Douglass; in form and nerve he looked as though he might have borne his plume victorious over the proudest Percy that ever splintered a lance on the border; and when he spoke his voice was so rich, and his imagination so soaring, I could not but bow to the sway of his spirit, as one of the authentic kings of the race. Yet would it be wise to take this evidence as conclusive on the whole subject, concealing the vast mass of the low and improvident? I state these remarkable instances that it may not be supposed I cannot see and feel, while I have before me daily the darker and more difficult side, which I seek to deal with patiently, kindly, and I hope wisely. Still there are portents of change which do not escape me; I am aware that it is growing to be a world question — and why is it? unless Providence is preparing for another step in the deep and wonderful design of the world's development.

"But, Mr. Featherstone, I have detained you longer than I ought; and I am very much obliged to you for your deference, and for giving me so clear a view of your ideas and consequent purpose. If you receive any further intelligence, which would be interesting to us, I shall expect to see you; and if at any other time it pleases you to call, it will be an acceptable attention."

CHAPTER XV.

They stood aloof, the scars remaining,
Like cliffs which have been rent asunder;
A dreary sea now flows between.
COLERIDGE.

ANTHONY FEATHERSTONE had been in New Orleans something more than four years, and in that period, by gift and acquisition, had become rich. That he was a man prone to self-indulgence, and had given way to his passions, almost without thought, — except as his ambitious views might help to control or hide, — is sufficiently apparent; yet the time of their sway had been too short to form inveterate habits, and he was still young enough to look to change and variety as the spice of life.

The death of his relative and patron had set him free to apply the power that came by his favor to whatever he might fancy to be for his advantage or pleasure. Hence — having no ties to the past, and no settled course for the future, save a desire for the new — he will soon shift the scene. In truth, he had quickly resolved to leave New Orleans, for a time, and visit some places and friends at the north; and, as he prided himself on his decision and rapidity of movement, it was only the fourth day after the interview in the last chapter, when he had made all his arrangements, and was ready to take the boat for Louisville.

On the evening previous to the day of his leaving the city, he met some friends, whom he had invited to a sumptuous entertainment in the St. Charles, and, as the viands kept up the renown of the house, so the wine kept up the hilarity of the company. Consequently the hour of adjournment got one or two extensions.

When the generous entertainer and the jovial guests separated, with ardent mutual admiration, and many times repeated farewells, Featherstone took a carriage to his house; not that he thought it might be difficult walking, but because repletion had rendered him inert; for such orgies exhaust rather than refresh, — which is Nature's design in all her gifts, — and are generally followed by bad nights and worse mornings.

Reaching the house, he made his way in, to find Flora awaiting him, as usual; and as she had changed somewhat in appearance since he first saw her, — having lost the sweet rose of youth, which was all that Featherstone had seen to admire, — so his treatment of her had changed also. Not that he could not feel, and duly appreciate, intellectual beauty, when he thought it rightly placed and appropriately exercised; but here, and by such a one, and in such relations, it was as unsuited and distasteful to him as it would be to a child to have the round and rosy face of her doll sculptured and paled into a likeness of Socrates.

A mere girl, brought up in deep seclusion, and talking of the most poetically colored of romances as though it had been, and might be, actual life, when she pleased the taste and stirred the passion of Featherstone, the few years that she had associated with him had been to her a full-leafed tree of knowledge. Under such influence her brow had expanded and elevated its arch; and if her eyes were less lustrous, they had gained in depth, and through them emotion came like flame. Neither were her lips the full flowing curves that they once had been, but close knit, like armor; and the upper one was so curling and flexible that a shadow dwelt above it, which moved in play or menace according to the nature of the thought or feeling which animated it.

Finding that she could not implicitly lean on her lover, she had been gathering strength to stand alone: reading much and meditating more, she was slowly but surely feeling out her relations to the universe. So came doubts with regard to her connection with Featherstone, and its duration — came to fill a heart which love was vacating. Thus she arose to see that he was growing coarse and low, while her upward and unfolding spirit was panting for a purer region. In fine, she had learned that male and female, those mysterious counterparts of nature, so tenderly and so divinely drawn to be one, must be absolutely one, or sever; aught less is debasing, sinful, woful.

Thus had she been musing when Featherstone entered her presence, gorged with food and flushed with wine. Seeing him in such condition, her eyes drooped and filled with tears — not drops of fond affection, such as in the earlier days so many times welcomed his coming, but tears of regret, sorrowful and bitter waters, such as no dead sea can yield.

Featherstone did not fail to observe her mood, for he was sharp-sighted at such times, and said, "What are you crying for now? It seems to me that this is something new" (for there had been a dry season). "Do you wish for any thing, that you take up these womanish weapons, hoping to win?"

"No," she mildly replied, holding her handkerchief to her face.

"Are you sick, then? I see that you are getting to be nothing but skin and bones. What ails you? Can you tell?"

"I do not know that I can," she answered, still grieving; "only that my life has long been growing sad, so that to think upon it is to be unhappy."

"Unhappy!" echoed he; "what have *you* to be unhappy

about? Is not every thing which appetite or even taste can ask provided and presented, as though you were the minion of fortune?"

Flora had suppressed her emotion during this reply; and turning a calm and penetrating glance upon him, she inquired, "Do you think that such materials can fill the measure of life? Has the heart no hope, no need, beside?"

"Is there to be complaint on that score? Well, this *is* amusing! Why, I have not remained away from here a single night since I first knew you, if not out of the city! Come, tell me, am I to be accused and tried for inconstancy or neglect?"

"Can frequent presence supply the want of continuous and ever-increasing affection?"

"Well, really, this is exquisite! Why, my lady, my friends actually laugh at me for the singleness of my love!"

"I am sorry that you have such friends — if those can be called friends who seek to sully things to their own taste by sneering at the unity of love, making their defilement their boast, and insinuating doubts on all virtue. You may smile; and I can well understand that you think I have fallen too low to talk thus; but, frail as I am, I can read Byron and scorn his despicable opinion of women; for, in my soul, I believe that it is not true; even my eyes refuse to look long on such scarlet robes."

"I believe it has been admitted that he wrote from experience."

"I do not doubt that; yet, vain boaster as he is, he sings only of his successes, and heightens those with all the hues of a gorgeous imagination, and the music of the most eloquent numbers; while he keeps secret — the only secrets he ever kept — the rebuffs and rebukes that should appear on his page, without which there cannot be full truth in the picture."

"I should think, by the color of your cheeks, that your health might be better than it was when I came in."

"It may be for the moment; but so long as the cause of pain remains, and continues operative, I have little hope of improvement."

"Ah! indeed; have you really any complaint to make against me?"

"Yes, I have cause of complaint even against you! and, if a slave may be permitted to speak, my thoughts are already ripe for utterance."

"Well, this is very romantic; but go on — I listen."

"Would it were romantic; but *that* dream has gone. Was I wrong in believing that those who love grow more and more to resemble each other, and must I give up my faith in the fond idea because our experience affords no confirmation of the doctrine?"

"Do you fancy it in my power to change my nature?" he inquired sneeringly.

"That you have been changing and are greatly changed is what I am left to deplore; for when we first met, only a brief time since if compared with the length of life, you had the power or the art to make your voice soft and touching — where is it now? Your flesh was fair and your expression kindly — what has so sadly changed them? You were tender and considerate — now you are harsh and hasty; simply a thing for your convenience am I regarded! Time was when you met me with, what I believed to be, the smile and the kiss of love; but they vanished long ago. Yet, having hope that these were but the opening bloom, I thought what might the fruit be; and, may I ask, what is it? Even the so fair promise is but as dust in my eyes; and am I expected to sit in the dreary waste and think it the garden of life.

"Have you found the end of your lecture?"

"I will hear you."

"You are rather emphatic! otherwise I do not know that I have any particular fault to find with your statement of the matter, as it seems to be a general charge of not coming up to a mere school girl's fancies — something which, among people of experience, would be passed with a smile; but you are so situated I think it well to stoop to reason the case, and so give you a practical view — for you have lived so secluded that you have had no opportunity to learn human nature, and particularly the nature of men. And I will say, for your instruction, and once for all, to impress it on your memory, that no rational person expects the things of which you speak are to continue; they belong to the honeymoon, and naturally wane with it. Therefore these changes, of which you complain, occur in nine families in ten, and are the contemplated results of years of intimacy; such years are apt to be a little disenchanting."

"Then advancing years, to nine in ten, are only steps which lead down to misery, perhaps to hell."

"Well, if it be so, it will do no good to whine over it. So you had better accept life as you find it, and take a view of things that you may hope to carry into practice; for all this, of undying affection and what not, is but the vision of poetry."

"If the poets have brought down from heaven a life more congenial to the heart than that which mortals live, I desire to close my eyes and dream their dream."

"If you think of dreaming, we had better retire."

"I do not wish to, now."

"But I do."

"If you so choose I presume you can; at least I will not delay you."

"Are you not going with me, when I ask you?"

"Not immediately."

"You look very much as though you did not intend to come at all."

"Perhaps I may not; would you have me, unless it be my wish?"

"Do you dare to say to me that you do not desire it further?"

"Does it require courage to say so small a part of what I feel?"

"Courage!" sneered he; "do you know what you are? Are you aware that a bill of sale can pass you whenever and wherever I please?"

"It may be so; yet I see nothing in that which can change my sentiments, or prevent me from uttering them."

"If you undertake to bully me, you will find it rough work before you get over the consequences of it."

"If I had any still lingering feelings of fondness, such breath might well wither them! Is it possible you have sunk so low as to think that threats of force can command love, or pass even the border of her dominion? Strong as you boast yourself, and feeble as I know I am, do you believe that, having once been excluded from her realm, you may ever soar her height again?"

"You are quite lofty to-night, my queen! It may be you expect that I shall humble myself before you: perhaps you have deluded yourself into the belief that you have the command here?"

"I claim no right of yours, I presume to no rule beyond myself; yet this extends so far, that, when I am forced to the sad conviction of misplaced and misused affections, I know no power which can prevent them from returning to my own bosom."

"This is very fine; but isn't it rather a small occasion for quite so much display? for I am not aware that I said or did any thing to warrant such a performance. Yet, as it appears to be over, I am willing to let it pass without further notice, for I am fatigued and sleepy. I suppose that you got out of patience in waiting, and I believe I did come in somewhat later than usual; perhaps I was to blame, but I could not well avoid doing as I did."

Thereupon, rising up, he continued as he took a light, "Come, let us retire, and you will feel better in the morning."

"Morning has already dawned on me; and I hope that I am fully awake: I have had a long dream, but when even a dream grows too distressing, it breaketh sleep; and mine was such."

"Do you wish to quarrel with me? Have you the presumption to extend your flurry further? and that too after I have intimated forgiveness of the past?"

"The storm in me is still. I have only been relating the story of its devastation — a devastation which, certainly, no rude gust of the same gale can ever revive to bloom or verdure."

"It does not become me to hear more of this. So now I leave you; and you can do what you please; but I give you warning that, if you do not repent, you will come to feel the retribution in every bone of your body."

"I hope that I have repented."

"Then why don't you rise up and go with me?"

"I have repented that I ever did go; and in the serene calmness of my soul I see the sign of forgiveness."

"O, you are getting pious — are you? You had better become one of the Sisters of Charity!"

"If I were free, I know no vocation that would be more soothing to my heart, or could sooner heal its wounds."

"The devil take me but I will make you feel that you are not free, and never shall be, unless you lower your tone amazingly! Are you blind? Yet I have said all that I can say. I stoop no further. I leave you to reflection, commending to you a careful review of your conduct and position; taking into consideration also that I am your sole judge, having power to cast you as low as the brutes, and your imp along with you, and to bind both to lie there until you lie in the grave." And, closing the door with a jerk, his heavy tread at length died away in his chamber.

When all was still Flora rose up and took the dirk, which was Park's parting gift to Featherstone, from the mantel-piece, where it had long lain as an ornament, and placing it in her bosom, sought the room in which her child was sleeping; where, only partially disrobing, she nestled down beside him, and slept the troubled sleep of those who fear a disturbing hand; but apprehension was her sole visitant that night, as nothing more real came to molest her. Featherstone's sleep was heavy, and stretched far on with the morning. The mosquitoes had ceased their music, and drawn off from his "bar" to seek some deeper shade from the yellow day, when he aroused himself and slowly gathered his scattered senses, so that, recollection having fully mastered the closing scene of the evening, he rose partly up, and looked around to see if there were any signs that Flora had been with him. But there were none to be seen; the bed was marked only by his form; and no kind hand had even raised the window that he might breathe the morning air.

So, gathering the evidence and comprehending its import, fiercely, he muttered a curse, and laughed a bitter laugh — when, looking at his watch, he arose hastily and hurriedly dressed himself.

Having made ready for his departure, he completed his appropriate work by taking the few jewels of value, that lay on Flora's dressing table, which were his gifts, with the diamond cross that was Merton's, and placing them in his pocket, he drew out a newspaper in which was a notice of his benefactor's death, and, marking the article, left it in the place of the things he had appropriated.

Although he took the valuables from the table with some degree of savage satisfaction, yet, when he turned to the latch he lifted it with the stealth of a felon; and, so descending the stairs, passed out at the open door where, a few years before, the moonlight had fallen so sweetly, and beauty and innocence arose on him so charmingly, without a single lingering glance or parting word, or sorrow for the sullied and trampled bloom.

CHAPTER XVI.

The sea of love that lies before
He does not calmly, coldly shun;
But guarded walks its sunny shore,
Until some shining goal be won.
ANON.

BRIAN PARK had so risen in these years, that great questions began to feel the grasp of his intellect. Yet he had not won that position, income, and influence, which he felt not only to be desirable but indispensable, before making a formal declaration of his love, and saying to Miss Vernon, the hope of his heart was that she would be his bride; although he saw himself advancing with sure steps along that upward path.

Thus, not being declared lovers, there were occasions when they did not quite understand each other; still there was strong sympathy between them, so that they met gladly; for in many respects they were congenial spirits, and moved to the music of the same chords.

The nobility of one's nature, with its delicate sense of honor, is frequently in the way of that success which takes the world's applause; hence that self-control of which Park was so studious in his attentions to Aurelia. For he had some respect for the hope or desire of parents; so that he could not clutch at their fruit, although it might lean to his hand, when a few more months would bring those golden rays which kindly part it from the bough. With such views he rarely called at the dwelling of Miss Vernon: their meetings were at the residences of mutual acquaintance, by friendly invitation, or at the house of Mrs. Summers, who had found opportunity of renewing their acquaintance, and took especial pride and pleasure in having her for a guest.

Those were thrilling moments, moments not easily obliterated from the memory, when, on leaving the place where they had passed the evening, he drew her arm within his, while they turned towards the quiet and shadowy street on which Aurelia lived. The fair form so near, yet so sacred and so sweetly trusting, and leaning so softly, yet somehow so magically, that it quickens the pulse with the fond whispers of the tender passion, — these are forever of the mysteries of creation, which the heart yearns to solve with something of divine ardor.

Had Park been of the common mould he would have reached betrothal long ago, or separation — for the one thought would have swallowed up all others; making their walks silent until the hope of possession had struggled up to utterance, so to be quenched, or to become the flame that consecrates the altar. But, being more delicately organized, and more widely developed, he could feel this thirst of the soul, and make but far-off sign — only some tender tone running through the music of his conversation, some loveliest dye, as it were, just tingeing all his thoughts.

It was a warm night in June when, as they turned away from his home, Park said to Aurelia, "Then you think of leaving us, for a time, to enter into the more exciting life of the watering places?"

"Yes, such is my mother's desire; and I expect to go in company with your cousin, by whose favor we first met — do you remember?"

Park saw the opportunity, but self-respect curbed him, and whispered, "Wait!" So he simply replied, "Yes, it was a bright hour," and paused; when he should have added, "and I can never forget it; for, from the hope that arose in me, on that evening, come electric messages which have kept my heart, and exalted my ambition." Yet he suppressed this, and what would have inevitably followed thereon; not that he did not feel it, but because he thought his manner sufficiently demonstrative, until his preparation was more full, and his power more widely conceded.

Aurelia had hoped that he might carry the suggestion on even to a declaration; and, being disappointed, she regretted having made the allusion. So when she took up the conversation, as she did immediately, she changed the drift of the theme, and said, "I suppose you like the city so well, and have vowed yourself so exclusively to your profession, that you will remain here quite through the summer, as I believe you always have done."

"I have not thought of going away; for the chase of what is called pleasure has never attracted me. Besides, the 'Lady Common Law' is a jealous mistress; consequently, I must win her complete confidence before I shall venture from her side."

"Do you find the study and the practice of the law so fill the mind as to satisfy?"

"Satisfaction, for any length of time, I imagine, is not often found; yet I think that one of my profession may win it as frequently as those of any other."

"That I can well believe; receiving, as it does, the most striking recognition for its long and laborious days, in triumphal hours, in the world's proud arenas. Whenever I think of the laurelled chiefs of your order, I desire to be a man, that I might try to master the weapons and join the march; hoping to so cleave my way as, at length, to champion some great cause of the trembling state."

"Yes, there is something dazzling in its mighty passages at arms; yet you little dream of the fatigue of the preceding march, and of the dark and loathsome ways through which it leads, wherein most must tread who reach those bannered lists, so charming to the eye of the distant gazer."

"Is the practice, then, so repulsive? I have never heard you complain."

"Why should I, when it becomes him who resolves to accomplish a purpose to do it cheerfully? Yet I believe that nothing, save the sanguine heart of youth, can go through it thus; and even the most hopeful and gifted of the young must often close their eyes to the actúal, and dream of the star that shines afar."

"Are there no soothing circumstances, no pleasures, and no worthy rewards, flowing from the early practice?"

"When the novelty of the situation and subject wear off, the initiatory business is not particularly pleasing. It does, indeed, have some relief; it is not a never-varying gloom, like the circles of the Inferno; for you will sometimes have it in your power to redress a wrong; yet to-morrow you may be called upon to change sides, and defend it. Then who, for the most part, are the clients? A really high-minded man feels as though he had committed a blunder, if, by any means, he is compelled to seek his own amid the mazes of courts. There may be, and I know that there are, marked exceptions; but the general aspect of litigants, even in the civil business, — to say nothing of the criminal, — does not come up to the average of the race. And when, by your industry, your skill, or your good fortune, you have drawn those around you, they not only take possession of your ear during the progress of the trials, but they haunt you in all the passages of the halls of justice, follow you to your office, to your house, and even waylay you at the corners of the streets; and that too for no purpose but to ask, "What do ye think about my case, 'squire?" — a case that, nine times in ten, has had all needful preparation, and to which the party has been fully admitted; while the action cannot be reached on the trial list in three days, and he knows it; and he also knows that your attention is due to another matter, then in hand."

"How little do we understand, or see even, of the steeps and perplexities of any path except our own! What tapestry you have hung in the temple of Themis! Yet I ought to have known, for I see that it must be grouped with the conflicts of the wayward, the wicked, or the unforgiving. Indeed, I should pity you, if I did not think that you had passed through these to less repulsive scenes."

"Your thought is almost true, in fact; for a glance backward is, to me, a sufficient spur to press on. I am like some lone traveller, who, emerging from the forest's gloom, begins to feel the sun that warms the cultivated plains and hill sides, and, in the distance, beholds habitations into which he may enter to find peace, and comfort, and domestic joy. Yes, let me not be unjust or ungrateful; there were alleviations; there have been many bright hours so mingled in as to soften the shadows; and this walk, which we have many times taken, shines warmly among them."

When Park paused, Aurelia did not make an assenting remark. Indeed, her arm rested lighter on his, because in her heart she hoped that he would declare himself further, and feared, if she spoke, or stirred even, that it might interrupt or lead him away. But he misunderstood her listening silence for want of sympathy; and, when he resumed the conversation, the feeling had vanished with the subject; for he said, "I return to that which should more interest you. I have no doubt that you will enjoy your pleasure trip very much, as a great variety of people are to be seen in the places you will visit, the most of which votaries fancy themselves accomplished in something, and no doubt are. If there be any, on exhibition, who have poor ideas, they may have proud horses; and a drive with them is sometimes as desirable, and it may be as exhilarating, as to walk with Apollo among the flocks of Admetus. You will also meet those who can talk, with some who excel in dancing; and yet more, who, in many minor ways, may help to amuse; while well nigh all of them are cunning in putting on apparel,—no mean or trivial accomplishment,—for a well-dressed company is, to me, as pleasing as a parterre of flowers; the chief fault being, it soon cloys in the drawing room as in the garden; so that we seek to return to more serious and dignified nature for strength and repose."

"You speak of the gay world as though you had passed your life in its precincts, glancing through all its mazes."

"I have visited there occasionally; but as the halls are designed only for momentary attraction, so the show is quickly exhausted, if one is disposed to think within its glittering circles."

"You make me regret that I have consented to go there."

"Then I have given an impression which I did not intend to give; as this so fascinating appearance is one of those that we must pass through before we can be entirely free of them. For this reason, if my wish could incline you to choose, you will keep the way that you have chosen; as there are many lessons to be learned there,—perhaps more rapidly than any where else,—yet it is to be graduated from, like any other place of learning; in truth only folly continues on, and takes pride from the slowness of its acquirement, and the length of its matriculation."

"Although you appear to approve of my going on this excursion, still your words make the summer seem long, and divest the places of their attraction; so that, if I do go, I fear I shall regret it."

"Then you must forgive them, and call to mind the heat and dust of the city, from which you are about to escape, and take into view that the places where you are to shine for a season are points of observation from which you may catch the varying aspects of surrounding nature, not yet all tamed down to use. The steep, rising hills, far sweeping and solemn, which wait there to meet you, are still kept mysterious by the shadows of the primeval forest, where something Druid yet haunts and hallows the leafy gloom. There you will behold mountains also, and their broken ridges, with here and there the frowning face of a bold, precipitous rock, its full, antlered front tossed against the sky, as if it had been, that instant, pierced and thrown on its haunches by the far-flying shaft of some mighty hunter; and, high over these, some heaven-scaling Titans, transfixed for their audacity, yet so great in their chains as to keep silence, and impose it on the gazer.

"There, too, you will see many a sweet valley, refreshed by the tears and protected by the limbs of those giants bound, with cattle amid the luxuriant green, or standing in the winding streams; while on the plats the mowers swing their scythes in the grass, (which to me is a fascination;) where happy children gather strawberries, or playing with the swaths, shake them to the sunshine; and, more pleasing still, their white and smiling homes, hushed in the sweet bosoms of orchards. All these make a picture which is taken away on no canvas, and one that fills the mind with peace and tenderness which no poet has sung. But these you will find, and more, profusely strown along most of the line of your journey; and, if you look on them with a loving heart, they will keep you and teach you their wisdom; indeed, I believe that you will not fail to see, and rejoice in, their refreshing and inexhaustible sublimity and beauty."

"I would not for any thing miss them; and I cannot do so,

for I shall be looking for your pictures in every vale and hill; they appear now even, in vivid distinctness, on the distant verge of the horizon."

"I should be better pleased if you would search for, and study, those which differ from mine; and, kindly bearing in mind that I remain within the city's circle, remember to retouch them for me when you return."

"Why need you so confine yourself here? I wish you would join our party; and I do not see why you cannot meet us for a little time, before the summer has quite passed, and lead me into the temple, and unfold to my apprehension the mysteries of nature."

"I should like it; in truth I am inclined to do so, yet I know that, if I make the attempt, I shall see before me the stern gaze and the restraining hand of the one to which I have vowed myself for many moons. I roamed widely over the earth at one time, but when I made up my mind to look for position and power here, I resolved that I would be lured into no other chase, until I had made them secure. The hope for full communion with Nature has not passed away; once touched and awakened to a perception of her beauty, we can never forget, or become indifferent; we leave her presence without fear of change, and return as to a desiring bosom. And I still cherish her features with affectionate memories, although I hide from her face. Yet even here I am not quite excluded from her charms, as my office gives much of the harbor from its windows; and a glimpse of flashing water sends them to me fresh and vigorous from the Author — while a pleasant Sabbath sunrise leads me where the grateful birds pour forth their morning joy. And not in vain, for she soothes, and heals, and continually discloses her enticing beauty to my desires; making each succeeding cloud-decked sunset seem more lovely than the last, and the stars move intelligible and inspiring —

teachers of faith, bright messengers from the heavens, their beams are saying, We traverse the infinite space in perfect security; despair not thou of the safety of the soul."

"You make the visible world appear the most glorious of temples, and fill it with the song of your praise. Indeed, love and faith are religion, penetrating, or rather flowing from, all noble natures — natures which the whole army of polemics and dogmatists cannot intimidate by summons, or carry by assault. Yet they have wronged me of some of this natural worship, robbed me of these divine smiles of which you so fondly and so charmingly speak, by their leading, by their despairing cry of 'Pantheism!' but, heeding it no more, I shall look for God in every bush. Still, having seen so little of what we more especially call nature, I feel like one who, pent within dim and cloistered walls, hears a story of knights and tournament, and the wreath which beauty braids and binds around her hero's brow."

"It is in such a spirit, and with such a hope, that I wish you to go forth; for then you will drink of the most ancient and sacred wells, and may return whole and refreshed." Taking her hand he retained it a moment, when, saying farewell, he yielded it up and departed.

Aurelia ascended to her chamber, sad and troubled; and, without a glance at the mirror, she took out a faded rose, the rose that was Park's first gift so long ago, and, reclining on the lounge, mused and doubted whether he still kept the leaves and flowers which she had given. At length she said, with a sigh, "No! men do not preserve such things, and it is weakness in us to do so. Ambition takes the heart of the gifted, and bears it above the region of flowers. Yet how he sees and loves nature! such pictures can be drawn only by a vivid imagination from a full heart and a fine understanding. Ah! did he so love me, could he be silent?"

But after a time, having thrown off her bonnet, she rose up, looked in the mirror, carefully smoothed down a stray lock of hair, and returning the flower to the place where it had so long been treasured, slowly disrobed to seek forgetfulness in sleep.

CHAPTER XVII.

The secrets only to be told by fire
Starry or beamless, central and extreme,
Burn to be born. FESTUS.

IT was towards the last of July that Anthony Featherstone, having nearly arrived to the end of his journey, turned aside to visit one of those charming places of summer resort, which, in this growing country, are every year increasing in number or beauty. He knew that many of his familiar acquaintance from the Crescent City were there, and, a votary of pleasure now like them, he hastened to participate in their diversions.

The persons with whom Aurelia was a summer guest were also passing the remainder of the season in the same house at which Featherstone alighted; and on entering the parlor after dinner, he recognized Mrs. Fardel, the cousin of Park, and renewing the acquaintance, was introduced to Miss Vernon. He was not aware that he had ever seen her before, and could hardly have been made to believe it, so struck was he with the power of her charms; and from the first moment he devoted himself to her with all the skill of an experienced tactician.

Soon after his arrival, he was invited to join a party of his southern friends at table; and as they sat over their wine, he informed them that Merton was dead, and that he inherited; upon which they filled their glasses, and drank a bumper to the successor's health and happiness. This news was caught up and borne about so rapidly that, before many hours had passed, every person in the house who could be supposed to take any interest in it had heard that Mr. Featherstone, the fine-looking and accomplished gentleman from the south, was rich, unmarried, and in every way desirable.

The watering place, where some of our characters had assembled, was one of that class which are planned for the amusement of vacant minds — people who, if they do not absolutely hate, have a very mean opinion of their own company, so that they sigh and yawn, from mere dulness, when alone; people who, being really nothing of themselves, feel that they must *go* somewhere and form a part of something. As the establishment was arranged, more especially for the wants of such, every hour had its allotted pastime; they drove, they shot, they bowled, they bathed, they dressed, and they dined, whereon music's voluptuous strains invited to the twining dance, stimulating the blood and blinding the heart with its wily enchantment, so softly poured, so brightly hued, that it seemed the wine of the gods. The rooms, if we except the public ones, were so small and warm that they appeared to frown on all study or retirement.

Still the place evidently had some powerful attraction, for it had drawn the rich and the gay, and those who follow in their train, from great distances, and in such numbers that the house was full to the roof-tree.

Aurelia, like so many others in the innocence of a first visit, had taken some books with her, which having received no attention, they, as it were with mortification, had crept away to the very bottom of her trunk. One, however, "The Princess," Park's last gift, had been looked carefully through for marked passages; but none were found, which making her too sad or too thoughtful to read, that also was closed; and at length it came to lie undistinguished among the others. And almost the thoughts of former days had gone with the habits; for her mode of life, with its associations, during those past two months, had tended to fill her mind with the shows of things, obscuring things themselves — she being part of an exhibition wherein the accidents of fortune were first in esteem. In a tournament the prowess of the knights make glorious the hour; but this place rather resembled a swift and exciting race, where the horses attract more attention than their riders. At such times, in hearts grown sterile, as they will in low devotions, a pretender can take a king's honors, and even paraphernalia is bowed down to in a kind of Fetichism.

That the tone of Aurelia's mind had greatly fallen since leaving home, was quite apparent; yet it was in full accord with the place and her companions. She might recover when she returned to a calmer sphere; but then she was in the material and of it. That was certainly an ungenial round for her nature, for light and lively were the hours, with no frown for any thing save serious and soaring thoughts.

On the other hand, it was no less apparent that Featherstone's accomplishments all came out there, as though it were their appropriate place. He dressed with care and elegance; he was a skilful waltzer, a bold rider, a good shot, and quick of perception, possessing a temperament warm and impressible also, with vivacity and point in his remarks on passing things. Before the first evening was over, he had waltzed with the most distinguished ladies in the company, said pleasing things to each, and if to some he spoke with such warmth as made their hearts flutter, he was kindly excused on account of the fire of his southern blood; if one of the more experienced, however, slightly menaced him with her fan, and said, "I am surprised, Mr. Featherstone!" he invited her to ride with him, and that appeared to restore her confidence.

He did not notice Aurelia at first, although he entered with alacrity into the dance, but left her to the attentions of others, until he saw by her manner — as he passed her with his arm half encircling his partner — that she was thinking of the omission, she being too studiedly unobservant of his presence. The chaperon also had similar thoughts, and a furtive glance; hence, as she stood by Aurelia's side, and saw Featherstone lead his partner to a seat, linger a moment near her, and then, bowing, turn towards them, she murmured, "The new star is drawing near."

In a brief time Featherstone joined them, and engaging in conversation a few minutes, at length he prayed for the pleasure, which he had so artfully delayed, in phrase and tone that gave token of the warmth of his nature, and so touched Aurelia that her acceptance was in accordant form.

"You must be very fond of waltzing, Mr. Featherstone," said Mrs. Fardel, "as I believe I have seen you with nearly all our choice young ladies, this evening."

"O, no; that is an unkind exaggeration. And Miss Vernon," he continued, turning to that young lady, "you must not listen to her, for I have only danced with three or four at most; and all of them from my adopted state — daughters of gentlemen who deign to call me friend; worthy scions of families whom I have long known and admired, alike for their charms and their characters."

"They are pleasing persons, and very rich also," said Mrs. Fardel.

"As I have but little of either beauty, or grace, or accomplishment, so I seek their presence and their smile; but the wealth, if it ever visited my thoughts, has ceased to be among my desires."

"Do you wish me to praise you?" inquired Mrs. Fardel with a smile.

"I think it would be sweet from your lips," he replied, bowing.

But at that moment the notes of a favorite waltz inviting,

Featherstone and Aurelia glided into its charmed circles, and yielding to its softly whispered, yet most glowing language, were soon silently and thrillingly listening to a tale more emotional and suggestive than words may hope to breathe; while, in their united grace and mastery, they fixed the gaze of the company, for they moved the very dream of motion, like the bright rings that play round rocks in flowing streams. At length the music ceasing, he led her to the side of Mrs. Fardel, while speaking warmly of the pleasure she had bestowed; and, leaving them with kindly compliments, he disappeared for the night.

On the next day he took his southern friend to ride, and returning late in the evening he joined the company in the parlor, though only for a short time, and did not dance.

So, for some weeks, he played his part, not often paying particular attention to Aurelia, yet giving the moments so devoted all the grace and attraction of which he was capable. Assiduous in his attentions to the other belles, and riding with them frequently, he did not extend the invitation to her until she had confidentially remarked on it to Mrs. Fardel, who, of course, on the first opportunity made allusion to it. Still he appeared not to heed it for some days, though more frequently in conversation with them, which led the chaperon to speak of a delightful drive which they had recently taken, when, appealing to Miss Vernon, and she assenting to the beauty of the scenery, he asked the favor of her company and guidance.

It was towards evening when they started on their excursion, and Featherstone soon entered into conversation on the warmth and luxuriance of the southern clime, and of the princely domains and generous hospitality of the planter — themes so captivating to an imaginative and luxurious nature, and into which his companion passed with quick sympathy, so that before they returned he felt that she liked to be near him. Lingering on the road, the evening was nearly spent when they alighted, and, with well-turned thanks and expressions of regard, he parted with her and retired to his room.

Miss Vernon soon retired also; yet lay long thinking before she slept, and even after, though so much more swiftly and wonderfully that she paused not to reckon with time and space, but oversoaring the present, had vision of the future in what we name a dream. And in that slumber she dreamed that she was married. To whom she knew not; yet felt that the deed was done; for around her were the evidences of the attending ceremony, and some still lingering guests or bridemaids; to those she appealed and entreated for information, but they turned and vanished. Then she strained her eyes to see something in the shrouding darkness, and so intense was the effort that she caught the outline of a form, and at length traced the lineaments of Park — distant, indeed, and not advancing; whereon, after long waiting, she signed to him, but he heeded it not, which led her to think that he was not the bridegroom. So she looked again, and beheld a form emerge from the blackness, and, passing by Park, come towards her. Full of the intensest agitation, she sought to discover the face, and in a moment she saw that it was Featherstone's, as, smiling, he drew near her couch. On this she felt an impulse to shrink back, to raise her arm in resistance, and tried to call Park to her rescue; but he appeared to be too far off to hear, while a chill shuddered through her veins and her bosom trembled. Then she heard a whisper to be calm and put away her fears, and she knew it to be her mother's voice. Whereon Featherstone murmured some tender words, and, taking her hand, leaned over her, when his breath and eyes were so warm that they dispelled the chill which a moment before had seized her; and still drawing nearer and nearer, he finally pressed his lips to hers so gently that she did not wake.

In the morning it flashed forth a picture of the memory; and one so vivid that, on meeting the glance of Featherstone at breakfast, the blood mantled her cheek, and her heart shook with the fear of losing its secret. And when he joined her in the parlor, there was a tenderness in her manner which gave him hope. Is it thus that our inclinations make our fate; or is there some mysterious leading that dreams should be so singularly in favor of the participant?

Thereupon, Featherstone became more particular and more tender in his attentions, though still for some days quite as much so to his southern friend.

At length it was rumored that he was about to leave the place; and in the evening he waltzed with a number of the ladies, and finally led Miss Vernon to the floor. Long accustomed to the art, and attuned to the music, on they circled, tasting, sipping, quaffing this most seductive wine even to intoxication; so that when they paused, and he led her through the press, she clung to his arm as if she could never more leave it; so much will the wild and pliant impulse of such moments outrun or oversweep discretion. Passing out they walked down the broad piazza, for Aurelia wished for air; and there, while to its fanning breath they moved, he talked of the fairy scene, the fascinations of the place, the pleasure of such society, and how her presence and kindness had made it an enchanted bower.

"I am sensitive to the charm of festal splendor," she replied; "but this seems full of attractions, and will long reign in my recollection."

"May I hope to be kindly remembered, sometimes, when you call it to mind?" he tenderly inquired.

To which question she not audibly replying, he took her consenting hand; and, turning, they moved down on one of the many shadowy paths together — moved in silence, until

Featherstone said, "Will you listen to one who can no longer refrain while he speaks of love? a love that knows no future time, but cries, now! and trusts its hope, its life, on a word. I have wealth; it shall lie in all profusion at your feet, and bear you wherever inclination can lead, though my desire will be you, only you! amid the grandest and loveliest scenes, or in the presence of warmest and divinest art."

Aurelia whispered something which he did not distinctly hear, and leaned her burning brow against his shoulder. On this Featherstone bent down to catch the accents; and finding that they crowned his passion, he twined his arms around her, kissed her again and again, and breathed into her ear, as with a breath of fire, how deep, how undying was his love for her. Yet still they clung and murmured in the shadowy circles of the summer night, and ate the lotos to the song of the sirens. When at length she roused herself and whispered that she must return, they clasped hands and kissed, and finally parted as though hope went out with vision.

In a few moments after they had separated, Featherstone gained his usual composure, looked carefully to his apparel, rearranged his locks, and entered the parlor as though nothing had happened.

Aurelia sought her chamber, and did not descend even at her usually late breakfast hour. Being missed from the accustomed morning promenade on the piazza, Mrs. Fardel went up to learn the cause; and as they met, she perceived that something of importance had occurred, and her instincts leading her to the right conclusion, she exclaimed, "Well, this is funny in the extreme! I hope that it does not make you *very* weak to have a lover, or quite sick to have an offer of marriage!"

"Do not, for Heaven's sake, speak so loud," said Aurelia in a suppressed voice.

"Dear me! I hope you do not imagine that you can keep it secret here? Such a thing is perfectly impossible."

"I wish that I might, even after marriage, for a whole year. There is something coarse in making public proclamation of that which seems so unspeakable."

"Nonsense! Come, have the goodness to dress and descend, for he has already inquired, and so kindly that it induced me to seek you; and if you do not make your appearance soon, he will think that you are troubled with regrets. But permit me to recommend that you leave your over-anxious face here, and take down your brightest one. Really, if I were to judge from your confusion, I should conclude that you were not more than sixteen."

They soon after descended; and, Featherstone joining them, they walked out to take the air, where he moved beside Aurelia with complete self-assurance, and covered her evident embarrassment and agitated feelings with easy fluency of remark on the topics of the hour. Under such treatment she resumed something of her natural grace of manner and flow of speech, which her attentive friend perceiving, she excused herself, and glided away that they might have a moment alone; for Featherstone's horses were at the door, and he carried a whip in his hand. When Mrs. Fardel had vanished, the lover said, "I began to fear that I should not see you this morning, as I promised, in the early part of last evening, to drive out one of my southern friends; and you know that one must keep his engagements."

"Certainly; I desire you should by all means," she replied.

On this Featherstone smiled, and gave her so warm a glance that she glowed under it; and turning away, her eye caught, in the outline of a passing cloud, the features of Park. And so spectral were they that her cheek blanched; yet she compressed her lips, for the intoxication of the night had led her too far down to recede, if she so desired; but she had otherwise determined.

Park, in truth, had not been entirely excluded from her thoughts during the night, for deep in her heart he had impressed his lineaments. Yet she could not help contrasting his circumspection with the ardor of Featherstone, his chastened tastes with the glitter and garniture of fortune — the god to whom her mother prayed, and towards which her own eyes were not infrequently inclined. Besides, one had proposed and the other had not — indeed, he might never do it; so calmly did he meet and part from her, so delicate and deferential was his touch. So gentle had been his wooing, also, compared with that of Featherstone, that she began to doubt its genuineness; that it was intended for no more than polite attention, while enjoying mere intellectual intercourse; such, at least, was the conclusion to which she came before she slept.

Then, too, Aurelia thought that she liked Featherstone well enough to marry him. She, at least, had been deeply moved by him; and it was a brilliant offer, not likely to be declined by any wise person. It must be borne in mind that she saw him not as he really was, but as he appeared in the midst of affluence, and courted by the beautiful and accomplished; while, in intellect and bearing, he was the peer of any man who revolved in the circle of gayety where she encountered him. And let it also be remembered that he was one of those who please many women, — if it surprise the gentlemen who most respect them, — for he had that kind of "animal magnetism" which leads to matrimony, not by the lofty and chastening steps of admiration, but by the impulse and inclination of passion. From this wild influence Aurelia was not free; in truth it was a portion of her inheritance, and had something of her secret thought, and at times seized the reins and swayed supreme. Yet there was that in her nature which gave it resistance; hence the seclusion of the morning, and her embarrassment on meeting Featherstone; and thence the nervousness which had conjured up the apparition of Park, and so saddened her spirits as to bring tears to her eyes.

Seeing the change that came over her, and misinterpreting it, he said, "I hope you are not jealous!" On which she gave him a look that made him inquire in a less confident tone, "Has any thing happened?" and, feeling a dread that something of his secret history might have reached her ear since their last meeting, he appeared like a culprit.

This, however, she did not observe, as her eyes were weighed down with her own secret; and, wishing to escape further inquiry, she replied, "O, it is nothing — some slight affection that will pass away with a little exercise."

"Then let me drive you out this morning; I can arrange it."

"No, I thank you; I choose to walk."

"May I hope that you will accompany me this evening?" he urged.

"If it be your pleasure;" and turning down a shaded path, — while Featherstone retraced his steps to join the lady who was to take the seat beside him, — in a few moments she heard the carriage dash away. Threading the secluded walk, her agitation increased rather than diminished; for the features of the landscape, in their sunny repose, as well as the gentle caressings of the morning air, reminded her of Park. And such were her thoughts, that, could he have met her and tenderly encouraged her long-cherished hope, were it necessary, she would have fled with him to the ends of the earth — could she but have seen his outstretched hand, she would have clasped it and been safe; otherwise, too weak for self-sustaining, she is trembling to her fall.

Although no word had been spoken by any one on that morning, concerning the engagement, loud enough for the most expert eavesdropper to have heard, while in all communications the strictest secrecy had been enjoined and most earnestly promised, yet it was apparent, from every glancing eye of the guests who had gathered for dinner, that the event of the season was known to all; for there

> "Was never secret history
> But birds did tell it in the bowers."

When the ladies had withdrawn from table, one of the friends of Featherstone replenished the glasses, and lifting the wine to his lips, said, with a significant glance at the happy man, "*Veni, vidi, vici.*"

"Very good!" said one of the group. "Capital, capital!" cried another; while a third set down his glass and tapped his thumb nails together several times, with an air that seemed to say, "My applause is the crown." On which, all laughed; and Featherstone ordered more wine — a seemingly appropriate and acceptable acknowledgment of the compliment. As the Madeira circulated, one said, "When may we expect to receive her in the Crescent? and what will Anthony do with Cleopatra?" but, observing Featherstone's brow flush, he immediately added, "I meant no offence, by Jove, my dear fellow! It was only a spark of envy, from thinking how beauty seems to rise to your lips, like the beads on your wine."

Seeing that his delicate associate had no intention other than to compliment him, Featherstone filled the glasses, and said, —

> "Here's to beauty, young beauty, all over the world!"

Tossing off their wine, they poured and drank again; and one said, as he set down his glass, "That was devilish good!"

Whereupon they filled afresh; for, a little confused, they thought the praise was meant for the wine — being oblivious with regard to the poetical sentiment. In this way they soon finished the bottle and their cigars, and, rising up, Featherstone went to prepare for the drive with Aurelia.

When he had sufficiently cooled his brow, flavored his breath, and carefully arranged his dress, he ordered his horses to the door, and sent a messenger to Miss Vernon. Completing her array, she descended, and, though paler than usual, smiled on those around, while approaching the carriage, as if she were about to ascend the throne of her desire. And having taken her seat with studied composure, she looked at Featherstone with a predetermined expression, as he placed himself beside her, which was calculated to give the observer an impression of fondness. In truth, she did take some satisfaction in the elegant finish of the "turn out," and looked with a degree of pleasure on the proud steeds, as they bounded away, with their steel harnesses flashing to the sun.

If Featherstone had entertained doubts in the morning, he now felt reassured. Yet it was his whim to avoid conversation, for a time, unless she should introduce it. So feeling, he put his horses to their mettle, for three or four miles, over the somewhat rough, wild, and wood-shadowed road which it pleased him to choose. At length, in the thick of the forest, he slackened out the ribbons, and speaking soothingly to his foaming coursers, they immediately dropped into a walk, hanging their heads low to relieve the pain in their necks, champing the bits to ease their aching jaws, and flirting out their muzzles to throw off the slightest pressure of the reins.

But Aurelia had made her election. And, finding opportunity in the course of the day, Mrs. Fardel had so painted the advantages of the alliance as to confirm the opinion. Hence she rose superior to the weakness of the morning, and set her will on carrying out the contract, and that too as speedily as he might propose. Thus prepared for business, she was the first to recur to the scene of their last meeting. And so completely had she gained the mastery over herself that she said lightly, even playfully, "I hope that you enjoyed your ride this morning?"

"No. I was thinking too much of you," he replied.

"Did that destroy your pleasure?" she smilingly inquired.

"But you appeared so changed, and were so cold."

Thereupon she told him that she had had much to think of in the dissimilarity of their situations. This led her to speak of the circumstances of her parents, of their broken fortunes, and that being an only child she ought not to be far divided from them.

To this — being anxious to remove every obstacle in the way of his passion — he replied, "I have no wish to return to the south, and we will live wherever you think you can be happiest." Thereupon he pleaded for immediate union with all the force that passion could infuse into the phrases of love.

At length it was concluded, after Aurelia had conferred with her protectress, although the season had not quite closed, to depart for the city within three or four days; and Featherstone determined to leave on the following morning.

As he was about to say adieu to Aurelia, he clasped a chain around her neck, to which was suspended a jewelled cross, flashing with the subduing light of diamonds and rubies. So the cross of the mustee — which, it will be remembered, he took from her dressing table with other valuables, on the morning of his departure from New Orleans — came again into use. Strange change! Has it the power to calm this tumultuous heart? Can it charm away thought, or erase fond recollection from this glowing breast? And, in view of all the circumstances, may we not confidently inquire in what particular, either in the splendors of the mind, or in purity of affection, has it been exalted?

In the morning, as Featherstone was departing, Mrs. Fardel appeared, and gently, but very expressively, accosting him, said, "I could not permit you to leave us without a word of congratulation."

"You are very kind," he warmly replied; "and I shall remember to be grateful to one who has so helped me haste to the wedding. And permit me to hope that you will so continue your good offices as to appear at the time indicated. I shall await your arrival with impatience."

"You may rest assured that I shall do what I can, as Aurelia is under my protection, and I feel a deep interest in her welfare. She needs just such a husband as I am sure you will make — one who can take her into society, and feel proud of the admiration she receives; for she is too beautiful and too attractive to be lost in mere household dulness and duty. So, if nothing happens to prevent, you shall see us at the time appointed; indeed I like to lay a train to a wedding, for 'marriage is honorable.'" Then leaning still nearer and speaking lower, she added, "If you are going to the city you must have a care of yourself, and not fight my cousin Park before we get there to take charge of you."

"What reason have you for such a caution?" he inquired with surprise.

"O innocence!" exclaimed she. "As if you did not know, you naughty man! that you had charmed away a heart from him. But I do not care, for he deserved to lose it, the cold creature! I have not the least mite of sympathy for him — to go shilly-shallying along as he did, thinking that she could wait forever! Now, I think it is always perfectly ridiculous to do so, and I see that there is more sense in your course; therefore I wish you joy."

CHAPTER XVIII.

He jests at scars that never felt a wound.
SHAKSPEARE.

As the carriage bore Featherstone away, he thought of the caution of Mrs. Fardel, and called to mind the incidents of the party at her house, and Park's attentions to Miss Vernon on that occasion, with his conversation the morning after, and felt some elation on thus finding that he had at length carried off one prize from an old and able competitor.

So, taking his seat in the cars, he went on restoring, touching, and coloring the past, bringing out the dimly-seen forms, regrouping the characters in the foreground, — himself in the blaze of light and the embrace of beauty, — and at length placed the picture where Vanity might gaze upon it in moments of leisure.

Again and again, in the course of his journey, he turned to look on the canvas with a kind of mischievous satisfaction, as he felt more pleasure in gain when he could measure it by the loss of another.

He had also that coarseness of sentiment, and sense of enjoyment in another's mortification, which led him to play practical jokes. Hence, as a part of his accidental triumph, yet with no thought of seriously wounding, he resolved on a little amusement with his friend, whenever he should find opportunity.

Entering Park's office soon after his arrival in the city, he was received kindly, though with some surprise that he should come on so late in the season, as he said, "I thought that you southern gentlemen generally appeared to us in June."

"It is usual; and it was not my intention to come north this year, but important changes came to alter my decision. Merton has died, and I have succeeded to a condition wherein I can afford to take my leisure."

"So the first aim has proved successful! Yet how do you propose to employ your leisure? for it is good only in so far as it gives you that choice."

"I think I shall marry by way of beginning."

"Well, if love leads, I hold that to be a wise course, so soon as one can see his way clear. But you must have found something very sweet to lead you to so serious a step! Nothing less than a sugar estate, I fancy."

"Very refined! Yet, to be candid with you, I am intending to espouse that Miss Vernon — you may remember her — whom we met at your cousin's, Mrs. Fardel's; and I shall be pleased to see you at the wedding."

"You are very thoughtful; and I will try to be one of the party."

"I fancied that would be your pleasure, and we shall be happy to welcome you on the joyous occasion — so you may expect due notice of the day and hour. And, by the way, how is the widow?"

"O, she is blooming and obliging, and would like to see you, undoubtedly; but come home with me and judge for yourself."

"No, you must dine with me to-day," replied Featherstone, smiling.

And, deferring to his wish, they walked out together.

"How soon do you return south?" inquired Park, as they ascended the steps of the Astor.

"That is uncertain. It is a point which I have yielded

to the inclination of another. You can inquire of the lady."

"Shall I have the pleasure of her company at dinner?"

"Not to-day, but in the course of two or three weeks she will be happy to meet you."

They had quite a social repast, touching, however, only on the surface of the times, as befitted the place and crowd, until the company in their immediate neighborhood had departed, or gathered into lively groups, when Park, filling the glasses, said, "We will drink, if you please, to the joy of Mrs. Featherstone, that is to be."

Featherstone received the compliment with beck and smile, as he raised his glass, and seemed to have peculiar pleasure while he lingered over his wine.

In a few moments Featherstone, having replenished the cups, said, "We will drink to the health and happiness of the beautiful Miss Vernon, if you will allow me."

On this Park touched his lips again to the wine and said, "I think the lady would esteem it so flattering a recollection that I may venture to thank you."

"You, of course, know best how she would accept the attention," replied Featherstone, masking his countenance with difficulty; "yet, when you again meet, you may say that I retain a vivid impression of her beauty, and hope to see her married soon, and her husband, that is to be, in Congress."

To which Park replied, "It will give me pleasure to present your compliments when I have an opportunity. But the political eminence, of which you speak, I am not likely to reach."

"Why not? I hear of your triumphs at the bar."

"The way in which it is usually sought, in these piping times, is not suited to my taste. And, were I elected, I should not like to be publicly 'instructed' in statesmanship; for, if there should be one of the constituency capable of instructing, he would be entitled to the place. Yet only in fearful crises will such hereafter reach it; it was the terrors of the revolution that brought out and elevated the giants who made our senate so august. Those times are passed. Still the slavery question may be so urged as to shake and arouse the people to a recognition of their true leaders once more."

"Ah! have you turned abolitionist?" inquired Featherstone.

"I love liberty and desire its diffusion. And it is worthy of observation that God has given it to mankind as he does food, so that, if it be justly apportioned, every one may have all he can truly enjoy. Hence, whatever of these is taken from one class in a state not only leaves them to suffer, but makes the taker licentious, to the further and still deeper injury of both."

"Do you intend to dissolve the Union as a means to such a result?"

"I strike against wrong, however fortified," Park replied. "If the constitution does not foster freedom, it is not what the founders of the government intended, and not what the great body of the American people will demand."

"Then you propose to destroy that incomparable instrument which gives us such dignity abroad and security at home?"

"I propose to inquire if it be not the will of the majority of the American people to have whatever is doubtful in the constitution construed in favor of freedom. And I propose yet further, if there be any thing in that instrument which sanctions tyranny, or throws a shield around the slavery propagandist in any of our territory, or makes the men of the free states a portion of the police to enforce the local laws of southern servitude, to do all that lies in my power to present to the country the necessity of taking the prescribed steps for its amendment."

"If you succeed in striking down that pillar the whole fabric will fall, and liberty and order along with it," said Featherstone.

"That is to doubt that we have benefited by our institutions; it is to deny the advancing intelligence of the people. If, when overthrown, it be so by endeavoring to eradicate a wrong, I have no fears but something nobler will arise on the broad basis of the Declaration."

"Then, in a certain contingency, you would side with the destructives! Do you think that the people of the north, and east, and west, if they are not satisfied with the interpretation of the constitution, will give their votes to change it?"

"Most certainly. Their very reverence for its many commanding excellences will lead them to remove whatsoever dims its glory or endangers its perpetuity."

"When do you expect a two thirds vote in Congress to initiate the measure, and three fourths of the states to ratify it?"

"Not soon. Freedom advances slowly; the future historian may count ages between its footprints; yet the goal will be reached. From darker doubt, through deeper perils, the long processions of our ancestors were called to march by their indomitable love of liberty, until they made the British constitution perfect in its personal protection. The planters are in the position of the feudal lords, yet where are they?"

"I care nothing for what may happen ages hence. I go against disturbance now; for the south will not submit to be instructed, much less controlled, by any other portion of the Union, however strong. They will sooner withdraw from the compact, peaceably if they may, forcibly if they must. They inherit an institution of the fathers more tangible than any which you boast; therefore, in extremity, it will be more desperately defended."

"That step, if successful, can yield them no additional security, for a dissolution of the Union will not relieve them from the effect of eternal laws. Do they think thus to escape from the operation of that title to lands which underlies, and eventually overrides, all others, namely, that he shall have who can best occupy? If they heap dishonor upon labor, do they hope to gather its fruits in peace? Is it possible for them to bar the spirit of the age from all their borders? No, arm as they may against these subtle forces, there can be no doubt which will finally prevail. Yet I am so far a conservative that I look searchingly at change, and ask for the most minute and mature consideration before it be accepted. But growth will continually demand it, however disturbing or painful may be the process. 'Before the eagle can have a new beak,' says Carlyle, 'he must beat off the old upon hard rocks.' Hence the best sign of the times is the dissatisfaction with existing constitutions and enactments, however Traffic may deplore it; and he who doubts this may fawn on the people for some selfish purpose, but has no faith in their capacity for self-government, and no desire to see Liberty make broader the arches of her Temple."

"So you are really an abolitionist! However, it may serve your turn in a local way; but for any place in the general government, you might as well be a native of Congo. Do you go in for philanthropy in general — the amelioration of the condition of criminals, &c.?"

"I believe in being merciful; for man has no mercy so tender as the Infinite Justice. I have learned that kindness alone can win its way to the soul and elevate it; all sterner messengers find it rock and leave it adamant. If this be true, — and no observing person can deny it, — what change must come! And, in view of it, no man is fit to legislate for this age, or the coming generations, who does not feel such impulse at his heart, and strive to give it organization."

"If such service was expected, I fancy that but few men would seek office," said Featherstone, laughing.

"Office is not to be sought; the purest motives cannot sanction the solicitation, as beggars do not often preserve their self-respect."

"If you are so scrupulous as that, I may stand a better chance, if Mrs. Featherstone should persuade me to remain here."

This recurrence to the prospect of his marriage seemed to fill Featherstone with pleasure, which he strove to conceal. Observing it, Park pleaded an engagement, and in a few moments they separated. Yet, while walking down to his office, he thought of the mystery, and came to the conclusion that Featherstone was really about to be married, as he could think of no other prospect which would have so tickled him into continual smiles and laughter.

As Park moved away, Featherstone turned into the reading room, still hotly smiling; and taking up a newspaper, he looked upon it and laughed audibly, two or three times, which so attracted attention that he tossed it away and went out, to more freely vent the fun and enjoy the joke.

On the passage down the river, Aurelia was fitful; at one moment very gay and then seated apart, gazing silently into the bubbling water. When, however, they reached the pier, and Featherstone came on board, she received him so cordially that a profound observer would have perceived that she was playing a part. Indeed, when she finally rose up from looking on the fleeting waves, she had so resolved; and well did she carry it out, in the presence of Featherstone. In this Mrs. Fardel ably assisted her, as she had persuaded Aurelia to remain with her for the few weeks previous to her marriage.

The neighbors of the Vernons were surprised one morning, soon after the foregoing arrival, to see the windows of their mansion all open, with a throng of painters and other renovators busy in every part. Mrs. Vernon, too, appeared to have awakened as from years of sleep, for she was listening to suggestions, looking at plans, and giving directions, from morning until night, and seemed to gain new vigor with each succeeding day.

In the course of two or three weeks these renewers and decorators disappeared, and the furniture began to arrive. During those days the family that lived opposite had many callers, who, as they peered through the closed Venetian blinds, and saw the costly cabinet work which continued to come, aired their recollections of the dark and dismal house, which for years they had known it to be, and wondered, and remarked, and conjectured in this wise, "Who, do you suppose, has bought Aurelia?"

"I have no notion, I'm sure; but I'll warrant that it is some man old enough to have a large estate and a short lease of it."

"Do see what lovely things he is giving for her; and paying in advance too!"

These shrewd and knowing observers were aware that the daughter was their most valuable possession; and if their tart words are worth little as a judgment, they are valuable as an unconscious, and therefore a true, confession; for when one speaks of another, it is of the nature and character of the person speaking that we are likely to learn most.

The old gentleman came out as usual, appearing to give little heed to what was going on within the house. Yet the new influence had not only reached, but penetrated him; so that he appeared more fresh and bright; and instead of emerging and looking out furtively from the back passage, he issued from the front door, and carried his gold-headed cane more frequently under his arm, as if he were growing stronger day by day. His white locks — he had not yet gone to the length of dyeing his hair — seemed to be more particularly cared for; and his skin was deeper colored, whether from an increase of stimulants, or brighter hopes, or both, we will not pause to inquire, as it was a pleasant sight; and when not wrung from the heart of another, or in any way too dearly bought, is like returning sunshine after long lingering mist and cloud.

The gazers were greatly surprised at Aurelia's absence during all this preparation; and the mystery deepened and grew august, when a carriage, with driver and footman in livery, began to draw up before the door, daily, taking Mrs. Vernon out alone, to return alone.

"What could it mean?" they looked and asked.

On this, some of those who had expressed themselves the most confidently with regard to the matrimonial sale, commenced to "hedge" their opinions, by suggesting, "These Vernons are one of the old families, and a great many of the members are rich: perhaps some one has died and left them a fortune."

"Yes; or pride of name has induced them to contribute, so as to keep up appearances," said another.

"Ah, that is not probable," said one of a more selfish turn. "It is far more likely that Mr. Vernon has been appointed to some fat office; and now that I think of it, it appears quite possible, as he has devoted his time, for over twenty years, to reading the newspapers, which are the teachers of politics, you know. You may depend upon it, he has got hold of the people's money, and they are flourishing away on that. Now, there was Mr. Overdrew and Mr. Bezzlem, both did it; and their daughters caught rich husbands by the game — so now they live at their ease. I declare it always makes me angry when any thing like this reminds me how we had to contribute to it, yet were never so much as invited to the parties which they gave in consequence. And, what is more aggravating than all, they keep up the same style now that they did before they broke."

"Why shouldn't they, when they prevented any thing from running out which their creditors could lay hand on?" said the lady of the house. "But you will find, if these Vernons have got hold of money in any way, that the lawyer who used to walk down here with the daughter will discontinue his visits; for she will carry her case to a higher court. It is mysterious enough now, certainly; but Aurelia must be along in a few days, and then we shall learn more about it — as she will surely drop straws into the current, so that we can see the direction in which it is setting. As for the mother, she is perfectly impenetrable. She enters and alights from her carriage in a way that would lead you to suppose that she had practised it every hour of her life; and wears her rich apparel, and reveals as little curiosity, as she would had the ride never been interrupted for a single day."

At length, under the directing care of Mrs. Vernon, the various preparations for the nuptials had been made; every portion of the house was in the approved order; no trace of the past remained. Even a faded rose had been shaken out, and swept from Aurelia's room, with other litter, by a mother's order; and if the mandrake shriek when torn from the earth, that rose might well sigh for the one who had so long cherished it; yet its plaintive spirit passed unheeded, for her ear was inclined to another voice; and though her heart will yet catch and echo its sad tone, it may then be too late.

CHAPTER XIX.

All's over then — does truth sound bitter,
As one at first believes?
Hark, 'tis the sparrow's good-night twitter
About your cottage eves!

BROWNING.

FEATHERSTONE'S business, together with the many duties and pleasures incident to his approaching bridal, so occupied his hours that he had not seen sufficient leisure to call on Park, had he so wished, since the day on which they had dined together. He, indeed, looked in on the widow Summers several times; but, as she had reasons for keeping the visits to herself, Park did not hear of them. Hence, as no circumstance suggested it, it had not entered his mind for some days, that Featherstone might be still in town, until, one morning about a fortnight after the meeting described, he received the following note, enclosing the usual card for such occasions.

"WEDNESDAY MORNING.

"My dear Park: In accordance not only with my promise, but my earnest wishes, I now more formally invite you to be present at my wedding; which is to take place — as you may see by the enclosed card — on this day week. You, of course, must not fail to be with us, for Miss Vernon and myself will both feel that we have lost a pleasure if you do not grace the gay occasion with your presence.

"Yours, truly,

"A. FEATHERSTONE."

On first looking at this missive, Park was disposed to treat it as a jest, rude and rough though it was even in that aspect; but he soon saw that to be altogether too profitless a play for Featherstone to be likely to engage in. Thereupon he turned the card over two or three times and scrutinized it; read the note again and again, and cross-examined it; and finally folded it up with the conviction that it was possible. Then, leaning his brow on his hand, he gazed deep and long within him; and at length a stern, even a pale, thought came up, and spread into every line of his countenance, as if he were putting on some fine armor, all white from the fire of his spirit, to meet the shock of an advancing foe.

Soon after so arming himself, he was under the necessity of going into court to present a case to a jury; and never before did he make an argument so clear, so cogent, and so concise. There was no ornament, no finishing touch. His thoughts were molten and moulded into terrible missiles, as statues of bronze have been in great emergencies, which went directly on and overwhelmed whatever he chose to aim at.

As Park was aware that it was about the time for Aurelia to return, he had walked over to the pier on two or three previous evenings, in season to meet the day boats down the Hudson. Yet now, when night came, with opportunity for investigation, he did not turn his steps in that direction, neither did he go down the quiet street which led by her father's house, but up towards his cousin's, where he had first met her, and with whom she had gone forth to revel in summer gayety.

Drawing near the mansion, he saw that it was open; and moving on, he soon heard voices, and those so lively that there seemed to be guests as well as family within. Crossing to the opposite side of the street, and passing by slow and observant, in a moment he distinguished Featherstone's voice, and, thereupon, the gay tones of Aurelia in reply; and they appeared to him gayer than ever. Arrested as by a hand dread and resistless, he stood and heard, not the words, but the note and accent, until the conviction came home to his understanding and went down to his heart, that the myrtle wreath which they were twining would be the crown of her desire — that even hope looked not beyond the bridal.

Well nigh stunned by the truth he had sought, and then shaken by conflicting emotions, he at length curbed his bounding blood and calmed his throbbing brain so as to think and utter to himself, "Strange infatuation! Yet not strange! only in *her* is it strange. Ah, how far she must have fallen! for this is steep down, sheer below the venture of my imagination! There are beasts which manifest a purer sentiment than this can be, and one that will not wither and die so quickly. What a blinding malady is passion! O, she was a glorious creature! capable of the crowning things, both in the realm of thought and emotion; and capable of *this* also! It seems but yesterday when I walked in her radiance on the height of life; and now she has gone where it makes my brain reel to gaze after her! What is love, if she were free? yet freely she has chosen, and making choice of flesh, I can leave her to Time, who will strip it to a skeleton.

"*He*, indeed, is only working out his own nature — a nature that had no entrance, or key, to any secret place in mine. Yet he calls me friend! and how has he given sign of it? No! we were thrown together by circumstances, not drawn by sympathy; and have kept up a kind of companionship which was refreshing to neither of us, but had a tendency to harden each. Hence I have seldom met him without wearing a secret cuirass; and, standing at guard, played only with the muscles of the mind; yet of *this* he has taken advantage to thrust at me! Seeing a blasted heath, he comes to 'palter with me in a double sense'!"

So he turned firmly away; although his thoughts still visited their presence, as he continued, "Had I found her mute, sad, or reluctant, I would have contended even on the last step of the altar; but she prays for no rescue — trembles rather at the thought of interruption. Well, it is a severe, though it may be a salutary, lesson; for I had fondly dreamed that I could fill one heart, and many sweet tokens whispered, this one; but I see now that they were only light and deceptive appearances, which kindred flesh has more truly interpreted. Yet, after all, there was something great, as well as captivating, about her; she was capable of the loftiest moods; the spirit of thought could take her into regal regions, and bear her up starry spaces, for which nature has given him neither wing nor inclination. If he whistle her to his hand, can he smooth her pinions to the perch, or hood her piercing eye? will she not soar away 'though her jesses were his heart-strings'? Now they are but thoughtless evening revellers, who drink their fill to awaken to a dismal day! No sweet peace, no ever-deepening friendship, can spring between their hearts to twine them into a hallowed retreat from the world's rude shocks. Neither will their flame be a continuing fire on the hearth, ever warm, ever cheerful. I can look on its fitful blaze without envy, as I shall yet look upon the ashes without surprise."

Thus had Park — though with a lacerated heart, yet one capable of applying the cautery to its own wounds — reasoned himself into his accustomed calmness, so that he entered the house and the presence of the widow, with no visible sign of that which had stirred him so deeply.

Taking up an evening paper, he seated himself near the table, where Mrs. Summers, with a light-hued dress in her lap, was looking over some laces; and when she found one which was sufficiently long or short, wide or narrow enough, she laid it on to some particular part of the dress, and so held them up to see what the effect might be.

Park observed what was going on without moving his eyes from the paper; so he inferred that she had been invited to the wedding, and was busy with preparation for the event.

At length, after many trials of different varieties of trimming, while holding the garment in many views, now front, now back, and in changing perspective, she said, "O dear!" and dropped the parts as though she was out of patience in trying to make them take elegant and pleasing form.

On this Park looked up, and appearing for the first time to notice her occupation, inquired, "Are you preparing to be married, Mrs. Summers?"

"I think of going to a wedding; and I expect to have a delightful time, if I can ever get this dress to suit me."

"Is the bride, that is to be, an acquaintance of mine?"

"Yes, indeed, and a very particular acquaintance, too."

"As there are so few who bear that relation, you must mean Miss Vernon."

"I do," she answered, while her keen eye searched him, but found nothing.

To which Park carelessly replied as he turned to his newspaper, "I supposed that to be an old story, as the lover invited me some twelve or fifteen days since."

"Has Mr. Featherstone been in town so long?" she inquired with well-affected surprise.

"Ay, truly; I think that I dined with him a fortnight ago to-day."

"What a strange man you are, Mr. Park, never to tell me! It seems so odd not to speak of that which could do no harm to any one, and might be a satisfaction or a gratification to many."

"Don't you think secrecy a good quality, Mrs. Summers?"

"Why, what do you mean, Mr. Park?"

"I mean, if one can read another, would you like to have him read aloud?"

"I don't know what you allude to," said she, coloring; "but you have made a mistake *once*, and you may again."

Park smiled, for he was somewhat amused at the keenness of the retort, yet saw no reason for further remark; while the widow thought him as uninteresting in conversation, as he appeared to be destitute of that warmth of heart which she had seen in Featherstone, and so admired in any one.

At length the evening for the marriage ceremony came, and the widow Summers, dressed very becomingly, — thanks to her own ingenuity, — had been set down punctual to the moment, as she was anxious to see all. She hovered very near, during the ceremony, and on the first opportunity for congratulations, she said very softly to the bride, "I have been through it all, and know precisely how you feel; but you controlled your feelings perfectly; there was not the slightest agitation, and I never saw you look so smiling and beautiful before."

Then turning to one of the bridemaids, and continuing in the same half whisper, she said, "How fine-looking Mr. Featherstone is! and how perfectly he has caught your southern manner, which is *so* captivating! I wish you would persuade him to wear a mustache, it gives one so distinguished an air."

"They do give a peculiar expression; they have a kind of chivalrous look, and make one think of knights and deeds in arms."

"Yes, indeed," said the widow; "and of the Turks, and of those beautiful creatures who come from Italy to play and sing the operas. And he would be quite like those, if he only had that last touch; and then it attracts attention, just like a flourish under a name on a subscription list. What a pity that he has none!"

"They are very easy of production," said Featherstone, who had heard many of her words, as she had intended them mostly for his ear.

"What if I object?" queried Aurelia, playfully.

"I should say that your objection came too late to be part of our contract."

"But in so trifling a thing you would not refuse me."

"Trifling things are not to be insisted upon," he answered with a warm smile, yet in a way to close the conversation.

If this made Aurelia look sad for an instant, she quickly vibrated to merriment, and seemed to have no serious thought.

Mrs. Summers was so elated with the attention which she had received, that she felt like patronizing some one; and seeing a lady of her acquaintance standing alone, she, rather superfluously it might be, excused herself to the group, and joining her, inquired, after the usual compliments of such an evening, "Have you seen the beautiful bridal presents?"

"No, I have not; although I am aware that they are getting to be the chief attraction of such occasions."

"Well," said the widow, putting her hand within the arm of her friend, "you must go with me and feast your eyes. Do you know Aurelia? O, yes, I remember now, you do: what a perfect creature! and she is a particular friend of mine, and so is Mr. Featherstone, and he is so generous. But they are all generous; only see what generous friends they have. I do really wish that it had been the custom to give so when we were married — don't you?"

Her companion, who was rather of a practical turn, replied, "They are pretty costly ventures; and I have no doubt that many of them will prove to be gifts or losses, which in this class of cases is the same thing. But can you tell me what they intend to do with twenty fish trowels, when one or two are quite sufficient for housekeeping?"

"O, I noticed that, and have thought it all over. It is just as I should like to have it, were it my case; for no one will be likely to feel compelled to make more than eighteen or nineteen wedding presents in all their lives! So they can do these trowels up and deal them out as occasion may require; and, in that way, they will get every thing else for nothing."

Here their attention was diverted to the company, who, gathering densely in the parlors, began to press around the plate and jewelry tables, where they lingered, and silently gazed, as if dazzled and overawed; or breathed low-murmured admiration until their souls seemed small and dim beside the minutest and most feeble gem. Never did golden calf receive more true and heart-felt worship. Yet how few of those who so adored, like the unselfish daughters of Israel, would have devoted their trinkets to the formation of their god!

The stillness of the guests during the ceremony, and the low hum and measured words of the first moments of reception, had heightened into mirthful sounds from every part of the large and well-filled apartments. The tide of life had ceased to flow towards the bridal group; and Featherstone, as there was nothing which absolutely required him to stand there longer, abdicated his station to meet his more intimate associates in the refreshment room, where he appeared to be relieved, and grew bright with glad exhilaration, and tarried long.

The bride still remained on the spot where she had made her vows. And although her beauty was so perfect of outline that even regal apparel could neither lend grace nor improve proportion, yet, like the evening star, she seemed more lovely for the half-veiling vapor. If there was a slight appearance of tension in her features, if her lip was like a bow partly drawn, it was too joyous an hour for any one to analyze for the cause. If she was profuse in smiles, few saw that they were almost as much a surface quality as the gleam of her gems, and none suspected that her lively remarks were intended to be a screen rather than an exhibition of her heart. Little as she had heeded it, in that secret place there was a shadow which no outward light could allay, and no turning away of the ear leave its whispers unheard. Such a visitant may be made to rest from troubling, for a time; it may yield, for a season, to the intoxications of life; but, when weariness comes, it will arise to haunt the soul, and amid woes, however direful, it will vindicate its preëminence.

Beside Aurelia stood one of her maids of honor — a creature fair and young, who listened to the vivacious but fitful conversation of the bride admiringly, for Nature had fashioned her mind, as she had formed her person, in one of her fondest moods. As they stood there, near each other, they presented a fine contrast; one seemed a garden growth, while the other had the characteristics, and something of the timidity, of the forest flower. One had the full and regular form of the warm-odored pine tree, which we select and place for ornament, while the other was more like a whispering birch by the brink of some clear and sweetly-secluded water. They were nearly of the same height also; and, judged from their outline alone, the bride appeared much the stronger; but when you saw their motions and their glances, you would learn that one might bear Diana's bow through all the sylvan scene, while the other was dreaming with Venus in her bower. In keeping with this, the eyes of one had the hue and the light of morning; those of the other, the darkness of night and the gleam of stars.

At length, in the midst of their conversation, Park appeared. He had considered the invitation carefully, even painfully, and came to the conclusion that his absence would be much more likely to cause remark than his presence; and one of his maxims favored the course, which was — "Look fate in the face."

He was dressed in black, though not specially, — for it was the only color in which he felt perfectly at ease, — and, contrary to his custom, his coat was buttoned across his chest, as if feeling the necessity of a shield, and making more apparent his sword-like form. His face was calm and impenetrable as marble; yet he entered with the feelings of one who searches, amid the murder and the moan of the battle field, for a fallen brother.

It was some relief, as he crossed the apartment, to see that Featherstone was not with the bride; for he had shown himself coarse and callous, to say the least; therefore he feared that any words of greeting which he might feel compelled to utter to him would be but a half-subdued echo of his contempt. With this abatement it was a heavy hour. Yet, bitter as was his own disappointment, he could feel some pity for the bride; for he knew that the materials of the marriage would never form a union; that the deeper thirst of her nature could not be long satisfied at this fountain, however it sparkled now.

As he caught her eye he had a glimpse of her heart, as we behold a landscape in the black night by a flash of lightning; and as deeper darkness follows thereon, so she shrouded it, for the moment; and on the next instant, while extending her hand, a smile spread over her features as soft as the light of a serene heaven, and she spoke volubly the commonplaces of the hour.

But Park's discovery — so entirely unlooked for *then* — had thrown him into such a tumult that he could not catch her tone, — and he would strike no other, — which seeing, she came immediately to his relief by saying, "It gives me pleasure, Mr. Park, to introduce you to my friend Miss McRae; and you may take his arm, Annie, to the refreshment room, while I speak to my mother."

As they turned away, Park felt that her eye was on him, and, raising his, he saw its deep once more open, with a vast space which seemed vacant and lone, yet it instantly closed as before.

Walking towards the refreshment room, Park tried to think of something that he might say to the lady who accompanied him; but his thoughts were tumultuous, and would follow only Aurelia. So he was compelled to the simplest form, and inquired, "Do you reside in the city, Miss McRae?"

"No, I do not; though only so far out as Greenville."

"Ah! I have a client of your name who lives in that town."

"He is my father; and I have often heard him speak of you, as he has great hope that you may gain his case."

"If we can ever get to trial," said Park, glad to take refuge from his feelings in so familiar a topic, "I think we may succeed."

"You must not be too anxious for a decision, for my father has busied himself with it so long, that, when it shall be finally determined, he will feel that his occupation is gone; therefore I give you full liberty to continue, and continue, to the extent of your ingenuity."

"That, in many cases, would be a valuable privilege; but in this, as my fee, for the most part, depends on success, I am somewhat anxious to have it concluded; and I think that I must go out there soon to see what kind of territory I am about to own."

"My father will be pleased to see you, and point out your domain. I walk over it, with him, almost every pleasant day; and while he searches for boundaries, I seek for berries or nuts, or stand silent within the gothic cathedral of the woods."

"You well name the forest thus, having felt the awe that whispers through its arches. When the ancient Germans gave up their sylvan worship, they shaped the rocks of God's house into the form, and traced them to the semblance, of that first temple; and what of wildness they could not transfer, was a loss of solemnity; indeed, no work of man's hands can give the thrill and impressiveness of the old woods."

"Truly, I feel that to be so; while the scream of a jay, or the chirp of a squirrel, within its solemn aisles, stirs me deeper and makes me more thoughtful than any note of organ or melody of chanting."

They soon after returned to the parlors, when Park, observing Mrs. Fardel, left Miss McRae with a group of friends who had gathered around, and joined her. That lady looked a little disturbed on seeing him approach, but quickly commanding herself, she smilingly alluded to the interesting occasion, and said, "Brian, you are getting to be my bachelor cousin. I should think that *this* would remind you that it was time to turn your thoughts on the subject of marriage. Now, if you had only been with us this summer, I could have introduced you to two beautiful young ladies of fortune; and, really, I wish that you had been there, for I know you would have liked either one of them well enough to have married her — and I have not the slightest doubt but that I could have arranged it nicely. Indeed, this to-night is mostly my handiwork; and isn't it a triumph for Aurelia?"

"Do you desire my opinion in relation to it?" inquired Park, in a warning voice.

"Yes, certainly; for you cannot but think it brilliant," she replied, though with a startled air.

"You may prepare yourself, then, to listen, not to compliment, but to truth. If there has been a triumph, it was over virtue; and the brilliancy that you speak of is a consuming flame. The world, doubtless, will congratulate her on the apparent success; yet she seems to me to have been bitten by a tarantula; and you think her happy because you see the glowing excitement of the insane dance; but it will pass soon — pass utterly; and when the virus has done its final work, the *friends* who enticed her to the mournful step may have an opportunity to look upon the consequences of their folly."

"I hope you do not think that I did it!" said his surprised cousin.

"I believe that you laid claim to it a moment since."

"I did? I'm sure I meant no such thing!"

"Why do you seek to evade a confession of the truth? You are a mercenary match-maker, and have to descend only one step lower to earn the vilest name which I know."

"What is *that*, pray? I never heard any one talk as you do, Brian, in all my life. I think *you* are the one who is insane! What word do you mean?"

"Do you wish to hear it — or do you fear it? Yet, in either case, I shall not utter it. But you may consult the dictionary; and permit me to advise you not to pause in the search until you think that you have found the worst."

So ending, he turned and left her with a theme for meditation.

Seeing that some persons were taking leave, Park approached the bridal group; when, hearing Mrs. Summers say to Aurelia, "I believe that I must bid you good night," he immediately offered her his arm, — for he saw in it a fine opportunity to make his escape, — which she accepted with evident surprise and pleasure; maintaining, forever after, that he was one of the most polite and elegant men that she had known, or seen, even in the "higher circles."

CHAPTER XX.

Drain off the soul
Of human joy; and make it pain to live —
And is it then to live? When such friends part,
'Tis the survivor dies. My heart, no more!
YOUNG.

IN the course of the day on which Featherstone left his house so like a thief, — I say so *like*, because all that the slave hath belongs by law to the master, — Flora went up to the room, and seeing a newspaper spread out over her dressing table, she took it up and, looking upon it, her eye immediately fell on a marked passage — a passage relating to the death of Rufus Merton. Reading it, her eyes filled; not on account of the generous and appreciating spirit of the article, but in unison with the thronging recollections which flowed through her heart; not one of which but was either grateful or tender. And long she sat and wept, thinking of that lonely sufferer so far away, with no soothing voice to revive the fading light of his eye, no loving hand to clasp in his, as he hung over the steep and fearful declivity.

At length, recovering something of her usual composure, she cut the paragraph from the paper, and having made it secure, her gaze rested a moment on her dressing table; when, observing some disarrangement there, she examined further, and finding what had been done, came to the conclusion that Featherstone had gone with the intention of returning no more. Over this she fell into another abyss of thought; but finally ascended from it, something agitated, yet closing with deep satisfaction. For she knew the fierce determination of Featherstone, and his dogged persistence; and they well nigh dispelled all fears of any further molestation from that quarter, which, in so short a period, had put on horror's shape: whatever else might come, this was a reprieve for which she gave sincere and glad thanks to the Father of mercies.

So, after a time, she went down to the sitting room, apparently calm and strong; and there, continuing her musing, Fred came softly to her side, and looked up into her face inquiringly. On this she took him into her lap, and held him long; the while frequently pressing him to her heart, and kissing him often, being scarce willing to let him return to his play. And, when she loosed him, he chose to remain away but a moment; for he would look up from amid his toys, and see something in her expression that drew him again to her side, to be again taken to her bosom.

It was not long, however, before he fell asleep in her arms; and then she said to Madam, "I think Mr. Merton"—for that was the name which she had been taught to call him, instead of father—"remains abroad a long time, mother; did he contemplate being absent for such a period when he departed?"

"My dear child, I have no expectation of seeing him while I live," replied Madam; "for although he did not say that he should return no more, still, from the many ways in which intelligence escapes, I had little hope that he would come here again; while now he has been away so long that I have ceased to watch for him. Indeed, when we parted, I felt that it was final; so that I followed him to the door feeling each dividing step like a dying groan; and if I ever see him dead, I know I shall find the same expression on his countenance."

"Why did he leave, mother, if it so cut him to the heart?"

"He had some trouble preying upon him, which he would not disclose. It may be that he thought our way of life wrong, and went forth to avoid it further. That, in truth, was what I suspected for a long time; yet his sudden and singular departure surprised and astonished me."

"I imagined, long ago, that it was something more than a desire to see foreign lands, something stronger than the ties of business," said Flora; "for I knew that his heart was here, as I never heard a tone from him, when he addressed you, which was not the very breath of love."

"Yes, that is most true; no coldness or doubt ever came to divide us; he went out sorrowing — went as though he saw no friendly-shining light beyond."

"Yet he may have found peace, mother; for when we follow the monitions of conscience, the sky clears and the heavens open."

"It cheers me to hear you speak so, my daughter; for I believe that you have strength and resolution to carry out your conviction, let it lead where it may; and I have gathered consolation to myself from observing it."

"He, too, may have found rest," suggested Flora.

"Do you think that he is dead?" asked Madam, agitated; for it had looked out from Flora's countenance. "Have you heard any thing?"

"There is news of him, from Naples."

"Is he sick — is he suffering? O, I would have followed him through all the world, had it been in my power. Pray tell me what you have heard."

"Dear mother, he does not suffer now."

"Then he is surely dead! O that I should be so severed from him — would that I might have died for him, or closed my eyes with him! Can those who so loved be forever parted?"

"In a few brief years — years necessary for healing and preparation — He who placed us here will call us home."

"Yes, it can be but a little time; the hour is not distant."

"Dear mother," interposed Flora, "we should walk this round of Time with a firm step; and the thorns which grow there and pierce us will let out life when it is better to die than to live. My path also appears dark, but I shall not shrink from it, for I know that the Father leads me; and although that path seems a broken curve, from the clouds which gather around and obscure it, yet I have faith that I can look back, when my course shall be closing, and see a perfect circle."

"I hope you may, my daughter; and it relieves something of the heavy weight on my heart to know that you so feel; but I grow weak under it, so that sorrow is my companion."

"It is not well, mother, to be continually counting the beads of woe; you should rather call to mind how many among us are compelled to grope and toil in infinite darkness; while we, by favor and education, can lay hold of the thoughts of all the wise, and soar on the hopes of all the righteous."

"Do you call that a blessing, child, which gives us wings only that we may beat them to bleeding against the bars of our prison? Could I have struck off my chains, might I have reached liberty, do you think that thought, or hope, could have held me back? No; I would have followed him, as they say the seal does the songs of the sailors. O, had I been so favored as to be with him in his last hours, to have received the last light of his eye, the last sigh of his love, I could have returned to the cotton field, or the cane field, and handled the implements of such hot and exhausting labor, for the remainder of my life, as though they had been the dear memorials of his unchanging heart; but this sweet and holy gift of nature has been taken from our race, to make my heart bleed always, and at times rise up in wild defiance."

"But, dear mother, that terrible bereavement, you know, is at an end now by the will of Mr. Merton."

"Such provision may be of advantage to you, Flora; but for me it comes too late."

"Yet you have told me, mother, that he offered you freedom long ago!"

"True, he did; but then I feared that it would be separation! Do you think I could so much as look at it, when it put on that aspect? No! Were it the world, or love, can you believe that I would have paused, for an instant, to try them in the balance? Why, every morning since his departure I have long looked to the east, but have seen neither waning star nor ascending sun, for I was lost in him."

"I have seen that yours was a deep bereavement, dear mother; yet we, who may not know what is best for us, should not look frowningly, or even doubtfully, on the irresistible current which sweeps us on. It is, indeed, hard to be divided from those whom we love; still, they are strongest who walk alone, for all great achievement is the growth of solitude."

"That may be true in the development of your life, but, if it ever might have been in mine, I feel it now to be too late. I am like a vine, that, long clinging to the tree which gave it most generous shelter and support, suddenly finds it prone and uprooted; and finds, also, every tendril of its nature so entwined with the limbs of the fallen, that it feels ashamed of its own greenness, while the leaves of the other are sear and departing—and may I not spurn at the flexibility which still keeps me rooted to the earth?"

"Mother, if God has fixed his canon against self-slaughter, they break the commandment as surely who nourish a wasting grief as they who strike into their own bosoms, with quick stroke, the gleaming weapon of despair. I know that there may be instances where even that would be a rightful protection from violence. Roman Lucretia was slow with the dagger that could alone have saved her from the lust of Tarquin; still, for all grief over separation, or the grave, there is nobler and diviner solace. We, indeed, in our youthful days, believe that only in another can we find sweet happiness and continuing joy; yet she who founds on any other rock, than that which the Creator has placed beneath each individual of the myriad race, may come to find herself an intruder or an outcast. I think that there is capacity, in every rational soul, for a charming life within its own peculiar realm; and the more cultivated it is, the more glorious will be all true companionship; no false or unkind one can ever make it desolate, for he will be closed out before he is aware, and triple brass will forever defy his return."

"I am proud of your strength, my daughter, and when I look that way I am calm. But, when I retire alone, I enter a gloomy cell, relieved only by a faint light from above; long, long have its walls been damp and cold, and now it seems drear and desolate. O, can any one think that I ought to continue there?"

"No, not there, dear mother; but to my heart you should come, and live for me and my child."

"O Flora, if you knew how much, to me, you resemble your father, you would not desire it; for I sit and fix my eyes on you until I seem to see him; yet no tears come, though my aching heart bleeds over this haunting spectre of bereavement; and, when it vanishes, I have no wish but to follow it, even were it to enter the grave and descend to torture!"

"For moments, for months even, I can conceive of one's being so lost in another; but for a lifetime, that is the fulness of hope. O, what must that man be who so takes possession of the heart and bears it, as did Douglas that of Bruce towards the Holy Land."

"Mr. Merton came to my side when I saw something before me, glaring on me, which was more dreadful than death to the young; and he pitied, relieved, and loved me. Thence, for twenty years, he made my life more sweet than any dream which agitates a maiden's bosom, or any hope that genius feels when he is fashioning his thoughts into immortal forms. I would not exchange even the memory of it for all the exchequers of kings, or all the expectations of the just. I know that love leaps from innumerable thoughtless lips in words, and melts away in kisses, to return no more. But bliss, unspeakable and unquenchable, is still a visitant below; yet it is born only of the union of those great hearts whose affection is so full and perfect that it forms an atmosphere around its object as elastic as the air, and soft and warm as summer sunshine."

"You have seen, mother, what I have not seen, found what I have not found; yet I feel that I have acquired strength as I advanced, while you appear to have lost it. Strange is the destiny which takes each of us by the hand, and leads so near, yet so diversely, that my theories weigh nought in your scale, as your experience affords no clew to guide me on my way. Indeed, if we reflect, we shall find that we can have but little help from one another beyond that which is merely temporary, for out from each private soul does the chart of its true course unroll; while the Infinite Father hides the footprints of his children, who have passed over this strand of time, and gone out on the unfathomable deep, as effectually and as wisely as those of ships upon the ocean. It seems to me manifest that he has appointed to each one of us a particular way, with an inclination to walk therein; and the brave will keep it, let it lead where it may; at least so life opens on my vision."

"Such views are not for me," said Madam, mournfully. "I cannot reason upon my loss to weigh what remains; neither can I see my way, for my light has gone out."

"Dear mother, all I meant was consolation."

"I know and feel it, my child, but when I look for it I can see only a grave."

So flow despondency's dim tears,
Amid the ruins of our years,
When the loved one is cold and low,
And in the clouds no beaming bow
Upbears our hope to where appears
The inspiring faith of bards and seers.
If death more tenderly endears,
Is Love so blind as to deplore
The parting from the changeful shore?
Can she not see, within the mind,
The wings for deepest heaven designed,
And in the storm that darkens o'er her day
A field to form them for the glorious way?

CHAPTER XXI.

> Riches are oft by guilt and baseness earned,
> Or dealt by chance to shield a lucky knave,
> Or throw a cruel sunshine on a fool.
>
> ARMSTRONG.

THE levee at New Orleans presents the finest view of a mart of commerce, all open to one sweep of the eye, which the trade of nations has created. Over all that vast and extended border of the city, the merchandise and the manufactures which have arrived, with the staples and produce that are going, — those to find their ways to the heart and extremities of the continent, on the myriad steamers of the rivers and bays; and these to go down to the gulf in ships, thence to thread their courses over all the globe, — give this strange town in the water an attraction which once drew the merchants to Venice, and, crowning her with riches, helped to nourish that gayety which still sings along the lagunes, and is fast opening into vigor and splendor here.

Adventurers from a wide region gather to this city; and among them are found the rude and ignorant, as well as the refined and polished: to the number New England contributes many a shameful, as well as many a noble specimen. If you step into the low rum shops to see who poisons and plunders the sailor, alas! too often you will find him a Yankee. Yet, if you pass over to the ships, you may mark the same pervading and persistent race, walking their quarter decks and filling their places with undisputed preëminence.

Bill Frink, the proprietor of one of the aforesaid shops, was born in New England, in a family which had been reduced to poverty by drunkenness. So, at the age of thirteen, he became a bar boy in the village tavern, partly out of pity which the landlord felt for the family, but mostly to work out a debt which his father owed him for drink. He remained there until he was sixteen, at which time he had acquired a stock of knowledge and of experience that it is full soon at twenty-five to know, if, indeed, it must be known at all. At that period, the keeper of a New Orleans saloon saw his skill, and learning his condition, privately engaged him to go out and mix liquors in his bar.

Bill's parents had but one child living besides himself—they had lost many from want and exposure—when he left home, according to his agreement, without giving due notice. The name of that one was Joseph, although at that period of his life Joe was the extent of it—it grew afterwards. Joe was a stubbed, shock-headed urchin, of five years' standing, who could and would spend half a day beside a mud puddle stoning a frog with exulting satisfaction.

The mother of these hopefuls had so hard a life of it that it was difficult to tell what she was, or might have been, under less depressing circumstances. As it was, she had a bewildered look, as though she sat in the shadow of a wilderness which gave no outlet. Yet, in the midst of a weary struggle for daily bread, which was not always successful, she tried hard to fix Joe's attention on the Bible; and continued, through many years, to read portions of it to him while he stuck pins through flies, or set fire to the flax on her distaff; for he at that age, and indeed long after, would never give his full attention to any part, except to the account of the plague of frogs in Egypt; and even that he did not appear to enjoy unless he was allowed to grasp a stone in each hand.

The drunken father roused up somewhat after Bill disappeared, and contrived, by a little extra exertion, to steer clear of the poorhouse, although he drifted around in full sight of that port on the lee shore of life, now standing off and now on, with tattered sails, and half swayed up at that, for the remainder of his pilgrimage, which was not destined to be patriarchal.

Bill continued in his new position in the saloon for two years, looking sharply about him, and managing to save all his own income, with part of his employer's also. At the expiration of that term he took a small shop, fronting on the levee, and fitted it up for the purpose of selling liquor on his own account. It was not a striking place, except in a bruising sense; indeed, it was low, — for it is more than twenty years since Bill went out there, — having two rooms on the lower floor, with nothing over, only a kind of garret chamber, as the roof alone covered it.

In this place Bill sold every variety of liquor which was in vogue, or inquired after; although he never purchased any kinds but pure spirits and whiskey. His stock was all native production, except a few drugs and dyewoods which he obtained of the importers, and which gave color to the statement that his rum, gin, wines, and brandy were all, as he swore they were, from foreign ports, and were the choicest that could be had. This shows his natural aptitude for the business; and add thereto his stock of jokes, yarns, and anecdotes, which retained the sailors and loafers that the spirits drew there, of course he prospered.

As Bill got money, he bought slaves, and set them at work on the levee, lading or unlading vessels, and fed and lodged them in the chamber of his store — the only entrance to which was a trap-door opening through the floor, and reached by a ladder, which he took away at night, on closing the shop, ere he turned into his own bunk below.

Continuing to increase in substance, which he, in common

with so many others of the ignorant, thought to be position and distinction also, he began to talk to his gaping or boozy audience on politics — he having picked up a few cant phrases and hackneyed expressions from the "stumpers." Yet, when he had dealt those out with particular emphasis, and played the part of parrot to his party newspaper, he generally found himself "snagged," for he had few ideas of his own, — however native to him might be a narrow vein of coarse wit, — and so, with an oath, he would end off in this wise: "Gentlemen, I could talk on them p'ints a week, if I on'y had words; but my arely edication was neglected. Now, if they'd on'y sent me to college, I'd have dead beat the man what made the universalist." Bill's education was limited, for he meant the university.

Bill Frink was one of that very numerous class who imagine that there is a great deal more in education than there really is; inasmuch as it never yet gave an idea, and never will. It can only give *forms of expression;* the thought to be expressed Nature gives; and she will continue to be the bestower of that commodity wherever it is found. He, however, supposed it to have talismanic power; and, consequently, when he felt that he was able, he wrote a letter to one of the deacons of the church in his native village containing a check of value, and also the following directions: "I want you to catch my brother Joe, and dress him up, and send him to school, and have him put right through in tip-top style; for, damn me," (I quote from the record,) "I, Bill Frink, can afford it! If they've got any thing ag'in havin' poor boys, I'll buy their old college, or burn it! damn me if I don't. Now, what I want o' you is, to see as how he's put through right, and you'll git your pay for the job. I reckon it's high time somebody by the name of Frink blowed out; and I'd done it somehow if I'd had half a chance; but I s'pose all the pews war jam full; at any rate, I warn't warned to train in that company; if they'd on'y done it, I'd beat the man what made the college."

In virtue of these instructions, the boy Joe, being about eleven years of age, was caught, and taken away from the frogs, from stealing birds' eggs, and worrying cats, and sent to prepare for college. He was not troubled with home-sickness. Finding much better food, and more of it, than he had been accustomed to, he digested well, and was contented.

Bill continued to come down handsomely, as he expressed it, until he saw Joe settled over a parish — although he was rather knocked aback when he found that the educated Frink was going to turn out nothing but a minister. He, however, did not think meanly of the clerical calling in all particulars, as he was in the habit of saying, (Bill was an observer,) "It is the surest dodge to git a woman as is rich for a wife that was ever scared up; for they hover round, or kneel down all along on the track, and look so solemn, tu, all the time, I swow! that 'tis enough to make a feller snort right out in meetin' — 'tis, by thunder!"

The deacon had given Bill, from time to time, very satisfactory accounts of Joe's studies; for he was pertinacious and plodding, and, consequently, took fair rank as a scholar. He liked, also, to pick over the cinders and sift the ashes of ancient fires, which gave him the notice of some learned doctors, who, particularly favoring dry subjects, spoke of him as a promising young antiquary. He was commended by some, too, for independence; he having a brusk manner to the common people, which shallow observers so name, just in proportion to its rudeness; but this was in his nature — a scar of his origin.

Bill Frink was a large and powerfully-made man, standing over six feet, and had been gradually taking on flesh for some years; so that he looked to weigh two hundred and fifty pounds. Joe, on the contrary, was short — which may be traced to the leanness of the larder in his father's house while a child, or to the tightness of his clothes, as his lower limbs appeared to have been cramped by some process. While Bill was a boy there was a more ample supply of cloth and cookery.

As the elder brother went on prospering in business from year to year, he, of course, increased his stock of whiskey and negroes, and became the owner of the estate of which, in the outset, he was only the lessee. He raised and extended the building, also, and consequently enlarged his scale of living; and, among other things, purchased a shining Congo woman to do the cooking, or, in truth, any thing which he might desire her to do.

Bill aspired, too, in other ways, affecting style and leadership; and although, somehow, he could never keep himself quite clean, particularly his big red hands and rosy face, as they were so moist that they caught all the dust which came near, yet he believed in his charms; for he dressed expensively, and always in bright colors and large figures; and wore so many chains and rings withal, that a Californian might have found "good diggings" almost any where on his person. His success led him to take his meals at one of the fashionable hotels, and pass most of the evenings in places of amusement, and much of the night in the saloons, where he always found a hearty welcome; for he was open-handed, and when he "treated," which was often, he invited the crowd; and he meant it too — being as active in bringing up the laggards to the line of the bar as ever Mr. Hackett was in forming his militia company on the stage.

At the time when Bill Frink's story began to flow into, and mingle with, the current of this narrative, his gang of negroes were about to discharge the cargo of a vessel belonging to New York, and late from Glasgow.

Frank Elery, the captain of the ship, was a native of the Old Colony; and, though still a young man, was every inch a sailor. With square shoulders, full chest, slim waist, straight limbs, and nervous temperament, he seemed formed both for strength and activity; while the flash of his eye, when aroused, was like a gleaming banner to lead his forces on; and nature and habit had bestowed on him the full port of command, so that he could govern without severity, and be kind without appearing weak. He had left school, and his father's house, at sixteen years of age, — leaving in the minds of all his mates a recollection of his brightness, kindness, courage, and scholarship, — to become a child of the ocean. Drawn away from books, and the professional life which his parents had intended, by that restless longing which the Sea awakens in those whom she would entice to her bosom, he went out to enlarge and liberalize his views in the observation of the various and opposite forms and customs of many people, who, it must be conceded, are striving, as best they may, however imperfect the progress or doubtful the result, to come into harmony with eternal right.

When Bill Frink went down to go on board Elery's ship, with his gang, for the purpose of breaking bulk, a pair of black, long-eared, powerfully-made dogs stood in the gangway and threatened them, and seemed to be especially spiteful towards the negroes; although they would not permit Bill himself to pass; for the crew and officers were all at their breakfast, and the dogs, of course, were on duty as ship-keepers.

Hearing the music, Captain Elery said to his steward, "Francis, step up and see what kind of game Luff and Trim have opened on."

Returning, the steward replied, "The stevedore and his men, sir, are here to discharge the ship; but the dogs won't let 'em come on board, sir."

This was what he had supposed; so, having finished his coffee, he went up on deck, and whistling once, it laid the hair on the dogs, and drew them to his side to leap up with more friendly notes; when, gently pulling their sleek ears, he said, "To the galley, and speak for your breakfast!" At this they started off very deliberately for the designated place, and, giving one bark, were admitted by the cook, and paid for their watchful care.

As Frink came over the ship's side, he said, "I reckon you've got some smart dogs, captain."

"They will do to keep meat from spoiling," said Elery.

"I guess they'd sooner spile meat if they on'y had their own way about it!"

"O, they won't hurt you," said the captain, smiling.

"In course not. I never knew a man to say any thing else of a dog what he owned. Now, I'll tell you what, captain, I'll bet a thousand dollars that they'll light on ary one of my niggers and throttle him, at the word 'Go!' and we'll settle it on the spot if you'll pay for the boy if they spile him — I will, by thunder!"

"As that would be no great sport to me, I think I shall not try it; although I will engage to pay all damage which they may do your men."

"O, yes; I s'pose they're chained up by about now!"

"They are lying round loose, nights, and are apt to hail every thing that heaves in sight, particularly if they attempt to cross our hawse."

"O, I know by the looks that they're dogs as is dogs; and I like 'em all the better for bein' up and dressed when any body calls. Where'd ye raise 'em?"

"They were raised in Scotland, and are the sharpest-scented breed in the world."

"You don't say so! What! be they hunters and watchers tu?"

"Look at their ears; the heavier those are, the more perfectly they exclude sound, and, therefore, the more cultivated and keener the nose. An ancestor of these dogs hunted with St. Hubert; and one of the line tracked Wallace into the fastnesses of the Highlands; and another led pursuers on the trail of Bruce."

"Whose niggers were them, I'd like to know?"

"They were not negroes, but men whom tyrants would have bound with chains, for their love of liberty, and bravely daring to struggle for its blessings."

"Wal, ye see, I guessed putty clost, if I didn't know but leetle about it. Now, I reckon you must had putty good schoolin'; but I hadn't the first sprinklin'. If I on'y had that, captain, I'd beat the man what made the college — I would, by thunder! But I've got a brother that ought to be struck clean through with it, for the pickle cost me enough, any how; and he turned preacher, and is holding forth in Greenville, right near York; so I guess as how you must know him."

"I may have seen him, as I have been in the town several times; though I remember hearing that one of their ministers had gone to Europe."

"That's him. He writ to me that he could do it without cost, and he was goin' to expose the winkin' virgin; and I laughed right out — I did, by thunder! to think he was goin' to du it when she on'y winked! But you don't mean to tote them dogs to sea agin, du ye?"

"I thought I should take them round home, and have a little sport in hunting foxes, or following the deer, in Plymouth woods."

"You'll find it too hot to hunt hounds when you git there; it'll be hissin' hot — it will, by thunder! So you'd better leave 'em with me, and when you're here you can go out with 'em jist as ye like. I'll keep 'em in shape."

"What will you give me for them?"

"Give! now ye don't ask any thing for dogs, du ye?"

"Sometimes; and we think these worth a trifle."

"Wal, that beats me! About what do they vally at, in cash?"

"Seeing it is to you, I will sell them for fifty dollars."

"Is that so? Now, by thunder! you don't mean any sich money!"

"Yes, certainly; nothing shorter."

On this, Frink drew out his wallet, and taking from it a fifty-dollar note, with a five, also, handed them over to the captain.

But Elery was evidently taken aback, and said, "You do not intend it, do you? What! pay such a price for dogs?"

"Yes; that's the way I play for tricks."

"But what is the extra five for?"

"For them collars and chains, as I s'pose you'd like to sell the tacklin' with the pair; and if that's not middlin' fair for 'em, let some body else bid, and p'raps I'll raise on 'em."

"O, that is ample; but I was thinking about the dogs, for I believe that I have got attached to them; and, although you have given me much more than I expected, if you choose to leave them you may now, as I am willing to sacrifice something to liking."

"You're mighty careful of me! but, the fact is, I've fell in love with them are dogs tu; and when that disorder fastens to us we don't care what we pay to cure it — we don't, by thunder! I know I've forked over rather stout, captain, but I guess I won't take any on it back, onless you're mighty anxious about it?"

"I see that you are drawing out to windward of me, and I suppose you mean to keep your luff; so all I can ask now is, that they receive good care, and when you wish to part with 'em let me know it."

"I'll do that clean up to the handle — but what's their names?"

"We call them Luff and Trim. The truth is, that while we were becalmed on the coast of Scotland, they chased a buck into the sea which we shot; and on taking it into the boat they whined to come on board; and having the wind heavy on the beam, the next day, they slid across deck into the lee scuppers so often that the sailors called on them to luff and trim, to fetch out — and the names have stuck to them."

At night, when they struck off work, Elery loaned Frink his gun — for hunting dogs readily follow that instrument — and unchaining the bloodhounds, placed the leashes in their owner's hand. But they divined from other appearances that it was something more than a chase — that it was a final separation; and, so feeling, they turned to him with a sadly reproachful expression for such unkindness; and then Luff laid his muzzle in Elery's hand, while Trim licked it in emulous affection. Yet, as they were his no more, he felt compelled to say, "Go," and they went without hesitation, or ever a look behind! What their thoughts were we may not know; but the sailors were sorrowful as they watched their going; and the captain felt that he had done wrong, in doing violence to their attachment to place and to him; for, however fierce their natures were, they had ever strove caressingly for his preference, and knew the meaning of his glance by the instinct of love.

Some few days after the discharge of the cargo, Captain Elery, meeting Frink in town, inquired how he liked the dogs.

"O, they're keen as a knife; I hunted with 'em yesterday."

"Did you shoot any thing before them?"

"No; we didn't take no guns."

"What did they follow? did you find out?"

"Wal, they followed one of my niggers."

"Run away, I suppose?"

"No, by thunder! they know better than to try that; we turned one out jist to larn 'em a lesson in the higher branches."

"How did they work? are they promising scholars?"

"They performed fust rate: we let the darkie run down into the swamp, arter tellin' him, when he heard the hounds, to climb a tree. So, when he was clean out o' sight, we led down the dogs and put 'em on; and they took the scent right lively, and went whoopin' on the track into the swamp, raisin' music enough for a country muster, they did, by thunder! and right arter that we heard the nigger yell! So we followed like horses, expectin' to find him laid out cold; but he was in a tree arter all the fuss; though, when the hounds got there, he hadn't clum so high but Trim grabbed him by the heel and tore off a 'spectable piece. Hows'ever, there 'pears to be 'nough left now to keep him from fallin' over back'ards when he looks up."

"Is it for such a purpose that you wanted my dogs? Is that the kind of game you intend that they shall follow?"

"We s'all let 'em have a leetle amusement, in that are line, once in a while."

"Do you call that hunting? are you such a devil as that? You've got the bloody heart of a wolf, if that's your game; and, if you follow it, you'll be pulled down and torn by your own dogs, or something worse."

"What hurt's that any more'n to run down a deer? They

ain't human; the hounds know their scent from our'n as quick as they do a bear's! That's the way I found out they wan't *our* kind. And our doctors say it's in their bones, tu; but I don't know nothin' about that, for, you see, I've no edication; if I on'y had that now, they wouldn't be nowhere. If I'd on'y been to college I could beat half the Congress men; I could, by thunder!"

"Certainly, I should think you might, judging from the size of your fists."

"Damn 'em! I could lick 'em with my naked tongue, I know I could!"

"O, I have no doubt of it! Yet I do not think it would be in good taste; and I fancy that you would get sick of it before you finished the undertaking, if those whom I have seen are as spotless as the average."

"Wal, you reckon as how I could du it, don't ye?"

"Yes, most certainly! I have an idea that you are up to any thing in that line."

"If I'd on'y been to college I would du it; I would, by thunder!"

"College could only smooth down your tongue, and make your appetite delicate — things which would prevent you from doing it so effectually."

"Now don't, captain; you spread it on a leetle tu thick! but you're tip-top; and I'm glad to see somebody who can understand Bill Frink, and has some notion what he mought have been, if he'd on'y gone to college. Come, let's take a drink."

CHAPTER XXII.

Existence may be borne, and the deep root
Of life and sufferance make its firm abode
In bare and desolated bosoms; mute
The camel labors with the heaviest load,
And the wolf dies in silence.

BYRON.

THE spring was fast opening in that southern climate, so that, at the doors of all the places of entertainment, in the passages of the courts and post office, and on the corners of the streets, innumerable bunches of the most perfect roses met the eyes, and, by their fragrance, sweetly solicited the attention of every passenger to their beauty, during all those temperate hours when, glancing through the dew, the silver-footed Morn appeared, or sapphire-sandalled Evening came.

But trade began to grow languid under the heat of day; and the waters in the deep gutters were taking on the hue of the forest foliage, — the ominously unfolding leaves of the pestilence, — warning those denizens, who take their annual flight north, to prepare for migration.

Among that number was William Rutledge. A few days previous to his departure, to be absent for the summer, some business called him into the Probate Court, where he found Mr. Steel — the husband of the late Rufus Merton's sister — making application for letters of administration on the deceased brother's estate.

Having heard his motion, Rutledge said, "Although, may it please the court, I have not been employed to appear in this matter, yet I should like to inquire if all the effects and papers that belonged to Mr. Merton have been received from abroad."

"We are so assured," Mr. Steel replied; "and they have also been carefully and thoroughly examined. I say this, because the gentleman was a valued friend of the deceased, and may have some ground to suppose that there should be a will among them; but no such document has been found."

"It was that of which I was thinking," said Rutledge, addressing the court; "for I have reason to say that he once gave effect to such an instrument; and, as it can operate no serious delay, I ask that a few days be granted for further search elsewhere."

"I, certainly, have no objections," replied Mr. Steel, "if the court so direct."

"Then it may be passed now," said the judge, "and taken up the first thing next week, if you are so disposed, gentlemen."

To this proposal they expressed assent, and left the court together.

On reaching the street, Rutledge inquired, "When did Mr. Merton's papers arrive, Mr. Steel?"

"Only four or five days since," he replied.

"Was there any writing of his that you found, which could throw any light on his condition or his desires, or disclose if he had any anticipations that he was near his end?"

"No, not a single line or word! There was nothing for a memento even, except some hair, — a long, black, glossy tress" (it was Madam's,) — "which Mrs. Steel thought, indeed was quite certain, must be a lock of their cousin's, a lady whom he once loved; and she is having it set in brooches for herself and daughters, as she wishes that some token of mourning should be worn."

In the course of the following evening Rutledge called at

the house where Merton had so long lived, and where he himself had so many times been received and entertained so kindly. He found Madam and Flora very glad to see him, although they were evidently depressed and anxious, and particularly Madam was so. Yet, after the usual forms of friendly greeting, she said, "It is a long time, Mr. Rutledge, since you were here; you used to come, once in a while, to to inquire after *him*; but I suppose you tired of it, as you found that we could give no information on the subject."

"It is true that I was disappointed in not hearing from Mr. Merton, either through the post, or you, or any one; yet this would not have deterred me from paying that attention in which I always found pleasure. But," he continued, looking at Flora, "you appeared to have a nearer friend, in a person who was a stranger to me; so I ceased to come often; knowing, however, that if you wished for advice or assistance, in any form, you had a right, as well as a sincere and reiterated request, to send for me; and I hope that you have so regarded it."

"We had not forgotten it, Mr. Rutledge," said Madam; "for we received it as a kindness, and have often thought of its value, as we knew that we might depend upon it. Indeed, Flora and I were talking, this very evening, of sending for you, as we wished for some information concerning the will which you once read to us; hoping to learn when it would be acted upon."

"Did Mr. Merton leave any papers here when he went abroad?"

"O, yes, many; there is a trunk quite full, and some in one or two drawers besides," Madam replied.

"Have you ever looked them over?"

"No, I have not, for I could not bear to do so."

"Then you do not know whether that will is among them or not?"

"I had no idea that it could be, as I thought it kept in some office when made; I did not know that he might retain possession of it."

"It is not expected that it be left in the office of which you are thinking, until after the decease of the maker; it ought, however, to be deposited there soon, and for that reason I came to see if I could find it here."

"We will bring down the things in which he kept his papers, and you may examine them."

Thereupon rising up and taking a light, she said, "Come, Flora," and in a few moments they returned bearing the trunk and drawers.

Rutledge and the daughter immediately began to look for the desired instrument; but Madam could hardly be said to render any further assistance, for the first paper which she took up, although of no earthly consequence then, had Merton's handwriting upon it; and, by it, her roused thoughts were taken captive and her mind absorbed while the anxious search continued. Through such aperture her heart went out aching with sad and fond recollections, while her tearful, gazing eyes seemed exploring for a lost form, like Orpheus, with hand-shadowed brows, through steep abyss in spectral realm! Yet her soul bore no musical, immortal hope that could lull to sleep the triune terror, and charm far past the dreadful gate.

Flora occasionally dropped tears over some awakened recollection, but made no delay; and Rutledge searched on in silence.

When they had examined the last sheet in the collection, Rutledge looked up to Flora and said, "Are these all?"

"I know of no more," she replied.

"Are you quite sure? for it is important that a thorough examination should be made at this time."

"Mother, are not these all the papers which Mr. Merton left?"

But seeing she did not heed her question, — for she was still in that mysterious interior world, — she continued, "Mother, Mr. Rutledge wishes to know if there are any more papers?" and Rutledge added, "Yes, if any more remain I should like to see them."

His unaccustomed voice startled Madam from her reverie, and raised her to the surface; when, looking out, she said, "Have you found it?"

"No, not yet," Rutledge answered; "and we want you to bring down the rest of his papers."

"I know of no more, except a letter which he once wrote to me from New York, and that I shall keep as long as I live:" then, hastily pressing her hand to her bosom to feel if it was still safe, she continued, "I could not exchange it for the kindest will that was ever made."

"Dear mother, we do not wish you to part with that; all we ask is, if you can think of any other place where he might have laid the will?"

"No, I cannot; I believe that he left no more papers here."

"May I look through your room, to see if it is there?" she inquired.

"You may;" and giving her the keys, Flora went out.

When she had gone, Madam said, "I feel that life has nearly closed with me, Mr. Rutledge; but, if that paper is not found, what must be the fate of my daughter and her dear child? O, she has one of the sweetest children that ever lived; and with no one but us feeble women, slaves ourselves, perhaps, to protect! O, what will become of him!"

"But the father of the child," interposed Rutledge; "I learn that he is wealthy."

"He has been away many months; he left us suddenly, and I think that he intends to desert us."

"Where is he?"

"I believe that he is in New York; and I should not be surprised if he had married since he left here; for — but you will not allude to it before Flora, as I think that she does not know of it — I saw in a newspaper the notice of the marriage of a person of the same name, and as it was longer than usual, and profusely adorned with such phrases as 'High life, beautiful bride, and connubial bliss,' I have but little doubt that it related to him."

"He is a man whom I never saw but once, and for some reason I did not make his acquaintance, so that I have even forgotten his name."

"Featherstone — Anthony Featherstone."

Rutledge took out his memorandum book and noted the fact, saying, as he placed it back in his pocket, "I expect to be in New York in a few days, and if the gentleman is to be found there, I shall have a few words to say to him."

"I do not think you will find it an agreeable visit; indeed, he did not please me at first, although Mr. Merton praised him, and he very soon disclosed traits of character which deepened that impression."

"How does your daughter feel towards him?"

"She has breathed no word of him to me; she seems to have the capacity to contain her sorrows; in truth, her wounds never cried out; she has the power to bear them in silence, if not to heal them."

"How have you lived since this Mr. Featherstone left; that is, permit me to inquire, how are you supported?"

"For a time our bills were paid at the counting room; but it is now some months since they refused to do it further, under his directions."

"How did he expect that you were to obtain food?"

"He ascertained in some way that Mr. Merton had given me some money when he was about to leave us, that we might have the satisfaction of possessing it, (such were his words,) even if we did not find a use for it; and his object was to force us to live on that; but it will last only a very little while longer, although we have guarded it with the strictest care; and when it is gone, Mr. Rutledge, what can we do?"

"If the will be found the court is authorized to make suitable provision for you, until such time as you may receive your legacies."

"If it be lost, what then can we hope for?"

"If that instrument should not come to light, the legal heirs of Mr. Merton are not without consideration and kindness; they certainly cannot forget, in their abundance, those whom they know that he would have shielded with his life."

"I have impressions which make that a dark and doubtful prospect."

"Surely the father of Flora's child will not permit the iron law to take its course."

"I fear he may; for he appeared to hate the child, and I think grew more rough and hard to Flora in consequence of its birth. Then he is far away, and none of those around him know our circumstances, so as to look into his face and make him hear our cry for help; otherwise he will not heed it, as all that he could ever have felt for her must turn to ice at such a distance. Indeed, he never loved; he is not capable of it; and if he has married, as I think he has, he will not only cast us off, but be anxious to thrust us out of sight if he find it in his power to do so: of this he is capable."

"It is possible; yet I am loath to believe that, when he shall calmly consider from what source he received his fortune, he can act so basely."

"He may think that he has some cause, as Flora must have seen that he had no love for her; and there may have been something said which hurt his self-esteem, for he went away very abruptly; hence, if he have any power over us, he is sure to use it for torture."

Flora here returned and said, "I can find no other papers in the house, and we may safely say that the will is not here: might not Mr. Merton have taken it with him?"

"He was not likely to do so, and I am persuaded that he did not."

"Have his papers, which he left abroad, been received?" Flora inquired.

"I am so informed; and, further, that there is not only no devise, but no wish or intimation any where expressed with regard to the disposal of his estate; and I infer from this that he believed he had made ample provision for you, and thought it secure."

"Where else then are we to search for the instrument?" inquired Flora.

"May it not be in Mr. Featherstone's possession?" Rutledge asked.

On this the blood hummed in Flora's ears, and flashed crimson even to her forehead, as she replied, "It may be."

"It is my intention to go to New York soon, at which time I shall make it a point to see him; and as I believe that he must know something of the matter, I may persuade him to disclose it."

Thereupon, Rutledge arising to depart, Madam inquired, "What day do you think of leaving for the north?"

"On Saturday, probably."

"May we hope to see you again before you go?" asked Madam.

"I fear that I shall not find an opportunity; yet, if I learn any thing more of this business that would profit you to hear, you may depend upon seeing me."

Drawing back as he spoke, she thanked him for his kindness and attention, and replying to his good night, Flora attended him into the hall and to the door. On reaching that she said, "Mr. Rutledge, I came out because I desired to say a few words to you from which I would spare my mother's feelings; for I fear that her own sorrows are more than she can bear. As you have expressed your intention of calling on Mr. Featherstone, I felt that I could not permit you to do so without informing you of our relations to each other; as they are such that, I think I may safely say, neither of us wish to see or speak to each other again. Certainly he can have no desire to see me, for he has married since he left here, and I could not meet him as I once did, as my affection for him is gone; therefore I hope you will make no appeal to his feelings, as that seems to me a degradation to which I cannot consent to submit. If there be no will found in our favor, he well knows what were Mr. Merton's views; and, if he do not heed them, nothing can move him. In truth, under any circumstances, I could not pray for mercy at his hands; rather the most hopeless bondage and the severest tasks than that. Unused as I am to work, I yet have tried to look at all its repulsive aspects, and I see nothing that should make me tremble, if it were not for my child. O Mr. Rutledge," she continued in tears, "if he must follow me into slavery, O, will you not see, when you return, if there is humanity enough in any or all of those who, while Mr. Merton lived, felt the golden touch of his bounty, to save the last of his blood from chains?"

"I shall seek you at once, when I come back to the city; and, if there has been any disastrous change, you may rely on me to speak and *do* all I can for you; but I trust that these clouds will pass, and I shall find you free and kindly cared for. Do not weep," he continued; "your child has the same tender and infinitely-sustaining arm to lean upon without which the mightiest cannot take a step or form a thought."

"O Mr. Rutledge, I know that you will remember us, for you are kind and good. And you will forgive my momentary weakness, while I glanced down the dark way."

"Feeling and emotion are not weakness," replied Rutledge, "but springs of action and inspirers of courage."

So taking leave he thought, as he moved away, "It is, indeed, a gloomy prospect. If the dreaded change come, what a change it must be! — passing from downy ease, dreamy luxury, and devoted love, to reeking drudgery, squalid poverty, and rigorous domination; and this, not only for a year or a life even, but leading down a long line of chained and bleeding generations. Can man so clip, and curb, and crush human aspiration, and not tremble for himself, remembering that sovereign Justice will surely some time arraign him? Did I say justice? The conscious, immortal soul, hurt and suffering with the wrong which she has inflicted, will, if not here, yet somewhere in the circle of the ages, seek judgment on herself, and meet the penalty to appease the dreadful recollection; and even then, when God hath pardoned the sin of breaking down the protecting will, and all the sweet hopes of a fellow-creature, to our lusts, I think I should wander sorrowing through the universe, until I found and won the full forgiveness of the wronged."

CHAPTER XXIII.

Trust not the treason of those smiling looks,
Until ye have their guileful trains well tried;
For they are like but unto golden hooks,
That from the foolish fish their baits do hide.
SPENSER.

AURELIA'S honeymoon was neither bright nor long-continued; it did not ascend the heavens, but, circling far below the zenith, soon began to edge and wane away, and yield its light later and later on the night. Indeed, how could it be otherwise? as Featherstone's habits seemed to gain power over him, so that he found the club very attractive; and besides, he was already paying his addresses to a new mistress, in the form of political ambition.

Still, for a time, the bride derived much pleasure from the happy contentment of her father, and the gratified pride of her mother, as they opened, refreshed and renewed, upon the altered scene. The wealth had yet other attractions also, or rather distractions — such as fine equipage, rich, overflowing wardrobe, and a round of fashionable amusements: these she had to profusion, if not to satiety.

But if the craving heart be left vacant, how will it at length come to scorn all this, and, it may be, despise the bestower of it, because it would have a delusive vision of something beyond which comes not! When the ineffable glories of love's young dream have all been bartered for bawbles, to become symbols of withered hopes and frost-nipped affections, the sad recollection does not awaken grateful thoughts, neither does it seem even *worldly* wise! Not thus do the birds line their nests in the summer bowers; not for such gifts do they momently gush forth into joyful song.

If, when such a sale and purchase are completed, the contract could always be acquiesced in by the promisors, there certainly might be more decent order in society; yet dim and dismal clouds would trail across life's morning star, and the music which elevates and glorifies our march would be tranced in every string. The heaven-descended dream of love, like that of liberty, fringes life with divine splendors, making it godlike and worthy of its Author. These two emotions and aspirations of our natures, that count all else as nothing in comparison, that give all and sacrifice all, if need be, show our being and our story to be touched with all the glory with which inspired penmen have blazoned it, either in its origin or its destiny. Indeed, Love and Liberty are pendulums of such sweep that they vibrate from God to God! Other machinery may mark the revolutions of time on its axis, but these alone beat the progress along its immeasurable orbit. Desperate Sappho leaps from a beetling rock on the Lesbian shore, and the most love-lorn heart that ever sighed to the lyre is still; and Brutus stabs his bosom friend, and strikes on, in the sacred name of Liberty, until tyranny triumphs, and the sainted assassin so despairs of the republic that he falls on his own sword; yet they have borne the world nearer to heaven, and drawn down upon it a warmer smile and a deeper sympathy from the spirits who mark the devotion of a human soul.

In reality Aurelia had prized the intimacy with a noble mind too highly not to feel its loss; and being left too frequently to think of it alone, the recollection soon came with a sigh, a regret, and at length a kind of hope; so that, on one fine afternoon in the opening spring time, she called to see Mrs. Summers.

The excited widow arose to meet her, saying, "Is it *you*,

Mrs. Featherstone? I can scarcely believe my eyes, for I did not hear a carriage stop at the door."

"I walked down, as I used to do; and you must give me some tea before I leave."

"With the greatest pleasure; but I am afraid that we have nothing which you can eat; yet if you will only tell me what you would like, I shall be delighted to set it before you, if it can be procured."

"I have no desire to find any thing more than I used to find."

"Now, really, I do wish to do something more. If you had only thought to have sent one of your servants to let me know of your intention, or had come earlier, I would have tried to prepare the best."

"You are very kind, but truly I came in late to prevent exertion, and surprise you by fulfilling a promise which you may have forgotten."

"No, indeed; and you shall have it just as you say, if you really prefer it so. But I do wonder why you did not come down here in your carriage, when you have such elegant horses. I am sure that I would not walk a step if I had them."

"One cannot always say what they would do, and there may be more pleasure sometimes in walking than in riding; at least I have found it so."

"Yes, such is the way of the world; indeed, I have often noticed that those who keep horses frequently take long walks, and boast of it even, while a great many who do not, because they cannot quite afford it, hide away at home and go out only from necessity."

"It is even so; for we sigh after many things which, when obtained, we find to be of little use; the observer is usually more charmed with them than is the possessor."

"That is just what you rich folks always say; you like to disparage the beautiful things you have much better than to part with them. But how beautiful you are! and what a beautiful dress! and do let me lay away that love of a shawl where it will not get injured."

As Mrs. Summers stepped into the hall, she met Park coming in, and said, in a suppressed voice, "There is some one here whom you used to like to see."

"Ah, who may it be?" he inquired.

"Don't you know this bonnet and this cashmere?"

"I am not aware of having made their acquaintance."

"I should think that you might see that they are a bride's."

On this Park laid aside his hat and outer garment, and entered the sitting room; while the widow, having deposited the garments, slipped softly into the adjoining parlor.

As he came in, Aurelia arose with a smile to meet him; and extending her hand, which he took, said, "Do you think that leaving your name at our door *once* is sufficient excuse for six months' absence?"

"Have I broken any of the laws of fashion by so doing?"

"I had thought," said she with some agitation, "that our intercourse might be entitled to the name and the forms of friendship."

"Friendship is a rare flower, and one that I have doubts of finding; for it opens oftenest in the morning of life, and is apt to close in the meridian hour; yet I begin to see that it would be sweetest and most precious in the evening of our days."

Aurelia's lips quivered and her eyes gathered moisture, not so much from the words that he had spoken, as from the tone of his voice, which, although not meant to be reproachful, made her feel as do the Swiss when they hear their home songs far away from their mountains.

Feeling much moved, she did not trust herself to reply, but turned to the window, and gazed out upon the sombre stones of the adjacent building without noticing, as they were in unison with her thoughts, and Park took up a book; so, for a minute or two there was silence. Upon this the widow came in, and seeing them, said, "How still you are! and Mr. Park reading a book!"

But the summons to tea mingling with her words, they accepted it as a reprieve, and were soon seated at the table. Yet there was only a thin sprinkling of conversation during the sitting, notwithstanding the laudable exertions of the widow, amid her many apologies for not having any thing tempting to her visitor, as she appeared to have no appetite.

Park sat but a few moments, though he gave no sign of haste; yet he arose alone, returned to the sitting room, passed through and left the house.

Soon after Aurelia entered the room, and finding that Park was not there, she felt relieved, yet grew sad with the thought that he had gone. But, as she saw that it was not from indifference, after a while her spirits arose, and she passed as agreeable an evening with the voluble widow as she had ever done since their acquaintance commenced.

Having anticipated that there would be a kind of conversation that might require some light work to fill the pauses, or give weight to the themes, Aurelia had taken a purse which was partly knitted, and seemed to be kept for such occasions. On this she leisurely took a stitch, or dropped one, or ravelled down, as though it were Penelope at her loom beguiling her thoughts from the absent Ulysses; while Mrs. Summers was busy with button-hole stitch on the edge of some white garment, apparently shaped after the style of the Turk.

As they wrought, they talked of many things; but mostly of dress, — for the widow thought Aurelia an oracle in that, and the bride was willing to indulge her, — of what was, of what is, and what probably would be, the prevailing fashion. And they laughed over the *border* warfare — which the widow's work suggested, and which was then raging — between points and scallops; and spoke of the powerful supporters of each, and which appeared to be the victor of the moment; and how, after all, it mattered little which triumphed, as the plaid was so over them all that it was but a petty strife between clans; and that, too, for supremacy in a district so obscure as to be known only to minute explorers.

Thus nine o'clock came round, and, shortly after, Aurelia prepared herself; and as she was about to leave with John, the widow's man servant, she said, "I have enjoyed my visit much, and you must return it soon."

"I am charmed to hear it; and I should be delighted to do so."

"Then you must name an early day on which it will be be convenient to come, so that I may be at leisure."

This arrangement was gladly made; and it may be easily imagined that there was punctual and delighted compliance, with admiration and praise for every thing which she saw or tasted.

The profusion and display, and continual round of amusement, of their first winter, had failed to fill the heart of the bride; and Featherstone had taken no true steps to occupy it himself, if it were in his power to do so.

The wedding was high tide with him, as it is with so many others, and soon the rocks and shallows became visible, and showed themselves more and more, as the current ran ever lower and lower in its ebb, with no returning flood that fulfilled the promise of the first. Hence Aurelia began to feel alone, and consequently craved excitement; and, going to a distant church on one evening, some few weeks after her visit to Mrs. Summers, she accidentally met Park there.

Drawn by the brightness and freshness of the day, to seek for that Sabbath stillness which dwelleth not in cities, Park had crossed on to the island, towards evening, and strolled into the country. There he caught the pensive tone of nature, and mused away the hour, apparently without aim or object to those who were flashing by in their slender vehicles; yet to him it was a bath most delicious to the sense, most purifying to the man.

Aroused, at length, by night's flitting shadows, he turned towards the town, through which he had passed; and, on reaching it, he entered the thronged church of a popular preacher. Pausing at the foot of the aisle, an attendant came and conducted him to a pew, in which there was but one vacant seat; and settling into the place, which he quite filled, he turned towards the lady at his side to find the eyes of Aurelia upon him; and they were bright with unexpected pleasure, while the glow of quickened blood was on her cheek.

Yet, throughout the service, he sat and thought of mutability and change, — the theme of the preacher, — and she, who was pressed to his side, was only so mingled up with his meditations as to give keener point and more touching emphasis to the eloquence.

Aurelia had emotions rather than meditations, for he who was beside her filled the first place in her mind; while the sermon seemed but a haze of splendor around him, and the tones of the orator only thrilled her to tenderer sentiment towards the paramount object of her thoughts.

Never before had they been so near, for so long a time; yet Park felt that there was an impassable chasm between them; that some moral earthquake had shaken them asunder;

and whatever agitation still lingered from the shock, or gloom brooded around, he saw that his habitation was not yet a ruin, although his once most charming prospect was closed up forever.

She, too, was exquisitely sensible to the proximity, and trembled at every pause in the discourse, through fear that it was about to close. Yet her heart grew thirsty every instant! like him, who, amid the flames, had a vision of Paradise, and cried out, to one whom he had neglected, for a single drop of water to cool his tongue, all-unmindful of the gulf that divided them.

When the ceremonies were completed and the crowd gave way, they walked out together; and Aurelia's carriage being drawn up near the door, Park attended her to it; on which she said, "May I have your company?"

Handing her in, he followed and took a seat beside her. But they rode silently until they reached the ferry, when Park feeling the necessity of some common theme to still his busy fancy, or to "wreak his thoughts upon," inquired, "How were you pleased with the sermon?"

"Very much. Were you?"

"Yes, I often hear him, and never with more satisfaction than I have received on this evening."

"It is my first visit to his church," said Aurelia, "but I intend to go frequently for the future, as I enjoyed the hour exceedingly. Yet, don't you think that his tone and manner might be improved?"

"I know there is a certain roughness about him which strikes one at first as a want of taste; still I fear that, if it were polished away, it would diminish the weight of the diamond more than mere smoothness or lustre of surface could repay."

"It may be so; and, after all, one cares little for the

ungainliness of the motion when every thrust is mortal; it pleased me much to see him charge into the host with such courage."

"Yes, he is a knight without fear, however much he may suffer reproach."

"Of that, no doubt, he will get his full share, as he must wear 'his beaver up' to have so looked into every thing."

"Yes, that must be very small which escapes his eye, or very subtle that eludes his analysis; and he is not only a natural artist, but a well-trained one. Observe with what skill he paints, leaving out no minute thing which belongs to the background, even; whether it be a picture on which the sunlight falls, or a view of the vista that opens in the soul to the divine smile; whether it be a description of a mountain brook at play, now stealing round a sheltering rock, and now laughing from pool to pool in the glance of day, or of mistaken life and the resistless sweep of Time's submerging wave. I like his free speech also, which scouts all conventional shelter, and knows no neutral ground, but marches straight on the ambush of the enemy."

Emerging from the boat, they moved on in silence once more, until the horses were drawn up at Park's home, when Aurelia inquired, "May I hope to see you at our house soon?"

"I intend to call; yet my engagements are such that it is difficult to say when."

"Can you not forego some trifle of business in my favor? You used to do so once."

But as the footman stood at the open door when she finished, Park arose without replying; and, holding her hand while saying good night, stepped out with a calm pulse and a heart still loyal to lofty ideas; and the carriage bore away one who would have been very unhappy, had she not been sustained by a wild and delusive hope.

CHAPTER XXIV.

No general gauntlet-gatherer for the weak
Against the strong, yet over-scrupulous
At lucky junctures; one who won't forego
The after-battle work of binding wounds.
BROWNING.

HAVING obtained an appointment with Featherstone, Rutledge presented himself at the door of the mansion, and, on giving his name to the servant, was immediately conducted to the library. As he passed in, a gentleman arose, and, advancing, said, "I believe I received a note from you yesterday."

"I addressed one to Mr. Featherstone," Rutledge replied.

"That is my name," said the person; "take a seat if you please. You are from the south, I think you informed me."

"I came from New Orleans a few days since."

"Ah! Are you from that interesting city? I resided there once myself for a few years, and a very gay and agreeable place I found it. I think that a young man may learn some of the ways of life, and get clear of many of his prejudices, there, sooner and more safely than in any other town with which I am acquainted. I cannot call your countenance to mind, but I presume that I must have met you frequently; perhaps in the St. Charles, or at the opera."

"It is possible that we may have met in both of those places, although I have no recollection of seeing you. I, however, knew your friend and relative, Mr. Merton, well, I may say intimately, having been, for many years, his legal adviser; and, among other instruments, I drew a will for him, which he perfected in due form of law; and it is concerning some of the persons mentioned in that testament, and for whom ample provision was therein made, that I wish to speak with you at this time."

"I remember hearing that there was such an instrument as you mention; and I recollect that we made very diligent search for it, and very wide inquiry was had, also; but they all came to nothing. Therefore we arrived at the very natural conclusion that he must have destroyed it; and I can scarcely believe it has turned up since I left; if so, my agent is singularly remiss in not having instructed me. I presume the will was not committed to your care?"

"It was not; and I do not hesitate to say that I think it utterly lost; not destroyed, however, as you suggest; unless it were for the purpose of providing still more bountifully for the persons in whose behalf I appear here. Indeed, to have put away that will without feeling that he had, in some form, protected them from want and the inexorable law would have wrung every fibre of his generous nature. He could not have so done; it did not lie within the range of his power. Were it to have bought bread for his own mouth, he would have contended unto death with the hunger, if thereby he could have saved them. I well remember how deeply he was moved while we were elaborating the provisions for the protection and support of those to whom he was bound by the 'Higher Law,' and how cheerfully he rose up when they had been drawn out to his liking. On their completion, he took my hand, and said, 'Rutledge, come and dine with us to-day, and bring up that document, for I want *them* to hear you read it.'"

"I also knew Mr. Merton, knew him intimately; and I see, in your account of him, a degree of weakness of which I thought my friend incapable. Certainly, while I was with him, I saw no such trait. Hence I am very naturally led to suppose that a will such as you intimate could not long have survived the making. Had he died a mere youth, it would seem more probable; but the experience of nearly sixty years of life is apt to harden or reason a man into something less romantic."

"If there be no will found is it your wish that the law should take its painful course?"

"Am I to understand that you appear here as counsel for those persons?"

"I am their friend here and every where; and no less yours when I say that then, and then only, does wealth appear to be a ministering angel when it gives us the power to make full restitution; when it smooths the path of one whom we may have tempted to err; or more omnipotent still, when it melts chains of iron from those who dreamed that they were bound to us by the golden links of love."

"Mr. Rutledge, when one is willing to meet the facts of a case, allusions or portents, however forcibly or felicitously applied, have but little weight; and I believe that I should do you great injustice if I thought for a moment that I could instruct you in the answer. Yet, as it is not within the rule of the profession for you to rejoin, I shall be under the necessity of doing so myself. You are aware then, in the first place, — I have no doubt, — that Madam and Flora are quite well educated; sufficiently so, at least, to know the consequences of their own acts; that Madam's associations with Mr. Merton gave her ease and affluence for more than twenty years, at the expense of his heirs; and that his death only renders her back to the condition from which he so long raised her. You may say that she has a child, yes, a grandchild if it so please you; and *here* there would be good and valid reasons why the heirs of the deceased should do something for their support; but the laws of the Southern States preclude the necessity for such action; they do more — they discountenance it. Certainly, my learned friend knows that such goods are in demand in the Crescent City. Indeed, I was offered a persuasive price for Flora before I left your town; yet at that time I thought of returning; but marrying soon after I came north, I concluded to settle here. And, on the part of her child, I see no call for charity, as he is worth fifty dollars at this moment; for the reason that the law takes entire possession, thus rendering him safe and serviceable. This I believe to be the purport and complexion of your servile regulations; and if they are not agreeable to you, why not devote yourself to the work of changing them, and so strike at the root of the tree to whose shadow you point?"

"Would to God that I could change them, at least so far as to protect the weak. Am I to infer that you estimate these persons simply as property, Mr. Featherstone?"

"As to that I have not yet made proclamation. But I will say this much, if you have any desire to purchase, you may do well to see my agent."

"Mr. Featherstone, if I know aught of myself, I came here out of pure humanity; came to soften, if not prevent, the fall of those who thought that in strict justice they might look up to you for protection. But I find it to be a delusive dream. Still I feel that I have discharged a duty, and in a way which you will not be likely to forget, whatever may be your course of action. If you yield to right feeling, you will, some time, seek to thank me; if you take the broader way, the laws of the land, indeed, cannot reach you, either to hinder or hurt; and you may think that you wear impenetrable armor to all higher commandments, yet the fiery darts of conscience shall at length rive and penetrate every part to stretch you in the dust. Low as the victims may fall, and chill as is the shadow in which they may be doomed to walk, it will be light and cheerful compared with the woe of him who awakes too late to implore forgiveness on this side the grave. You may harden your heart for a time against their plaint; but come it will, in the hours of inevitable weakness, or amid the strokes of fortune, dismantling all the towers of your strength, to leave you prone and bleeding among the melancholy ruins of life."

"You manifest such a philanthropic interest in this matter, Mr. Rutledge, perhaps you had better appeal to Mr. Merton's sister when you return."

"It is but a few days since I waited upon Mrs. Steel, at which time I learned that the titles to this property were in you; and I have no doubt—as I believe you have none—that they were given that you might have the opportunity of reaping the pleasure which springs from generous deeds."

"Your doubts do not disturb me, Mr. Rutledge. It is not my habit to judge hastily; and all the circumstances of this case which were known to me were duly weighed and considered to the maturing of my decision. Now, I believe you have not disclosed any new facts, nor do you pretend that there are any. Therefore, to continue in the forms of your profession, how can you expect me to restore it to the docket? And into that future, to which you point, I have neither time nor inclination to gaze; and if I had I should not see what you imagine. The practical mind moves on steadily, and sleeps calmly, amid your 'Gorgons, Hydras, and Chimeras dire'!"

"You may so look upon life now, Mr. Featherstone, as your experience is only of the opening scenes of the drama; but if you attempt to play out the play, as you have indicated, you will find the hand of fate upon the curtain."

On the following morning Rutledge was introduced to Park,

for the purpose of taking his opinion, and retaining him in a matter which had been committed to his care, as suit had been threatened in the city courts. Having laid open the case, and examined the law on which it rested, and the decisions that illustrated it, they soon passed into conversation on the relative prosperity of the north and south.

"I know that nature is on your side, for a fruitful soil is the most permanent wealth," said Park; "yet it will not be unfolded as in the west, for the just stimulus to labor is wanting."

"True; give the Anglo-Saxon liberty to do, with the award of the fruit of his doing, and he will clothe the waste places of the earth with verdure, and build up institutions to protect him in the enjoyment of his possessions."

"Then you do not think that free society has proved a failure here?"

"In some things I regard it as eminently successful. The life of republicanism is visible over all your landscape, while the torpor of aristocracy is equally apparent on ours. Yet in one essential particular I should say you had failed, if you were not continually failing; that is, in not electing your ablest men to office. In this we have kept the nobler and the wiser course."

"I concede the general truth of that charge. The dereliction springs, in a measure, from our great prosperity; this offers opportunity for the unblushing demagogue, or the possessor of mere money, to seize that which the people should scorn to bestow on any but the foremost champions of their cause."

"If you would inculcate that doctrine, and live up to it, you would be incomparable. But as it is, if your institutions breed better men than ours, they are shorn of their influence; and you have as bad specimens as any that we produce. I called upon one last evening, who can more coolly weigh money and misery than any man born in our latitude. Made wealthy by one of the most generous and gentle of men, he is using the estate to thwart his patron's views and desolate those who trusted in him. This gentleman, whose name was Merton, had a quadroon slave, who, in every thing save form, was to him a wife. By her he had a daughter, who has a son by this Mr. Featherstone; yet he has not only deserted, but doomed them, and will convert their price into pleasure."

"I am astonished at the capacity of man for evil," replied Park, "and this is the terrible thing in your laws, that they offer such opportunity to the base. Acting so oppressively towards a class, is there no hope of changing these statutes?"

"Not soon; for power was never vested in a more vigorous or a more united body. Only as it exhausts the soil will slavery recede — annexing new territory ere it forsakes the old. Did not the southern border offer centuries of conquest and expansion to the planter, you might put a period to his domination, for the bond of the Union is stronger than the chain of the slave; but as it is, he will only march on."

"Do you think there will be nothing gained by agitating this subject?"

"Yes, much. It will keep alive the spirit of liberty among yourselves. With us it is failing. We shall lose freedom of speech and of the press; they will be surrendered to a dread necessity. And you, seeing that there are institutions with which they cannot long coexist, will the more vigilantly guard them."

"By the same rule the principles cannot coexist in the federal constitution. They are antagonistic in their nature, and the knights of each grow fierce in their jousting."

"Those are only passages at arms within prescribed lists; the Missouri compromise is a sufficient barrier."

"That will be borne down, or voluntarily withdrawn, on pretext of giving a free field to the combatants. To this step I have no objections. For the mass of the pioneer emigrants to the territories are those who wield the axe, guide the plough, and aim the rifle; and by the very nature of their honest and hardy occupations, and the consequent simplicity of their lives, they are the indomitable conservators of liberty. Slavery requires the line of thirty-six thirty, not Freedom; and if ever southern statesmen are so unwise as to trample it down in their struggle for dominion, they will be outflanked. Yet, in such emergency, the federal court will come to their aid."

"That can hardly be possible. What are your data for the opinion?"

"Knowing that the possessors of disputed power never cease to fortify their position, I have watched the executive and senatorial tendency in the selection of judges, and so studied their characters, that I am satisfied to what conclusion they will come when the question shall be presented. They will yet declare the constitution a pro-slavery instrument."

"Such a decision would be a greater stigma on the nation than slavery itself."

"It may be. But as evils they bear no comparison — one is real, the other theoretical. Nevertheless, the fact is inevitable, and the sooner it is solemnly enunciated the better, for then the American people must see on what false courses they have been steered; and I cherish the hope that the ship is yet stanch enough to breast the gale and draw off from the fatal shore."

"When that hour comes you will find me an abolitionist," said Rutledge, rising up and walking the room. "In truth, I am now in favor of gradual emancipation, and the preparation which is necessary to make it a benefit. To that *timely* result I have nothing to object. Deprecating only rash words and rough conflict, I accept the full discussion, hoping thereby that wisdom may unfold the way. For however slavery has affected the African, it seems to me to be hurtful, in many ways, to the Anglo-Saxon, and therefore dangerous to the nation. It tends to degrade all hand work, and so menaces the republic — for the dignity of labor is the corner stone of Liberty. Hence I could no more censure a laboring man for being an abolitionist than I would a church member for desiring to preserve the purity of the communion. Indeed, look at it as we may, slavery has sad prospects. The day of undisturbed possession has passed. The irresistible diffusion of intelligence rebukes the master, and is making the bondman a conspirator. The institution must recede from the light, or fall. From the very first it has shrunk from the line of the free states; and an inherent law, which we can neither repeal nor successfully resist, is accelerating its steps."

"God grant it!" said Park; "for as I read history, it seems the most fatal of temptations. Leading to ease, to luxury, and to lust, it has shorn the locks of every nation that has yielded to its embrace. If it reared the pyramids, it caused the sands of the desert to drift around them in devastating waves; overwhelming a strength and grandeur the bones and dust of which, as they are slowly exhumed, amaze the mind, and give awe and mystery to the name of Egypt. Where, too, are the sovereign cities which were set like gems in the Scriptures of the Hebrews? Their kings conquered but to enslave; and over their ruins some solitary column mourns. So, one after another, it dimmed the starred states of Greece, and finally quenched Rome herself — that glorious orb which so long gave law and learning to the world!"

CHAPTER XXV.

To bear too tender, or too firm a heart,
To act a lover's, or a Roman's part?
Is there no bright reversion in the sky
For those who greatly think, or bravely die?
POPE.

FEATHERSTONE was in frequent correspondence with his partners in New Orleans, the subject of which was the providing of means to meet their business engagements, rather than an account of profits; in fact, the traffic had not paid since leaving the management to others. This was owing, in part, to the loss of his sagacity; but chiefly to the low state of the water in the rivers, which had prevented the crops from coming forward by the boats to market. With such weight on his mind, it was certainly an unfavorable moment to make an appeal to his liberality. The expenses, also, which he had incurred by settling in New York, together with his luxurious mode of living, were surprisingly large; so that, on looking over the bills, and inquiring of Mrs. Featherstone if such articles had been actually purchased, and at such prices, and receiving, as he generally did, a concise and affirmative reply, he did not suppress his astonishment, not to say indignation. Perhaps the want of ready money to meet them caused him to effervesce more than the magnitude of the outlay; yet that fault he could not well lay at the door of another.

Environed by such circumstances, and occupied with such thoughts, Featherstone was not charitably disposed — indeed, who would be? To say truth, he had been thinking, the very day on which Rutledge called, how he should "realize;" and, as he reasoned with a single eye to business, he came to the conclusion which, all things considered, any thrifty trader might — namely, that it would hardly be right to draw on the commission house of Featherstone & Co. So he was compelled to look elsewhere for the needed funds; and where would he more naturally turn than to that property for which Rutledge had appeared? especially as it was unproductive, and perhaps deteriorating — at least, part of it was of a perishable nature.

It may do Featherstone no injury, in this connection, — for the same reason that we plead drunkenness in extenuation of murder, — to say that he belonged to a class of people who are so lavish on themselves, that, however large their income, they have no means to minister to the wants of others. It has been observed, also, that such persons are apt to become callous, and are liable to that peculiar pride which seems to live entirely on the surface; and, being so exposed, it is quite likely to get touched, and when touched it winces, for proud flesh is sensitive. Then, too, the only art of healing which they know for such hurts is a counter-irritant; so they touch back again, and, it may be, with a trifle more of emphasis. Some people may, and I am aware do, denounce this way of proceeding; but they can scarcely suspect that they are crusading against a long-prevailing fashion among what are termed the ornaments of society.

Judging from this trait of his character, perhaps the way in which Flora had met Featherstone, in their last interview, might be still remembered, and made his purpose firmer, although it could not much accelerate action: bills payable gave the impulse, means available determined the selection; consequently the appearance of Rutledge had no other effect on

Featherstone, for the moment, than to hasten the consummation of the thing which he desired to avert.

Soon after Featherstone precipitated himself into matrimony, he wrote to a shrewd acquaintance in New Orleans, an estate broker, constituting him his agent, and, stating to him confidentially all his interests in that city, requested him, particularly, to have an eye to the property in and about the house, and to dispose of certain parts of it when he had opportunity.

On the next day after the interview with Rutledge, he communicated further instructions, to wit: "See if you can find a purchaser for the house, and all the appurtenances and contents, at ——— thousand dollars; if not, you may strike down towards these figures, ———; but on no consideration may you descend below this last sum." He further stated, "I have no doubt that the property would bring a better price at public auction, as there are some articles which seem calculated to make the bidding lively and the market buoyant; but as it might swell to an event, and so get into the newspapers, or become conspicuous enough for Scandal to whet her beak upon, I prefer to avoid that method, as there are relatives in your town who might take offence; and I would rather make some sacrifice than risk the chance of their displeasure. There is, also, another point which I wish you to take into consideration; it is this: I hear a great deal said against dividing such families; and, although I hold that every admitted feeling will be found a foe to the 'peculiar institution,' if you can do it without loss, you may lump them; as I like to fall in with public sentiment so far as I can conveniently.

"Now, I want you to take this matter vigorously in hand, as I must have the funds; so you see that the terms of the sale are to be *cash*, or something readily convertible."

On receiving the above orders, the broker cast about in his

mind who there was among his acquaintance — and he knew nearly every one in the city who possessed the means for such outlay — that would be likely to desire the property. So, at length, fixing upon two or three, he took occasion to see the gentlemen in the course of the day, and broached the subject.

One of them, a young man who had lately come of age and into possession of a large estate, replied, " I have no objection to looking at the goods, if Fed will go too."

Thus appealed to, his companion, who was also rich, and recently from Paris, said, " Now, my dear fellow, I have no idea it can amuse *me;* it must be doosed tame, I fancy, after what I have seen abroad. Still, Carlo, my dear fellow, if you wish for a sight, I will exert myself to please you; but you mustn't bore me, my dear fellow."

" Did you ever know me to, Fed? besides, *you* are turning auger now!"

" Ah, Carlo, that is mechanical and coarse; but I admit the augury, and if it do not come true, my dear fellow, we will encore the play."

" At what hour will you go and take a view?" inquired the broker.

" It is very immaterial to me," replied Fed; " any time — now; then I shall not be bored with the memory that 'this thing's to do.'"

" No, not by daylight, Fed," cried Carlo; " let it be after dark, at least."

" Well, gentlemen," said the broker, " suppose then we fix on eight o'clock this evening; and I will meet you here with a carriage, you know."

To this they assented. And at the appointed time they met, and rode up to the house together.

As the season was warm — it was near the last of April — they found the front door of the house open. Walking in without ceremony, they met Madam in the hall, who, having heard the sound of a carriage, and afterwards voices, was coming forward somewhat hastily to close the door. But seeing that they had already entered in, she paused and said, "Gentlemen, I think that you must have mistaken the house."

"O, no, Madam!" replied the broker; "we are perfectly aware whose house 'tis, you know — once Merton's, now Featherstone's, and, perhaps, to-morrow it may belong to one of these gentlemen, you know."

"I do not know you," said Madam, "and we have no desire to see strangers."

"Ah, indeed! allow me, then, to make your ladyship acquainted with the agent of Anthony Featherstone, Esq.; said agent, you know, havin' full powers to tradė, traffic, sell, and convey, this house and its contents, not exceptin' even your sweet self!"

But as she stood silent, he continued, "Come, lead the way into the parlor; for it requires more light than you've got here to ascertain your value, you know."

Seeing that the scene could not be avoided, Madam reluctantly returned to the sitting room, with the gentlemen following close upon her steps. She went sorrowing and thinking of Flora, and of the dreadful day when she herself had stood in the market, and how Merton came and rescued her from distress and doom.

Flora had been silently expecting such a visit, during some days; for she had gathered from that fruitless search for the will, and from the manner and words of Rutledge, the conviction that such an event was impending. Being so impressed, when she heard the voices in the hall, she felt that the crisis was approaching; and, when the rude speech of the broker fell upon her ear, she rose up and stood upon the hearthstone, pale but calm, and fixed her piercing glance on the leader of the group as they entered.

The broker flinched a little under its flash, but, turning to the inspectors, he said, "This is the flower of the family, gentlemen, and has the reputation of being one of the most beautiful and desirable of her class, you know, and not to be had for money often, either."

Madam, advancing, took a place beside her daughter, and stood there more agitated and fearful, yet as silent as she.

Carlo and his elegant friend were there for amusement, rather than with any serious intentions of purchasing; consequently they stood like actors who had forgotten their parts, and looked frequently towards the door as if they were anxious for a prompter.

But the broker had called in the way of business, and felt that he had a handsome commission depending on the sale; so he said to Flora, who still awed them by her bearing, "Don't you feel a leetle higher than usual, to-night? Now I reckon your flag is rather sarcy, considerin' how no nation, not even Hayti, you know, has acknowledged your independence."

"The nation or the individual," replied Flora, in tones so firm that Fed and Carlo trembled, "that is determined to defend her inherent rights to the last gasp, has but little need of the recognition of power."

"If you pitch your tune that high," said the broker, "there'll be some mighty sharp notes afore the music is over, you know."

"And I have no doubt that there will be base ones, also," retorted Flora, "if you stoop to carry out the instructions of your employer, or even if you only follow the inclination of your own nature."

"Your spite," replied the broker, "can't hurt my reputa-on, you know. But——"

"No, I should think not! as your expression shows that no act could add infamy to it!" said Flora, interrupting.

"But your owner being absent," continued the broker, "I am bound to say, in the presence of these gentlemen, that he is liberal in his instructions, and more considerate than is usual in such cases, you know."

"Then he is a coward, as well as a knave," replied Flora.

"I shall treat him to your opinion," said the broker; "perhaps he may vally it, from an old lover, you know."

"You will earn my thanks by so doing," said Flora, "and you may say to him, at the same time, that he would not dare to lift a finger, or so much as breathe a rude word in this direction, if Mr. Merton still lived. If, in becoming heir to my father's estate, he has become master of all whom he loved only to crush them, tell him to look for a day of accounting; tell him if he had only been just—for generosity he cannot feel—the boon would have so surpassed my expectation as to have rolled the blood over me in a flood of shame, for thinking that I could have so wronged him as to doubt his fealty to so bald a virtue! And tell him that I know him,—know him so well that had he shown any disposition less rabid than revenge, it would have overstrode my comprehension,—and that I even fear him to be too callous and corrupt for the stings of remorse to torment and terrify into better courses."

"Gentlemen," said the broker, after a minute so long that the clock seemed to stop after each tick, "we will now go over the house, if you'd like to inspect it?"

"I should like to see the outside of it, doosedly!" replied Fed.

"So should I," said Carlo, "and that right soon!"

Thereupon, the pleasure-seekers started for the door; and as the broker turned to follow, he growled to Flora, "The next customer that I bring here, if I don't damn'dly mistake, will make you wish you'd received *these* a leetle sweeter, you know!"

As the surprise party seated themselves in the carriage and drove away, the agent broke the silence, by saying, "Now ye see, gentlemen, what edication does for sich articles — the A B C's are rank pison to the institution, you know."

"It is all a doosed bore, 'pon honor!" I give you my word, Carlo, my dear fellow, I never was so deeply bored in my life — never!"

"Now don't fret at me, Fed; I wanted to leave as much as you did; but I couldn't help pitying the girl."

"I did not see any thing to pity, except my own poor ears; for the play is a bore any time, a doosed bore, my dear fellow! our set in Paris, *la belle* Paris, voted it a bore — if she had only sung it, I might have been amused, as that refines and tones down the horrid ranting, my dear fellow — it does excessively!"

"It was a little too dramatic, Fed, I must admit; and then we had no opera glasses to hide behind. What is the matter with her, broker?"

"I'm a trifle puzzled myself, you know," replied the agent; "but they have been livin' here, considerable of a spell, putty much as they'd a mind to, you know, and I've near about concluded that the gal has picked up a lover; her actions kind o' let it out, you know."

"Doosed likely, and very lately too, by the way she gave tongue! 'Pon honor, I never was so bored before in my life — never!"

"She expects some backin' from somewhere," said the broker; "and the lover may have told her how he'd buy her when she's put up for sale, you know. There must be somethin' of that sort to make her so uppish and offish, you know; but I'll teach her that the string of her kite is in my hand!

And, gentlemen, although this has been rather a sink-pocket job to me, you know, still I'm most disapp'inted on account of its 'mountin' to no great fun for you, you know."

"It is all a bore, a doosed, horrid bore! Carlo, my dear fellow, let us alight at the opera; for I feel nearly broke down under the weight of, *you know!* YOU KNOW! I do, my dear fellow, 'pon honor!"

In a few moments after, the carriage drew up before the French opera house; and our gentlemen alighting, "Bore, doosed bore!" wandered back, and into the coach, when they disappeared.

As the driver closed the door and mounted to his seat, the broker said between his teeth, "Of all damn'd bores, a squirt who has been three months in Paris is the most sappy! Now that spooney reckons he's French! and yit to be a Frenchman is to be a game cock! while he's nothin' but a squab, with the pinfeathers all a hangin' to him, you kn—!"

While the carriage was rolling away from the house of the slaves, Madam went out and closed the street door; and, when she returned, Flora inquired, "Is there any thing remaining, mother, that you fear to lose?"

But as Madam did not reply, Flora continued, "Yet it may be well to shut out even the free air, that we may not hear it sigh around us. Do you think that the worst is to come, mother?"

"There can be no after-stroke for me; but you, O my dear daughter, it may touch you further."

"Dear mother, weep not for me, fear not for me; I have measured the height and depth of it, in thought, and have marked out my course. They have but little to fear, mother, who do not fear death."

Long they communed; and mournful and low were their words as they wandered through the once sunny, but now waste places, of memory; and, at length, turned even to the future with no cringing weakness. So, late in the night, they parted with a kiss to their respective chambers.

Flora retired to weep over her child, and pray for his deliverance, as she lay down beside him and drew his cheek to her bosom; when, after a time, sleep kindly came to take her from the dim eclipse of hope. It was late in the morning when she arose and went down; yet seeing no sign of having been preceded by her mother, she ascended to her chamber, touched the door, and called, "Mother!"

In a moment after calling again and receiving no answer, she lifted the latch and entered — entered to find a breathless stillness! to find her over-wearied mother taking a secure rest; for she had passed beyond the oppressor's power, and was cold even to the touch of filial affection.

Was it a visitation of Providence? Who can search so deeply as to say that it was not? although in the centre of the room there stood a brazier containing ashes and some half-consumed charcoals, which revealed the design, as did the lifeless form the successful termination. There, indeed, forever still, lay the hand which had executed; but the guiding hand! ——

"Son of St. Louis," said a priest of Holy Church — who believed in her power to forgive sin — over one of the outcast monarchs of France, in his dying moment — "Son of St. Louis, ascend to heaven!"

"Daughter of a slave," said a layman, — who believed in God, — when he saw the more than "maimed rites" of this burial, "Daughter of a slave, ascend to the bosom of the Infinite Mercy."

CHAPTER XXVI.

> If I stoop
> Into a dark, tremendous sea of cloud,
> It is but for a time; I press God's lamp
> Close to my breast — its splendor, soon or late,
> Will pierce the gloom. BROWNING.

THE broker was something startled when he learned the fact of Madam's death, and ascertained the probable cause; but, beyond that, the catastrophe made no sensation, for, her life and society having been limited to the walls of the house, so the mourning was confined there. Even curiosity about the nature of the disease, or the sudden dying, was not awakened, although a few persons who lived nearest had seen the deceased at the window, or the door, on the previous day, as they were aware that people who are very unwell may make such appearance; while they could remember that she had long looked sad and worn, so they thought that she might have declined into her grave. Thus a familiar form had passed from their sight, to soon fade out of their memory.

No enlightened jury was called to investigate the case, and gather and collate the facts, to merge their total ignorance of the cause and motive of the tragic act in the word "insanity," which

> "Resolves all doubts so eloquently well."

In consequence of this pecuniary loss to that portion of Featherstone's estate which had been intrusted to the broker's sagacity, he became anxious to dispose of the residue immediately — fearing that "insanity" might be epidemic, and still further reduce the value of the property. Yet, in urging the sale to a conclusion, he did not forget how sharply he had been bearded by Flora; and he called it to mind the more readily because that he felt it to be in his power to repay, by finding a purchaser who, he knew, would be disgusting and relentless. And, in this connection, he bethought him that probably Bill Frink might fancy the property, as some time before he had said to him, while drinking together, in reply to a remark which he had made, "Wal, if you git any tasty article in the yaller line, I'd jist like to inspect it."

Thinking over the matter, he was very soon satisfied that this would suit him, as he believed that he could make it appear to be a good investment, at the lowest price named by Featherstone, after deducting the market value of Madam.

Acting on his thought, he met Bill that day, and, drawing him into one of the saloons, called for drink, and over it talked of the estate on sale.

When Bill had heard him through, he said, "I reckon as how it tastes a leetle too strong of the money for my use."

"But you must look at the real estate, you know; for I think it is worth every picayune he asks for the whole concern."

"Now don't du that, for I shan't think your woman worth nothin' if she ain't high cost; as, somehow, the vally of every thing seems to me to be in dollars; and I'd like to know how you're goin' to reckon it in any other way? for nothin' else has got the vally stomped on to it."

"Well, that's good enough for another drink; you are a practical man, Mr. Frink, and I must give in that your way, arter all, is the only practical way of gittin' at it; the government stamp is the thing, you know."

"'Tis that. But what color's your beauty? Du she come up putty well to sugar, or run mostly to molasses?"

"She's a mustee, you know," replied the broker.

"A musty woman! Du ye call that are a good sort?"

"O, yes, they bring the tallest prices, for they're paler than quadroons, you know, and sometimes pass off for white, you know, where there ain't no good judges; and you've on'y to say that they're Spanish to travel with 'em or go with 'em any where ye like, you know."

"That's handy; for I mought want to carry a handsome piece up north, sometime or other; I guess I could come it over 'em some."

"It would be slick; and you'd be hard to beat, Bill; and I reckon she'd do you exactly, you know."

"Wal, if you say so, I'll jist look over the goods, and then if we can hit any where near in figurin', I shouldn't wonder if it's a go."

"That's the talk, Bill. Will ye take a turn round there this evenin'?"

"Not I. I takes daylight to du my business in."

"Well, you be cunnin', Bill. Then s'pose we go now?"

"Agreed. Off hand's the word, by thunder!"

"Them's my sentiments, arter we've had another 'smile,' you know."

When they had taken their drink they departed on their errand, caring for no wrong, however deep, if it stood within the clear and complete sanction of the law.

In all his pleasures Bill had a keen eye to cost; accordingly, when they arrived at the house, he preferred to make a thorough examination of the premises outside before looking at the interior.

When they had completed that part of the review, they entered in, and, proceeding up stairs, inspected all the chambers and furniture; then descending, they went through below in the same manner, until they came to the sitting room; on reaching which the broker, in a suppressed voice, said, "We shall probably find the woman in here, you know."

"Wal, she ain't dangerous, is she? Haven't got her chained up, have ye?"

"O nothin' o' that kind," the broker replied; but he involuntarily knocked at the door.

"That's smart now. Du ye own any goods that ye're afeard on?" when, lifting the latch, he pushed the door wide, and they stalked in, the broker falling to the rear.

Flora sat with a book in her hand, from which she did not raise her eyes, and Fred stood as though he had approached the door for the purpose of opening it; but seeing them enter, he backed away towards his mother, though without haste, seeming rather to dislike the appearance of the intruders than to have any fear of them.

"How d'e du, marm?" said Bill, in a tone of voice which he thought was tender and insinuating. "You live in a fust-rate tenement here, marm; and tall furniture you've got tu; you must have rather a swell go on it. Is that are boy yourn?"

But as Flora did not reply, he continued, "Wal, mum's the word; I understand it, I du; 'nough said, marm; silence says consent; all right, my duckey!" and looking round at the same time, he saw the sideboard, and nudging the broker, he stepped up to it, opened, and, taking out a bottle, drew the cork by his teeth with two or three twists of his head, then pressing it to his nose so as to take the odor, he nodded and winked to the broker, and saying, "Here's luck, my leetle beauty," tippled off something of the contents, as a large bunch in his bare red neck moved up and down several times, like the wattles of an old gobbler when he spreads his tail and prates of his domestic consequence.

Having thus quenched his thirst for the moment, and fortified his courage, Bill wiped his mouth with the back of his hand, and, passing the bottle to the broker, drew a chair up beside Flora, and seating himself, said, "Du ye know how to read, marm?"

"Yes; and I believe that gift cannot be stolen or torn from me."

"That's so. Now du ye s'pose, marm, as how ye could larn me some of the higher branches? for all I lack is edication. I haven't got none o' that, nohow; if I on'y had, I could beat the man what made the college. I s'pose ye know how to turn out all sorts of fancy things, marm; can ye du darnin' and sich like?"

"I can, and I am willing to work; indeed, I would not shrink from the hardest labor, if by it I could support myself and my child."

The broker had set back the bottle where Bill found it, and thinking the pause opportune and fearing further discussion, said, "If you're ready, Mr. Frink, we'll take leave now."

"Why, what's your hurry? I want to du a leetle courtin' fust."

"But I must go, you know, though you can stay if ye like."

"Wal, if you're a goin', I s'pose I must go along tu," said Bill, grinning. So gathering himself up and saying, "Good day, marm," he shambled out in a gait as unnatural as the tone of his voice had been affected; for, conscious of his own meanness and of her superiority, he became a *lie*, hoping thereby to appear more lovely in her eyes — a frequent performance of many other pretenders.

When they had emerged from the house, and were moving down the street, the broker said, "Well, Mr. Frink, how do matters and things strike ye?"

"Putty fair," Bill replied, in his natural manner, which he had then recovered. "The gal is a brick, a reg'lar brick, a pressed brick, but I don't care any thing about that; and Bill laughed at the conceit, and the broker joined in, as he thought the trade hopeful; "and she looks smooth enough for any part of a house, and talks as how she was most willin' to be stuck in the chimney corner. Yet Bill don't quite swaller it, for it's gammon, by thunder! for I'll bet she'll cry half the time, if she can't have fifty dollars' worth of things a month; and she'll throw away more gloves in a year or so than I ever had. Now, I don't say, mind ye, as how Bill Frink can't afford it, but I du say he'd better buy cheaper colors."

"If 'twas 'cordin' to instructions to put this property at public sale, you know, Mr. Frink, I wouldn't ask you or any man to buy it at the figures I've chalked, you know; but the owner hasn't yit so instructed."

"I s'pose I can make ye a bid, if that'll du ye any good."

"I'm cornered as to price, you know, Mr. Frink."

"Sartain; I reckon I know all about that — I've been there. But I'll give ye — now I'm goin' to make my best offer, and let that be the end on't — I'll give ye —— thousand dollars, and that'll more than clean me out; it will, by thunder!"

"It's no use to talk, you know, Mr. Frink, onless you come somewhere near my limits — so I'm afraid we can't trade."

"Wal, I'll give ye five hundred more, but not another picayune; and Bill Frink 's a fool to throw away so much as that on fancy."

"That's no price, you know; so you can't want the property much, Mr. Frink."

"Wal, what du ye say to two hundred and fifty more? but not another cent, by thunder!"

"Mr. Frink, you've come so near I don't mind namin', privately, ye know, his price to ye, which is two hundred and fifty more than your last bid, and if you'll toe that are mark the property is yourn."

To this he soon agreed, although he had offered five hundred more in the outset than was necessary to become the purchaser; but the broker saw that he was in for it, and so he stuck him for another thousand.

In the course of a day or two the papers were drawn, the money paid, and the property conveyed — thus Bill Frink became the lawful owner of the house and home of Rufus Merton, and of all his lineal blood. "To what base uses we may return, Horatio!"

The business was completed on the premises, when Bill took possession and the keys. Thereupon the broker said to Flora, "You're now, together with the boy, house, &c., you know, the property of Mr. Frink, here present, and I hope you'll have a pleasant time on't."

On this, Bill grinned, and said, "Ye won't be so kind o' lonesome now, marm, as I shall take a turn round here, in the evenin', for a leetle tender talk, and jist to see if you're willin' to make yourself useful. You'll love me when ye come to know me — all on 'em du."

But Flora making no reply, the gentlemen departed.

The broker was well satisfied with his success; and Bill felt nicely, for every thing appeared to run smooth, and, as he thought, wore a prosperous look. So he invited the broker to dine with him, and as he furnished an abundance of liquor, they both drank deeply, and were warmed into a confession of their true natures without disguise — yea, with pride; thereby revealing a moral pollution well nigh past hope, as it could be seen that they were already condemned and burning in the fire of a sensual hell.

In the course of the evening Frink came to his house;

when, fumbling some time with his key, he at length got the door open, and entering, found Flora alone, with a book in her hand, and occupying her usual place in the sitting room.

Fred had gone to sleep in her arms, some time before, when she had carried him to another room than her own, and laid him in bed without awaking him. She had done this because she was expecting invasion; and having completed her other preparation, she sat, when Bill came in, sadly but firmly awaiting the assault.

Frink took a chair, and, seating himself beside Flora, said, "I hope you're glad to see me, ducky; ha'n't been cryin' for me, have ye?" And, as a fitting conclusion of these questions, he put out his arm as though it were his intention to encircle her neck; at which she drew back, and gave him a glance as sharp as a knife. Feeling the cut, Bill desisted, apparently surprised, and asked, "Ye ain't a goin' to act offish, be ye? Now, I wouldn't, ducky; for I reckon it won't du no good, no how, 'cause I've bought and paid for ye; so I guess you're mine, marm, in the tightest kind of a way."

"Bought me! you've bought me! You may, indeed, have made the poor purchase of this body; yet I deny, and utterly scorn, the title which you hold for any purpose but labor."

"Now, don't ye think you'd better hold your hosses? I want ye to understand, I didn't buy ye to work, my duck! I can git three niggers for what you cost that will du six times more luggin' nor you could. So you'd sooner go in for scourin' knives than pleasure, would ye? Wal, you're a good 'un! Now, how many new gounds will it take to satisfy ye, my ducky? Come, say it, for I feel mighty liberal now, and you'd better strike while the iron's hot; so out with it, now, right off, for it makes me kind o' savage to wait; and you'll never find an easier time to git round Bill than now."

"I have said that I am willing to labor; and I shall be ready with to-morrow's rising sun to apply myself to any work, however hard, to which you have the power to condemn me."

"Now, ain't you actin' putty considerable tall for so thin a house, marm? Now, don't fancy you're goin' to put Bill Frink off with that sort o' stuff! Du ye see any thing green enough about me for squash bugs to eat? P'r'aps ye think Bill ain't sharp, and can't guess what the case is! May be somebody 'll rush in to help ye! won't ye call 'im now, if he's round, and would like a lively turn? Or if ye want to slip out and run, you sh'll have a fair start, for Bill's got two of the sweetest dogs as ever barked on track; and he's fond o' huntin', tu, 'specially when the game 'll pay — now, wouldn't ye like to try it?"

To this Flora made no reply; but rising up, and taking a light, she moved towards the door.

"Where 'bouts ye goin' now? ain't off for good, be ye, my beauty?"

"I am going to my own room; for I have too long endured words against which I have the power of closing my ear."

"O, wal, that's all right; we'd as good's go to bed now as any time;" and he straightened up to follow her.

Turning on him, Flora gave the red and half-intoxicated giant a look which made him quail, for an instant; but he rallied soon, and said, —

"Go on, my duck — don't trouble yourself to wait for me; go up to the bower; I'll be round there in time."

Flora's cheek paled, yet her form visibly dilated, as she moved silently away, and ascended to her room, with no sign of haste; and, without closing the door, she placed the lamp on the table, when she paused a moment, as if plunged in thought or hushed with prayer. But the spell was broken by footsteps; when, looking up, she saw Bill approaching to enter. On which, moving quickly towards him, she thrust her hand into her bosom, when a gleaming dagger flashed across his eye to be poised high and threatening, as she said to the invading miscreant, "Come, if you think it wise! yet we cannot breathe the air of *this* room together an instant in peace!"

"Ah, ha!" growled Bill, nothing daunted, as he drew forth a broad, heavy bowie knife; "that's a game which two on us can play at!"

"Then strike!" cried Flora, as she clutched her left hand into the bosom of her dress and rent it deep down, while she drew towards him. "Strike! for I prefer your steel to your smile. Strike! and then I shall be *free!* but pass not that door for any other purpose."

On this, Frink slunk back a step in astonishment, and said, "You don't want to die, du ye?"

"Of what value is life, on your terms?"

"So you r'a'ly don't fancy Bill, don't ye? 'drather hack away with cold steel, ha? ready to pitch battle with him — well, you be a trump, you be, by thunder!"

"I did not draw a weapon to strike you except in extremest need — rather my own heart than that; but this room is sacred to me, and blood is a cheap defence."

"Now, if ye mean it, I s'pose I can put it off a day or so; but, let me tell ye, you'll fare better, in the long run, to back down right off, for Bill don't swaller slights easy."

Yet, as Flora neither made reply nor changed her attitude, he added, "So ye mean to stick to your text to-night, du ye? If ye du, I won't crowd. But I want ye to understand that when Bill comes here ag'in, he expects to be better accommodated; for if his temper fires up, he's hell! And he'll let this here go, and call it courtin'; but the next time he comes round, he comes for a weddin' or a funeral — he will, by thunder! So he'll say good night now, and hopes it's all pleasant."

During his talk, Flora closely searched him, and she saw that his brutal purpose and determination were neither adjourned nor abated, for the leer of lust was in his eye, while its smirk spread out over his vulgar visage. She saw, also, that he was desperate, and knew that he was meditating treachery, so that his words of leave-taking were not the snare which he hoped they would be, as he sprang forward and clutched at her wrist, thinking to disarm and overpower her. But, great as was his strength, and swift as was his bound, they did not avail him then; for she saw the fell thought, when it flashed up from the hell of his passions, and drew back her arm so suddenly that he caught only the keen blade, which laid open the flesh of his hand; and darting aside at the same instant, she dashed out the light, and, from the midst of the black darkness, cried, "You vile wretch, look to your own life now!"

Bill made no answer, but, leaping like a tiger to the place whence the voice appeared to issue, flung wide his arms, and struck out with his weapon; yet it clove only the air, and all was still.

Flora, indeed, barely escaped his stroke as she glided noiselessly away, palpitating with dread and loathing. He even had a glimpse of her vanishing form; and making one more desperate plunge to lay hold of her, he struck a piece of furniture, which threw him heavily to the floor, when his bowie knife broke from his grasp, and bounded, rattling, far beyond his reach.

After the whirl of blood and brain, which the shock of the fall occasioned, had subsided, he felt that he was still whole, yet lay abject and trembling, because, being weaponless, he was completely in her power. With that thought the beads of sweat gathered thick on his forehead, and his skin tingled, in twenty places, as though the fatal steel was piercing him. On this, his blood boiled, and his breath came thick, making him to feel all that a dastardly culprit can undergo when the hangman adjusts the cord to his neck, and the waiting coffin arrests his eye, while he listens for the click of that spring which will hurl him over the fathomless precipice.

Yet, after a few moments, finding that he was still alive, Bill began to crawl away, as softly as he could, in what he hoped to be the direction of the door; but he did not strike it, while every touch against the dead wall gave him a pang; and, hearing a rustling very near him, he gasped with horror as he jumped aside from the sound. This fortunately threw him before the opening, for he was full of despair, and was as weak as an infant. So he passed out, and went groping on, feeling for the stairs; when, touching the balustrade unexpectedly, he well nigh lost his senses, but recovering in a moment, he hearkened with every hair. Catching alarm once more, he sprang, and, being on the brink of the stairs, went down, carrying most of the balusters along with him — half screaming, half groaning as he fell. But, realizing what had happened, he jumped up, on the instant, and overturning two or three chairs, finally reached the front door, and getting it open and himself out, he locked it, to sink down on the step and laugh in very weakness, and think himself a favorite of fortune.

However, in a few minutes, another feeling came over him, and he said aloud, "Now, how many times will Bill Frink stand bein' bullied by a woman—and a nigger at that? Will he sneak off ag'in? No, by thunder! he'll go loaded with arms fust; and he'll be here to-morrow night to make this here house the hottest or the coldest place this side o' hell!"

CHAPTER XXVII.

The tuneful noise the sprightly courser hears,
Paws the green turf, and pricks his trembling ears;
The slackened rein now gives him all his speed,
Back flies the rapid ground beneath the steed;
Hills, dales, and forests, far behind remain,
While the warm scent draws on the deep-mouthed train.
GAY.

From the open casement above, Flora had heard her master's words, and felt that in the end the battle would be a losing one for her; felt that it was a field in which heroism itself could have no hope; felt that there was nothing left to her but flight; and, although that must be through a multitude of foes, it were better to venture forth, however dark the prospect, as struggle itself is a reprieve, and on the most forlorn path is sometimes victorious.

So, having watched Bill go up and out of the street, Flora entered the room where her child was sleeping, and there prayed the Almighty for his guiding hand through the thick darkness that environed her.

Still bending over her son, she kissed him, and as he roused to consciousness she said, "Mother is going out to walk; does her dear little boy wish to go with her?"

"It be all dark, mother — isn't it?"

"My dear child the dark is our best friend now; and it is cool and breezy at this hour, which makes it more pleasant walking than by day."

"O, I want to go if you be going," said Fred, rising up.

But a few minutes had elapsed ere she made him ready, when, arraying herself for the adventure, she took a cup and some bread, with a few other needful things. Then, softly opening one of the front windows, she gazed over the silent street, and seeing nothing to deter, lifted Fred out, jumped out herself, closed the window, and taking her way towards the lower suburbs of the city, at length reached the levee, and continued to walk hurriedly on. When daylight appeared, fearing to be questioned by those whom she might meet there, she turned away from the river, and sought the cover of the bordering forest; there, beneath the shade and through occasional tangled undergrowth, she pressed on, skirting the cultivated ground and following the course of the Mississippi — now leading her child and now carrying him, still strong with resolve, if not with hope, and anxious to put space between her and the city from which she had fled.

In this manner she urged on her steps until the heat and stillness of midday found her so weary that she sat down on a little rising ground, — it being somewhat less damp than the surrounding country, — beneath the shade of a far-spreading, towering live oak, which was curtained dark with long mosses, pendent from every limb, and seeming as if the dryads that dwelt there had dishevelled their locks to veil their charms from mortal eyes.

During the long march Fred had made no complaint, for Flora watched him carefully through all, and when she thought that he might be weary, took him cheerfully in her arms and carried him on until he desired to get down; in truth, his attention had been so taken with novelty, that he found no time to think of himself. As they walked along the child had made inquiry about every thing which he saw in the woods; yet new objects thronged so thick that he could not wait for answers, and his "O mother, what is that?" passed with the vision, as he watched the continually unrolling panorama with its ever-new attractions.

He, however, soon fell asleep after the halt; and in a little time Flora herself slept, for it seemed a secure place, and she thought it necessary to prepare her for the journey of the night; so, beneath a large shawl which protected them from the thronging mosquitos, they took their rest.

Thus, for three or four hours, they found repose. But at length Flora was aroused by sharp notes and the near rustling of the undergrowth, when, starting up, she saw, and was seen by, some boys who were searching for the young of the mocking-bird, which inhabit those woods in great numbers. It was the voices of those birds, now shrill, now mournful, as they darted near and around these devastators of their happiness, which gave the first warning of danger, and startled Flora from the depths of sleep. The marauding party consisted of a white boy, of about twelve years of age, with two, apparently, attendant blacks some few years older.

As they came through the brush, near the tree, they saw the child as well as Flora; so they gazed curiously for a few moments, but finally passed without question; and when they were fairly out of sight she lifted up her boy and hurried on.

In this manner she continued to press forward for more than an hour, when it became so dusk that farther progress was difficult. Then she halted and watched until she thought it nine o'clock, for there were occasional dwellings along the course of the river, and masters or overseers might be out in the early evening, who would observe, question, and detain her until duly advertised and claimed. When that hour had fully arrived, she crossed the cleared land, gained the levee, and kept on by the edge of the descending current.

Where she was going Flora had not paused to consider; she felt that she must go — it might be some mysterious leading. She only knew that she was flying from something more dreadful than death; so that she could look down upon the dark flood beneath her feet with composure and a feeling of calm trust, for into its silent bosom she might sink, when men should rise up to scourge her back to violation; even this was to her a hope and a place of refuge.

The boys, consulting together, soon after returned by the knoll where they had left the fugitives, but finding only the trampled grass, and a few crumbs thereon, they went home; and the white lad, being the son of a planter, reported to the overseer what he had seen.

That keen official made but few inquiries before he ordered his horse saddled; which being brought, his foot was quickly in the stirrup and his spur against the flank; and, in less than an hour's time, the pavement of the city rang to the tread of his smoking steed.

Seeking an acquaintance immediately, he spoke of the matter, and was directed to the broker, as one who would be most likely to know, or soonest learn, something of the ownership of the fugitives.

The overseer was not long in finding that person, when he gave the information and his own suspicions.

"Nearly white, you say she is, with a boy three or four year old. How fur down from here were they scared up?"

"Between eight and nine miles, I reckon," the overseer replied.

"What kind o' goods did they have on — spruce or common lookin'?"

"I didn't have a sight at them; and the boys didn't seem to know, for all that they could tell about it was, their clothes were lightish colored, and they had a large light shawl."

"S'pose we cross over to the saloon and take a drink; and p'r'aps we may dig out somethin' more about it there, you know."

When they entered Bill Frink was at the bar with his comrades, and seeing them he called out, "Come on, broker, you're right in time, and jist bring up your friend, tu; for we've got to drink all they've got in these here decanters; we have, by thunder! so the more help, the lighter the jag."

Having emptied their glasses, the broker, taking Bill aside, asked, "How does it go up *there* — how do ye flourish in the tender line?"

"O, so so; she acts a little rusty about startin'; but I guess she'll go well 'nough arter she gits warm. Come, let's take another drink, for I'm fittin' to go and court her."

"What! haven't you paid her a visit to-day? you oughter be very 'tentive at fust, you know."

"No, by thunder! I go in for business in the daytime."

"Was she sweet on ye, last night?"

"What's that to you, by thunder! What the devil be ye so pryin' about — haven't ye got your pay for her? But come, I'm dry; so let's wet down ag'in."

"Now don't git into a pucker, Bill; for nothin' short of a matter of business could have led me to call ye one side, you know; and I reckon your woman has stepped out."

"That would be a swell go!" exclaimed Frink. "Now I'll bet a hat she hain't; and I hope she has, for I'd like to slip my dogs on her tracks; I should, by thunder! Du ye r'a'ly think she has gone and done that are?"

"I guess we'd better go and take a squint. There's no knowin' what'll they do, you know; and there's cause to suspicion somethin's broke loose."

"You hain't seen her sence I bought her — have ye? Now what the devil be ye so kind o' private about?"

"If we find she's vamosed the ranch, you know, you shall have the whole story."

"Then I s'pose I'm bound to go; and while we're up there we can finish that bottle in the bureau — you remember it?

By thunder, what the devil was that? It tasted like there was tansy in it; but let's go and git done with the job."

So the three started off together, while Bill said to those whom he was leaving, "Boys, hold on here for me, for I'll be back in less than no time."

When they had fully satisfied themselves that neither Flora nor her child were in the house, and Bill had expressed great astonishment and indignation over the wreck of the stair rail, and had slyly recovered his bowie knife, he turned to the broker and inquired, "Now, where the devil is she? for I s'pose you know. O, won't I give her some! Won't she catch it, ha! by thunder!"

"This gentleman, you know," said the broker, indicating his companion by a jerk of his neck, "may give ye a leetle more light on the subject."

Thus appealed to, the overseer related the facts which had brought him to the city.

On finishing his account, Bill said, "That's she; and a right lively hunt we'll have on her tracks to-morrow. Won't she catch it, for she can't git away nohow; her chain is more nor a thousand miles long, by thunder! And you desarve well of Uncle Sam, and me tu; so ye may reckon on your pay, and I'll be down to your coop, with the right sort o' company, by seven in the mornin'."

"That will be in good season," said the overseer, "and you will find me ready to p'int out the place where she was seen, and foller the hounds."

Soon after they separated, Bill went round to three or four of his intimates, and acquainted them with the expected sport; and they, being eager to participate in it, engaged horses for the coming day.

When the arrangements were all made, Frink did not return to the saloon, as he had promised, but retired to rest; or rather to labor with a dream, in which prospect and retrospect were strangely mingled. As he sank to slumber, he started off after the hounds with an exulting heart; but soon his horse was flying along the terrible edge of dark and precipitous rocks, down which, after many times nearly losing his footing, so that the rider was in paroxysms of fright, at length he fell! But, as they were hurled over the steep, he caught hold of something which seemed to him a balustrade; yet it was so frail that it flew to splinters in his grasp as he went crashing down, down, down! until, seeing that he was about to plunge into a yawning chasm whose dizzy deep was alive with serpents, writhing and glowing like flames, he screamed and started, half awake, though not sufficiently to shake off the demon, for it led him, night long, amid recollections and portents which made his hair to stand on end and his flesh to creep.

By the dawn of day the hunting party were stirring, and, mounting, reached the plantation at the hour appointed, when the boys led them to the knoll where they had seen the fugitives.

On being shown the ground, which had then well nigh lost all trace of step or pressure, Luff and Trim were led to the spot, and soon made to comprehend what was wanted of them; so that, after snuffing, whining, and whimpering around a few moments, Trim gave a short, sharp bark as he took up the track, and Luff struck in behind him with a bellow, and Bill shouted, "It's a start!" when the plantation dogs were let loose, and taking the scent, they followed with full voice; and the horsemen, wheeling in pursuit, galloped down the woods to what they called glorious music.

The hounds worked slow and were occasionally bothered at wet places, probably because over those spots Flora had carried Fred in her arms. They soon, however, passed out of the forest, crossed the cleared field, and mounted on to the levee, down which they followed eight or ten miles, when they once more struck across the clearing and in among the trees; but these began to draw nearer the stream, and in many places approached quite to the brink of the water. The hounds grew more and more lively as the scent became fresher, and over that swampy flat led the horses at long distance; so that Bill called out, "Ride clost! We shall be on 'em soon! If the game don't tree, the fur'll fly! We must jump down the dogs if they fasten; I don't want 'em torn up right off hand; for I shall feel as if I hadn't got half satisfaction; I shall, by thunder!"

It was a strain of high enjoyment to those fiendish hunters, as they pressed on their plunging horses; and Frink's face glowed with ferocious triumph, for he expected, every instant, to hear the despairing screams of his victim.

His brain so fired with this thought that he fancied he heard a cry, and shouted, "Hark!" In suddenly checking his headlong course to listen, the overseer tripped his horse, so that he blundered and launched him against the limb of a tree, which caught in the corner of his mouth, and tore his cheek open to his ear.

Bill laughed, with the rest, as he saw him roll in the mud; but the woods were echoing with the full wild joy of the hounds; so on they dashed again, their steeds foaming and smoking beneath the burning sun, yet as eager in the chase as dog or rider.

"There! there!" shouted Bill; "the hunt's up! the hounds are still! We'll have 'em, dead or alive, in a few shakes; we will, by thunder! Hooraw! hooraw!"

So the riders shouted, "Hooraw!" and the trees caught up the unfeeling cry, yet more faintly repeated it, and the dogs replied far down through the foliage.

CHAPTER XXVIII.

Fate made me what I am — may make me nothing —
But either that or nothing must I be;
I will not live degraded. BYRON.

As the first signs of approaching day began to pale the eastern stars, the notes of preparation on board of the ships which were ready to depart from New Orleans broke cheerfully on the ear. The rich, deep voices, incident to the full, strong lungs that the great sea gives its votaries, were growing every minute more predominant and decisive, over the echo of the trampled decks and the shrill screams of the blocks, as they swelled up in command or remonstrance, jaggy with oaths and piquant with epithet.

There, near by, paused the steam-tugs, hoarse, hot, and oppressed in their breathing, and seeming to wait with restless impatience, while grappling to the leviathans which they were to bear down through the passes and set free in the waters of the Gulf.

Casting the eye aloft, men were to be seen lying out on the yards of the ships; and top-sails and top-gallantsails were escaping from their gaskets, on three or four, that were about to try their own wings; for there was a leading breeze from the south, while the vapory fleeces which were rising along the north-west gave indication that it would veer to that quarter as the day advanced.

One after another, those vessels sheeted home, filled away, and stretched out into the silent, swift, and turbid current.

Who is there in whom a ship does not awaken admiration? The most perfect are very dreams of beauty, with charms that never cloy; for still we gaze whenever their white bosoms woo the wind. Even the most uncouth are attractive, when, under a press of canvas, they look to the wind and cleave through the broken ranks of opposing waves, or stagger before the gale and reel amid the billows; while those which are modelled with art, and clothed with grace, leave their pictures in the mind to rise occasionally to sight, on the illimitable sea of memory, long after they have "veiled their high tops lower than their ribs, to kiss their burial."

The last of the ships which left the levee, on that morning, was one to be remembered — long, sharp, and full sparred, she divided the waters without disturbing them, any more than does the fin of a shark as he prowls for his prey. When she swept into view, it could be seen that she was one of those triumphs of naval art which give to the ocean an interest not its own, but akin to that which the beauty of Mary has left in the otherwise gloomy halls of Holyrood.

As her signal mounted to the main, and unrolled on the breeze, it disclosed her name to be the Muse; while her appropriate figure-head was a female form, draped in white and girdled with gold, and in her hand she bore a golden lyre. She seemed a flowing curve in every part, except where the quarter blended with the stern frame, which was slightly rounded and gracefully raked, and decorated with a single wreath of laurel dipped in gold.

When, under a cloud of canvas, she gathered way, with every thing braced sharp and swayed home, she looked away to the windward of all those which had got off before her, and was overreaching them at the same time — revealing to the nautically trained eye that, when her cap was full of wind, she cared but little from what point of the compass it came.

With the ease and celerity of a pilot boat she glided down, tacking and tacking until nine o'clock, when, having made nearly twenty miles, the breeze failed under the heat of the sun, — for it was the first of June, — so that she scarcely had steerage way in the descending current.

The crew of the Muse were hiding in the shadows of the sails, or the bulwarks, from the fierce heat of that southern latitude which crinkled to sight in the air, and seared the flesh like a mist of molten gold; and the mosses on the mighty oaks, that skirted the river, hung as though they were cast in bronze, although the faintest whisper of the lightest and idlest zephyr has power to agitate them.

Captain Elery — for it was his ship — was slowly walking along her quarter-deck, scanning the white clouds, — which still continued to float out of the deep blue of the west, — glancing, occasionally, over the ship's side at the water, and then aloft, as if at a loss to know where the Muse got her headway. But her skysails towered far above the forest, and met the first advances of that western breeze which the "scud" of the morning had prophesied.

At length the captain said, "I believe our signal has caught a fair wind, Mr. Jones, though there's not much to brag of yet; but if I know the quality of those 'sheep-skins,' along the nor'-west, we shall have a pelt or two before the day is over."

"I hope so," replied the mate; "for I want to steer clear of this mud creek before night comes on; as it's so near the color of the land that in the dark you can't tell which is which; and I don't want to be cast away in a swamp; give me either land or water; they're too much mixed up here to suit me. They say that Lafitte, the pirate, used to navigate all through these woods in his craft."

"Very likely, Mr. Jones; but then you know that she was

fore and aft rigged, and so might sheer round the limbs of the trees easier than we can. Yet, under full headway, I think that the Muse could go in any-where along here, two or three times her length, easy."

"That's what I'm afraid of, sir; for, in the dark, we can't see the turns in the river, and if there's a good breeze she'll make a straight wake, and tear her copper half off in ploughing through."

"And then," said Elery, "when we come to haul her on to the ways in New York, — as we should be obliged to do, — we might find blackberry bushes, instead of sea-weed, hanging to her bottom. I would as soon be caught with hay seed in my hair, as have 'em see that! But hark! Do you hear that music? Some devil is out with the hounds this hot morning. Hark! they're heading this way — driving right down on us. What voices they have! Were it an October day, and the grass all silver with frost, and the leaves all the colors of the rainbow, I should think that I had lost something of the glory of life in being cooped up here. But hear them come — they are almost down to us! Francis, give me my gun! Something will break cover in a moment! if it's a deer it may take to the water. Get the downfalls of the quarter-boat tackles clear, men, and stand by to lower away! Mr. Jones, where the devil are you now? If a loon had squalled, a half a mile off, you would have been tiptoeing the deck, or skulking along under the rail, with your old king's arm, in less than no time!"

"There, there, the bushes move!" cried Jim, — one of the men, — who had been quietly watching; "something *is* breaking cover!"

The captain saw the motion, also, and dropping one knee on the stern coop, he brought his eye to bear along the sights of his double-barrel in an instant; when something did break cover — something which brought the captain to his feet, and the but of his gun to the deck, with a ring! for it was a woman, wild and dishevelled, with a child, whom she seemed to bear as though it were but a feather in her grasp! Springing up the levee, — some six or seven feet above the level of the land, and two or three higher than the river, — she dropped her child, and stretching out her imploring hands towards the ship, she cried, "O, save me! save me! Save us from those terrible dogs; save, O, save my boy!"

She ceased; yet there, upon the bank, she stood with her arms still outstretched to the Muse, as though that winged thing were the last faint hope which then lingered above the grave.

The captain, gun in hand, leaped into the boat, and, as he did it, called Jim and Jack to follow; when, "Lower away, men!" was the order and the work of an instant. Standing in the stern sheets, — the tackles having been unhooked, — he said, "Now spring to your oars — spring!"

As the boat swept out from under the shadow of the ship's quarter and headed for the object, Elery turned and said, "Francis, rig the companion ladder! Mr. Jones, do you hear those dogs? There, there! That's Trim, — and that's Luff! I should know their voices among a thousand, by the richness of the metal."

The next instant the men were resting upon their oars, for the boat had reached the feet of the supplicant.

Marking, at a glance, the delicacy of her hands and the style and texture of her dress, torn and soiled as it was, Elery said, "Lady, what do you implore at my hands?"

"Life! protection from those terrible dogs, and more terrible men! O, do you not hear the fiendish pursuit, and will you not have mercy and save us from death?"

"They will not molest *you!* They are on the track of some

wild inhabitant of the woods — you have nothing to fear from them."

"It is my trail which they are following! It is I and my poor boy whom they are hunting down! O my God, is there no compassion for the outlawed? Can you feel no pity for a slave?"

"*You* a slave? Why, there is not a tar on blue water who is not browner than you are. You a negro! well, my God, that alters the business! it puts it beyond my reach, for it is a peculiar institution, and I don't want to burn my fingers with it. You see it is a matter in which somebody, at some time, agreed for me that I should never interfere." And, turning to his men, he added, "It makes my blood boil to say so, but this is something which we are bound not to meddle with; so back your oars, for we must leave it;" and, on the word, the boat shot twenty feet from the shore.

The next moment, seeing that last earthly hope depart, Flora caught her child to her heart, and raised her eyes far above the tall top-gallants of that stately ship. Silently there, for an instant, she intensely gazed; then, as if she saw some beckoning finger from out the infinite blue, and obeyed its summons, she leaped into the eddying flood and sank from sight.

The captain stood with his eyes fixed on the spot where she had disappeared, as if paralyzed; and the men at the oars sat breathless. Then there was a void space, as if time paused, or a minute was stretching to an hour. On this, a shout broke forth from the deck of the ship, not from one alone, but from many; it was no single thought; it was the swift, impetuous impulse of all, "Save her!" "Save her!" And the man at the wheel was heard to say, "They'd better be quick about it, too, for there's a breeze coming."

That cry broke the spell; and dipping their oars into the water, they rested over the spot where she had plunged, but nothing which bore the semblance of humanity was visible; the strong, eddying current had drawn them under, and in a tide so turbid that it seemed impossible to see any thing below the surface.

Yet there they gazed — all gazed; how intently, how fearfully they gazed, while slowly pulling the boat down the river! At length Elery saw something playing in the rings of an eddy; a bubble or two broke on the surface; he thrust down his hand, — it was the hair of Flora, — and in a moment she was drawn into the boat, still pressing her boy to her insensible bosom.

In taking them on board, the child's hat and Flora's shawl had fallen off, and lay floating on the surface, which one of the men seeing seized to draw them after, when Elery said, "Throw those things back! they are chattels; but I have made up my mind that these forms are not — so help me, God!"

The Muse, during those agitating moments, had forged ahead, for the wind had come fair and was freshening; yet she was not out of hail, and seeing his ship's name roll full on the breeze, Elery called, "Mr. Jones, strike the signal! I would not have that seen now, by these landsharks, for our best bower, though Hope leaned upon it!" Then tremblingly unclasping the arms of the mother, and taking away the child, he laid her on her face along the quarter seat of the boat, with her head and neck drooping over the afterthwart.

Thus leaving her, he took the boy across his arm, and, inclining his chest, the water trickled from his mouth and nostrils. In a moment, as the flow subsided, he pressed the child's nose so as to close the passages, put his lips to his, and went through the action of breathing, three or four times, into the drowned lungs — bracing firmly against the breast, when he drew back the air, to start up the natural motion. Then drawing another deep breath from the atmosphere, he repeated the expiration and the pressure again and again, until the boy begain faintly to catch his breath and to whimper; when, opening his eyes, he commenced crying — so it became evident that he was safe.

They had then reached the ship; but as the companion ladder was an impracticable way with one so helpless as Flora, and to rig out a chair would cause delay, they immediately hooked the boat to the tackles. Seeing this, as their anxious faces were all bending over the bulwarks, the men sprang to the falls, ere the order to do so was given, and ran the freight up to the cranes with a will. Leaping on to the rail, the instant that it was within his reach, Elery clasped the lifeless form, and, bearing it to the deck, placed it on the trunk of the cabin; when, turning to the men who were pressing near, he said, "Fall back, boys! I want air; and don't stifle the child, either!"

Quickly thereon he proceeded to treat the asphyxia of the mother as he had done that of the son; and frequently he repeated the action without sign of reviving life, until he became so exhausted that he thought of calling for assistance. But, as he paused and looked around, they all stood so mute and motionless, and with so despairing an expression, that the yet latent force of his nature was aroused, and he bent with new energy to his method of resuscitation. So working, for a brief time, he thought that he felt a muscle quiver! In a moment there followed a slight shudder of the frame; then a low gurgle — a groan — a convulsion!

The sailors started at the sound, and many of them listened and looked with bright tears coursing down their bronzed cheeks, and the hearts of all were softened and touched with tender compassion. Yet, as she gave fuller signs of life, their feelings changed and their brows knit, for the lion within them was rousing, at thought of an oppressor who could be more dreadful than death.

Flora had, apparently, lost sensation so soon as to have had no struggle with the King of Terrors; yet she came back to consciousness slowly, falteringly, and by the gate of pain.

When Elery felt that she was out of danger, he took her in his arms, and, carrying her below, laid her in the upper berth of one of the starboard state rooms — that being the windward side; and spreading some blankets over her, he opened the port, that she might feel the fanning of the westerly breeze; and telling Francis to watch by her, and call him instantly if he saw any change, he passed out and ascended to the deck.

CHAPTER XXIX.

Play with your fancies; and in them behold,
Upon the hempen tackle, ship boys climbing;
Hear the shrill whistle, which doth order give
To sounds confused; behold the threaden sails
Borne with th' invisible and creeping wind.
SHAKSPEARE.

THE first thing which attracted the captain's attention as he reached the deck was the boy, who was lying down in front of the hencoop stirring up the fowls with a belaying pin, and crowing louder than any of them, while his wet clothes were smoking under the fierce rays of the sun.

But the sailors were all looking at the spot where they had made the rescue, which was then nearly a mile distant. For there, some minutes before, even while they were hoisting the boat to the cranes, the hounds had come to a stand, and, foiled and panting, were awaiting their masters; though at this moment two or three of them, having slid down the bank, were swimming off from the shore as if attracted by the shawl and hat, which, floating, were still circling around in the eddies of the current.

"Francis," said Elery, as he turned his eyes that way, "pass me up my spyglass."

As the steward laid it in the captain's hand, he inquired with a jerk of his neck to the starboard, "How is she?"

"She's breathing short, sir, and wheezes some, but I guess she's coming round, sir."

"I hope so; but you must keep a sharp lookout."

On this he raised the glass to his eye, and, having brought

it to bear, said, "Yes, these dogs are after that hat and shawl, for I can see where they float, and they are heading for the objects. There, they grab at them — it is a shawl! and they are trying to jerk it from each other as they make for the shore. There stand Luff and Trim, with their tongues hanging out as long as pump-spouts! and they are snuffing the air and looking right down towards us as if they knew every timber in the Muse by the smell! There come three or four horsemen struggling out of the bushes and up the bank. One is Bill Frink! which is just what I expected, when I first knew the voices of the hounds. There, they dismount, and pull the dogs out of the water. Now Bill takes the shawl — he spreads it out and shows it to the others as though he knew it — I can almost hear him swear! — There, he slings it off into the river. Hark! I believe that I did hear him say, 'by thunder,' then; or else it was something about going to college! Now he's watching us — now he's looking at Luff and Trim as they run down the bank towards us and back again to him — he understands! he's pointing to the ship and speaking to the others — I can certainly hear him swear now! — There, they swing into their saddles — and there they go up the levee at a round pace with the dogs stringing along after them."

The captain closed his glass, and began walking to and fro on his quarter-deck; and though not fast at first, his pace fell slower and slower, as if his limbs were getting entangled in the thread of his thought. While moving thus, Fred came up softly behind him, and taking hold of the spy-glass, which was poised in the pendent hand of the sailor, closed one eye and squinted at the brass shove an instant, when, discovering nothing that particularly interested him, he danced back, and resumed his performance at the hencoop.

Elery, however, was too much absorbed to notice the manœuvre of the boy, or observe the smiles of the sailors. But at length he turned to the mate and inquired, "How fast do you think the Muse can sail, Mr. Jones?"

"Well, I believe we have crowded her fifteen knots, sir."

"Then it shall be done to-day, if we can find wind enough; and there's a pretty stiff breeze now well on the quarter, and it is pricking on every minute; but we must pack the canvas on to her; so put out a whole suit of weather studding-sails aloft, for we must look for most of the wind over the tops of the trees." And turning to the men he added, rather unusually, as they had overheard the order and were dispersing to the duty, "Now bear a hand, boys, and let's see how quick we can get them on to her."

As they sprang to the work, Elery said to the man at the wheel, "Tom, keep her as close to the eastern shore as you can, and not get out of the strength of the current; for this shaggy forest will take all the wind out of our lower sails if we don't give it a wide berth."

"Ay, ay, sir," answered the steersman, as he gave her a spoke or two more of weather helm.

"Francis," said Elery, stepping towards the companion-way, "what time is it below there?"

"Ten o'clock, sir."

Then looking up, the captain said, "Lay out, lay out aloft there! reeve your halliards and rig out your booms — be lively!"

"Ay, ay, sir," came ringing down and echoing from the deck.

Taking a turn along the quarter, he was soon back by the mizzen rigging, and looking aloft he cried, "Hoist 'em up; sway 'em taught; that main-topmast studding-sail isn't half up;" when quickly glancing to the helmsman, he said, "Tom, let her come to a little."

"Ay, ay, sir, there she comes."

"Stand ready there, men," said the captain, as he saw her luff; "have your turns all off. There she shakes! now work lively. There, belay all that. Give the fore a small pull, Mr. Jones, while you're about it. There, make that fast. Keep her off now, Tom; there, steady! Now coil away your rigging, clear the decks, and let her slide."

As every thing was done that could accelerate the flight and complete the fashion of his ship, Elery walked along by the coop, and, stooping down, took Fred from his play, and held him up in his arms. The boy drew off a little from so strange a face so near his own without his consent, although a warm and heart-felt smile lit up the manly features, and, bracing one of his small fists against the captain's shoulder, while his eyebrows drew down and his lips quivered, he asked, with half-reproachful accent, "Where be my mother?"

"Do you wish to see her?" inquired Elery, in a tone of voice so tender and touching that it startled the sailors who were near, and who knew him only through the decisive emphasis of command. Yet, strange to say, it was a spell of power upon them, more potent for the handling of that ship, in the hour of peril, than aught or all which they had known of him before.

"Yes, I do," the child replied; "I want to see her right away."

"Well, then you may," said Elery; "and we will go down into the cabin together, and see if we can find her."

As they turned to descend the stairs, Fred wound his little arms around the neck of the captain, as though he had tested his quality, and felt that he might entirely trust in him. So they went down where the mother lay.

When they had reached there, Francis, who had continued to keep his watch, stepped softly away, and ascended to the galley.

They found Flora in seeming slumber, and apparently free from pain; and when the child saw her so lying, he relaxed his hold, and, looking on her and then on the captain with a smile, said, in rather a ringing tone, "Mother be asleep."

But that familiar and heart-opening voice had power to break the spell and unseal the sight; although, but a few brief moments before, the dread shadow of the eternal curtain was upon it.

Seeing her closed lids struggle to open, Fred cried, "Mother, where you been?"

On this the eyes of Flora, looking out so bewildered at first, began to gather light, which in an instant flamed into intelligence, and overflowed her face with a smile. Then came a quivering, and a slight agitation of the muscles, as if the will was once more assuming sway. Thereupon she slowly and feebly lifted up her hands — her arms; when the captain gently laid the child within them, and she drew him to her lips, to her bosom, while Elery, whispering, "You are safe here," stepped out into the cabin; yet paused a moment there to brush a tear from his cheek, as though it were some weakness, rather than the evidence of noblest emotions, ere he ascended to his hardy crew. As he came on deck, he cast his eyes aloft, and then looked over the ship's side with evident satisfaction.

While he stood on the weather quarter, looking at the clouds, Mr. Jones, walking along near him, asked, "What do ye think of them to'-gallan'-stu'n-sail booms, sir?"

"O, they're good wood, I believe," Elery replied, turning his eyes on them; "although they are not quite so straight sticks as I thought they were. They appear to be pointing down river."

"And it's my guess that they'll be goin' there soon if they ain't taken in," the mate followed up with.

"Perhaps," replied Elery; "and when they go we'll rig out new ones, for this ship has got to show every rag of canvas to-day which she can carry; and I want to see those booms break, as then I shall know that we have found all the wind we can use."

"You'll have that satisfaction shortly, if I'm any judge of spruce poles; for it looks to me as though that fish was a leetle too heavy for the tackle. There, look o' that! see him spring!"

"That was rather a screamer of a flaw," the captain replied, with a half-doubtful smile; "but it's smooth water, and you will find your neck aching before they snap, if you undertake to watch 'em."

"But why do ye want to drive her so, sir?"

"For a number of reasons, Mr. Jones. But chiefly because we have a valuable cargo on board; and most particularly on account of our having one or two things which were not in season to be entered on the manifest, and therefore they require despatch; for, before the sun goes down to-night, we shall see a 'high-pressure' in hot pursuit of us, or I'm no judge of signs. When those horsemen left the spot where we spoiled their sport, they started for New Orleans, with a determined purpose; and they will go there in an hour and a half from the time they left, unless they meet a steamer on the way that can do the work, for there are planters along the whole route, and many of them will eagerly give their best horses to the service, which they regard as a common defence. Consequently in two hours from that time, they'll be in our wake at the rate of sixteen or eighteen knots, at which point we may have about forty miles the advantage; and it is not an inch too much, for by my reckoning she will be so near us at that, before the sun sets, that we can hear her pant! And if we keep this breeze, or even get more, we shall be able to see the smoke of her wrath, from aloft, by four o'clock. So you perceive that prudence, safety perhaps, says, 'Carry on, until every thing cracks again!' Then, too, we are loaded just right for sailing, as we are a few inches by the head, and the Muse only drops her quarters, as if crouching to spring, when you press her — which brings her about on an even keel, the true condition for great speed."

Standing by the mizzen rigging — the mate having crossed to leeward to clear his mouth and take a fresh quid, wherewith to ruminate the conjectures of his captain — Elery called, "James!" This was the sailor who had pulled the bow oar in the rescue.

As James approached, he appeared to be less than twenty years of age, with a fresh and bright countenance, a small and agile body, which was dressed with that careless neatness that makes the sailor's costume the most pleasing of all.

On his coming quite near, the captain said, in a low voice, "I want you to lend me your best blue jacket, the one with twenty bright buttons on a side, and the trousers to match; also some shirts, — white ones, mind, — with a black ribbon to tie the neck, a black belt, and that sennit hat which you made, and take them down to my state room."

The young sailor turned away with a pleased expression playing over his face, and entering the forecastle, he, in a few minutes, having filled the order more than full, conveyed the clothes to their destination, or, rather, to the place designated.

Soon thereafter the captain descended; and, as he passed on to his quarters, he heard a pleasant prattling, that seemed to remind him of something; on which, he opened his locker of private stores, or the medicine chest, and, taking out a decanter of brandy, poured out a portion; when, having filled the glass with water, he entered the apartment of his passengers, and said to Flora, "I have here a draught which I ought to have thought of before; but, if you can forgive me this time, I will try not to be caught napping on my watch again."

Flora looked into the countenance of the sailor, so full of generous purpose, and still radiant with the light of a noble deed, as he said this; but her heart was too full for speech, so that her eyes overflowed, her lips quivered, and her shoulders heaved; when, stretching forth her hand, she clasped Elery's iron palm, — gauntleted, as it was, by his glorious calling, for any and every emergency, — and, burying her face in the pillow, wept aloud.

The sailor also wept — wept silently, wept great drops, like the first of a thunder shower; and every drop so shed seemed to choke his utterance; he thought soothing words, but could not say them.

The child, hearing the sobs of his mother, turned away from the port, where he had been intently watching the flying shore, with all its waving woods, and, nestling down, worked his little arms around her neck, and kissed her cheek again and again in silence. Yet as she appeared not to notice his caresses, he said, "Don't cry, mother; what be mother crying for? Don't cry any more, mother." But seeing that she still continued on, with increased rather than diminished emotion, he lifted up his head, and looking at the captain, said, "You kiss mother!"

There was high-swelling agitation and awe, even, in that scene, which the child, if he saw, must wait many years to fully feel and appreciate. For notwithstanding Elery's lips had joined hers, so recently and so closely, in the process of resuscitation, that stage had passed now, and they seemed to him as unapproachable as the immaculate stars.

However, the proposed remedy aroused the weeper. When, withdrawing her hand, she stilled all visible emotion, and, with an expression of countenance such as only great deliverers can win or appreciate, said, "I thought to thank you" — and then the tears flowed again; yet, in a moment, and with a faltering voice, she concluded, "but now I fear that I never can. To be a slave no more! O God! can it be? Never again — never!"

To this the sailor tried to reply — tried many times; and at length he said, "You need not fear for your freedom; when you are a slave again, I shall be; and your tears are more expressive than any words — they've swept down on me like a tropic storm. It's the heaviest blow I was ever out in, so that I'm completely waterlogged, and don't feel like making a single move to get seaworthy. If the swell rises any higher I believe I shall go under."

Veiling her eyes, Flora said, "It is so noble, so marvellous, so much more than I dared to hope, that in climbing to thanks I am swept down by tears; for I am very weak, and I hope that my deliverer can wait till I am stronger."

"Yes, forever! But your weakness — it was that thought which led me in here with this brandy and water; so pray oblige me by rising up and drinking it. I think that it will do you good."

Flora, after a moment, did as he requested; but as she swallowed only a part of it, he placed the remainder near the bed, and left her, saying, "I must go on deck now for a short time, and hope to find, on my return, that you have finished the draught."

As he came up from the cabin, Mr. Jones said to him, "I have just thrown the log, sir, and she's only going eleven knots. I thought she was slipping easier than that."

"How should she, when her lower sails don't get wind enough to straighten the tacks, except by flaws?"

"It's more likely to be the muddy water; but I guess she'll keep out o' the way of any bloody tug they can start from the city, at that rate."

"She may — yet there's still a long stretch of river ahead; and, until the Muse takes a white bone of the Gulf in her mouth, I shall spread every pinion for flight. And you must send a man aloft, occasionally, to see if there is a smoke-cloud astern, and after four o'clock keep one there."

Just then, the steward passing from the galley, the captain said, "Francis, what has become of your dinner?"

"It has been ready some time, sir. The men have got through a long while ago, sir."

"Well, you may set it on, now, and we will eat at once."

"You've no occasion to say *we*," said Mr. Jones, "for I staid my stomach in the caboose more than an hour ago. I don't wait till this time when there's grub cooked and I've got a jackknife in my pocket."

To this the captain replied only with a smile; when, looking aloft a moment at the booms and skysail masts, — leaning like trout rods to the darting, dying beauty of the brooks, — and casting a furtive glance over the taffrail, he disappeared from deck.

CHAPTER XXX.

'Twas twilight, and the sunless day went down
Over the waste of waters like a veil,
Which, if withdrawn, would but disclose the frown
Of one whose hate is masked but to assail.
BYRON.

SEEING the table spread, as he entered the cabin, and observing the child, — who had resumed his watch at the port, — Elery said, "I want you, my boy, to come to dinner now." And stepping to the door of the state room, he inquired, "Will mother have something to eat also? But — and I should have attended to it before — you must change your wet clothes; and, as we are where female apparel is scarce, you will be under the necessity of accepting something a little different."

So going into the after state room, he returned in a short time, bringing the suit which the young sailor had furnished, and, laying it down near her, inquired, "Do you feel able to get up now?"

Looking at the clothes a moment with evident embarrassment, Flora replied, "I hope to feel stronger to-morrow."

"Then you must take dinner, or I fear you will not."

"I should like something to eat, if you will be kind enough to bring it in to me," said she, with a faint smile; "and, if you please, you may take Fred to the table."

The boy stretched out his arms at the word, and Elery, gently receiving, placed him by his side, where he soon felt at home. Thenceforward the past was as nought to the elastic child; the present was all.

Having dined, the captain still remained, leading Fred to ask questions, and answering them to his particular satisfaction and the delight of the mother, who was near enough to hear all, when the man at the mizzen-topmast-head called out, "Smoke astern!"

On this announcement, Elery ascended to the deck, yet without hurry, and hailing the lookout, inquired, "Is it a steamboat?"

"Ay, ay, sir," cried the sailor; "I think I make her out. I believe I see her smoke pipe, sir."

Thereupon Elery swung into the mizzen rigging, and, going up eight or ten ratlines, looked long and intently. Then, slowly descending to the deck, he walked musingly along the quarter for some time. At length the pitchy billows of smoke from the pipe of the tug caught his eye where he stood, and glancing up, he said, "Aloft there! Come down." And, turning to Mr. Jones, he continued, "Thank God that we have got clear of the woods, and night is coming, with clouds to help; and, do the best they can, it will be dark before they reach us. Yet it will be close work, and they may lay us aboard; so you must call the men aft, as I have something to say to them."

When the sailors had gathered near him, Elery said, "I summoned you because it is evident that we are pursued, and in a way which may lead to extra duty. In the rescue of the morning we have broken the laws of this land, and our straining sails are witnesses that we desire to interrupt still further their execution. Yet I cannot find it in my heart to back a single cloth of canvas; on the contrary, I would see it swell to the wind until it can bear no more. And, if that will not save those whom God has committed to our protection, if the pursuers overtake and attempt to grapple, I am for resistance. I have reached that point; and, if you feel as I do, we will meet them with arms, and defend the fugitives with our lives."

But observing their eager faces, he added, "Don't shout, boys; there isn't room here! wait until we open the Gulf. I see that you are ready to stand by them to the last gasp, and I am with you; so we must prepare for it by seeing that those four-pounders are well cleaned and loaded; and, James, you go down with Mr. Jones, and get out the cutlasses, and give them an edge."

As they went below to attend to the sharpening of the "boarding brands," Flora looked out of her state room — for she had heard some of the words of the captain — and, seeing the mate take out the weapons, inquired, "Do you apprehend any danger?"

To which that officer made answer, "There's a steam-tug comin' down, which looks as though we're chased; and, if she overhauls the Muse, and is sarcy enough to grapple, I rather guess there'll be a leetle bit of a fight."

By the time that the warlike arrangements were completed, the dimly seen sun had set, and it was growing dark apace — for in that latitude the twilight is short.

At length down came the night, which made visible the flame of the lighthouse on the point of the Pass; and soon the ship began to feel the motion of the Gulf, and, gracefully bowing to its greeting, seemed to press on more ardently, as if she heard in the voices of the waves the tones of loved companions.

There, too, right in her wake, grew ever louder and louder the sullen roar and crashing tramp of the swift pursuer, and redder and redder glowed her eyes of fire, out from their iron lids.

The winds wailed through the cordage of the Muse, but all human sounds were hushed in grim expectancy, as these brothers of yesterday were about to grapple unto death because that the Higher Law, having been rudely and wantonly aroused from its embers, had illumined the darkened mind to the assertion of its supremacy.

On the first intimation of danger Flora had arisen from her couch, disrobed, and put on the young sailor's apparel; when — with the addition of the dirk, which she placed in her belt, and upon the hilt of which her left hand rested — she ascended to the deck and stole unobserved, under the protection of the friendly darkness, to the weather quarter and to the captain's side, where he stood watching the wrathful approach of the smoking, panting foe.

At that time they had reached so far down as to open the South-west Pass, where the greater rake of the wind, blowing across the current, had set in motion a chopping sea, which the long ship disdained to notice. But when the steamer came ploughing into the "rip," it tossed her like a clam shell; so it became evident that in a sea way, with the breeze then blowing, she might look for the Muse's tracks in the morning, yet her sheeted form would have glided beyond their vision.

"She has gained nothing for the last five minutes," said the captain; "if any thing, we drop her; but she will smoothen her water shortly, and then she'll come down on us like lightning! She's not more than three hundred fathoms astern now, and when she strikes over this 'rip' she'll leap nearly that distance; so have those guns wheeled to the weather quarter, and clear away the ports; and, Jack, you take charge and direct them. James, you see that a match is ready, and await my orders. Mr. Jones, give out the cutlasses."

Seeing that the person who stood beside him — whom he had taken to be James — did not start, he looked round rather sharply, when, discovering that it was Flora, and observing her hand upon her weapon, he said, "Do you get up for *this*, when you thought yourself too weak to take a seat at table?"

"O, I am stronger now, and you must let me stand where

you stand, and strike when you strike; for I should scorn myself if I thought that I could shrink from my own battle, believing, as I do in my inmost soul, that extreme resistance to their force will be just."

The sailors heard her ringing words, and there was not one among them all but felt that he would give his life for her, in that impending struggle, as freely as he would drink a glass to her health, when, on leaving the ship, he can gain the license of the shore.

At that moment, also, there was a slight relief from the strain, as the ship, being in smooth water, was evidently drawing ahead fast, while the steamer was in the roughest part of the passage.

But little time elapsed, however, before the tug stood steady on her keel; and then it became apparent that she was putting out the uttermost of her strength to close with the chase; for smoke, like storm clouds, rolled above and to leeward, while the blaze gleamed and darted from the summit of the pipe, as if it were the hand of the Olympian, launching his thunderbolts. So on she rushed, bounding.

Then, breaking through all the din, arose the fierce barking of enraged dogs! and Flora clasped the captain's arm, for she knew, as well as he, the voices which so pursued her steps on that terrible morning. Then there came sharp, quick growls, as if they were pulling down their prey; and then half-choking sounds, seeming as though they ravined blood! Men, also, were seen rushing down the stairs, and moving swiftly before the fires, and massing together with shoutings and cursings, and springing and striking at the same time, as if they wrenched off the dogs or beat them down! Yet the boat rushed furiously on, and was within three times her length of the chase.

"Sight your gun!" shouted Elery, "and level just above the

fires, dead on the boilers! she comes no nearer without answering — be ready with your match!"

On this, he brought his speaking trumpet to his lips, to hail her; but ere the wild, defiant tones struck their ears, the boat opened midway through all her length, like the yawn of a volcano's crater! shooting dark masses and myriad fragments high into the air — some gleaming red, all tipped with flame! And rushing after it came a crash, a roar and rolling thunder of explosion, which, cracking the bending booms, and shaking the Muse in every spar and timber, made the "Father of waters" quake in his lowest bed, and flee, trembling, through all his marshy passes!

As the last splinters hissed down and were quenched in the flood, to the dazzled eyes and deafened ears of the appalled watchers, the place where, a moment before, the steamer had strode over the sea with steps so mighty, seemed as dark and silent as the grave — they could discern no vestige of wreck, hear no voice of any "strong swimmer in his agony."

Thus shielding the fugitives, and those who gave them "aid and comfort," came the thick bosses of Jehovah's buckler — so struck and pierced the dread shaft of the unseen Avenger!

To the benumbed ears of the spectators how deep seemed the stillness! as if Nature had said, "Hush!" and was listening for the footsteps of an earthquake! Slowly they recovered their sense of hearing, while the waves were heard as if sighing, and the winds moaned as though for the dead and the dying. Long, without speech, without motion, awe-struck and paralyzed, they stood; for they felt that a weapon mightier and swifter than theirs had transfixed the oppressor in his exultant hour, even at the moment when he was making his swoop on the wave-cleaving quarry.

Yet on flew the Muse, with a straining pinion; and, at length, the clouds broke and fled away from the brow of the night, when the moon came out to welcome and cheer them, and charm their recent terrors into pensive dreams. Then they looked up and saw the serene heaven glancing approval, from its myriad eyes, of their deed and their determination; while the west wind fanned and calmed their tumultuous pulses: thus the voices of nature, which are always in harmony with great actions, breathed over them a benediction. So sustained, they began to move about, then to speak low to each other, until, after a time, the tones of all came up to their natural pitch; when they talked of the scenes of the day, the fate of the foe, and the freedom of the sea — for the light, on the point of the Pass, was already on the Muse's quarter.

Soon Elery's voice was heard in command; when the broken booms and split studding-sails were secured, the yards rounded in, — as the ship was running nearly before the wind, — the larboard watch called, and the course given.

There, too, was the lamp of the lighthouse fast sinking in the waves; and, as Flora stood watching its fading beams, the captain, having completed his directions, came to her side. Seeing where her glance was directed, and observing that she appeared downcast, he inquired, "Are you sad then, after all, with the thought that you're leaving this land?"

"O, no! I was thinking how the word 'forever' is mingled up with the separation; and what deep and deadly wrong that must be which can change home into the most loathsome and terrible of places; so that every breath of wind, which helps to waft me from it, seems like the waving of the wing of some protecting angel."

"I am glad that you feel so; and I will take a parting glance with you; for when it vanishes behind the waves to-night, on me, too, it sinks forever! I value my freedom too highly to venture there again."

"That, indeed, is what I feared. O, you have made a great

sacrifice for me and my child, to-day! and would that I could express how grateful I feel, or that I could see any way of repaying you."

"Is not glory its own meed? You must not think that we have made a sacrifice; for, although the port is closed to me and the Muse, I consider it of little account, as the world of commerce is wide, and invites us to traverse every parallel."

"Truly, I hope and pray that you may not suffer for your devotion to me."

"Suffer! Why, you have this day ennobled me in my own esteem. It was your distress which flamed through the darkness of my understanding, and taught me how full of hell is that law which puts a scourge in the bloody hand, and clothes with irresponsible power the lusts of the oppressor. No! I would not have this day blotted from my memory, though with it might go all that I could desire to erase from that mysterious register."

Flora strove to reply, but her heart was too full; which the sailor perceiving, he drew her arm within his, and turning towards the cabin, they descended in silence. On reaching her state-room door she looked up, and, smiling faintly through her tears, gave him her hand, while she whispered a trembling, sweet good night, then vanished to her place of rest; there, night long, to sink to slumber, from which to be startled and hunted by pursuing dreams, until she awoke to feel herself cradled on the deep, and welcomed by the shouting waves to the wild liberty of the ocean.

CHAPTER XXXI.

Upon the gale she stooped her side,
And bounded o'er the swelling tide,
As she were dancing home.

SCOTT.

MORNING came forth in all its beauty over that summer sea, while the unflagging wind still bore the ship gallantly on her course. And when the sun ascended from out the waves, pouring the wine of life from an urn of gold, the glittering tide seemed a libation to the Muse; for, so far as the eye could range, she was alone on the deep.

At such times it is a charmed existence; a life in which the old Sea Kings revelled, and their lineal blood take to it as a child seeks its mother's breast. Of this strain was Elery; and he was up and walking the deck early, for his beautiful ship had laid hold of his affections, so that he never tired of watching her motions, or perfecting her finish; every rope's end was fashioned into beauty; every sail was graceful, and, when spread, swayed exactly to its true place; while the rake or squaring of every spar and yard yielded obedience and pleasure to his eye.

He observed every thing which related to her; not the minutest escaped. If there was a rope-yarn on her polished deck, his hand found it; and if her wood was marred in a single place that he could not reach, you might note him often turning to look over and down upon it; and, if he could get near it, you would see him sharpen his knife and pare it away with the tenderest care, as though he were smoothing the locks upon a daughter's brow.

As the Muse had captivated Elery at first sight with her beauty, so she had kept him by her singular excellence, and even made him proud of her qualities as a sailer. For, in speaking of her, he said, "The ship is not yet launched that can lap her weather quarter on a taught bow-line, or show her the rake of her stern-post when going large." Even a careless eye could not pass her without observing when riding at her anchors; while here she rose on the sight, a bright consummate flower, as if the waste ocean had unfolded into bloom.

The morning was far advanced when Flora ascended to the deck, for her late slumbers had been calm and deep, so that she awoke refreshed. When she emerged from the companion-way, she paused to look on the right hand and on the left, as it was the first time in her life in which she had beheld illimitable water; all around the glad waves were tossing their white caps and laughing in their play, while among them the Muse clove her way with swift and graceful motion, as some queenly beauty glides through the measures of a dance to soft and melodious music.

"Is this the sea?" said Flora, as the captain came near her; "the creature which I imagined to be so full of dread, so wild and savage of feature. Never have I seen the sun ascend so royally the morning, or take such complete possession of the world of vision. Then this is the ocean — and how gorgeous in its beauty! I can see now how it inspired Byron to sing so eloquent a song; and how as a boy he loved to wanton with its breakers and be borne like its bubbles onward. O, if this be a fair specimen of voyaging, my chief regret will be when I find it drawing to a close."

"It is a grand picture to a few, though not to many. I feared you might be hoping the cruise would soon end."

"O, no; yet I should like to know where we are bound, and when we are likely to arrive."

"If fortune favor us, the voyage will be completed in the course of ten or twelve days, in the port of New York."

But observing her face grow thoughtful, and then sad, he resumed, saying, "When I saw you come on deck you seemed full of the joy of the hour and the brightness of the season, and I was glad. Was it a mistake, or have you changed?"

"I was thinking," she replied, with a sad smile.

"I shall not object to that. Yet let me hope that you will not allow any thought of the future to press in and perplex you, for an escape which opened with such striking fortune I do not believe can darkly close."

"O, it was not the future, but the past, which rose up before me; and, although it can have none other than a sorrowful reception, I fear that neither the security nor the peace of coming years can wholly charm it away, —

'For I am as a weed
Torn from a rock, on ocean's foam to sail.'"

"I have imagined that yours was a sad, perhaps a terrible, story; and you must tell it to me some time. I should like to hear it, and besides it may be some relief to you."

"It gives me pleasure to feel that one who is entitled, by the circumstances which have placed us near, to know that story, has a right by nature as well; and, on some suitable occasion, you shall learn all which is mine to communicate — in some brooding night, or some stormy day, perhaps, when images of sadness more naturally possess the mind; but it is too sunny and cheerful now. Pray tell me, is *this* life on the ocean? Do you often see such a day as this?"

"O, yes, frequently. At this season of the year it is so common that it may continue through the passage as bright and cloudless as to-day; and you must cheer up and take the enjoyment which it offers. But, by the way, where is Fred? I have not seen or heard of him this morning."

"I left him looking out of that little round window, for I could not find his clothes; and I should think that he had tossed them all out through that place into the water, if my own appropriate apparel had not disappeared also."

"Francis," called the captain. And the steward making his appearance, he inquired, "Do you know any thing of the boy's clothes?"

"Yes, sir; I took them away, and have washed 'em, sir."

"Are they dry yet?"

"I believe so, sir; but I was just trying 'em when you called, sir."

"That's well; and take them below as soon as you have them ready. You took away the lady's clothes also, I suppose: are they dry?"

"No, sir; I hung them in the sun; there wasn't room in the galley, sir."

"Well, you will return those, when dry, to the place where you found them."

"But I starched 'em, and they'll need ironin', sir."

"Is that all? At the time when I noticed them last, they appeared as though some one might have to handle a palm and needle, for a watch or two, before they would be fit to set again."

"I can do that too, sir."

"See, then, that you do not discredit your ship."

On this Francis turned away, smiling, and disappeared in the galley; and Flora said, "I am afraid that he will find it a difficult task."

"It may be; yet I think he will repair them so that they'll do to spread when we go into port; and in the mean time you must wear such gear as our chests contain."

To this Flora made no reply, other than to look her thanks and her embarrassment together, as she turned to follow Francis below for the purpose of dressing her child.

She soon returned with Fred, who bounded away from the caresses of the captain, after a few moments, to see his old acquaintance in the coop. So Flora sat down upon it to gaze out over the ocean, and Elery, joining her there, said, "I have some books below, if you choose to read?"

"O, not now, not to-day; for this great volume, which is thus open to me, seems more novel and more charming than any book; it may tire in the perusal; indeed I have heard that it does, yet I cannot conceive how!"

"You talk like a true sailor. In all my cruising I have never felt what is called the monotony of sea life. I cannot read on deck while the ship is under way, for my attention will not stick to the lettered page. I try hard sometimes, but only to find myself lured off by the motion of the vessel, the music of the waters, or the whispers of the winds; and there is an exhilaration in the air, also, which will not allow me to sit still, but keeps me moving about deck. Yes, you may well prefer this page, for it is more suggestive than any that man has made, and flashes with gems which genius can neither quarry nor polish. Borne up by the breeze and illumined by the sunshine, the waves take captive my eyes, and lead me to hearken to their voices. Yet a first voyage will hardly win one so to view it, and most people will never do so; for great things improve on acquaintance only to those who can appreciate them. But do you not dread sea-sickness?"

"Never having experienced it, I have not the best knowledge of its nature; yet if, as I suspect, the feeling spring in a great measure from fear, I intend not to be infected with it."

"I have never thought of that as a cause; still there may be something in the idea, as the way to avoid the disturbance, according to my experience, is to offer no resistance to the motion of the vessel, but go with her, wherever she tumbles, without a thought; and I suppose, on the whole, one must have no fears in order to do that. Yet I have heard of those whose trouble custom could not alleviate, and no application but the firm earth would effectually compose."

So passed the hours; so came to her sight, for the first time, a tropical sunset at sea — the most gorgeous picture which Nature displays in the rotunda that bounds our vision; for it is only there that she unrolls all her banners to welcome the regal orb from his victorious march; only there that the King of Day, in royal profusion, strows choicest purple and gold over the heavens, as he retires into his pavilion of clouds.

On the third morning out, there was a cry of "Land, ho!" and Flora, hearing the words, hastened to the deck, when there it lay, in full view, with the green waves rolling and leaping around, as if to hang their white fringes on the rocks. And, inward from the coast, the pale blue vapor, with which night had clothed hill-side and valley, was rising and vanishing, or awaiting the touch of the sunbeams to be transmuted into silver and gold. Then, as the mist rolled away or melted into air, the palms — the fairest conception of the teeming earth — appeared waving their royal branches in the breeze, and seeming a giant race of Indian braves, decorated with their war plumes, and advancing through the fog to look upon the wondrous bird of the deep, as erst their ancestors gazed on the white-winged ships of Columbus. To Flora's mind the scene opened with all the freshness of discovery, while to her eye it gave a most lovely picture; for the Muse was just at that distance which made it seem

"A silent isle on which the lovesick sea
Dies with faint kisses and a murmured joy."

"This," said the captain, as he came to her side," is the most enchanting region that we shall see on the passage."

"O, there is a sweet witchery as we so approach! It seems as if coming to meet us. Just see how those waves leap up like dogs in emulous fondness, and touch their lips to the faces of the rocks! What land is it?"

"It is Cuba; and we are fast opening the Moro. If you will step a little farther to starboard you can see the Havana now, with the ships at their anchors."

"Which way is starboard?"

"Excuse me; but looking forward, as you do now, it is on your right hand."

On this she went over to the side indicated, with the sailor, and there lay the white city; perhaps the most charming winter residence on the globe, to him who wishes to give some time to communion with nature, as well as to luxury and amusement, and loves the sun's smile and the south wind's caresses.

"Keep her off, now," said Elery, turning, as he had hauled in closer than usual for vessels not intending to enter the port, that Flora might have a full view of the place, "and let her run down by the lay of the land."

"Ay, ay, sir," replied the helmsman; "there she goes."

"Square the yards; we're running dead afore it."

When that was done, turning towards Flora, he said, "That studding-sail has rather cut off our prospect. Suppose we walk forward."

Flora gladly assenting, they went on to the top-gallant-forecastle, where, standing in the shadow of the head sails, while the fresh breeze from the foot of the swelling foresail fanned them, they saw that island which Spain taxes, and the nations covet, set in the flowing girdle of the sea.

"What golden light floods all the landscape!" she exclaimed;

"how strange, how beautiful, and how exalted above any which I have viewed, the land appears! as in all my life I have seen no hill until now."

"The Lower Mississippi is not the most favored portion of the earth in some particulars," said Elery; "and I think myself, that this would be more agreeable to live on, or be buried in, than the reeking swamp which is known by the name of Louisiana."

But catching a glimpse where she stood of the sheeted foam that flashed on the parting waves beneath the Muse's prow, Flora stepped forward, and, leaning over, saw those pearly splendors on which the lover of the sea never tires of gazing. In a few moments she became so absorbed that she reclined by the anchor and said no more. So the sailor left her to gaze on the ocean's charms, the severing sapphire, the crystal and purple foam bells, with the dolphins dividing the sunbeams into all beauteous colors as they darted lithely on; and when filled with these to be borne far away on the wings of her musing.

Long was the view and sweet the dream, as when she rose up and looked around the island had nearly faded from the horizon — that island which we do not need now, and therefore, if wise, could see pass to any or every power in Europe without a stroke of war or even a breath of diplomacy. Indeed, when it shall become necessary to us, it will matter little who has possession; we can go and take it; and not that alone, for when the limits of my country are defined, when she completes her coronation robes, every gem of the Antilles will be found on the hem of her purple.

CHAPTER XXXII.

I will send his ransom,
And, being enfranchised, bid him come to me;
'Tis not enough to help the feeble up,
But to support him after.

SHAKSPEARE.

FLORA was fast becoming a lover of the sea; so that onward to the close of the voyage, when Fred had retired for the night, she might be seen taking her place by the cathead to watch the flying waves, the seething surge, and the phosphoric flames; and there, too, on nearly every time of her watching, as if conscious of their admirer's presence, came a shoal of porpoises, playing and snorting, and leaving long trails of fire in the clear blue water, as they darted onward or around in their races with the Muse.

One evening, when Flora had been looking over the bow some time after the porpoises had closed their wild play, and departed in a direct line for another ship whose dusky form was dimly seen on the horizon's verge, the captain went forward, and leaning down by her side, said, "I have come, hoping that now you will tell me your story."

Flora thought of it for a moment, and then, speaking low, so that her words were muffled by the moaning of the solemn sea, she narrated her early life, her love, her sorrow, and her oppression.

The sailor was startled into exclamation a number of times during the narration; and when she had fully finished, so that she looked up to his face inquiringly, he said, "It is more than

I had imagined, both in light and shade; in truth, the artist who adds any thing to the human form when he paints a devil, has but little knowledge of man!" and then, pausing a moment, in that diffidence which checks the admiration of the noble, he added, in tones pure from all tinsel of compliment, "and yet more shallow is the idea in drawing the outline of an angel."

Flora was so struck with the lofty and sympathetic nature of the sailor that she confessed to it in silence; and for a moment her heart inclined to him with the tenderest emotions.

But soon Elery said, in a low and even an agitated tone, as if he arose from much deeper thoughts, "You have made me a brother by your confidence; and, now that I have been admitted to an acquaintance with the past, let us glance towards the future; let me tell you my scheme, that which is in my mind for you to do when the voyage has closed. I have a cottage, pleasantly situated in the town of Greenville, not far from the city, which needs attention; and I want you and Fred to go out and live there, to take care of the fruits and flowers while I am at sea; for when I sail again I may not return in two years, and, if no one live in it,—and no one will unless you do,—I shall come home to find the fences carried off, the trees broken down, and all the vines torn from their trellises."

"Is there any thing that I can find to do there by which I may earn a living?"

"The care of the place will pay for the living; that, of course, is for me to see to and provide for."

Flora looked at him a moment, searchingly, when she said, "My way of life has been so secluded that I am ignorant in such things, and you must not help to deceive me. If you respect me, as I hope you do, you will not consult your generosity, but rather my independence, when, having given me freedom, you are about to open to me a fairer field and a higher life. I know that I can work, and it is my desire to win my support; so much so that to point out and help me on that path will be to answer my most constant prayer, and be remembered as the instrument of a guiding and protecting Providence. I shall know how to make labor welcome, for I leave that behind me, the memory of which will carry cheerfulness into toil, and link patience to hardship. Indeed, personal liberty seems a pearl of such price that all beside appears trivial. I would not speak too confidently, seeing that I have accomplished nothing; yet, if time and circumstance leave me strength and freedom, I hope never to be heard complaining."

"But you are not strong, and I think that you are not in good health; although, whenever I inquire, you say you are quite well. Then they who have not been accustomed to work will find any place difficult to fill, however humble it may be; and female labor is ill paid at the best, for the employments to which woman is restricted are over-full; consequently desirable situations are not easily obtained, and sewing is said to be wholly unremunerative, unless night and day are devoted to it."

"I have some skill with my needle, and it is such employment that I hope to find."

"Yes, and keep housed until you lose flesh and spirit, and become so diseased that the green earth shall be unwholesome and the fresh-bracing air a torture! Do you think I can see that after my bloody cold-heartedness in letting you nearly drown?"

"Did I? I have hardly had time to recur to it."

"Well, God knows I have! and I think always what a savage you must thought me, when I shoved my boat from your bleeding feet, and was deaf to your beseeching prayer. It seems to me now that I could never have approached or spoken to you again, if over that barbarous act there had not opened a prospect for generous purpose; and nothing can ever reconcile me to myself if you refuse the terms of my redemption. I will seek after no excuse for what I then did, as there can be no semblance of one except in the long catalogue of subterfuge. Yet this I may say, that, having no connections save those who were in easy circumstances, and being myself always in perfect health, and never seeing or suffering shipwreck, and no striking distress ever turning to appeal to me until this came, I had grown incredulous of great calamity. But, at length, I hope that I am awake; and will you say that I have aroused too late? I have the means and the desire to place you in a comfortable condition; and, seeing this as you should see it, how can you close against me the only path by which I hope to return to humanity?"

Flora was too much moved to reply; and observing it, he resumed, saying, "Grant me this and you will give me a motive for exertion. Then I can spread my canvas to the winds with a stout heart, and meet the shocks of life with an elastic spirit. The memory of those who have trusted in me will keep me on noble courses, and be as a magnet when all landmarks are lost and the stars obscured. This hope, let me impress upon you, is no impulse of the moment; it illumined my soul when I first stood beside you, in the hour of your weeping, with your hand in mine; and, sheer wreck as I was, it kept me above the waves! To that, as to a spar, I have clung; and can you now wrench off my grasp to see me go down in the abyss?"

On this Flora sobbed through her tears. "It shall be as you wish; I am satisfied; O, how satisfied! Was it selfish in me to doubt? How could I believe in such generosity in a stranger, seeing what I have seen! Yet how natural, how necessary you make it appear! so that I feel it would be ungrateful in me to refuse. Still, as the way of payment is all dark before me, your kind words make me both sad and glad; although I know that it is only adding a trifle more to the weight of obligation; for the fate from which you snatched my child and me is a mighty debt, not to be thought of now, or ever, without streaming tears, nor whispered save in benediction. But that is passed; while the sentiments which you have expressed to-night shine over the future in clear and cheerful light — making the clouds which hung there, and the distress that full likely lurked beneath their folds, to vanish away. It may be all weakness, yet my heart presses me to sanction your generous purpose."

"Say, then, that you accept my proposition, and make me strong again."

"It shall be as you will; and O, most thankful am I, to you and to Heaven, that my way is made so smooth before me."

Reclining there they were silent, silent long; and in silence the moon in the mid heavens flung around them the wan witchery of her beams, while the winds whispered, and the sea half suppressed its moan; though, after a while, the dull notes of the porpoises were heard, as they came blowing through the swell, to kindle their trails of fire around the softly-moving Muse — yet they heeded them not; for they were rapt and gazing into that interior, more august and glorious, world that opens beneath the many-colored bow of hope which is rounded by an Orb, that we cannot behold, on the passing clouds of life.

At length there were a few murmured words between them, when, rising up, they went to the cabin. And not one among all whom the proud and prosperous envy passed down, that night, either on land or sea, to the realm of dreams, with more chastened spirits, more holy purpose, or more grateful hearts, than did this sailor and this slave.

The weather continued fine until they were nearly up to Hatteras, when they had a heavy gale, with occasional showers; yet Flora, in rubber coat, boots, and sou'wester, kept the deck — for it was a new scene, and, to her, singularly attractive.

The wind was fair, but furious; so that the Muse had reduced her canvas to a short jacket, showing only double-reefed topsail and foretopmast staysail. The sea was not "wicked," although it ran high; so that, when the sun broke through the smoke of the Gulf Stream, — as it did frequently, flashing on the raving surge, and transforming the waves to emeralds, — it became a glorious as well as a thrilling spectacle. But the sails, which they were occasionally meeting or overtaking, were the crowning charms; now plunging or rolling deep down, — as their courses might be, — their bright sheathing gleamed in the sun almost to their keels; while far out on the slim yards the sailors, handing or reefing, were tossed to the clouds, or bowed to the billows; and, beneath and around, the brine was all white with the wrath of the warriors of the deep, at seeing their crushed ranks and cloven crests; yet on and over them rushed and bounded the ships, victorious as Murat when he broke through the hostile horde of mamelukes in the battle of Mount Tabor, thick sprinkled, but only with the blood of his foes.

Fred had long since become the pet and companion of the sailors, and took his rations in the top-gallant forecastle whenever he chose, which was nearly as often as the hour came round — for he was afraid that they would do something which he should not see. From the first day out he had watched the splicing of every rope and halliard, the tying of every knot, and the platting of every rope-yarn; and in oakum-picking he had come to be at home. But, more fascinating than all these, or aught else, his particular friend James, in his leisure hours, was rigging a little ship, an exact model of the Muse, and upon which the child's heart was set with absorbing admiration.

It being a stormy day, James was in the forecastle at work upon his craft, while Fred was closely watching as he set up the royal rigging, rove the braces, and gave the completing touches. At length, putting away his balls of thread and twine, and closing his knife, he held his vessel off at arms' distance, and took a careful and pleased survey of the miniature; which Fred observing, he inquired, "Be she all done now?"

"I believe she is, bub; her riggin' is all on, and set up."

"But where be her sails?"

"O, she isn't launched yet; it'll be time enough to bend sails then."

"What is launched, Mr. James?"

"Floatin' on the water, little freshy."

"Who did you make her for?" Fred further pressed, leaning in the sailor's lap and looking up anxiously in his face.

"I made her for myself," James answered, turning his glance aside.

"O, you've got a great big ship; and Fred want the little ship — he wants it dreffully."

"I've had a boy in my eye some time, who, I suppose, must have it, if he wants it as much as I think he does."

On this Fred's face drooped sorrowfully, while he glanced at the prize; which James observing, said, "If you want to see that little boy you must kiss me, and look for him in my eyes. Then you may ask him for the ship, if you think he'll give it to you."

So encouraged, Fred scrambled into the sailor's lap, kissed him, and looked sharply into his friendly orbs; when, in an instant, he cried out, "I know who it is; it is me! isn't it me?"

The kiss and kindly smile of James were full confirmation of his sight; and, while straightening his back to slide down from the knee, he said, "I want to go and tell my mother." So off he darted, through the rain, to the quarter deck. Catching Flora's hand in both of his, he swung round by that support, saying, "I've got a little ship, mother!" when, pulling her with fiery impatience, he added, "and I want you to come right away and see it."

James had kept his eye on Fred, and seeing him leading his mother towards their quarters, — though not very rapidly, as the motion of the ship made their course rather devious, — he called out to the men who were lying about, some in their berths and some on chests, "Boys, you'd better turn out, for the lady's beating up, and she'll fetch in here with a tack or two more!"

On that announcement the sailors hove short quick, catching up and hastily using little looking glasses and combs; while Jim hurriedly brushed the litter into one corner, with an old shoe, and turned a kid over it.

It was all pretty rapidly done, however; for, when Flora and Fred entered, they appeared to be deeply interested in ancient newspapers and tattered books, which last seemed to have done their chief duty as razor strops.

"There, mother, there 'tis!" cried Fred, as he drew her into the forecastle. And looking at James, he asked, "Isn't it mine?"

"Of course," replied Jim, smiling; "I said you might have it."

"It is very beautiful," said Flora; "but I am afraid, Fred, that you have been begging for it."

"I didn't! did I?" cried Fred, emphatically.

"Now tell me," said she, gently, "did you not tease for it a little, a *very* little?"

At that Fred hung his head to one side an instant; then taking hold of the sailor's hand, and looking up in his face with a smile which was dewy with emotion, he said, "I didn't much, did I?"

"No, not so much as I wanted you to, as I was finishing it for you."

"There, mother! isn't it mine, now? O, how I wish it had some sails!"

To meet that wish, Jack said, "I'll rig him a schooner next voyage."

This was the sailor who, having pulled the after oar in the boat, went to the steward, the first day out, — it being the wish of the men, — and requested him not to send any of the fresh provisions forward, but to save them for the cabin, except when the boy ate in the forecastle, and then some one would come for his mess.

"You are very kind," said Flora, "but I am afraid that Fred will trouble you, for he is here all the day; or at least I do not see any thing of him, only for a minute at a time, except at night."

"We want him here," Jack answered. "It comes near to making men of us, when we see a child who takes a liking to our ways and leans on our hearts; and, if you can let us have him, we'll adopt him, as the soldiers of Boney did the child of the regiment, calling him the child of the Muse — then we'll give our last dollar to school and clothe him."

By that time the tears were streaming down Flora's cheeks; when Jim, seeing them, said, "Jack, what do you want to talk about taking away a child from a mother for?"

"I didn't mean any hurt! We'd be tender with him. But, if we can't have him, she must let us pay for his clothes and schooling, and send us word by the captain how he gets along. And on the stormy days, when she thinks of the sea, tell him how we loved him; and let him come on board sometimes, so we can have a look at him. Then I wont be spending all my wages for rum and tobacco, to end in some bloody scrape: and I speak for every sailor here, if it was heart's blood she needed as well as money."

Under that Flora sank down on a chest, and, with her face buried in her handkerchief, was sobbing aloud.

More tender than women to a woman's tears, the sailors sat distressed but silent, and half doubted their own nobleness; when Fred, moving two or three steps towards Jack, said, rather defiantly, "What you been making my mother cry for?"

This misapprehension of her champion roused Flora; and, starting up with recovered strength, she said, "I know that you helped to save me and my child; and, in that armed and threatening night, I saw that you all were ready to die for me. Then I felt your heroism to be so lofty that I dared not trust myself to speak of it; while now you have risen so much higher, that neither time nor the grave can efface the memory of your kindness. I should think myself colder than the clods if I did not accept something of your proffered assistance; yet I want time and hours of composure before I can decide how much; for which I have no words; poor even in thanks, poor in all things save tears." Here she again melted, and gave free way to feeling; but, in a few moments, she stifled down her emotion; when, taking her child by the hand, she said, "We will go now."

Fred drew back, however, saying, "No, mother; I want to stay and see my ship and eat my supper! Now do let me, mother; for *they* want me to, and I want to, dreffully!"

Flora smiled on the listening group, as she released Fred's hand and turned to go; when they said, "God bless you!" and never did angel bear a nobler or a sincerer prayer up the bending heavens.

CHAPTER XXXIII.

She comes majestic with her swelling sails,
The gallant bark; along her watery way
Homeward she drives before the favoring gales;
Now flirting at their length the streamers play,
And now they ripple with the ruffling breeze.

SOUTHEY.

FLORA awoke early on the following morning, although she arose late; for her mind was filled with thoughts that charmed like dreams, yet were real as life, and wielded a power which held her long in the circle of their spell.

When, at length, she ascended to the deck, the sun was lord of the scene; while the clouds of the broken storm were torn and flying like rent canvas on the breeze.

The wind, still strong, had veered to the westward; and, having loosed the courses and boarded the tacks, the men were on the yards shaking the reefs out of the topsails, and, while doing the duty, were talking and laughing in a cheerful and unwonted way. Mr. Jones was speaking freely, and even ventured a joke with the second mate; while the captain seemed to have stooped down from his quarter deck to be familiar with all; and seeing Flora emerge from the cabin, he greeted her with the phrase of the hour, but more heartily than usual; when, taking her hand, he shook it cordially, saying, "You keep your room late on such a morning."

"It is, indeed, a very fresh and charming morning; although, to me, it is not more so than many that we have had on the Muse; and yet there may be something connected with it which I do not see or perceive, for I observe that every one appears exhilarated. You ought to have called me, if there was any thing more strange or beautiful than has been displayed to my view, so that I might have arisen to watch and enjoy it with you."

"O, you have not lost any thing worth sighing for; it will be just as good news to you now as it would have been two hours ago, and you will not have so long to wait. We're expecting to give our sails a port furl to-night; we're drawing near the end of the voyage, so that the hills will soon rise up from the sea to welcome us."

"I like to rejoice with those who rejoice," Flora replied, after a pause; "yet I have found hearts here that, being more gentle and warm than the summer air, have given me a place of rest and refuge which falls to few, even of the most favored, and one that awakes no wish for change."

"That is singular! as, I have no doubt, much of the cheerfulness of the men arises from the opinion that you must have been lonely and uncomfortable here; while now they imagine a very agreeable relief to be nigh at hand for you."

"How strangely we are misunderstood! Do you think there is a face here that I can ever forget; and the words which I have heard, can they die? No; the ship herself is a holy shrine, and sanctified in my heart as no altar can be. There is not a thing on all her deck that is not burned into my memory, and I shall feel her cradling motions all the days of my life."

"Neither can we forget! Yet it is near the middle of June; the time when the green earth is in its glory, and invites us to eat of its first fruits — while the ocean, after all, is but a desert, and the sailor a homeless wanderer on its waste of waters. Even those who think that they love the sea are filled with fonder emotions when their native land looms above it; and you must not be sorrowful while our gladness is for you; as there is not one of us but will lay bare a strong arm to make your path easy and your burden light."

"It is that which, most of all, oppresses me; as I know not how to refuse, while I feel that I can never repay. Even the sailors came near to breaking my heart last night with their generous words — words which I can neither forget nor repeat."

On this, as the tears were starting down her cheeks, Elery said, "You have no need to repeat them, as I know their substance now; for Jack came to me, after you had retired, and gave an account of your visit to their quarters in his own graphic manner. He said, 'The lady came forward with the boy this afternoon to see the ship which Jim had given him; and while she was there I thought it my duty to speak her, seeing that none of the officers were present, which I did as tender as I could; for, you see, we liked the boy, and she, you know, we wouldn't mind dying for. Yet, somehow or other, my words struck her like a squall; when I tried to take 'em back, and that knocked her on her beam ends; but the boy showed fight, and she righted. Then, after a minute or so, the clouds appeared to break and roll off, and she smiled on us quite sun-like.' There he paused, but soon added, 'I believe that's all, though I feel as if there was a good deal more of it; but I only come to speak about the way it was done; so I can ask you to explain it, and let her know we didn't mean any hurt.'

"This seeming to be the close of his description and apology, — for he was turning away, — I told him that I would take care that there was no misunderstanding; when he finished by saying, 'There's one thing, that I a'most forgot, which we want you to navigate for us, if you'll take the con of it. We've all voted to give what wages may be due us at the end of the voyage to her; and we'd like to have you draw the money from the agent and pay it over."

"Truly, I hope I am incapable of that; what, take all and leave them destitute — what will they do?" exclaimed Flora.

"O, they'll ship and go to sea again in a few days, I suppose."

"Do you think that I can be thus instrumental in driving them forth to wander on the desert, away from that green earth of which you have so feelingly spoken? No; in so doing I should feel as though I had robbed my protectors and benefactors."

"But would you slight their gift? I think that might be their interpretation of a refusal. You have had an opportunity to see something of the sailor's heart and hand, I know; yet you have not learned how lightly he values money; and let me say that I believe they take more pleasure in laying their earnings at your feet, in this way, than in all which they have scattered from many a long cruise. So you must not refuse a part of the offer of my men; and it may be both unwise and unkind to decline any of it, for I think that they consider the money so appropriated that they will never accept a dollar of it for their own use, whatever may become of it. However, I can talk the matter over with Jack, and learn what his notions are."

"I wish you would; as I feel that it will be ungrateful not to receive some portion of it, and cruel to take all; so *do* try to make them see how improvident they are." And, listening a moment, she added, "That is Fred's voice — where is he? for I believe that he is calling me."

"I think he's in the forecas'le — the sound seems to come from thence."

As the boy was nowhere in sight on deck, Flora walked forward, when again the word "Mother!" came tinkling on her ear; and, glancing up, she saw him looking down and laughing through the netting of the foretop; upon which she inquired, "How came you up there, my child?"

"Mr. James bring me up; we be looking for land."

"Have you found it?"

"Yes, there it be! Land, ho! Land, ho!"

"Where away?" called the captain, who had now joined Flora.

"Two points on the larboard bow," replied Fred, after a moment.

The sailors, then making it out from the deck, laughed and cried, "Land, ho! Land, ho!"

Not long after they raised Sandy Hook; and then a pilot boat, fair as some snowy albatross of the "Stormy Cape," came winging down. But the pilots, knowing the ship and the custom of her captain, only inquired after health, and answered the question of news, as their beautiful craft flew across the Muse's quarter; when, trimming their sheets aft, they stood to the southward, and soon seemed no more than a wreath of foam on the wave.

As the ship drew on, under a press of canvas, the hills appeared to be advancing to the very verge of the ocean, where, at length, they stood out bold with their feet in the foam. The gulls were sailing slowly along, and looking into the sea as if searching for something which they had dropped, or swooping down to recover it. Occasionally a land bird shot by on rapid pinion, as though, dwelling among the people, he had caught their unrest; like the fishermen whom they were passing, whose arms were in constant motion, although no fish nibbled the bait. The scene was getting more and more animated every moment. They were entering into the midst of a fleet, overhauling ships, brigs, and schooners; some naturally dull, while others, being commanded by old sea-dogs who shy, and fly from land, were under short sail; for having taken it in at twelve o'clock the night before, they had shaken out nothing after. So they went sagging up the passage towards the port, appearing as though they had blown away their canvas, or sprung half of their spars.

Yet further on, yachts, steamers, and sailboats were coming in sight and cleaving the swift tide in every direction. And rising on either hand were green slopes rich in waving grass and grain, with shadowy trees, and cattle upon a thousand hills; while the signs of industry were every where around. Even down to the very brink of the brine men were busily gathering the storm-torn tresses of the deep.

At last the port opened, and lo! under way, riding at their anchors or lying at the piers, there were a thousand ships displaying the flags of the nations — not in sullen folds and with whispers of defiance, but the true emblems of Peace, the proud tiara of all-conquering Commerce, wide waving over a diversified landscape, and crowning a varied beauty which no city by the sea surpasses.

Having been boarded by the customary officers as she came up, and duly permitted to go on, the Muse reached the pier, and made all fast, just as the sun's last beams were soaring from the spires of the city.

On landing Elery went immediately up town, to make some necessary purchases, as well as to notify the agent of his arrival; and, returning in the course of two hours, he descended to the cabin to find Flora in female costume, which was clean at least, and if you did not scrutinize too closely, quite passable.

Francis thought so, as he had done his best to repair it; and, when he saw her arrayed, he was surprised at his own success, so skilfully had she overfolded every imperfection.

"Well," said the captain, smiling, "are you ready to go ashore?"

"I am content to remain here or go any where you say; believing, as I do, that you will take the wisest course."

"Then I determine that we ride out to the cottage this evening; and you can leave on short notice, as it will not take you long to pack your trunks."

"That is very true; yet I am loaded with obligations which so weigh upon me that I find them difficult to carry."

"You are sad," said the sailor, "while my spirits are of the brightest."

Upon this Flora rose up, and said, "Let us go."

And the captain, seeing the tears starting from her eyes, drew near her, and whispered, "Do not weep."

But Flora, looking up in his face, said, softly, "May I not give tears, who have nothing else to give?"

"To those who can appreciate their value," Elery tenderly replied, "they are gems which so pay and overpay, that all other tribute seems poor beside them. I see that you cannot away with the thought of your indebtedness to us; but have you ever considered how much more blessed it is to give than to receive? You must permit us to enjoy that pleasure now, and the time may come when you can more than repay it."

"That is a fancy, a dream, a fond suggestion," said she, rousing, "which I will not look at too closely now, but leave it to shine, though it be only the mirage of a star in the dim heaven of hope. It is cheerful to think, to believe so; and I dare not frown away so welcome a consoler. Let us go; but where is Fred?"

"We shall find him with the men."

Thereupon they ascended to the deck; but it was all silent, not a sailor to be seen, as Francis had told them that the lady was about to leave. So Flora called, "Fred!" when he came running from forward; but he came alone.

"Where are all your shipmates, my boy?" inquired the captain.

"They be away out there," Fred replied, pointing towards the forecastle. "Mr. James, Mr. Jack, and all on 'em."

On this, Flora, looking up to the captain, said, "I must see them a moment before I go."

"I'll speak to them." And going to their quarters he looked in and said, "Come, boys, the lady wishes to say good by to you before she leaves the ship."

After a moment one of them replied, "You go, Jim; you and Jack; we can't — we don't know what to say."

"But she wants you all to come; and will you refuse a woman her parting wish? Come, heave ahead!"

So out they came, — for the captain's last words sounded like an order, — and followed him to the companion-way, where Flora and her child were standing.

"Do you think," said Flora, as they gathered around her, "knowing, as I do, that many of you I may never see again, that I could leave the Muse without taking your kind hands and saying farewell? you who have done so much, O, how much! for me and my child. I was stripped of all which makes life desirable, and so driven to despair that God alone can know how low and wretched I was; from which condition you saved me, to strow my path with peace and plenty. O my friends, I feel the greatness of your service, and I know the set phrases of thanks; yet I cannot say them, as I see that your generous natures shrink from such words — only this, that I can never, never forget you."

Pausing a moment amid her emotions, she gave her hand to each in turn, and, speaking kind things to all, separated, saying, "God bless you."

Jack, from diffidence or accident, was so situated that he

was the last to receive her hand; and, while it rested in his, he said, "Mine is a hard hand, but it is strong; and it will work for you, or fight for you, so long as its strength lasts; and so says every man of the ship's crew."

CHAPTER XXXIV.

His feeling wordes her feeble sense much pleased,
And softly sunk into her molten heart:
Heart that is inly hurt is greatly eased
With hope of thing that may allay her smart;
For pleasing wordes are like to magick art,
That doth the charmed snake in slumber lay.

SPENSER.

THE elegant, fashionable, and apparently fascinating atmosphere into which Aurelia, pressed by circumstances or blinded by desire, had chosen to enter, as the one wherein she could most fairly and fully unfold, was striking, chill or stormy, through her heart, and doing its legitimate work upon her nature.

Had Aurelia expected too much? If by temperament she was ardent and exacting, she was also capable of the deepest tenderness and the most single devotion; while Featherstone, as his gloss wore quickly away, showed himself coarse, capricious, indifferent, and at length overbearing and tyrannical.

With a lively faith in the design of nature to throw a never-fading splendor along the path of love, Aurelia could not avoid the conclusion that she had missed the way; and that too, irretrievably! She did not dream that she herself was partly in the wrong; she thought only how fatally she had been deluded. Though deeply moved, she yet had no sorrow for her own sin, but was nursing a rebellious spirit; so that she soon came to look upon the joy of others with something of displeasure, during the height of which there flashed up full many a keen or scornful thought that she did not restrain, and which showed but too clearly the bitterness of her own disappointment.

And, in truth, she had some cause, although Featherstone had only taken the common course of young men of wealth and leisure, such as keeping a fast horse, and having "fast" friends, and going abroad for pleasure, and coming home to sleep; which last, however, he did with great quietness when not questioned as to the where, and why, &c. If Aurelia ventured to make such inquiries he thought it an invasion of his prerogative, and answered accordingly,—at such times, reflecting more on what he had done for her than of that which he had neglected to do; and this was so natural to him that he always believed himself to be the aggrieved person.

When there is bitterness in the heart, opportunities are not wanting to vent it; so that, if Featherstone had even a whist party at his residence, which often happened, he was likely to be snubbed soon after it was over, on account of the noise of the game, or rated in the morning for the accidental injury and disorder of the room. But not being one of those who take a check of that kind quietly, although aware that he had gone wrong, he would protest; on which proceeding, after the first burst, Aurelia would restrain herself to silence; yet that was so unsatisfactory that he would try to spur her on, but with so little success that she usually turned from his fetid breath with more contempt in her motion, or looked at the wreck and soil with more pointed sneers.

But what need to say more than that love was not there? Unlike in taste, and dissimilar in aspiration, they had been lured together by false lights, which soon died down, to be kindled no more. He, indeed, cared little, for he had made other arrangements; but she felt the gathering darkness and the deepening desolation, and turned away into whatever of fashion would amuse or excite, only to find weariness and disgust at last.

Within such mire there is no wholesome rest, and yet out from it there is no clean path, except for the winged spirit. Ah! it is then that we turn to other days to recall early hopes, and, it may be, an early lover, with all his kind looks and tender ways, and place him beside the skeleton to which we are chained. *That* power of contrast will live with memory! Through her silent halls stalk the spectres of the wronged, to be our secret companions, however defiant or sorrowful their reception.

It was on a day after one of those social meetings — which had been more than hilarious, with a corresponding contempt and consequent imperiousness — that Mrs. Featherstone had engaged to take tea with Mrs. Summers. And although, when the hour for the visit arrived, she went forth from her door with a haughty step, she yet approached the plain house of the widow in a pensive mood and with a quickening pulse.

Mrs. Summers, having provided every thing which she fancied would please her guest, was on the watch for her coming, and received her with particular and unremitted attentions, and did not leave her except when the hour for tea had nearly arrived; then she made excuse and went out.

Yet Aurelia was not long alone, for in a few moments the door opened, and Park entered. He, however, was not to be taken by surprise, but calmly meeting, as though he had expected to see her, he greeted her politely, and, taking a seat, appeared as if in the presence of a client — no more; while he seemed to be waiting for the statement of her case.

Seeing this, and fully interpreting its meaning, Aurelia inquired, "Have you become so absorbed in your profession that you cannot find an evening, or even an hour, for society, or to meet the claims of friendship?"

"Men who follow my profession closely," replied Park, "can see little of society, and less of friends. They deal chiefly with enmity, and draw most of their support from it; indeed, it gives more freely than charity, and will go farther than the heart of kindness! If you wish to have some one search your ways and study your footprints, so that he may know them among a thousand on the remotest strand, and there, penetrating through all guards to your presence, draw your curtain, and peer in on your sleep, hope it not of Love; Hate alone can do it."

"It is painful to hear such truth, and from you. How different from what you were do you appear! I cannot believe that there has been such change in you."

"Have you not changed?"

"I hope that it is not in my nature to forget or turn coldly away from a friend — and especially the one whom I seemed to esteem the most."

"Am I to infer that you have the same feeling towards me now as when we used to walk together?"

Aurelia sat half reclining, her arm resting on the scroll of the sofa, while her fingers were nervously playing with the cross of the mustee. On this question her head drooped, her eyes were cast down so as to be almost veiled by their long lashes, and a tremor flitted over her features, when her hand wandered across her brow to shade it more completely, but it could not hide her tears.

Park saw, and said, "I regret that I have an engagement this evening; yet the business shall not detain me after nine o'clock. If you can remain here until then, I hope you will, as I have a desire to talk with you."

"I shall wait," she falteringly replied, after a moment, without raising her eyes.

There was no further conversation; and in a few moments, in which Aurelia recovered her composure, the tea bell summoned, when they arose and met the widow at the dining-room door. She manifested surprise on finding Park with her visitor, and said, "If I had dreamed that old friends were together I would not have called you so soon;" (she had waited ten minutes past the usual time;) "but I thought that Mrs. Featherstone was quite alone."

Park went immediately away, on rising from the table, and, returning at the time named, he entered into conversation with his accustomed ease where there were only two or three persons, and something of his old playfulness, so that it was after ten o'clock when Aurelia arose to go home.

As the attentive widow daintily touched her guest's collar, seemingly to arrange it, she said, "Shall I speak to John?"

But at that moment Aurelia was very busy with her bonnet; and Park, turning towards the hall, drew on a glove, and taking his hat, said, "It is growing quite warm, and is beginning to feel like summer."

"Yes," said the smiling widow, "I think you will find it a warm walk, yet a very pleasant one, I have no doubt."

"Will you join us?" Park questioned, rather than invited.

"I should like to have you do so," said Aurelia, "if it would give you any pleasure."

"Not this evening, I thank you," replied Mrs. Summers, looking roguish; "but at some other time I should be delighted."

Passing out, they turned up the street, when Aurelia accepted Park's arm timidly, yet hopingly. But, as he continued silent, she grew fearful, feeling that it was a pause in which to gather force or fix determination, so that she was not surprised when he said, "In the few moments that I was near you, on the night of your marriage, my heart was busy with scenes like *this*, as I thought that the curtain was falling over them which only sad Memory could raise again! You, at least, were voluntarily entering a world which I had dreamed was inaccessible to all save the chosen one."

Aurelia trembled, but replied, "I hope that I did not appear indifferent to you?"

"On that point I have no complaint to make. On the contrary, I hold that the mysteries and the music of the heart are for Love's ear alone; not only in the sunny moments of the bridal days, but throughout every succeeding hour. I, indeed, may not measure the feeling of others, yet I desire all of affection, of devotion even, that *one* can give, to appease my heart, and a true wife can ask no less!"

Aurelia clung to his arm in silence, and Park knew by the quick motions of her bosom that she was weeping over the picture. But, continuing his limning, he said, "I had dreamed of such love; and, although I have been forced to doubt its existence at times, still, in the depths of my soul, I believe in it, and still dare to think that, at some time in life, I shall meet it. It may never come, yet the fond vision shall warm me, and the hope shall keep me; for I know that God is just, and therefore that no longing of our nature is doomed to continuous disappointment, but rather to ineffable fruition."

"Do not, O, do not, talk thus!" she faltered imploringly.

"Have I uttered aught than what were once the hopes of your own heart? and why should they come to torture you now, unless it be that the brightest dream which life can entertain has been bartered away, or thoughtlessly cast out, to vanish up the sky a forsaking and accusing angel?"

"O, do not *you* turn coldly from me, in the hour of my need."

"If I can help you in any way, you may confide in, and still command, me."

Silently she wept, and clung to him, for some space; then came, falteringly and low spoken, a mournful story, as if of the wiles and glittering scales of a serpent; and then the cold coil and the fangs; so that there, where, had she been true to herself, she might have received the rich offering of most chivalrous affection, she came to implore assistance, or move that pity which is akin to love.

"When she had closed, and Park intimated that he saw nothing in her statement, sorrowful as it was, that would warrant success to the proceedings towards which she looked for relief, she inquired, "Is there then no escape from all this wretchedness?"

"We may pity and deplore your situation, but the law has opened no path by which we can penetrate to your rescue. Your husband may reel into your presence; he may invite the vile into your house, and 'make night hideous' with his orgies; he may cut you to the heart with the most cruel and insolent words; but, unless you can show the scars of his violent hand, no official arm can come to your aid."

"Then would to God that he might strike me, even though it should cripple or disfigure me for life! But is there no law against this direst counterfeit? no remedy at this stage of the fell disease?"

"There is none pointed out, except it be the gentlest forbearance or the sweetest submission," replied Park.

"If it be so, then there is nothing left to me but to steel my heart against all feeling, and, meeting taunt with taunt, bring on a crisis which may rend my chains. And O, when that hour shall come, which is now the height of my hope, life will stretch out a desert before me! Even you shun, and seem ready to forsake." Here she was interrupted by her weeping; yet, with an effort, she resumed, saying, "My other woes burn and madden; but *this* prospect is full of tears; it is more than I can bear."

"Did you not voluntarily raise the curtain on that view?"

"Might not your indifference ——"

But here her voice choked, and she leaned on him, so that he stooped to support her, (as they were in the arch of the doorway,) and said, with deep agitation, "Aurelia, can any reproach rest upon me, in your mind, in connection with this woe? Have I not suffered enough, but this must come also? O, there was a time, when, if I could have seen that you desired

'To say your sorrows in this bosom,'

or your joys, it would have opened like a city's gates to the one who had saved it from desolation, while strewing all garlands beneath your feet! but that time has gone down the unreturning tide."

"O," said she, still leaning upon him, "there was a time when I would have given my life for one hour of the bliss of those words!"

On this, Park gently disengaged himself, and said, "Did I turn away from you while there was hope? If, of late, I have avoided your presence, it was that I might go aside to meet my sorrow in secret places — for I had shrined you in my inmost heart; and when you were so suddenly and so astonishingly torn away, think you that I did not grieve and mourn over the slain love? O Aurelia! how have you wronged both yourself and me! wronged, too, in a way in which no reparation may come; so that all words of tenderness between us can now be only weakness and folly. Let us, then, here close the theme, as if it were a sepulchre — even though I bury within its damp, cold gloom the sweetest and the saddest of all mortal memories."

Aurelia was so shaken with this that Park bent tenderly over, and was about to put his arm around her, when, startled by Featherstone's ascending the steps, he turned away unrecognized; while the wife received the husband with the composure and bearing of Juno the protectress.

CHAPTER XXXV.

The trees were interwoven wild,
And spread their boughs enough about
To keep both sheep and shepherd out,
But not a happy child.
MRS. BROWNING.

IN the soft summer time a Sabbath in a country town like Greenville has peculiar charms; the long, quiet hours of the morning seem to be filled with the spirit of peace; the hum and the moan of labor are all hushed to sleep in the bosom of a day of rest; and the sun appears to rise up and stoop over the village with all that fond, ineffable tenderness which the great masters of the pencil have given to "Mary Mother" while she gazes on her wondrous child. And behold how still the leaves, the grass, and the blossoms lie, while they drink the dew which falls every night, a miracle of manna, for their sustenance! How grateful the odor, as if the air was filled with the ascending souls of flowers! and how dear, how emotional, the calls of the trusting birds which build their homes, and tell the tale of their loves, beneath the sheltering windows!

On such days, when all outward things are so touched with inimitable beauty as to woo the glance, and angels have so swung their censers through the heavens as to make it a luxury to breathe, who does not feel that Nature is our mother, and that her smile will unfold, in the bosom of a loyal child, a yearning after the Divine?

Flora, having arisen early, had drunk deeply of the overflowing fountains of the morning light, to be sweetly refreshed and made so joyful, by its influence, that her emotions and thoughts were praise and thanksgiving. Yet, amid this delicious musing, the duties of the hour had been so heeded and cared for that the table was set with plates for three, while "the sober berry's juice" sent an inviting odor out through the doorway and beyond the vine-clad portico.

Hark! It was just the faintest step, and the gate was very carefully opened; yet not so softly but that a quick and waiting ear caught the scarce perceptible sound; when the listener, rising up, met the gentle approacher at the door, where, with smiles and friendly words, she welcomed him beneath the portal.

They walked in together, and, as the captain was about to take a seat, Flora said, rather archly, "You ought to taste some of yon cherries fresh from the trees — they are sweetest in the morning." But, seeing that he was a little doubtful about going, she continued, "Now do go, if only to please me, and you shall have breakfast in a few minutes."

Elery, then comprehending, went forth, smiling, into the spacious and pleasant enclosure. There he found Fred, who, having become familiar with every nook and corner, came quickly to take the sailor's extended hand, that he might enact the proud showman to the happy owner.

"I'll show you my hens — I've got some hens! they be all black, with white caps on their heads. Where did they come from?"

"How should I know?"

"O, you know — my mother says you do;" and the sunny smile that flowed and rippled over his bright face, as he looked up to Elery, was rich in remuneration.

Having shown those, he took the sailor to see a bird's nest. But, as the bright eye of the bird shone over its rim, they kindly turned away to visit every part of the garden where nook, or thicket, or flower had struck the boy's fancy. Then he pressed him to eat of all the kinds of fruit, — whether ripe or green, — and especially each large and beautiful cherry which hung within his reach.

Soon Flora walked down the path, and, seeing them, she came beneath the shadow of the tree to receive the cherries, which the sailor gathered, as though it were her natural office. He, also, was equally pleased, for manly strength knows no deeper charm than to wait on a lovely woman who accepts the service with grace and kindness. After a few moments, however, they loitered, talking, into the cottage and to breakfast, where Fred claimed the eggs only that he might have the pleasure of giving them away.

Speaking of the cherries that were on the table, Flora said, "These are not so excellent as those I intended to set before you, for, seeing that there were larger and more richly-colored ones near the top of the tree, I lifted Fred on to the first branch, telling him to climb up and throw them down on the grass, — and you know that he can hold his weight any where with one hand; besides, you said that I must encourage him to climb, — which he did, while I continued picking, and thought no more of him until I heard him cry out, 'Land, ho!' as loud as he could shout. Whereupon, I ordered him down very quickly, fearing that he would raise the neighborhood. So you have not been treated to the choicest this morning, because Fred was a naughty boy."

On this the child looked a little embarrassed, and said, "Mr. James told me to say so."

"Well, he told you right, Fred; and you may say it, when you are on board ship, every time that you can see it," replied the sailor.

"I wish I was there now, if I can't speak out loud here!" But meeting the serious glance of his mother, he slid down from his chair, and, coming round, climbed into her lap to draw her ear down to his lips and whisper, "I want you to go too, mother."

"What!" cried Flora, kissing him, "leave this beautiful place, where my dear child has every thing that a mother can wish?"

"I wish I had my ship," Fred uttered, ruefully.

"You shall have her this evening," said the sailor.

"May I? O, good!" cried he, now full of expectation.

So glided the hour, like some fair, flowing stream just rippling to a breath of air; thus Flora was agitated as she contrasted the past and the present.

Before they separated from the table the bells in all the church towers rang out their sonorous song of good will to men — a type and far-off echo of the eternal harmony! So, indeed, it seemed to them as it arose on the free air, and chimed around their contented nook; while to all it was a peaceful voice, sounding along the hushed aisles of the Sabbath, and bearing joy to hearts which were true to themselves, as well as a summons to the indifferent, to join in the universal praise. Upon it there began to be a stir in the street, where many a grave face and formal tread, and many a gay ribbon and elastic step, were going up to the temple; and who may dare to say which was the more acceptable offering? for is not gladness the most grateful aroma of thanksgiving? Is not the happiness of the creature the design and the hope of the Creator?

On arising from breakfast Elery and Fred retired to a rural seat in the garden, where, having finished her morning duties, Flora soon joined them; and, finding the shade of the trees more inviting than the shelter of the roof, there most of the day was passed, where they could catch glimpses of that flashing sapphire dome which suggests the eternal temple, and disposes the soul to worship.

Gentle and cordial was their converse. Yet, after a time, when the day was declining, Flora said, "I saw that you brought out some books; let me go in and get one, and you will read to me."

"If such be your wish, I should like the first volume of Landor." This was a work which Elery had taken up in a bookstore in Glasgow on his last voyage, and was so struck with the passages at which he glanced that he purchased it.

When she returned he selected the Imaginary Conversation between Brooke and Sidney, and read; and then that between Marcus Tullius and Quinctus Cicero — strains of great and humanizing thought, in periods formed like diamonds, and finished to the translucency of that polished gem.

Pardon me, indulgent reader, if I linger long around this home of charity in a tender spirit, for to me it is a holy place; and I know of none where the grace of the All-giver has more manifestly descended. Peace dwells here and kindness aboundeth; while that love of which Plato dreamed is binding up a wounded heart and pouring its cheerful light on the path of the desolate. So Flora often thought, and the reflection was as a precious balsam to her hurts; while the presence of the benefactor poured it afresh, and the warm, low breathings of outward nature so heightened the charm and winged the passing hours that the day vanished ere they were aware.

It was one of those evenings of dark and crimson clouds, as if there had been battle in the heavens; and Nature, bearing the sun like a bleeding paladin to his pavilion, came with the pale twilight to mourn his dying, followed by the weeping shadows of night — a sadly solemn funeral procession moving along the landscape. This touched them with a melancholy which is sweeter than mirth, making them feel the worth of friendship, if not the witchery of love.

Fred appeared weary after tea; but, rousing up as with a new thought, and running to the sailor, he said, "Now where be my ship?"

"O, she's not far off," and, going out, he returned with her in a few minutes. It was a pleasant sight, for those who were looking on, to see how full the child's glad heart was, and observe how he hovered near, and many times spelled her name, — for Muse was lettered along her quarter, — and touched her tenderly, as if fearing to hurt her. Yet, after a time, becoming satisfied with handling, he asked to have the model raised to the mantel-piece, which was done; and never did ancient Roman place among his Lares a more significant object of worship than was that ship for that cottage.

Flora's eyes moistened when she saw the vessel; partly in sympathy with her boy, but chiefly because it called to mind a scene with which it was associated in her memory — the scene of the visit to the sailors' quarters. Whereupon she said, "I hope, Captain Elery, that my friends consented to keep a portion of that money."

"No, not a dollar; you could not force them to take it."

"Strange self-forgetfulness! What will they do?"

"O, they are not troubled; and, really, I think that they may be gainers by the gift. Certainly I am, for they've all taken a month's advance and shipped with me for Europe. And I'm very glad to inform you, also, that through their means you're now part owner of the Muse, as I have taken the liberty to buy a thirty-second portion of the ship on your account." When handing her some bank bills, he continued, "And there is the balance of the fund, which I hope you will use as freely as it was given. I made the purchase without consulting you, because I thought it necessary to attend to the business when I had a good offer; and I inform you of it now, thinking that I may not have another opportunity very soon, as *our* craft will be ready for sea to-morrow night."

On hearing this, Flora leaned her brow upon her hand, and the tears flowed in silence; and long they sat in that prayerful stillness, without speech, yet perfectly intelligent of each other, as though every breath had been a whispered word. At length Fred gave signs of sleeping; so that, after a while, Flora rose up, and taking the child, laid him in his bed.

On coming out, Elery arose to meet her; and, taking her hand, drew her arm within his, saying, "Let us walk in the garden."

Silently they moved over the path many times, while the soft south wind fanned them and calmed their pulses; and, when the waves of emotion had something subsided, Flora said, softly, "Are you really going away so soon?"

"Such are the orders. And, on the whole, I like the rapidity of the move, as business is good, and we want our ship to make money, so that you can have every thing which may contribute to your comfort."

"Have you any idea that I can ever be more happy than I am now? O, how this contrasts with what was! Even in the light of day I gaze from the window, I look from the door, for proof that I am not dreaming; and when I awake in the veiling darkness, it is long before I can believe in the glorious translation, so beautiful and so blessed is the land to which you have led me."

"If you could know how much protecting you has blessed and exalted us, I think that you would see how all the material aid which we have rendered is as nothing in our sight. Can you still imagine that you are greatly indebted to us, because such is the way of the world that they only name as a gift what they can clutch in their hands? Yet one would think that even the sordid might see that there are more glorious givers than Astor could be; when in his own counting house there was a clerk who fused in his fiery heart the victory of Botzaris into song, and gave it to mankind — among whom it will live, and be loved, long after the last vestige of the fortune or the munificence of his employer shall have disappeared. You, also, have given us the most ennobling voyage that we shall ever behold; and the memory of it will help to guide and keep us in all coming time. The earth, by its influence, has become more charming, and the sea more musical; while the stars shine brighter and awaken thoughts which they stirred not before. Hereafter I shall walk the Muse's deck, in the night's solemn stillness, amid pleasing recollections, and bear up against the furies of the storm, or, if it must needs be, go down into the ocean's bosom, with a more undaunted heart and a serener faith. Is it not something to have achieved all this from one action; and will you not let us make some poor return for it?"

It was many seconds before Flora could reply; but at length she said, "It is well. You have laid it open as I never saw it before, showing me how the charm of the gift reflects upon the giver; so that I feel it to be God's doing. He it is who touches right giving, and right receiving, with the hues of heaven, and breathes over them the same blessing. Indeed, I now see so clearly that I question no further, but accept the obligation cheerfully; and you may say to my generous friends, I receive their gift in something of the spirit in which it was offered; as your words have exalted me to feel, for the moment at least, like one who has bestowed great benefits. To-morrow did you say?"

"Yes, if the wind be fair, we shall go down the harbor in the evening, and perhaps put immediately to sea. But the months will quickly glide away, so that I shall soon be out here again; and, in the mean time, I want you, out of kindness to me, to take every comfort which money can procure. This is what I most earnestly desire; and, when I meet you at your door once more, I hope to see you looking as if you had found pleasure in complying with my wishes. Will you try to remember it, Flora?"

"O, how can I forget?" she faltered.

When feeling the motion of her grief, he said, as he gently pressed her arm to his side, "Do not weep."

Looking up in his face, she replied, softly, "You will not deny me the tears of gratitude, for they unfold the heart as the dew the flowers;" but noticing his wet eyes, she continued, "nor chide me for partaking of a luxury in which you indulge yourself so freely!"

The sailor brushed the drops from his cheeks as he moved towards the street, where, taking her hand, he whispered, "Farewell," when the gate closed softly, the door swung silent, and — he was gone.

CHAPTER XXXVI.

Alas! our young affections run to waste
Or water but the desert; whence arise
But weeds of dark luxuriance, tares of haste,
Rank at the core, though tempting to the eyes;
Flowers, whose wild odors breathe but agonies,
And trees whose gums are poison; such the plants
Which spring beneath her steps as Passion flies
O'er the world's wilderness, and vainly pants
For some celestial fruit, forbidden to our wants.

BYRON.

ALTHOUGH the changes of time are sure and unremitting, they yet come so softly that they give no shock, and leave scarcely a perceptible trace in passing; it is passion that ploughs and disappointment that harrows. Under such influences the queenly beauty of Aurelia began to grow dim and fade; even her voice was losing its music and becoming harsh: thus the silent Arachnes, that spin unrestingly in the brain, were clothing her with a new and a repulsive garment, which all the trappings of wealth could not hide nor its gems adorn.

It would have been surprising if Park had not seen so disenchanting a change. Yet, at first, he looked upon it with doubt and misgiving, though there came times when it struck him with amazement. Then, in thought, he would go down through all the past, and finding no trait of it there, he would say, "It cannot be." But when next they met, in the company of others, up would come the fact. So the vividness and certainty of present impression began to assert their power, causing to spring up in his heart, slowly, reluctantly, yet completely, the conviction that he had not only met with no loss, but some friendly Guiding Hand had led him bleeding from the path of danger. Thus, one by one, the silken fillets that bound Park to Aurelia were broken, as it were by a breath; and if it made him sad to see them sever, he at length rose up free, with a heart enlarged for humanity and a new-born hope for the future. He could then meet her as he met the world. She had taken her place among acquaintance, perhaps clients. Thenceforward she could be little more to him than a fact of human experience, to come forth on the tide of his thought to thrill or illustrate discourse.

"Well, it was singular," said Park to himself, when even the scar had disappeared. "I have had a narrow escape — how different she is from what I thought her!" But this, though a view which we are inclined to take, — it being the only consolation that may be left us, — is not kindly done, and more, it is not often just; for we are such creatures, and such victims of circumstance, that we cannot say what one might have been under other influences. Indeed, it must be evident to the discerning that had Aurelia wedded Park instead of Featherstone, she would have unfolded into all womanly excellence, and those who knew her intimately would have wondered at the continuance of her beauty, while seeing many an occasion to commend her love-overflowing heart, her sweet, low voice, and night-long vigils by the couch of the sick and suffering. Truly, it was a sad misstep which she had taken amid that thoughtless revel; entering upon a path rosy to the sight, but thorny to the sense, where the air soon blighted her one season, even in its spring time; and thereon had followed the nipping frosts that deepened ever more into winter with its desolating blasts.

Park, having got his McRae case referred, was before the referees. They had been in session some days in the town of Greenville; and, it being the pleasant autumn season, the gentlemen were disposed to hear the testimony leisurely, and view the premises frequently; so that it was rather an agreeable diversion when compared with a trial in the city courts.

Mrs. Featherstone was also in the village, passing a few weeks with a relative. She had chosen that time because she took an interest in the pending arbitration, as it concerned her friend and bridemaid Annie McRae. She, however, saw Park occasionally, at some social meetings on account of the court. And, on one evening, as the case was drawing near its close, he walked down the street, when accidentally meeting her by the steps of the house in which she was visiting, he talked with her a moment, and, accepting her invitation, went in. It was not long, however, before he inquired for Mrs. Howard, when she came down. In a few minutes after, Miss McRae and a Miss Graves came in, and they had scarcely entered into conversation before the bell rang and the Rev. Joseph Frink was introduced. He was somewhat squat in figure, and still shock-headed, as when a boy, with features which indicated pugnacity rather than nobleness of purpose. And having recently returned from Europe, where he had only added to his coarseness and self-conceit, he entered with the assurance which this circumstance is apt to give to persons of his stamp.

If it made Park smile to see so much sounding brass, it aroused Aurelia to ring a few changes on him, as she knew that her cousin, and, indeed, most of the parish, thought him a great man. And, as he had not talked two minutes before he mentioned Europe, she, knowing their prejudices, inquired, "How did you like the opera?"

Mr. Frink, thinking to please her, and caring little for the opinion of those members of his church who thought it a dubious clerical taste, replied, with evident pleasure, "It was capital! O, it was magnificent! You can know but little of the scope or of the art and appointments of the musical drama unless you witness the performance in Paris or Milan."

Slightly annoyed by the inopportune calls, Aurelia felt mischievous. And knowing that the parson had talked of his travels until they had become a bore, even to his friends, she said, "I should like to hear your adventures on the Desert, and your description of the Holy City."

Delighted with the compliment, the reverend traveller was just branching off, and had mentioned Egypt, — which seemed like sand in his mouth, and from which he would have passed on to Jerusalem by a route more tedious than that of the children of Israel, — when Miss Graves cunningly changed his course by inquiring, "Have you seen the Spanish lady, since you spoke to me about her, Mr. Frink?"

This being a subject on which he was inquisitive, he dropped the other, and bluntly replied, "No! Have *you* heard any thing new?"

"Mrs. Featherstone and I met her and the boy in a store this afternoon."

"Well, how does her color correspond with the report in circulation?"

"She seems to me more Moor than Spaniard; and I believe that there is negro blood in her veins. She is much bleached, I admit, yet there are certain indelible marks which cling longer than their skin. She has a peculiarly indescribable something in the eye that I never saw a white person with, or a colored one without. You may observe their finger nails, also, — and hers still retain the sign, — and you will find them marked with the unmistakable color which the sun of Africa engenders, and which neither clime nor circumstance can wholly obliterate."

"Perhaps she dyes her nails with henna," Park suggested. "It may be that she has escaped from some Eastern seraglio, as the corsair bore the favorite from the blazing palace of the pacha."

"She would have reigned in the sultan's, though like Lolah she was dusk as India!" said Aurelia. "And I should like much to hear the story of her life, for she is gentle yet strong, and has passed through that which develops character. Hearing so many conjectures about her, since I came here, I observed her attentively, and, whoever she is, she is no ordinary person. Her eyes have the serenity of truth itself, and her lips the firmness to utter it in any presence; while there is something in her carriage which reveals that, in extremity, she would front her foe with the heroism of Saragoza's maid. Did you visit Spain, in your travels, Mr. Frink?"

"O, no! no interest attaches to her institutions, comparatively; and she has no facilities of conveyance, so that, when one gets into her midst, he could not guess how long it might take him to finish her; and that is likely to be looked to by one who *did* the pictures of the Dresden Gallery in a day!" On this he swept his eye around the circle, as though he waited only to be crowned.

Taking the meaning of his expression, Park said, "You must read the works of art with singular facility! for to that hall Raphael has given the infant Jesus and the peerless Mother, on which canvas there is more Christianity than in all the wreck and relics of Jerusalem. Do you find nothing interesting in Spain? I could not see the Pyrenees and turn away from them. The very name of Iberia thrills me, for around it cluster the shades of Roman armies slain, and consuls led captive! Even her still seclusion has a charm that would lead me to linger with her muleteers through all the storied land. And where, down so many ages, has the blood of a nation flowed in such gallant and courageous current, adorned with knights and ladies who have inspired her ballads to be the best in the world; while their rent and ruined palaces, all tenantless though they are, would touch my heart like holy places. And if the Spaniard had not made his country glorious, if it were not immortal in the smile of Cervantes, the Briton has consecrated the Peninsula — every vale and mount are vocal with the bugles of Wellington."

"You must have been in Spain and staid a long time," said Frink.

"Yes, a very long time; for I was with Scipio when he gave up the captive maid, and went with Columbus when he sought the assistance of the queen!"

"Any body can travel in that way!" said the parson in a tone that savored of contempt for such ideal visitors. "But I have been on the banks of the Jordan, and brought home some bottles of the water!"

"That is something for which I have no thirst; as I hold it to be the initiatory stage of superstition, a link in that chain which weighs down so many nations, and chafes and scars well nigh every heart."

"I think that impious! for we use it to baptize with."

"I may be, in your judgment. Yet to so use it, is to lay the foundation for the worship of the wood of the cross."

This being too sacred ground for Mr. Frink to venture further upon with so profane a person, he made no reply. Or it might be that he saw, in a tray of cake and fruit, with which a waiter was entering, matter more worthy of his attention, as his digestive powers were still conspicuous among his faculties; yet in their exercise he had no sympathy with the plain and homely, any more than he had with those classes of his parishioners.

During the repast, Annie, taking a seat beside Aurelia, inquired, "Did you speak to the person whom they call the Spanish lady?"

"No, I did not; but Miss Graves found an excuse to do so, in asking her to join your sewing circle."

"Did she accept the invitation?"

"No. And it would have given you pleasure to have observed the manner of her declining, for the grace of her utterance I cannot convey."

"I desire to see her — particularly since she has so impressed you!"

"Then why do you not call on her? Were I living here, I certainly would gain her acquaintance, if possible."

"I have thought of it, and now I am impatient to know her."

The edibles being disposed of, the parson withdrew; and, soon after, Miss Graves and Annie took leave.

As they walked away together, Miss Graves inquired, "Are you much acquainted with Mr. Featherstone?"

"A very little; I have seen him only a few times."

"I hear that their union is not quite a perfect one."

"I do not see how it could be. Yet an unhappy marriage is an unspeakable thing; no vulture at the heart of Prometheus had so sharp a beak, or tore with such untiring talons."

"I do not think that she desires our pity, as her manner discloses her to be rather defiant than sorrowful, and her old lover is still attentive."

"He is here attending to my father's lawsuit."

"Perhaps she may be prosecuting a suit here; at least, marriage does not appear to have changed the current of her feeling, or called home all her tender glances."

"If Aurelia has found disappointment in marriage, my heart could bleed for her. But I have no sympathy for the idea that she finds in Mr. Park any thing but a friend."

"I have not said that she does."

"You certainly made such insinuations; and they are among the most hurtful of weapons."

Having then reached her father's gate, they separated; and, entering, she found him looking at plans and deeds; upon which he rose up, and met her with a smile and a kiss, for he had been musing of success.

Soon after the visitors had gone, Mrs. Howard having withdrawn, Park said, "You must have been quite taken by the lady of the cottage, as they name her."

"Yes, she pleased me much. Yet the child took my attention more, for he reminded me of Mr. Featherstone; not that their features particularly resemble, but their air and motion are similar."

"How old is the boy?"

"Four or five years, I should think; and I wish that you could see him walk across the store as I did; the likeness was in every joint!"

"I presume it was nothing more than one of those fancies which sometimes beset us, and may be traced to their causes; you were probably thinking of your husband shortly before."

"That, certainly, was not the cause; for no person was, and no one could have been, farther from my thoughts."

"Then you think the lady remarkable both for mind and beauty?"

"Yes, she really awed me by her manner, and pleased me as I listened to her replies to Miss Graves; for the words which she used were suited to the size of the thought conveyed, while her accent was native, and her pronunciation pure. Then, too, her features are fine, and so plastic as to herald and heighten her ideas. Even her color is scarcely an objection, as she is not so dark as many a northern brunette; but then their brown lies on the surface, while hers seems to strike up through, as Titian and Nature paint. And, over all, there is a veil of mystery, as if there were some romance in her story that may not be told.

'Yet who can keep in semblance long,
Or hide the key note of their song,
Or hope to mask in mourning weeds,
When glances tell love's secret beads?'"

Thereupon the conversation gradually died away, and they sat near each other, some minutes, in silence. Aurelia, in truth, paused through agitation; and Park liked to sit so, not thinking it necessary to be always talking or listening, if with discerning friends; yet he found such pleasure in congenial companions, that, when at leisure, he sought to be near one; this, indeed, was healthful to his nature.

At length, however, he arose to go, (they had been sitting in the back parlor, which connected with the front by sliding doors that were drawn partly back, and through which the visitors had entered,) and giving her his hand they moved on slowly together, when she said, "Why must you leave me now?" Seeing that he hesitated, she pressed as though she would retain his hand; and, turning, he suffered himself to be led to a sofa by her bewitching fingers, which were warm, agitated, and even convulsive; yet his thrilled to no emotion, warmed to no kindred pulse, were only passive and resigned; so that, in a few moments after they were seated in the dusky silence, she suddenly released her clasp of the lifeless thing, when it slowly slid down by her side. Yet, in an instant, she sighed over the loss! for she felt as if her last wild hope was taking its departure. With that thought tears came; and then a deep hysterical sob; when Park turned quickly towards her, and leaned so near that her head drooped in very weakness, or recklessness, upon his breast. On this he involuntarily drew his arm around to support her; but, her heart beating against it as though it would leap through her heaving bosom, he divined the nature of her excitement, and drawing off, said, "You must calm yourself, or I shall be obliged to consign you to the care of Mrs. Howard."

These words, spoken in a subdued but determined tone, and glittering all over with frost, transformed Aurelia to the coldness and rigidity of marble; and, starting up, she stood gazing at him as if petrified.

This swept painfully over Park's feelings; and, taking her icy hand, he said, tenderly, "Aurelia, will you permit me to be your friend?"

"*Friend!*" gasped she; and then laughing a bitter laugh, she caught away her fingers, again to regret it fearfully — for she was at direst strife with herself.

"Yes, friend!" replied Park; "it is too late for aught more. Think you that the love which was carelessly cast away can revive and return again?"

"Am I alone to blame that it was so lost to me?"

"Is any part of the fault mine? for you seem as if you thought so."

"Was it not wrong to leave me so long in doubt of your affection, so surrounded as you must have known me to be? yet I scorn all explanation. Friends! do you think that we can be *friends?* No, never! Where the fire of love has been spurned, and its ashes scattered, only hate can spring up!" and turning away she paced the apartment in tearless silence.

Park sat a few moments amid conflicting emotions; but at length, rising up, he drew near to her, and gently inquired, "Shall I go now?"

On this she came so close to him that he felt the breath of her words, and the despair of her heart, as she said, "Do you wish to part with me forever?" And then, "O Heaven, that I should still question!"

Park hesitated, while some sad drops of pity came; but, in a moment, he calmly replied, "That shall be as you choose."

"Then it is my pleasure that you go;" and on the word he departed.

Intense as was the gleam in Aurelia's eyes when she uttered those inevitably conclusive words, still more intense was the torture that followed thereon. Foiled, slighted, mortified to the utmost extremity, she threw herself upon the sofa, and spurned at the bitter and sickening thoughts which boiled up in her seething brain, and rolled burning through her rebellious heart. And full deeply, ay, pitiably, did she learn, in that hour, what many a beautiful but falsely-aspiring creature has found, and many a one will yet find — that love is its own most fearful and most desolating avenger.

CHAPTER XXXVII.

Bear welcome in your eye,
Your hand, your tongue: look like the innocent flower,
But be the serpent under it. SHAKSPEARE.

ON the following morning, the Rev. Mr. Frink called at the village hotel and inquired for Mr. Park. Mr. Frink had the politeness to call upon all distinguished strangers who visited Greenville, although they did not come with the expectation of such a favor.

In a moment the servant who received the order, returning, said, "The gentleman is in;" and Mr. Frink followed him to the room.

On being shown in, and seeing Park busy with his papers, he made an elaborate apology for the interruption, yet with the air of one who thinks his company the amplest remuneration. And drumming a moment on the arm of the chair in which he had seated himself, he added, "I have just received a letter from my brother in New Orleans, which I wish to lay before you, as therein he requests that I should see some New York lawyer and employ him to look after the matter."

"What is the nature of the business?" inquired Park, with cold civility.

"It appears that he has lost two slaves, a woman and a boy, both of them nearly white — the mother being about twenty-three, and the child four or five years of age. He believes that they escaped on a ship bound to New York, and probably are somewhere in this vicinity. He suspects so, because they formerly belonged to a man who lives in your city; and he supposes that they would naturally flee to him, as he is the father of the child. The names of the fugitives are Flora and Fred."

"Does your brother communicate the name of the previous owner?"

"I find that he cannot remember, exactly; but he thinks his first name is Anthony, and his last, Fetter— something, and what, he don't know."

"Fetter! do you say?"

"Yes; that is all I can make of it."

"The last syllable may be 'son,'" suggested Park; "or, at least, it would be appropriate. Let me look at the letter, if you please."

"It is written so badly that I am ashamed to show it. He used to do such things very well; but it seems that he undertook to chase the fugitives on a steamer, and was blown up in the scrape, losing an eye and parts of both hands; and this is the first business which he has been able to do since the accident."

"Does he give any particular instructions, or directions?"

"Nothing special; the whole letter is very indefinite. He simply wishes to have the matter looked after, and he will pay well — to do which, I may add that he is abundantly able."

"I think you must let me have the letter if I am to examine the affair with any reference to action."

"Well, I have no great objection, if you will observe secrecy with regard to the whole thing; for no one here knows that I have such a brother, and I prefer that they should not."

Park took the proffered letter, and, placing it in his green bag, said, "I will peruse it when I am more at leisure."

Mr. Frink inferred, from this remark, that it was time for him to depart; and, rising up, he said, "There are one or two public institutions in town, Mr. Park, which it would give me pleasure to show you, if you can find time to visit them."

"I am obliged to you; but I expect to close my business

here on to-morrow, and thereupon must leave immediately for the city."

"I hope we shall see you out here often, now that you have made our acquaintance. We think we have a very beautiful town, and we know that we have some of the solid men."

"And some of the showmen, too, from appearances," added Park.

"They do not belong to my parish. I have taken such frequent opportunity to preach against the vanity of riches as to keep down the ostentatious spirit among my flock."

"Then, I suppose, you find such preaching popular; and I have no doubt that, as they have no means for indulgence, the majority of your hearers like to see the more fortunate undergoing the penalty of success."

Feeling that his secret motives were rather too obvious to his examiner, (for no huckster in the town coveted money or the power which it confers more than he, so that all he could feel of love, even, appeared, from his proceedings, to be a kind of legal attachment to secure an estate,) the parson thought it best to withdraw without further remark on the subject; so he bowed himself out with a smile which was meant to be friendly, yet it spread out into obsequiousness until his face appeared flabby, if not foolish.

On leaving the hotel, Mr. Frink turned towards the cottage to make another call; for he was not slow of suspicion, or without curiosity, and sometimes indulged in them to an excess which was reprehensible. Arriving there, he gave quite an emphatic notice of the event, as he was a trifle perémptory; and on Flora opening the door, he bowed slightly, and said, "I am a minister of the gospel in this place, and thought it my duty to call upon you to inquire how you felt with regard to religion."

So announcing himself, Flora invited him to walk in.

Accepting a seat, he looked around a moment, as if taking an inventory, whereupon he said, "You have rather a snug place here, madam; much better than a great many of the lower classes find, and such as would make them thankful. Do you think that we are usually filled with so lively a sense of God's manifold blessings as is becoming such frail and perishing creatures?"

"I desire to be."

"No doubt, we all do; yet how make it manifest, unless we attend divine service? The meeting-house is the place set apart and dedicated to worship; and, short-sighted as we are, we may see that there can be no offering if the gift be not laid upon the altar."

"I have heard the glad tidings that there would come a time when every heart should be an altar."

"Certainly, it is so written. But I am an ordained interpreter of that word, and I say that the time has not yet come; and until it does come, the meeting-house is the place; that is the peaceful fold, aside from which there is no safety, for wild beasts rage without."

"It would ill become me to controvert the opinion of one who has been set apart to the sacred office. Yet I have seen two or three gathered together, in so kindly a spirit, as to hallow the place of their meeting — leading me to the conclusion that it is man who sanctifies the temple, not the temple the man."

"You speak of that meeting, madam, with too evident pleasure to have it stand to you for merit, at your final accounting. Sorrow here is the sign of joy hereafter; pleasure in this life is only the foreshadowing of punishment beyond the grave."

"I fear that I shall never be able to comprehend such a scheme; and to hear it urged would not help me to find out God, or strengthen my trust in his divine providence."

"Do you wish to be classed with infidels by the whole Christian world?" inquired Frink, while he darkly frowned.

"I see nothing in a name capable of leading me to do that which conscience does not call on me to perform."

"Well, I have done my duty," said the parson, who in reality did not wish her to come to his church; for if she was "colored," as to him she appeared to be, it was extremely doubtful if his society would allow her to sit among them. "But if you choose so perilous a course for yourself, you ought to send your boy to our Sunday school, and have *him* brought up in the way that he should go."

"I thank you, for I think that he would like it; and it would be agreeable to me to have him attend; indeed, I should have sent him before had it been requested."

"Then you must have him ready by nine o'clock on the next Lord's day, and I will see that some one calls for him — Miss Graves, probably, as on her way to the school she passes by here."

"I will do so with pleasure, as it relieves my mind from a point that has pressed upon it." And asking to be excused a moment, — as she performed her own domestic duties, — she passed out of the room.

Fred had been sitting very quietly in a little chair during the interview, with a small book in his hand, the pictures of which appeared to take his attention; yet he had not failed to note the expression of his mother's and the parson's faces, and draw his conclusions. Turning to him, Mr. Frink said, "Charley, you are to come to my Sunday school next Sabbath morning, and we will try to have you know something."

"I know something now, and my name ain't Charley, neither."

"What do you know, Fred?"

"I know my mother don't like you!"

"How do you know that, saucebox?"

"O, 'cause she don't look as she does when somebody else is here."

"Who else comes here?" insinuated Frink, sinking his voice.

"I shan't tell you, for I don't like you a bit!"

"Do not like me! Come here and see what a pretty thing I have in my pocket;" and his voice was very wheedling.

"No. I don't want a single thing you've got!"

Seeing that he could draw nothing more out of the child, the reverend inquisitor drew up to the centre table, and made an examination of Flora's books. There was not a volume among them but what came from some gifted poet, or some earnest and able inquirer; yet he found Byron, and put on a sanctified face; Carlyle, and seemed touched with fears; E——, and trembled with apprehension; P——, and grew scarlet with holy indignation! And as Flora returned on the moment, he said, "You have some very dangerous books here, madam! and when I think of the awful responsibility which attaches to my sacred office, I must say wicked, extremely wicked books!"

"Indeed; I was not aware of it; which of them have that reputation?"

So called upon, the reverend censor named them over with decisive emphasis.

Whereon Flora inquired, "Are you confident that you are quite just to those authors?"

"Yes, most certainly; for I have read every word which they have written; hence I know what I am condemning, and I say that no person can read them without being stained and corrupted, or led into fearful, if not fatal, error thereby."

"Have they stained and corrupted, or led you into error?"

This was so unexpected a turn, that Frink glared at her, while the blood flushed over his face; but at length he said, "With ministers of the gospel it is different. They expect to make great sacrifices, even their lives, if need be, for the salvation of souls. Therefore they are compelled, as it were, by Him who appointed them to the holy office, to examine this food for the mind, as the mother tastes of the cup ere she allows it to touch the lips of her child."

"I may not venture to reason with one so learned; yet it seems to me the principle on which you would exclude those works from the people is the same as that which induces the Catholic priesthood to withhold the Bible from the examination of mankind."

"No, madam, you are entirely wrong; for those which I speak against are bad books, while the Bible is a perfect and holy one."

Seeing that he had thus made an adroit escape out of the dilemma in which he had placed himself, by the habit of loose statement he had run into from rarely hearing or heeding a reply, he added, "This is an enlightened age, madam; women are presuming on an equality with men; but they will find that presumption is always a long way ahead of fact. They have no colleges yet; and how can they hope for any thing great until they have the institutions of learning which create it? I have no intellectual or spiritual graces that were not the growths or the gifts of my alma mater. When can *they* hope for such an incomparable mother? They may be nursed by an ordinary one, some day; but when they do we shall cease to protect them, and entering our field as rivals they will learn what life is. Now, we watch to supply their every want and gratify their every desire, for we have generously bound ourselves by law to do it. If, however, they persist in pursuing the rebellious course, they will finally have to contend with us for every thing."

"You are speaking of something to which I have given no thought; but is not your argument a defence of slavery also, in that it offers Protection as an equivalent for, or something superior to, Right?"

"Slavery, madam? I denounce slavery! Slavery is immoral, and I am a teacher of morals. No, madam, the laborer is worthy of his hire; if the servant earns money, he wants it; if I earn money, I want it; while it grinds both him and me, and all who have to toil as I do, to see the masters dashing out with splendid equipage, and rolling and revelling in luxury. And they would do well to remember, while it should be some consolation to all who mark their ways, and are free from their sin, that Dives and Lazarus exchanged circumstances when they changed worlds. I have denied myself molasses, madam, because it seems to me so like the the blood of the poor African;" and again he appeared as though he waited to be crowned; but as Flora did not condescend to do it, he turned and departed.

Immediately on reaching his bachelor apartments he lighted a choice cigar, without thinking that the leaves of the weed resembled the negro's skin, and were the product of his toil, for he loved tobacco as well as he ever did any thing; indeed, while inhaling the spirit, and puffing off the cloud, he had the air and look of a devotee in the presence of his idol. After the narcotic and poisonous plant had sufficiently soothed his restless and craving nerves, he wrote the following answer to Bill's letter:—

"GREENVILLE, *October* —, 184—.

"Dear Brother: I received yours of the twenty-fourth this morning, and immediately gave the business into the charge of a distinguished lawyer belonging to the city, — one being providentially with us, — who will give careful attention to it.

"I have just returned from a kind of parochial call on a woman and child, who have been living here in a very pretty vine-clad cottage for some time, and they closely coincide with your description of the runaways. The only difficulties in the way which I can see — and I have looked at the matter sharply — are, they appear too delicate and are too well bred for the class. But I know nothing about the case, although I believe that the boy's name is Fred, and I enjoin that no such idea shall ever be intimated, for you will see that, situated as I am, I can have none but the most secret connection with it.

"I hope you did not own the steamer that blew up in the pursuit; and I am sorry that you got disfigured by the accident. Your doctor's bill must cut deep; if you were only a clergyman now, you would escape without charge.

"Your grateful brother,

"Jos. Frink.

"William Frink, Esq.,

"New Orleans."

In the course of the evening of that day, the Rev. Mr. Frink called again at Park's room, and said, "I took occasion, after I left you this morning, to look in at the cottage of which we were speaking last evening; and, on close examination, I am inclined to the opinion that Miss Graves's conclusion is nearly right with regard to the negro blood, as they appear to me to be tainted with it; and they seem to tally almost precisely with my brother's description of those whom he has lost."

"If they should be identified as the same persons, what do

you propose to have done?" inquired Park, with severe accent and a severer glance.

"I believe it pertains to your profession, rather than mine, to answer that question, Mr. Park," replied Frink, with the look of a scared cur.

"Do you desire that an arrest be made and a trial had?"

"I do not wish to have any thing to say on those points; but I can write to my brother, and get his instructions."

"As that will probably be his course, I also wish to have nothing to do with the points. I cannot think my profession is under any obligation to commit a crime against humanity if it be sanctioned by statute; while ——"

"O, no, no, certainly not!" cried the parson, interrupting.

"While I thought that it belonged to your high calling," Park resumed, "to assuage sorrow; to let even the prisoner go free, who may be supposed to have broken a law which was enacted or promulgated for the well-being of society; and how much more those desolated ones whom the iron hand has crushed down to the grade of beasts of burden! Do you imagine yourself to be a teacher or even a disciple of Him who went about doing good? or of that One who struck with death those followers who gave only a moiety of their money to the common charity — can you believe that record and not tremble?"

"Have I done any thing wrong? Nothing was farther from my intentions."

"No, O, no! you are too cowardly to *do* wrong; you only suggest, you only subborn the deed."

"I do not desire that you should take hold of the matter, and I am sorry that I spoke to you about it at all; which I should not have done, had not my brother, to whom I am under deep obligations, written me concerning it. I moved at his suggestion entirely; and if you will return me the letter it shall be destroyed."

"Most willingly! But, if there should be any attempt to molest these persons, I shall inquire whose hand directed the iniquity. So you will bear in mind that, touching every portion of this discovery, I here place a seal upon your lips, which you are forbidden to mar even by a breath."

"I never wish to speak of the affair again, and I hope that *you* will not; in fact, I believe you are bound, in honor, to that course; communications to counsel being among the secret things of the law."

"Are you a client, or only a prowling witness? To *such* I shall make no promise other than this: that I hold you responsible for the safety of those persons, against all the arts of the kidnapping species."

The Rev. Mr. Frink said no more; but, placing the elegant letter of his brother Bill in his pocket, took leave without alluding to the public institutions in the village, or putting on the smile of the morning.

CHAPTER XXXVIII.

Who knows the joys of friendship?
The trust, security, and mutual tenderness,
The double joys, where each is glad for each?
ROWE.

THE bright season had just glided by, in which the hectic flush of the forest foliage betokens the dying year. The leaves were brown and sere, and went rustling down the breeze, or crackled beneath the feet; their life going out in an articulate monition of decay, as they joined the melancholy and myriad wrecks of summer beauty.

It was one of those autumn evenings when the frowning, cold, gray cloud-bank hangs along the east, waiting for the sun to depart ere it climb up to blot out the stars, and send forth its winds with whispers of winter. Yet these intimations of change, these moanings of the desolated year, are lessons of sympathy which are not all lost upon the air, but help to develop kindness and deepen friendship, thus favoring the growth and glory of man; so that, while the earth's pulse is still, it would seem as if the spirit of Nature turned in deeper and quicker current to the nurture and unfolding of her consummate flower.

Mr. McRae had won his case; and, having thus completely established his claim to a large and valuable estate, many, who had taken their titles from others and built upon the land, were coming to him to clear the encumbrance; and being generously dealt with, they were thankful, while he was more than usually serene and contented. Annie, also, was happy in her father's smile, and rejoiced in his liberality; for her heart was kind, so that it overflowed with sympathy towards those who suffered by the award of the law.

The cottage of Elery stood upon the property which had been in dispute, — that being the reason why it sold so low when he became the purchaser, although the sailor was not aware of it, — and Annie, fearing that the lady who lived there might hear of the change to her alarm or distress even, said to her father, while tying her bonnet, "I am going out to pass an hour or two;" when, folding a shawl around her, she left him to his evening newspaper and pleasant musings.

It was but a few moments after, that she passed through the cottage gate, and, upon her summons, Flora opened the door. Seeing, by the light shining from the sitting room, that it was a young lady who stood before her, she said, "Will you walk in?"

"I thank you; it would give me pleasure;" and, following her to the room, she found a cheerful fire on the hearth, which sang down the moan of the winds, and seemed to greet her with warm and inviting smiles. There was something in the tone of the reply to the invitation which touched the heart of Flora, and called forth her sweetest expression. Observing this, Annie added, while taking the proffered seat, "I came in to see if we can be friends — may I take off my bonnet?"

Flora's eyes filled with tears, for Annie's face was so full of tender and entreating interrogation, that it more completely opened her heart than is common to the longest course of trust and confidence; and she replied, "You have, indeed, taken me by surprise; for I did not dream that what I most needed was so near. A stranger in a strange land can hardly hope for that which is usually the slow growth of many years; and yet you lead me to believe in its possibility."

"Then let us accept the opportunity by trusting at once

with that unreserve which becomes those who have faith in friendship. For I, too, need a friend; as there come to my mind ideas, hopes, and aspirations which I cannot reveal to my father, — although he studies to make home dear and life delightful to me, — yet I long to breathe them to some one who will receive them with tenderest sympathy. Have you never experienced such feelings and emotions?"

So agitated and quickened to confession, Flora said, "My life has been one of great vicissitude. I have seen some of the darkest as well as some of the brightest days that ever blackened or illumined the path of mortal. I have been cast down, — so it seems to me now, — only to make my deliverance the more glorious; while impressing on my heart the infinite tenderness and the sustaining power of Him who leads us.

"I was tenderly nurtured by parents who were united by the ties of love; and, amid all the appliances of wealth, I was exalted by education to an acquaintance with the works of the great masters of thought. Yet thereupon I sank beneath a tyranny which made its first advances in whispers of affection, until I was not only sold as a slave, but 'bowled down the hill of heaven as low as to the fiends.' Then my deliverer came; and such a deliverer! I had seen kindness before; I had heard and read of sublime devotion, stars of glory all; yet this was as the sun in the heavens. I cannot, even now, make it other than seeming. I try to tread back on my own steps, when it appears to be some romantic and wonderful path, enchanted and brought down to earth by the gorgeous imagination of genius."

Thrilled to silence, Annie at length said, "We do, indeed, sometimes read of such exalted action; but it must be the height of life to have so realized it in the devotion of one."

There were more. One, certainly, was preëminent; still,

many were deeply devoted with their great hearts and hands as open as the day even to their own destitution! and not only for the occasion, for a week, a month, but even to this hour and beyond; so that I taste it in my daily food, yes, in the air I breathe — for I had ceased to breathe, and they restored me."

"You will not pause there: such glimpses only make me more impatient for your story; so that I may venture along the course, to see if it were possible for me to rise up as you have done: truly the difficult way is always the noblest; and dangers bravely met crown the brow once and forever."

At this point, Fred came timidly up to Annie, and put his hand softly in hers. She looked down on his sweet, upturned face, and, perceiving his desire, took him into her lap, accepted his kiss, and so tenderly returned it that he nestled near her, yet still kept his eyes fixed on hers: while encircling him with a gentle arm, she gave ear to the narrative of the mustee, in which she comprehended all, excepting names, from her school days with the Sisters of Charity to the hour when she arrived in the village where she was speaking.

Annie listened with lively sympathy, with tears, and with silence; and when the fugitive made a close of the tale, their eyes met, beaming with deep trust, but thrilling agitation; for the sea heaves high long after the storm has subsided. Silently clasping hands, they sat until calmness came, with smiles and words in the soft, low tones of returning serenity; on which Annie said, "I hope that you will continue to live among us."

"I desire to; yet it is all uncertain, as my home here hangs on one life, which the sea is liable to take any hour, and may have taken ere this."

"I trust in brighter hopes; but if any change threaten, if any trouble come, will you confide in me, that I may share the pain?"

Flora pressed Annie's hand, and replied, "My heart opens to your touch as if you possessed a charm by which to enter it."

"Then you must give me room there; and what is mine shall be thine, and that which is thine shall be mine; and if, perchance, this door should close against you, my father's house will open to you and this little boy as freely as to me; or if, by any vicissitude, we become poor, we can take a school together, and win that independence which we now enjoy as a favor."

Fred having sunk to sleep in Annie's arms, Flora took him, without awaking, to his place of rest. On her return, Annie said, "You have not told me where your deliverer is, or even how old he is."

"I do not know his age," Flora replied, smiling; "in truth, I have never thought of it before; but he cannot be much older than I am; and he is on the way from Europe."

"Do you expect to see him when he arrives?"

"Soon after, I have no doubt."

"I hope he will not remain long, to keep me away from you; for I found you, and you are mine."

"But he found me first, and may set up the claim of priority."

"Well, he shall not have you if I can help it."

"I do not think that he will contend with you; but, on the contrary, I believe that he would like to see you, and I wish him to do so very much."

"I am not quite certain that I desire to see him, for he is a hero; and they generally expect so much deference, so much worship, even, that they harden me into brass."

"It is not so with the hero of my story; he humbles himself even to me, and disparages his deeds so that they may appear of a less shining order. He insists that he is the great gainer, in that it has given sobriety to his thoughts, and elevation to his life. Yet, at first, I suspected that it was only said to lift from me some weight of obligation; but, on perceiving my idea, he bore it away as the flood bears whatever resists its sweep. I had, indeed, many times heard and read of the generosity of sailors; and I found them all and more than I had been led to believe. Still I cannot help thinking that the crew of the Muse, with regard to me, caught something of their self-devoting spirit from the chivalry of their leader; as in the most memorable actions it is always the case, so that Leonidas appears to be alone in Thermopylæ, and the single arm of Paul Jones seems to conquer the Serapis.

"Then, how dark it was — and what light flows over me now! I seem to have been driven out to pass from conflict to triumph. Even the fierce voices of the dogs grow mellow and musical as they recede; and the thunder crash that closed all reverberates in the distance like a morning gun which ushers in the day of freedom. Then came my first view of the ocean, and a ship in her glory; and I was spell-bound when I saw her casting great gems of sapphire from her, as though she spurned the gifts that would delay her flight. I even fancied, as I observed and was swayed by the motion of her career, that she had feeling for me, and flew on rejoicing that she was free, as well as the instrument of freedom. Not Columbus, when he bore home the offering of a new world, felt his heart more elate than was mine. The summer winds caressed me, the foam leaped up and kissed me."

"How differently trouble appears when it has passed!" Annie remarked; "and how danger changes its aspect when we look back upon its torn banner and trampled form! how it consecrates the life that we have lived, and arms us for the conflicts which may come! I desire never to forget that the fire which burns, is, at the same moment, testing and purifying, as the darkness that broods over many a human path is there only to form the background of a hero's picture."

Soon after, they rose up, and, standing near, they appeared of the same height, and strikingly alike in form, which they noticed with smiles and kindly words; and as they walked, with their arms intertwined, their motions seemed the same.

So crossing and recrossing the room, Annie, at length, said, "I came here, this evening, to see if I might do you a favor, or be of service in any way; and lo! you have given me the story of an Olympic struggle, with a triumph such as no wreathed Grecian has won! laid open before me a volume of inspiring life for which I must ever remain a debtor!—and is there no opportunity to make some poor return?"

"Have you not given me such friendship as to melt my heart and pour it into yours? so that I have no words to say how dear you have grown to me, Annie, (if you will allow me to call you so;) and whenever, hereafter, it may please you to pass within my gate,

'There is an eye will mark
Your coming, and look brighter when you come.'"

They continued walking without further speech, for their mutual understanding appeared to be complete; and when it is, presence satisfies, a touch can heal, and glances are revelations. Under the influence of friendship, for so brief a time, the cottage had changed from a quiet and secure, into a charming nook, where these two, together twined, seemed like the bright rings of some eddy wreathing and circling there, away from the surging current of life. As they thus moved through the silence, they heard approaching feet, then the bell; and, while advancing to the door as they had walked, the latch was raised, and the sailor entered — entered with kind words and a cordial greeting.

Passing on to the lighted room, Flora said, "This is my friend Annie, Captain Elery; and she has borne the relation so long that she knows all about me, and thinks she has learned much of you."

"You must be cautious, Captain Elery," said Annie, smiling, "how you believe in the picture, as she colors skilfully."

"Yes, I will be on my guard; and I owe her a little incredulity, for she was a stubborn doubter, even of me."

"You may forgive her that, for she believes in you now, heart and soul."

In the first tones and glances of these freshly-meeting natures Flora caught their fine accord. Instinctively she felt that some divine influence was mingling the subtler elements of a new creation, and, foreseeing the Paradise, on the moment she closed whatever of dream her own heart may have been indulging, and resolved at once to become its devoted guardian. Full of this generous purpose she quickly replied, "That is true, Annie, for my confidence is entire, like that of a sister's, and I trust that I shall be found equal to a sister's devotion. Indeed, that is my relation, by virtue of which I am mistress of this house and do the honors; so that if you will have the kindness to be seated, and inform me what refreshment you would prefer, I will try to procure it."

As she had directed her closing sentence to Elery, he replied, "Fruit is usually my first thought when I reach shore. Have you any?"

"Yes, and some which grew on your own plantation, and for that reason will have a sweeter taste."

Thereupon she brought out both pears and peaches; and, placing them before her guests, she said, "The pears I think you will approve; and if the peaches are not what they were at the time when I gathered them, you may reproach yourself, for they have been waiting and pining for some one."

Annie helped herself, saying, "I believe that I am fairly entitled to a part of these, as my father has a claim on the land where they grew."

"Is this Miss McRae?" inquired Elery. And gathering his answer from her smile and arch expression, he continued, "I heard before I came out of the city, that the case had gone in your father's favor; do you imagine he'll bear down very hard on me?"

"I fancy he may, if I tell him how luscious the pears are, and how long the peaches keep."

"But will you take such unkind advantage of the evidence which we have furnished against ourselves?"

On this Annie took one of the largest of the pears from the dish, saying, "I will take this home to him, that he may taste and be able to judge of their value."

Touched with her humor, Elery selected another, which was more perfect, and, handing it to Annie, said, "Take this one to your father, also; and say, when you present it, — if you will do me the favor, — that Frank Elery intends to call upon him, some time in the course of a week, for the purpose of perfecting his title to the cottage."

"It may be more for your interest to choose a small and hard one to send him, as I think that you will be surprised when you learn the terms of settlement."

"Perhaps so; but I purchased the estate at a low price, and you may say to him that the more a thing costs the higher some people value it."

"If that be your method of estimation, we will try to have you hold this place in particular regard." And, rising up, she proceeded to arrange her shawl and bonnet, saying, "I suppose my father is listening for my step; so, my friend," (here she took Flora's hand,) "I must leave you now."

"May I hope to see you again to-morrow?" inquired Flora.

"I know not how to refuse." And, turning to the captain, she added, "Then we are to have the pleasure of seeing you at our house soon, I think you promised."

"Yes, very soon; if you will allow me to act as convoy;" when, taking his hat, they passed out together. As they moved up the street, he said, "The pleasure of this evening has been beyond my anticipation, and chiefly because I saw that Flora had found a friend in you."

"I am sad with thinking how much more I have found than I can give," Annie replied. "She is a treasure; and I thank you from my heart for bringing her so near me."

"You cannot be more pleased with her than she appears to be with you, or than I am in finding that she has so fully confided in you."

"I admire her; for she is at once a mirror and a picture; now revealing my own hidden features, and now charming me with the depth and meaning of her own. Then, too, what a history is hers! Indeed, you did generously, you did nobly, in so rescuing her; and I honor the sailors, every one, for their continuing kindness and devotion. I long to see the ship even that bore her so gallantly away; for she speaks of her as a thing endued with life and capable of feeling."

"The Muse is all that she gives her out to be; but you must be cautious with regard to her praise of us, for we could have done no less; it did not rise above the line of duty."

"It may be so; for, with the noble, duty is a sublime height; it was all that Nelson asked, when he gave his last signal to the breeze, for he knew that it would call forth the utmost strength of the sailor's arm and heart."

"To have done well, even in one thing, will rift the clouds so that hope may shine on the storm which wrecks us. Would that I had had many such favorable opportunities, that I might feel more worthy of your commendation."

"You must not deny or disparage your deeds, or I shall persuade Flora to let me proclaim their excellence."

"I object to that; and your generous praise is equal to my ambition, while it gives me new motive for exertion."

Having reached her father's door, they soon separated with mutual esteem and a kind good night.

Returning to the cottage the sailor found Flora seated by the bright blaze of the replenished fire, with a large easy chair near her, evidently placed there for one expected. Accepting it without ceremony, he said, "I am very glad to see you looking so well; for in thinking of you I feared that you might have found life here not quite as you had hoped. Yet if I could have known that you had won such a friend as Miss McRae, the gloom which seemed to surround your abode would have melted in sunshine."

"She is truly a lovely person," Flora replied; "and possesses one of those natures which make us feel, at the first meeting, that we have known them long — so quick of sympathy are nearly related souls."

"I hope to meet her here often. I should have known from your appearance that you had found something valuable during my absence, and I wish you to enjoy it. Indeed, there is nothing more pleasing to me than the friendship of thoughtful women; men do not so trust each other — only a woman can twine thoroughly into *their* confidence."

"Yes, in friendship as in religion we must give all; to keep back a part of the price is as fatal to one as to the other."

"I know that any reserve springs from just so much lack of affinity. But how is Fred?"

"Dreaming sweetly, I have no doubt, as he fell asleep in Annie's arms."

"You must take him into the city while we are in port, and see your friends on board of the Muse."

"It would give me a great satisfaction to do so, and Fred would be delighted."

"If you thought she would like it, you might ask Miss McRae to accompany you; and, should she incline to go, you can take the cars some afternoon — only let us know of it the day before."

"I fancy that she will be pleased with the idea. And now I want to hear something of my old acquaintance the ocean, and my friends the sailors."

"The men are much as you left them; they kindly remember you, and that memory has greatly contributed to the success of the voyage; and the sea is the same dark-frowning, bright-glancing, storm-tossing, or tenderly-caressing creature as ever, I suppose, yet she awakens recollections now that give her a new grace, as they touch life with fairer and more attractive hues, or unseal and elevate my vision to behold them."

Flora's tearful smile was a confession that she could not gainsay his words, for she saw that his glance was clearer, his bearing higher, and his manner more refined and equal; he was, indeed, receiving his reward.

CHAPTER XXXIX.

> You have seen
> Sunshine and rain at once; those happy smiles
> That played on her ripe lips seemed not to know
> What guests were in her eyes.
>
> SHAKSPEARE.

AT the request of the Rev. Mr. Frink, Miss Graves called at the cottage to take Fred to the Sunday school.

Flora had made her child ready early, for he felt much pleased with the idea of going, as he had watched the prettily dressed children on many previous Sabbath mornings while they passed by, and wished to join them in their pleasant walk; so that, although he did not like the appearance of Miss Graves, he kissed his mother, and looked back with a proud smile as he took the teacher's hand at the gate.

If Fred was an object of curiosity to those who observed him on the way, he became much more so when he entered the school room, as most of the teachers and many of the older scholars had heard the doubt touching the purity and consequent respectability of his blood.

But the child shrank from their prying gaze, and seeing no friendly face among them all, he began to cry; on which they turned away to their respective classes. Yet one fair girl, near his own age, who sat beside him, was touched with pity, and gently took his hand in hers; and, as he looked up, smiling through his tears, kissed him, and whispered, "Don't you cry."

Upon this, the mob having dispersed, Fred dried his eyes;

and the rest of the hour wore quietly away, while many a timid yet sweet glance played between the children — a heaven-sent lesson for the morning. When the school was over, Miss Graves permitted the friendly girl to conduct Fred home, as she, with her gossips, had come to the conclusion that his blood showed the servile taint; and she feared that she might lose caste herself if seen with him any more; for society in Greenville was fastidious on the point of color, a cloud on the skin being worse than one on the reputation, inasmuch as it is more difficult to hide.

As the children went out, they locked hands and walked along the street looking at objects, about which they talked so musically that a Scotch terrier, that lay sunning himself at Annie's door, sprang up with sympathizing eyes, and came frisking playfully around them, as if desiring to share their happiness. Thus they went on until they had nearly reached the cottage, when they met a brother of the little girl, a boy about twelve years old, who said, hotly, "Let go my sister's hand, you young nigger, you! you're a smart darkie! trying to play white folks, be ye? Scat!" and giving his sister a cuff, she fled towards home, crying. On this the dog grabbed him by the seat of his trousers, and took most of it with him up the street; while Fred darted into the house, as he would not have done had he been anywhere near the young ruffian's size and age.

Flora was taken by surprise at his sudden appearance, because she had supposed the teacher would keep him through the morning worship; she saw, also, that he was flushed and seemed angry. So kneeling down before him, she untied his hat, and, while smoothing back his locks, inquired, "What is the matter with my little boy?"

"Nothing!" yet instantly he inquired, "Mother, what is nigger?"

"It means dark colored, or black."

"It don't! I know it don't! and I never'll go to that old school again, you see'f I do!"

"My child, has any one applied that word to you?"

"Yes! and I know who he is, and I'll fling a stone at him the next time he comes by here, you see if I don't!"

"My dear little boy will be wicked if he does that."

"Then I want to be wicked! and I will be when I'm big enough! When shall I be big enough, mother?"

Flora made no further reply, but, taking him into her lap, soothed him with caresses; and, in a little time, he became as bright and playful as ever; yet the battle of his life had commenced in that morning's skirmish.

In the evening, Annie called; and, receiving cordial welcome from Flora, Fred came to bask in her smile, as the lilies in the pond open their fragrant bosoms to the morning sun. Taking him in her arms, the adventure of the school all flowed out under her tender questioning. Whereupon she said, "You must never go there again, but come to me; and I will try to teach you lessons more in keeping with the spirit of Christ. Love and Devotion are his apostles: relying on their aid, I hope to lead you kindly and gently in the way of learning, so that you will like to study, and, may be, love your teacher."

"I'll do any thing you want me to when I've flung a stone at that boy."

"He is quite too mean for you to notice."

"Is he?" inquired Fred, rousing up to a new view.

"Yes, indeed he is! and I, certainly, will not notice him until he says that he is sorry for what he said to you."

"Then I won't! 'cause I want to do just like you do."

"I believe that you are entitled to be his teacher," Flora

smilingly remarked, "as your method appears to be very successful."

"He felt that he had been unjustly treated, so much so that to deny him any redress was still deeper to wrong him. I have pointed out what seems to me a better way of recovering his self-respect — which an impelling necessity urges and goads us to regain."

"But are you not cultivating pride when you give him the impression that this boy is beneath his attention?"

"The sooner he learns that generous actions elevate, and that mean ones degrade him, the better it will be for him and for society. I know how you yearn after equality under the law, and since I listened to your story I desire it exceedingly. Yet so long as nobleness and meanness of purpose coexist, so long there will continue to be a higher and a lower, by divine sanction. Who went with Fred to Sunday school?"

"A lady called for him, whose name I do not know; but the same person, some days since, met me in one of the shops, and invited me to join a sewing circle."

"Then it must have been Miss Graves."

"There was another person with the one I allude to at that time, — she wore a diamond cross, which attracted my attention."

"That was Mrs. Featherstone, a lady from the city; she is an old friend of mine, and once very lovely; but now greatly changed, and I fear by marriage; for she united herself to a man who appeared to me to be repulsive, although many called him handsome."

"Poor creature, I pity her from my heart. Indeed, I felt, the moment that I looked into her face, that there was something preying upon her, and now I can see the vulture."

As the hour of leave-taking came round, and Annie arose for that purpose, Flora said, "I think of going into the city, and on board of the Muse, some afternoon this week: have you any desire to go with me?"

"I should like to see the ship very much; yet I am afraid that I might be an unexpected guest."

"I will promise that you shall be a welcome one, if it be your pleasure to accompany us."

"On what day do you think of making the excursion?"

"You may suit yourself in any day after to-morrow."

"Tuesday, if it be fair, will please me, as it is the next one," said Annie, smiling. Thus the friends parted without separating; for each had become a shrined presence to the other, filling the once lonely hours with soft, sweet music, making the cares of the day cheerful, and attuning to fullest harmony the evening hours.

When the friends went into the city and down to the Muse, they were met, at the carriage steps, by one who was on the watch for them; and leading the way directly to the cabin, Flora followed to the door and preceded him down.

But a ship being a new sight to Annie, she paused to look at the long and polished deck, the shining capstan, and then aloft to her tall and tapering spars, with their intricate cordage, so sinewy and symmetrical; but, at length, yielding to Flora's repeated call, she went down; not, however, without observing the home feeling which seemed to animate Fred.

As he came on board, he ran aft to take hold of the wheel and strain at the spokes to port the helm; but as it was hard to the larboard, he found it difficult to move. Yet, feeling that Annie's eyes were upon him, he looked it over knowingly, for a moment, then turned to make an examination of the hencoop; but finding it empty, he cast a glance aloft, took hold of some of the halliards quite familiarly, and gayly skipping forward, disappeared in the top-gallant forecastle.

When Annie went below, Flora showed her the beautiful

home that she once dwelt in; and observing the hat which she had worn still hanging where she had left it, and remarking upon it, the captain replied, "You were the last occupant of the room, and Francis chooses to keep the things as you arranged them. The sailors, also, look upon it as a kind of shrine; and it is a salutary one, for under its influence they have become neater, more sober, and more capable; while Jack and James will soon be officers — Jack goes out second mate when we sail again."

"Where are they all?" Flora inquired.

"They are in the forecas'le, and I'll venture to say Fred has found them before this time."

"I've no doubt of that! Annie and I are going to seek them, also."

"The steward expects to see you soon, as he has some fruit and other refreshments in waiting," interposed Elery.

"He is very kind, but I wish to see the sailors first; and, if you are willing, I shall ask them to come and partake of it with us."

"I think you may do so, as they provided it," said he, smiling.

Ascending to the deck, the ladies moved forward, when Fred, seeing them advancing, ran out to conduct them on; and, as they came near, Flora saw that the room was clean and bright, as if prepared for their reception. Whereupon memory flashed another picture before her mind; so that, when she stepped over the threshold, her heart beat as though she was about to enter into the presence and receive audience of kings.

The sailors arose with warm and honest smiles to welcome her. Taking the hand of each, though not without tears, she called them her friends, her protectors, her deliverers; and turning to Annie, whose eyes were overflowing, and clasping her hand, she continued, saying, "This lady is also my friend, being true and noble, as you are; and I have told her of your generous sacrifice for the forlorn and destitute."

"Yes, and it is one of the most heroic of stories!" said Annie. "Your treatment of Flora and her child has made me love the ocean, because it seems to foster whatever is glorious in the soul."

After a moment of silence, Jack came near, and placed something in Flora's hand; when she, observing that it was money, said, "O, no, no!" and sank down on a seat, trying to restrain her tears.

To the words and the action Jack replied, "We're sorry to hurt your feelings, but it's not half what we feel to be your due; for we've all got three suits to our spars, where we had one before we saw you, and shot enough in the locker to ballast and trim with when we spread 'em."

"O that I could do something for you!" cried Flora.

"You've done every thing—you've given us all we've got! for most on us had nearly sunk when we saw that you felt for us and believed in us, which, somehow, makes us better, so that we're trying to right up and be men."

"You are men!" said Annie; "men fit to stand among the most worthy; and it is the fulness of your humanity which so overpowers her."

On this Flora, through her subsiding emotion, said, "It is so, indeed; and, for all your giving, I can hope to make no return. Yet I am persuaded that a more bountiful One has given his blessing, and that shall calm me." When rising, she continued, "I would not, my friends, that you should ever forget me or my child; but let me pray you still to retain some memory of yourselves. I should rather die than have either of you suffer on account of your charities to me."

"You needn't have any fears about us," replied Jack; "we

could ride at our anchors if we liked, but we'd sooner be under way."

"Then I wish you to get under way now," said Flora, "and go with us down in the cabin to partake of something which you have provided."

On this proposition Jack's sails appeared to shiver, and turning to his shipmates, he saw that they were all braced sharp, as though it was a head flaw. So he replied, "*This* is our place; we shouldn't feel at home aft; and the captain mightn't like it."

"He will, most certainly, like it; for we told him what we intended to do, and he was almost as much pleased at the idea as we were." But they appearing still to hold back, Flora continued, "Are you afraid to sail under my convoy?"

"Not if you've got that dirk with you which you mounted to repel boarders," Jack replied.

"Come," said Flora, smiling, "you cannot deny me this favor after having given me so much."

Thereupon Jack made sail slowly; when, one after another, the rest tripped their anchors and drifted out after him, though not exactly in the wake of the convoy; for half of them fell to leeward of the mainmast, while some kept broad off, until they reached the scuppers, and then went sounding along under easy way.

Flora and Fred led the fleet, while Jack manœuvred to fall behind Annie. But, seeing it, she said, "Do you intend to desert one who desires your company?"

The tone of her voice, more than her words, drew Jack up alongside again; when he said, "We want you to talk over her to take part of our wages, for somehow it makes the work lighter, and the watching pleasanter, when we feel that it is bringing in something which may cheer them as cares for us."

"I will — truly I will; for she loves you all like brothers; and it is your generosity alone which so melts her to tears."

"Somehow we do get a heavy sea on when she comes for-'ard; but it has washed out the fo'cas'le; and we want you to thank her for't, for we're rough, and don't know how."

"There is no need that you should make use of words where you are known by heart — yet I will do as you wish."

On entering the cabin, as they did in advance, — for Flora paused to bring up the rear, — Jack was quite as much at his ease as though he had been standing upon his mother's sanded floor on the Cape. And as they came into the presence of the captain, he looked upon them as though he thought that Annie had made a conquest; while her beauty was so heightened by the emotion of the hour, and her manner so subdued by heart-felt sympathy, that he became filled with her radiance, to be "saddened by heavenly doubts."

Throwing off her bonnet to wait upon the sailors, — which she did with easy attention, while speaking such words as made them feel it to be a sister's voice, — her brown glossy hair, in which there was no slightest ripple, lay like a shadowy jut around her temples, relieving their proportions as though wreathed by an artist, yet appearing as careless as nature; while the occasion deepened her color and breathing, as well as the whole expression of her flexible and perfect form — at least so she seemed to the master of the Muse; and never again can he enter that cabin without feeling something of the spirit of her presence.

Flora moved among the crew in generous rivalry, and Fred was not outdone by either; yet he only shouted "Land, ho!" twice, with the captain's permission, and much to the amusement of the sailors.

When the entertainment was over, they separated, as once

before they had done, and, entering a carriage with the captain, took the road to Greenville.

On reaching the cottage, in the dusk of the early evening, Elery said, "I wish you to introduce me to your father to-night, Miss McRae, if you will do me the favor."

"Yes, do, Annie; and then I can have tea prepared on your return."

"It will give me pleasure so to oblige both of you," said Annie, smiling.

As they turned up the street, Flora said, "Now remember that I shall await your coming."

"That will meet my wish," replied the captain; "so you shall be obeyed, if I have any influence, or any of the art of persuasion."

They found Mr. McRae with the evening news; and, when the introduction was over, Annie excused herself and left them. Thereupon Elery said, "I have called on you, Mr. McRae, for the purpose of arranging with regard to the cottage."

"I have been expecting you," he replied, smiling; "therefore I drew out the deed a day or two since."

"How much is the consideration?" inquired Elery, taking out his purse.

"You will find it there stated," he answered, while handing him the title.

Elery opened the paper, and finding it written, "For brotherly kindness," said, "But ——"

When Mr. McRae interrupted him, with — "You must not object to a little from my abundance, when you have so heroically given; for my daughter has revealed the story to me; and, since that time, whenever I look out of my window, your cottage seems to be the sunniest spot in the landscape; and I wish to keep it so."

"I shall try to have it continue a bright place; yet, as you mean the benefit for her, I accept it, with thanks, in her name; and it gives me pleasure to see that she has found friends here."

"The benefit will reach her, I have no doubt," said Mr. McRae, as Elery arose to go. "Yet, if any thing more be needed, we desire to be especially remembered; and whenever it may please you to call on us, we shall be glad to see you."

Thanking him for his courtesy, the sailor invited him to visit his ship, and took leave.

On this Annie came tripping down the stairs to join him; and, opening the library door, said, "I am engaged out to tea, father, and do not expect to return until nine or ten o'clock."

"Very well, my daughter, that may be as you please."

As they passed out of the gate Elery said, "That pear, which I sent by you the other evening, must have been very persuasive, or else the bearer of it was so."

"I hope not in a way to displease you. Indeed, you must permit us to take a share in your good work; for, while it makes my father more cheerful and more dear to me, it has given a joy to life which I had not found before."

"I did not mention it to chide. As you desire it, so I would have it; for I see that you shape your course by the stars."

"How could I else, when your deeds lead me to look so high?"

Having then reached the cottage, they entered to find tea awaiting, to be accompanied and followed by bright and cheerful conversation, which was just agitated by those charming emotions that rise to perfection only in the glances of friendship and love.

When the evening had thus swiftly sped, and Elery was returning with Annie, he remarked, "I think you rather devoted yourself to my men to-day."

"I like them, and particularly the one with whom I came to the cabin. I never felt the full meaning of the phrase, 'heart of oak,' until I stood beside him. The Muse, too, is a beauty; so her captain has reason to be proud; and I confess to having passed one of the richest days of my life this day. Yet how little did I dream it! It is a new revelation. Look there, above us, how deep, how glorious is night! still I think, as I gaze, that the human heart is deeper and more glorious than the universe, for I have seen that to-day which outshines the stars."

Though they walked slowly they soon reached the door where Elery bade her good night with a thrilling, but a silent heart, for he saw that his hour had not yet come — as her free and soaring speech gave sign that no master emotion had awoke to lay chains on her tongue, and break like stormy waves upon the shores of fear and hope.

Well could he wait while they passed many pleasant and ripening hours together in the cottage and at her father's house, — seeing that his presence brightened, if his partings did not sadden, — ere the Muse once more went forth to bear her lyre over the waves.

CHAPTER XL.

Hath vice a
Charter got, that none must rise, but such, who
Of the devil's faction are? The way to
Honor is not evermore the way to
Hell: a virtuous man may climb.

SIR W. DAVENANT.

FEATHERSTONE had closed up his business relations with New Orleans, drawn home his capital, and embarked it in other operations; which, if they appeared too adventurous to some, were generally attended with success, while they furnished him a pleasing and well nigh necessary excitement.

Being ambitious of political distinction, he aspired to a seat in Congress, and had been for some time moving to accomplish that purpose. When the day for the meeting of the nominating convention to fill that office drew near, such exertions were made, and such means used, that most of those who made influence in assemblies of that kind assured him that he would be the nominee. Yet there were one or two who feared and expressed their doubts, as it was the time when the question of slavery began to heave and surge, and threaten to sunder the great political organizations, although they, like the others, were conservative men, and loudly professed the Union, because it is dear to every American heart. These politicians worked for Featherstone with a will; for, on being called out at the rooms of the "Union Club," he had said, "It appears to me, gentlemen, that we are approaching an important crisis, one which for a long time must shape the course of this nation, and determine whether wisdom or fanaticism shall guide her; yet I hold that the chart by which we are bound to navigate is as plain as the way is safe. I need not speak, in your presence, of the large interests which not only rest upon, but are inextricably inwoven with, the 'peculiar institution;' or of the source of that prosperity which enables the southern planter to be patriarchal in his hospitality and princely in his expenditure — thus infusing life-blood into all the veins of trade and commerce, as well as gayety and tone into all our places of pleasure. Neither will I pause to picture to you the desolation which must stalk over that fair and fertile region if the tie which holds the ignorant and improvident negro under the supervision of intelligent and considerate masters should be cut asunder. I forbear, also, to open the view beyond, where appear indignity, violence, lust, and murder, pursuing our own race and kindred. I forbear, because any appeal to the feelings, while adjusting this question, should be discountenanced, for the reason that 'truth is a pearl to be sought after only in clear waters.'

"It was a saying of Pitt that all great questions are simple; and if examined, as it should be, strictly with regard to its practical operations and issues, this subject is a striking illustration of the doctrine, as there are but two or three points which rise into the clear, cool atmosphere for the light of reason to rest upon. These I shall examine in as few words as possible, as I desire to be understood.

"I say then, in the first place, that negro slavery in the United States has benefited the bondmen. Any man may see, if he will, that the African is better off in this country, as a slave, than he ever was in any situation in his own. Indeed, no one can show the facts that will shake this position, if he search back to the days of Jugurtha, or even to the pictures which represent the different races of men on the walls of the exhumed temples and palaces of old Egypt.

Such being the historical view, uniform and unchanged, until modern civilization stepped in to prevent their mutual destruction and turn them to use, it seems to me entirely to dispose of the question of condition; for we are not to compare or contrast their state with ours, — a common error, — but with that of their own race in their native land, if we are seeking truth.

"This being conceded, there remains a single question of policy, namely, the return or surrender of the fugitive; and when I say that they want him, while we do not, — than which there is nothing more manifest, so that even the blindest may perceive it, if he will but think of their social position amongst us, — it appears to me that I have indicated the only reasonable course to pursue amid the fanatical noise of the hour.

"These two points, the comparative condition, and the necessary laws to preserve their improved state or enlarge the sphere of their usefulness, are the sum of the whole matter. And the question now is, Shall this great system of peaceful life and binding law be sacrificed to morbid feeling, or be used for the purposes of agitation? the chief effects of which will be to float light and worthless things on the surface for a time, and make the waters opaque to him who would search their depths. I know not what course may seem wisest to others, but as for me, I shall oppose the counsels of such leaders, and seek to quench their torch ere they have accomplished their incendiary purpose."

Park was one of the delegates to the convention whose suffrages Featherstone had prepared the way to take. When a nominating committee had been packed to that end, and while they were out on the responsible duty, there came from various parts of the hall a call for Park. He had seen no occasion to take any conspicuous place in the proceedings hitherto, but sat with rather a sad countenance, apparently wrapped in meditation. As the echoes of the call subsided, he arose with an expression of form and face which hushed the assembly, and said, "Mr. President: If I believed it in my power to give direction to the thought or higher elevation to the action of this assembly, I should respond to the call with a more cheerful spirit; but I am aware that a warning voice rarely receives a welcome, although it be ever the province of wisdom to take of the passing hour some security for the future. Yet, from conscious strength, we are so little accustomed to forearm for any emergency, however momentous, that the alarmist is usually treated as either weak or designing. Still I feel that I cannot shrink from such office, however I may suffer thereby in your estimation.

"In following out the duty that thus devolves upon me, I can direct your attention to no new thing, but only to the more complete development of one which, having had many years of existence, is growing ever more impatient of question and belligerent of nature — and are we always to fall back before it? I know that this has been, and still is, by some among us, held to be hallowed ground; but I can no longer respect a veil that only conceals from the most careless glance that there is a struggle going on between Slavery and Freedom in this country which will shake the continent; and that they have been, and are, and must be forever, foes. Gentlemen may cry, Peace! and close their eyes to every thing but merchandise; yet the issue is already joined, and all our future will be but a prolonged or an adjourned trial, until one or the other party shall march on victorious. Do gentlemen see any signs of forbearance? Are not the concessions and compromises which we have made cited as precedents and reasons for granting more? Therefore does it not become us to pause and inquire where this shameful retreat is to end? As for me, although amid sad forebodings I must say it, I see no rampart in the distance save the human breast, and that is ours to-day.

"I know not how others feel; but shame comes over me when I hear it intimated that we are to yield to threats or acquiesce in encroachment; yet if it must be so for a time, while the men of the day lead us far from truth, we shall rise again and struggle back, through peril and with glory, to the old traditions; for the people of this nation love liberty. And is there any worth in any thing which can be offered in exchange for her gems? Do we not all hold them too sacred to allow of their being weighed, or even rudely breathed upon, where they glitter in the crown of the Union? If we may not speak of the constitution without reverence, how much more ought we to regard the spirit of freedom, which is its glory! Yet that spirit is a subtile essence, which no constitution has succeeded in retaining, for any length of time, in all its original purity and fulness; and great as is the one which was formed for us, and profoundly grateful as we are for the gift, what can they who shall follow us across the stage find of our enacting, I will not say to enlarge, but to preserve their work? while we know that the framers of that instrument had ideas of freedom which they could not embody, although they died in the faith that their time would come. Yet where are their prophesies? Is there any sign that the day of their fulfilment is advancing?

"Be not deceived; shrink not from the exigencies of the hour: on the past no man can repose in peace; for it is in the nature of Tyranny to encroach. Therefore there is yet to be many a convulsive distribution of power, and many a painful cremation of the phœnix, ere political institutions take that final form in which all the children of men can rejoice. I hear a voice from the clouds, which lower around, summoning us to duty, imploring us to put our talent of liberty into circulation, so that, when the Master cometh, he may receive his own with increase. Such only will be found to have been faithful servants of Him and the people."

Here the nominating committee entered, and reporting the name of Anthony Featherstone, Esq., it was put to vote and confirmed, in the convention, by two majority. On the announcement of the result the president said, "I am instructed that there is some other business to come before us, whenever gentlemen are ready."

The excitement of the members, on the vote being declared, gave Park an opportunity to depart without special observation; and when he had gained the street he turned down towards the residence of Featherstone, which was not far off. It being a long time since he had called at that gentleman's mansion, — although he still continued to return his salutation, whenever they casually met, — he thought he would avail himself of that opportunity to give him some timely instruction, as he felt sure of finding him at home, ready to receive the committee, who would soon come to surprise him with the fact of his nomination, and praying his acceptance. So thinking, he arrived at the house; and, on inquiry, the servant signified that Featherstone was at leisure, and, leading on, ushered the orator into the presence of the nominee.

"Ah!" said the political aspirant, as he arose with his blandest smile and advanced a step, "I thought you were at the convention, Mr. Park; I believe I saw your name among the delegates?"

"I left their place of meeting a few moments since."

"Have they made a nomination so soon?" inquired Featherstone, looking at his watch; "if so, it must have been done on the first ballot."

"It was so done; and they nominated Anthony Featherstone, Esq."

"That is an unexpected honor; and I am at a loss to find what should fix their hopes on me. Yet, on reflection, I think that it must be because there is a great question pending, the bearings, circumstances, and details of which, they know, are familiar to me."

But as Park made no reply or appeared about to do so, while his manner and expression were puzzling and portentous, Featherstone asked, rather dryly, "Am I to understand that you were delegated to notify me of the action of the convention?"

"I hold no place by their appointment; neither did I come here to declare their preference; but simply to say to you that, when a committee does appear to signify the action of that body, you are to decline the nomination."

The audacity of this direction stunned Featherstone for an instant; but recovering, he inquired, while feeling that some terror hung over him like the sword of Damocles, "Do you call this interference a friendly service?"

"I came here to perform a stern act of duty, to accomplish an aim of sovereign justice," said Park, with piercing coldness of accent. Yet softening his glance, he added, "But, now that you so remind me, I see it to be the height of friendship also, if thereby you will be counselled and curb your career."

"When I wish for advice in this matter, I may call you in," said Featherstone, while all the lawless acts of his life were tumultuous in his memory; "but until I do, you would do well to shun the office."

"I came here," replied Park, while his lip curled, "neither to advise nor persuade, because I knew that such mild applications would avail nothing; but to direct. I appear here for Flora and her child; and in their names I protest against your temerity in attempting to represent a free people after having sold your own blood into bondage."

"It is all a cursed lie!" Featherstone hastily declared.

"That," said Park, (as Featherstone's answer, although it denied, implied a knowledge of, the facts,) "is a blackguard's last defence, and worthy of you and your cause. I came here not only to save our politics from a still deeper stain, but to prevent the press from proclaiming the history of your relation to those persons; which it shall do to-morrow, if you venture to accept their offer."

"What can be done?" inquired the candidate, cowering under the stroke; "if you will name it, I may take it into consideration."

"Seek out those whom you have so foully wronged; then, when you have made the fullest restitution in your power, you shall have their forgiveness, and, what you consider of vastly more value, my silence."

"If you will bring me to them," said he, brightening up with the feeling that he was surmounting the obstacles, "and stand out of my way in this matter, I will do any thing that you can say is reasonable."

"Not that length! for this nomination must be declined, under any circumstances, as you are unfit for the post."

"Then," said Featherstone, his face flaming with passion and his lip quivering, "they and you may go to hell!"

"As the committee must be near here, I give place," said Park, turning to go; "but you will decline the honor they offer, for the same reason which compelled Cæsar to put away the proffered crown, after he had trampled on liberty."

On this the candidate's features overspread with spite, as his mouth overflowed with impotent curses; and Park left him to rage alone. Featherstone was still savage, almost frantic, when the committee were shown in, so that he received them strangely. And on their declaring the object of the visit, he replied, "The nomination of the convention is as unexpected as it was unsought: more pressing interests persuade me to decline the honor — I cannot accept!" Thus far the formulary, when his passions mastered him, and he cried, "Curse politics! a curse *is* on the purchased paths to office! and if the state were falling in ruins now, *I* could laugh: but you may go and tell your convention that I shall pay no more to accomplish it. Then *they* will laugh; for they know that moneyed fools are becoming more numerous and more liberal in their offers to those who finger the dice of every important election. So tell them to go on 'loading' and palming with all their devilish cunning, for they are the quick curse of the country!" and, starting wildly up he strode across the room.

But the committee still lingering as if in doubt, though really they were fixed with amazement, he turned upon them, saying, "Are you not answered? have I not been sufficiently explicit for your understandings?" Thereupon they huddled, and took wing, like a covey under the eye of a marksman. So gaining the street and returning to the hall, the convention was immediately called to order to hear their report.

This accomplished, the chairman was appealed to, who, rising, said, "Your committee have waited on Mr. Featherstone, the nominee, and acquainted him with the honor which this body had conferred; but he peremptorily declined being a candidate."

"I think that there must be some mistake!" ejaculated one of the members, without rising in his place, while many others looked what he declared.

"Order!" cried the president. "Is there no probability, Mr. Chairman, of Mr. Featherstone's acceptance?"

"Your committee have no doubt of the matter," the chairman replied; "they believe it to be one of the fixed facts."

This final announcement struck many with surprise, and a

certain few with blank astonishment. It drew the delegates from their seats, around the committee, to hear Featherstone's precise words, which being many times repeated, it at length grew to be the conviction that the man was insane. Then there followed brief consultations between a particular few, with low-spoken, but decisive words, out of which set came a motion to adjourn,— for the "wire pullers" were thrown into confusion, they having provided against no such catastrophe.

That course, however, did not appear to give general satisfaction, although it might be very desirable to some. This being observed by one of the more active members, he arose and said, "Mr. President: I think that I give utterance to the prevailing sentiment of this body by objecting to any form of separation, until the purpose for which we are here convened be accomplished; or, at least, still further sought to be. Therefore, I now move that we proceed to ballot once more, and with the single aim of the public good. With that high object full before me, and in order to stimulate the action of every man who hears me, I nominate to the consideration of this assembly Brian Park, Esq.," (cheers) — "a man, Mr. President, that even you need not blush to honor; a man worthy to take any place to which we have the power to call him; a man who loves that liberty which we all so loudly profess; one, also, whom God has clothed with the ability and the courage which become a champion. And, closing our eyes to every thing save the glory of our country, let us give our standard to his hand; then, though the night be dark, the morning will meet it still waving, the breeze find every fold floating free."

Immediately on the conclusion of the member's remarks, the motion to adjourn was loudly called for; which, being put, was voted down.

Then they proceeded to ballot, though not without two or

three attempts to take the business from the hands of the convention at large, and turn it over to a packed committee. But the time for that stale manœuvre had passed; for the members, many of them, had shaken off the common lethargy, and were breaking away from the routine of such occasions, so that they seemed to be in earnest, as if feeling their purpose to be worthy of their energies. Thus armed, they carried it through successfully; and when the vote was declared, it was found that Park had twenty majority.

On leaving Featherstone, Park had gone to his office, supposing that the business of the convention would be postponed. But, on being notified of his nomination, he again appeared in the assembly.

Thereupon, the many knots of delegates sundered, and each resuming his seat, the murmur fell; and amid the silence Park slowly arose, as if weighed down by the burden of his thoughts, and said, —

"Mr. President, and Gentlemen: I thank you for your suffrages. I honor you for the noble impulse of liberty and humanity from which they sprung. I hail it as an omen of the wide awakening which is to come. I perceive by it that the patriotic heart still throbs quickly at thought of peril to freedom. I see the thrill and the fire which beget republics. They fill me with the highest hope; yet I cannot permit them to blind me to the actual condition of public sentiment. I am persuaded that the people do not yet sympathize with the ideas which I have expressed, and you have so generously approved; and if so, how can I be a *representative*, in any popular or powerful sense of the word? I know that there are gentlemen who think Congress is the fitting arena in which to agitate and form public opinion. I have come to a different conclusion. I believe it to be a place for deliberation — for the full expression and final trial of that opinion ere it take the form of law. This being my conviction, how can I meet your wishes? If I yield, it will be through love of place or ambition of distinction; and no good could come of the mission — it would be without success and without honor. No; the representative of the truths which I have uttered must wait until the people are thoroughly aroused to their vital importance. He should enter those wide-echoing halls only as the foremost wave of an in-heaving ocean, grand in its uprising, and irresistible in its might. Though the signs of that flood are faint, its hour will yet come. In the mean time, the broad waters are to be troubled, and that, too, by far other hands than such as are clutching at Ambition's ladder. Our rulers are to be confronted, and their proclivities proclaimed to the people. This is a sad task; yet, like Hamlet in laying open her crime to his mother, —

'We must be cruel only to be kind.'

Nothing but the supremest devotion to the good of the country can sanction this course; and he who enters upon it will accomplish little unless he put aside all seeming private advantage.

"So understanding the nature of the office to which you would elevate me, I must oppose your voices until a more auspicious day. Would that such day had already arrived! But my words and your friendly reception of them are only a far-off sign of the advancing dawn. To the advent of that morning I henceforward devote myself, in social converse, in primary meetings, in lyceum halls, and through the press — these are the cradles and schools of great national questions: it is there that the hand is formed which is greater than the throne itself, and to which it must yield the sceptre, or, at length, be crushed."

This address caused those who had cast their votes against

Park, and who were not yet dwarfed and hardened into "hacks," to blush that they had so done. There were some, however, who received it with a sneer, and assailed it with ridicule. So there were a certain few, that had heard Featherstone's conversations on the subject of the nomination, and knew something of the amount of money which he had lavished to gain it, who gathered into a knot by themselves, and discussed him, only to become more puzzled, so as to end in the word "Fool!"

"And a green one at that," remarked one. "Who ever heard of any thing so verdant? He ought never to be invited to the public crib again; he evidently prefers grass. I think he'd like to work out Nebuchadnezzar's sentence."

"You may be right," replied another; "yet perhaps he declines because his taste is too delicate for cabbage."

An hour after the departure of the committee Aurelia entered the apartment where Featherstone still sat, with his elbows on the table, and his hands in his hair, glowering at something in the air which seemed to concentrate his senses, although it was invisible to all other eyes. When, however, in an instant, he became conscious of her presence, he started up and growled out, "Is there no room in this house where I can be alone?"

"Nothing could be more agreeable to me," she replied, "if you will only give notice what place you have selected for your meditations."

But as she continued to advance quite nonchalantly towards the table, where he stood in rather a theatrical attitude of defiance, — which she, however, did not appear to observe, — he blurted out, with increasing emphasis, "What do you want here?"

"At least one thing which I do not find — a gentleman."

"That is something which an intruder should have no expectation of finding."

"Can I be an intruder in any part of this, my mother's house, because you, for the moment, may have entered there?"

"Your mother's house! More tomb than house — wherein you were half buried among the bones and dust of departed splendor. I wish that I could change it back to the condition in which I found it, just to see how you would plead, and weep, and caress for its restoration."

"My dear, you cannot wish for that change more than I do, so that you vanish with the other gewgaws! Then Hope might once more return, though never again in my heart can she hold high festival. Do you dream that the gold and crimson of the decorator's loom, with all the upholsterer's cunning, can compensate for the lost radiance of her wing?"

"Indeed, one would imagine, from your tone and manner, that you thought yourself foully wronged in my having surrounded you with every luxury, while elevating you and your house to the circles of fashion; and permit me humbly to beg your pardon for so doing, hoping to gain it by confessing, as I do now, the sincerest sorrow over the foolish act."

"If your sorrow and supplication could restore, I should accept them with joy and thanksgiving, as the prelude to divinest harmony."

"Restore what?" sneered he, with venomous expression — "the poverty, the gloom, the intense longing for wealth and station, and the apparent passion?"

"Truly, it is a painful catalogue, but one that you, above all, should have spared me; although, when I reflect upon what you are, I am not surprised to hear it. Cold, coarse, and callous, you have chilled or blighted every tendril of my nature which turned to you, until my heart scorned the direction; so that through you, it has become a ruin, and its once bright world lies desolate, in all which you have deceived me past the expression of words — wronged me beyond reparation; even my peace of mind, which the lowliest and loneliest may keep, has gone, like the lost Pleiad, to be seen no more."

"This is rich repayment for all that I have expended on you. Yet it is some consolation to hear you confess how the gilded harness chafes, especially when I call to mind its strength, and the power that lies in my hand to curb you at will! Hence you may find abusive words a little too expensive for common use, although they appear to be as plenty as pennies were scarce before I was inveigled into giving you relief. I wish to God that I might be poor, for a time, just for the enjoyment it would afford me to look at you, when you saw the gaunt spectres of want and squalor returning."

"From my soul I desire it, as all my surroundings now cry out and reproach me; and yet for still other reason, it would so cover you with the contempt and forgetfulness of the world that I might feel some touch of pity for what I now despise."

"I have heard enough of this impotent railing," cried Featherstone, turning livid; "and if it does not cease at once, we will see if power can do any thing to suppress it. So leave this room instantly!"

"I defy the power to which you appeal as deeply as I scorn the possessor of it. And if I have abstained from expressing my thoughts hitherto, be assured that it was not from any fear, but because I took counsel of Prudence; to her persuasions I listen no more, as you are not capable of distinguishing between forbearance and cowardice. Neither will your emphasis, nor your bluster, move me from any room in this house until it be my pleasure to go. Yet, having finished the lesson for the day, I prefer to leave you, so that you may the more thoroughly digest it, my dear." When, taking the book which she had come to seek from the table, she quietly, leisurely, and with a slight smile even, turned away and left him.

But seeing that she was passing out without closing the door, and having been on the very verge of violence, Featherstone sprang forward with an oath, and threw the leaf against her so swiftly that she fell heavily to the floor; whereupon he locked it with a jerk, and returned to his meditations.

CHAPTER XLI.

Yet, freedom! yet thy banner, torn, but flying,
Streams like the thunder storm against the wind;
Thy trumpet voice, though broken now and dying,
The loudest still the tempest leaves behind;
Thy tree hath lost its blossoms; and the rind,
Chopped by the axe, looks rough and little worth;
But the sap lasts, — and still the seed we find
Sown deep, even in the bosom of the north;
So shall a better spring less bitter fruit bring forth.
BYRON.

FEATHERSTONE'S ambition had been struck low by the fear of disclosure, and thus all his proud hopes were suddenly baffled. He looked to the thick cloud which had so swiftly swept around him, but no ray of consolation penetrated it, neither could he discern any break in its folds for future outlet.

Then recoiling on the past, he felt deeply mortified that he had gone so far with the influential politicians; for he saw that they looked upon him as if they deemed his course to be inexplicable. And if at any time he met either of the members of the committee who waited upon him on that momentous occasion, he was put to burning shame that he should have so lost self-control in their presence. Neither was he without chagrin whenever he thought of the amount of money that he had expended to purchase disgrace. Ah! how often, as it sickened his mind, did he cry, "Fool!" to himself, with an indescribable loathing. Such sharp thoughts and haunting memories as these must be laid or overlaid.

Yet shaken as he was, it wrought no change in his scale of value, so that he desired, first of all, to make up his pecuniary loss; and hope sent him to the brokers' board, where he had been before with some success; but, entering without the same coolness and caution, he found the results adverse; so much so, indeed, that he became alarmed, and made an oath with himself and Fortune that, if she would only lead him back to whence he started, he would venture there no more. On this vow the luck seemed to take a favorable turn, so that he came nearly up to the point of departure; but then he fell back once more. Soon, however, it took another turn, and he rose again; whereon followed other fluctuations, until, after tossing upon a most agitated sea for many months, he saw himself winner. Yet at that stage he paused only to reply to the monitor which whispered of his pledge, with some sophistry about not meaning to swear to stop *there*, "That, of course, I intended to include the cursed electioneering expenses!" and, after a stormy voyage, he at length rounded that point; where, for a few days, he rested secure. Thereon came back the old, distasteful thoughts and sickening memories, with an increased craving for excitement, which his late habit had engendered. Neither did his friends fail to tempt him with brilliant prospects, while reminding him of his judgment and skill, so that he began to fancy that his success had come through knowledge — that experience made the path safe. Consequently he entered again into the play, with varying fortunes, yet ever higher stakes, until, secreting what he could of his property, he left his high-minded and adroit associates in the game with a taint upon his credit, that being thought less disgraceful than an empty treasury.

When Featherstone had cooled off, so that he was capable of reflecting upon his condition, he concluded to recommence the practice of the law; and, making known his determination, his friends procured him the appointment of United States Commissioner for New York as the crisis of eighteen hundred and fifty had just passed.

That crisis wherein Liberty took a backward step, even while leaning upon the arm of our mightiest statesman — the one who, through many years, had laid his hand upon these jarring states, whenever he pleased, and composed them to silence, if not to harmony, in the name of the constitution. Had he stood adverse to the fugitive slave act, it were barrier all sufficient against the encroachment; but he gave his great genius to its support, twining his large thoughts into, what he held to be, a bond of union, and therefore his most glorious wreath; and long, indeed, will it survive to lie upon the coffin of that measure, and draw the pilgrim to its tomb.

It was that statute which Featherstone had been selected to assist in executing; and it was thought to be a judicious appointment, as he appeared to be well qualified to carry it through. Besides, he had been unfortunate; and those who have the power of naming to office are apt to take such fact into their kind consideration; so that most of the places in their gift are filled with persons who have not succeeded in other things — a trait of charity in them which has not yet had its due attention and applause.

The enactment of the fugitive law drew men from the far south to visit us; and among them came Bill Frink. The day, almost the hour, on which Bill arrived, he went out to Greenville; not because he was particularly desirous to see his brother, but rather on account of something which he noted in a letter of his, although he had afterwards received one from him that seemed to have been written with a view to counteract or do away with the impression made by the first.

Entering the town a little before sunset, Bill left his horse in a stable, where, by inquiring, he was directed to Joe's residence; and, on reaching it, a summons brought Joe himself.

When the short brother opened the door, he looked up and down, and then up again to the long one. But, as a thumb and three fingers were gone from his left hand, with two from his right, while all one side of his face was ploughed up into red ridges, in the midst of which there was a scar for an eye, Joe did not recognize him, and said, rather surlily, "Did you inquire for *me*, sir?"

"Yes, boy, I did that. But you look as how you'd like to blow me up ag'in; yit I reckon once 'll du for Bill Frink."

"Come in," said Joe, giving him his hand, while growing red; "come in, and do not talk so loud; there is a person sick in the house."

As he entered, Bill said, "Then the boy Joe didn't know his brother — ha? P'r'aps he's lost some of his beauty, but he's tough yit."

Hurrying him into his room, and closing the door, the parson replied, "You ought to be thankful that it was no worse; you are a monument of God's sparing mercy."

"Now, hadn't ye better call it a fragment? But I'll remember your sentiment, and tell it to one o' my bloody niggers when I've lathered him within an inch of his life; I will, by thunder!"

"It is a very fearful thing to die," said the parson, professionally.

"Du ye never kill any frogs nowadays, Joe?"

"I hope that I have changed from my sinful courses, since, by divine aid, I put off the depraved nature of a child."

"If that's so, what be all these ere chunks of stone for on this shelf?"

"Those are the memorials of the sacred places which I visited while abroad."

"Now, is that what ye call comin' home with a pocket full o' rocks; or be ye afeard ye s'all forgit 'em?" said Bill, nudging Joe with his thumb.

"No, I can never forget *them;* for they are very great

helps to religion, with many. I have occasion to explain and discourse upon them, nearly every day, to some one of my flock. Even those Oriental pipes have a kind of devotional odor."

"Wal, I shouldn't wonder, for I bow down a leetle in that are way myself: but then I guess I'll take one of these ere cigars, as I s'pose it'll amount to about the same thing, some how."

"Yes, help yourself, and pass the box; I think that it may do me good to join you."

As the brother complied with the request, Joe exclaimed, "What a hand you have got, Bill!"

"It ain't quite so slick a flipper to swim with as it used to be; but I rather guess Bill can keep his head out o' water with it some time longer yit." And lighting his cigar, he drew a chair near to an open window, and looking out, said, "A real handsome place you've got here. Whose house is that are?"

"An odd old stick by the name of McRae lives there."

"Rich, I reckon?" said Bill, trying to wink with his blind eye.

"Yes, he has over much of this world's goods; yet he never comes to meeting to manifest his thankfulness — strange that he does not think what must become of him!"

"What cottage is that are down yender, with the pole-beans a runnin' all over the front on't?"

"Some widow's, I think; but I do not know her name — she does not attend my meeting."

"Has that old McRae got any gals?" inquired Bill, with a grin.

"He has one daughter, and she is an only child."

"Now, why ain't you a firin' up arter her? If you don't git married some time or other, I reckon as how I s'all have to; for it's tu good blood to let run out so; 'tis, by thunder!" Then, having finished his cigar, he took out a small flask, and, holding it towards Joe, said, "Will ye smile?"

To which invitation the parson, with a motion and look of disgust, replied, "I do not desire to take poison; the Lord deliver me from that sum of all wickedness." And lighting another cigar, he poured the fumes around him while appearing, and probably feeling, as though he had been caught up into the clouds, far above this sinful world.

Hearing him through, Bill carried the bottle to his own mouth, and trying to come the wink, which was a failure, he grinned once more, and said, "Ye look to me as though ye carried round a distillery of your own, Joe; now, don't ye keep the *worm* putty full? But I'd say jist so, if I was in your place; I would, by thunder! So, here's luck!" Then the bunch in his throat moved up and down many times, like a polite person bowing in a numerous and rapidly arriving company; so that, when he drew the "willow" away from his mouth, and shook it at his ear, he looked sorry.

As it grew dark, Bill, getting up, said, "I reckon it's time for me to be ridin' back to York."

"You make me a short visit," said Joe, with a pleasure that he could not quite conceal.

"O, ye needn't hope to dodge me so; for I'm comin' out here next Sunday to hear ye spout. I wants to see what college can du for a Frink."

So they separated; and, when the door closed between them, the Rev. Mr. Frink felt elated and relieved; for he had trembled at the recollection of the "seal" of Park, when Bill spoke of the cottage, and feared, during every minute of his stay afterwards, that something would lead to the subject again.

Yet, while Bill was moving down the street, he said to himself, "O, no, don't know her! hasn't heard her name! P'r'aps I've found a Frink what ain't for s'archin' into sich things — p'r'aps I haven't — we'll take a squint jist out o' cur'osity." So, turning down a lane, he reached the side of the cottage garden, where, finding a place through which he could pass without much difficulty, he entered; and seeing a light shining from the rear window of the house, he cautiously approached to find it half curtained, so that he could see no one therein with any distinctness, although the shadow of a female form moved frequently across the screen.

Withdrawing a few paces, he seized the limbs of a tree in his broken claws, and drew himself up to the point from which Fred had cried, "Land, ho!" where, with a sense of suffocation, he saw Flora, with a knife in her hand, preparing the evening meal, and a boy sitting by the fire. Gazing there, half breathless, he heard the door open; and then a man stepped out, who, walking down, paused to glance up into the tree in which Bill watched; but, apparently seeing nothing unusual, he passed on and looked at other trees.

While the person was away Bill felt for his bowie knife, saying to himself, "P'r'aps old Frink is treed at last; but they can't take him alive no how, by thunder! though he'll lay low for a minute, and let them bark fust;" when, looking up, he saw a young lady, with a bonnet on, come into the kitchen, who spoke to Flora and kissed Fred. Upon which the mustee opened the door, and, peering out into the dark, said, "Where are you? I want you a moment."

The person called replied, "I am coming;" when, walking up, he again paused by the tree on which Frink was perched; and, spreading open the low, hanging branches, looked up into the foliage — but turning away soon, he entered the house and closed the door.

Upon this, Bill descended from his observatory in haste and trepidation, and scrambling through the live fence, he stumbled over a rock into the road, thus meeting it face to face; but thinking that he had the worst of it in the encounter, he gathered himself up, and, while muttering curses, limped away as fast as possible to the stable, and, mounting his horse, took the road to the city. When he was well out of the village, he drew forth his flask, and, tipping off what remained of the contents, said, "Old Bill knows a leetle somethin' if he hasn't been to college; and I guess his scent is putty good yit: at any rate he don't knock under to ministers in that are line, no how, by thunder!"

On reaching the city, Bill had a social glass or two, but retired quite sober, for he felt that the business of the morrow required that he should be cool and wary. When he arose, however, he made it his first business to call on Mr. Mixer, of the bar; and after he had taken his somewhat late breakfast, and made that gentleman another call, he beckoned to the landlord, inquired for a United States commissioner, and was directed to the office of Mr. Featherstone, as the hotel keeper had some of that lawyer's cards and one of his notes of hand.

Finding Featherstone alone, Bill intimated the nature of his business, and, ascertaining that the commissioner was ready to act, said, "Now if ye undertake this ere job, squire, I want ye to draw your papers with all your might; for I expect there'll be some flutterin' and floppin' afore I git 'em back into the cage. And I know about how the thing's to be worked myself, as I talked it all over with my lawyer afore I took up the track; so, to start with, my name's Bill Frink, from New Orleans; and when you've writ that are down I'll tell ye some more."

Having minuted the name and residence, Featherstone said, "Now their names."

"The *servants'* names (he said how I'd as goods call 'em servants, while I was round here) is Flora and Fred, woman and child, and a'most white at that; but, allowin' they be niggers, I want ye to understand that they're jist the highest priced color in the market. Who ye lookin' at? why don't ye put down them are names? ye goin' to try to remember 'em?"

Recovering from his surprise, Featherstone wrote down the names, and inquired, in an indifferent tone, "Are the fugitives in the city?"

"O, they're within your beat, squire; and p'r'aps that's enough for ye to larn now; but Bill has seen 'em, and seen 'em flouishin'; and he kind o' aches to git a pull at their roots, 'cause he wants to transplant 'em to a hotter climate, so they'll bloom out 'arlier."

"It may be that, when we have caused them to be arrested, there will be an effort, on the part of the fanatics, to purchase their freedom."

"They ain't for sale; as they're particular favorites in my family, and they'd be enough sight better on't there, 'cause we all liked 'em ever so much, and was terrible sorry when they left; and I was cooped up in my room a mighty long spell on account on't. I tell ye, squire, when master and servant part in that are way, they're both apt to feel bad afore it's over. You men here, in the cold north, have no notion how strong we're linked to one 'nother. Now ye see, squire, its goin' to cost me a heap o' money to git them things back—a sight more nor any smart judge will prize 'em at; and why du I go it, if 'tain't for their good?"

"How long have you been the owner of the fugitives, Mr. Frink?"

"I've owned 'em jist long enough to git mighty fond on 'em, and not long enough to forgit what they cost."

"Who was their previous owner?"

"Du ye mean previous afore, squire?"

"Yes, the last owner before you."

"There, squire, that's the very thing I'd like to worm out — I should, by thunder! But, any how, the rascal what jewed me hails from this here city, and he helped 'em to run, for they'd never dug off so if somebody hadn't told 'em. Now, ye see, if I can once git 'em home, I can coax her to tell me who 'twas; and when I find out, I shall come on here ag'in, and p'r'aps I may want ye to defend me ag'in the law; for I shall mount him! I shall tumble down on him like a thousand o' brick — I shall, by thunder! Ye may be sure on't, squire, for Bill allers pays what he owes. I want ye to understand that he's considered about as ready a settler as you can scare up any where, or any how."

"Have you any persons with you who can identify the property?"

"How, squire?"

"I say," explained Featherstone, "is there any one here who knows the fugitives?"

"O, yes, we've got a large invoice jist arriv, and they're at the house I stop at tu; and one on 'em's name is Rutledge, a lawyer; and another's a flash chap they call Carlo, and he ain't a dog nuther. And they're both from Orleans, and will back up hard for the good o' their country. They're Uncle Sam's folks, you may bet on't, by thunder!"

"What is the age of the woman?"

"Wal, I reckon she's about five or six and twenty — ye may call her that much, and resk it, squire; and the boy's 'twixt five and six — and I guess them's all the p'ints that want explainin', squire."

"I believe that you have given me all the important facts."

"I should ruther guess as how I had; and now I'd like to know when I can have them papers."

"I can leave them at your hotel as soon as they are drawn out — which will be before the sun sets, certainly."

"Wal, that 'll be 'arly enough; for I likes night work, any how, 'cause I want to put these ere tender claws round 'em while they're sleepin'; then when they wakes up there 'll be such a lovin' meetin' of old cronies as ye don't often light on; and mebby she'll be so anxious to go back to her coop that I shan't ask for no more o' your help. But ye needn't look so scared, squire, for here's your ten dollars."

As Featherstone took the proffered fee, Bill said, "Now I shall expect ye to propel jist as strong, squire, as though ye hadn't got it." So, going out, he went over to his hotel to make another call on Mr. Mixer; and being pleased with his flow of spirits he remained with him until dinner time. At that hour, feeling the thing to be going gayly on, he called for a bottle of wine at the table, and had a very pleasant time, all by himself.

On coming out of the hall he saw a person whom he thought an acquaintance; and, feeling quite talkative, he gave him a little nearer look, when, putting out his fragment of a hand, he said, "How are ye, Captain Elery?"

Elery took the two fingers which Bill offered, and, looking at him, said, "Your hail is familiar, but I don't know the craft. What may be your name and port?"

"I don't wonder ye can't make her out, for she was blown up arter you saw her, and they couldn't find all the pieces; so we had to patch her up without 'em; but I guess Bill Frink is seaworthy yet."

"Is that a fact? why, you look as though you had been filibustering with Lopez! Then this is all there is left of the sharp who outwitted me in a dog trade, is it? Come into the parlor, and tell me how those hounds turned out! You must have had some exciting chases with them before this time?"

"Say *one*, and bet high on it," Bill replied. "I never had

on'y one right 'arnest hunt with them are dogs; but that was a ripper! and they died game — they did, by thunder!"

"How was it?" inquired Elery, as they took seats.

"Wal, it was this way: you see I'd bought a light-colored darkie, for fun, — you understand, — and she sot out to run. So we found her tracks, and them dogs, O, they took 'em beautiful! and never lost 'em once in the whole hunt; but when we reckoned as how we had 'em sure, we broke out o' the bush right on to the levee, and there them hounds was, fetched up all a stan'in'!"

"Had she jumped overboard?" asked Elery, apparently astonished.

"No; they'd got onto a damned abolition ship; and though they'd sailed more nor a half a mild away, them dogs snuffed 'em that fur; and I guess they heard me swear tu. Then we rode back to Orleans, and took a tug and blazed away arter 'em like thunder; and afore night we made 'em out; and then we strained every peg to overhaul her, but she sailed like a pirate. So, ye see, it was dark as a nigger's pocket afore we fetched her; and then we couldn't quite, for it grew rough; but we piled in the pine knots and the rosum, and we'd have jumped right on to her in three minutes, if them hounds hadn't broke loose. They'd been a whinin' a'most all the way, for, ye see, they smelt niggers — and rushed bellerin' for'ard and down stairs, where they throttled the ingineer and a fireman; and afore we could break up the row, any way, the b'iler bu'st; and a'most all on us as went up, ye see, didn't come down ag'in on'y in pieces; and them dogs went under, tu, in the scrape, and so I lost 'em."

"It must have been rather a rough time; and you were lucky not to get both of your binnacle lamps put out."

"It dowst one, and kind o' joggled down the wick of t'other

a leetle, I reckon; but not quite fur enough to stop me from spyin' *her* last night, any how."

"But you don't mean to say that she is any where in this region!"

"If I didn't climb a tree and peak into her nest last night, you may sell me for a nigger; and while I was thar, the man what lives with her — I guess 'twas him, for they seemed kind o' thick — bolted out and squinted up where I was, and I felt for my knife. But arter a minute or so he hauled off, and staid till she hollered to him. And when he come back he give my roost another s'arch, and then turned away jist as if he was arter his gun; so I clumb right down and left. But I want ye to understand Bill ain't bluffed off so. He'll see her ag'in to-night, and then he'll have the *papers* what'll knock her hand and pile tu, or else he'll give in that he don't know nothin' about cards."

"What do you intend to do with her?"

"Du with her!" echoed Bill, holding out his hands; "I want to see if I can cut meat enough out on her to mend *them* things."

"Would you punish her for loving and seeking liberty? You should remember that you are a republican, and that she may have aspired after the privileges of the free by seeing what a blessing they were to you. Would you stifle the hope of freedom in one who had so learned it?"

"O, no; but I may cut her up a leetle for takin' away my freedom. Ye see, I was shet up a'most tu long by her freak, and p'r'aps I didn't enjoy it particular. Now, captain, shouldn't ye love to go out and jist help me corner her? It'll be fun; it will, by thunder!"

"About what time do you intend to take the castle and seize the goods?"

"Wal, not till arter midnight; for, ye see, I want the town

to git still; and ye know we can't go on with the case, here, afore mornin', any how."

"I think that would be rather a late hour for me; yet I may conclude to go, for I believe that I could take her so easy that you would be surprised when you found it done."

"I want ye to understand I'm some at that; and I asked ye to go along jist 'cause I'd like for ye to see how I work in that sort o' harness."

"Well, if I fall in with you in the course of the evening you may rely on me to do any thing in the case that any man ought to do; and, on the whole, I think that I shall go."

"That's the talk; and we'll have a rum time when we git round her."

On this they separated.

It was not long before Bill went down to call on his friend Mixer. But, after a time, feeling refreshed by his social ways, he returned to the office, where, on inquiry, he found his papers, and requested the host to send out for an officer.

When that person came, Bill made him acquainted with his business, and thereupon they agreed to meet at eleven o'clock, and go on the expedition. Then, as a matter of politeness, Bill invited the officer into the bar room, and to the acquaintance of that spirit which enters in to charm, yet all too frequently remains to defile or to destroy. How apparently kind, but how deplorable in consequence, to those who lack self-control and have constitutional proclivities to its abuse! How many a glorious eye has it dimmed, how many a noble form has it cast down, until it seemed a mercy when the grave opened to shroud them from averted eyes!

CHAPTER XLII.

While amid the world's delights,
How warm soe'er we feel a moment among them,
We find ourselves, when the hot blast hath blown,
Prostrate, and weak, and wretched, even as I am.
FESTUS.

IT was nearly sunset when Elery parted from Bill; and, going out of the hotel, he took his way immediately to the Muse.

As he reached the head of the slip in which his ship lay, he met Jack, who was then second mate, dressed up, and hailed him with, "Where are you bound?"

"No where in particular, sir; only a short cruise."

"Then lay to here, a minute, while I speak to Francis." So leaving, he went rapidly on board. But, before Jack had got well seated on the cap-log, he returned, and, without pausing, said, "Come with me."

As they turned up street, Jack fell into the captain's wake; on which Elery said, "Draw up alongside; for I have something to tell you."

So Jack hauled out and came up abreast, when Elery said, "The man who claims to own Flora and her child is on here for the purpose of forcing them back into slavery."

"Who? Bill Frink! What can he do on that tack?"

"He can do much; for he has discovered where they are by some means; and a law has been enacted which will be a bloody weapon in such hands. Now, what I want of you is, to follow the devil, and stick to him through the night; and contrive to keep him in the city, if possible. But be sure and track him close, as I shall reckon on your arm; so you must take horses when he takes horses, and keep within striking distance, as we may meet on the road."

Having arrived nearly to the hotel, Elery, pointing to the building, added, "Frink is in *there*. He has only one eye, and parts of both hands are gone; for, you know, he has been blown up since you saw him; but you can easily make him out."

"If that's his course I'll overhaul him, and hold the weather gage, too, or I'll never steer another trick."

"He's a keen one," said Elery, as he left Jack; "so you must keep a sharp lookout."

"I'll try to lay along on his blind side," replied the sailor. Soon after he entered the bar room of the hotel, where Frink was drinking and getting noisy. Calling for a glass himself, he took a seat by one of the marble tables, and, taking up a newspaper, appeared to be busy with his own affairs. Yet his thoughts were of Bill and those whom he was hunting down; consequently his eye would frequently seek and fix sharply upon him, to turn away with a feeling of defiance or disgust, though Bill did not notice it, as he was in his element, being surrounded by the "suckers" who usually hang about drinking places to pander to the vices, and sponge their living from the careless prodigality of the intoxicated.

But there was one who had kept partly clear of the revel — although he stood in the group and seemed of them — whose business it was to observe and infer. This was the officer; and, drawing Bill one side, into an adjoining apartment, he said, "I am afraid that your affair is slipping through your fingers, and we had better be moving at once if you wish to succeed."

"I s'pose ye reckon I'm gittin' drunk; but you'll find me all the sharper for that are; ye will, by thunder!"

"I think you are watched, and may be outwitted."

"Who in hell dares to dog me? Show me the man, and I'll give him a lively whirl!"

"I can show you, if you will try to keep quiet, and have not already disturbed him. I have been observing him ever since he called for liquor, which he has not drank a drop of, but sits looking over a newspaper; and if you will slyly notice him, you must come to my conclusion."

But Jack was awake as well as the officer; and, seeing the movement, he caught enough of the conversation to learn that the outside of the house might be the safest, besides being equally good for his purpose; for if Frink remained it was well, and if he came out he could be as easily distinguished, and more quickly followed.

Consequently, when they returned, Jack had gone; and, on going up to the table, they found his glass empty. Thereupon Bill laughed at the officer, and said, "Ye see he swaller'd his rum afore he left; and I'm dry; so I reckon I'll take a smile with you on this ere."

"But there is the place where he poured his liquor," persisted the officer, looking under the table; "so I am now certain that he was watching you, and, hearing some of your loud words, thought it best to escape from scrutiny; therefore, if you wish to accomplish your purpose, you haven't a minute to lose."

At length Bill perceived that it might be so; and, turning to two or three, who appeared to be his particular admirers, said, "Gentlemen, I've got to be off, a few hours, on a leetle scout; but, if you'll jist hold on here till I git back, we'll have one of the times; we'll set 'em high; we will, by thunder!"

On this, the persons addressed having signified that he would find them on hand for any thing, Bill and the officer went out; and, taking a hackney coach, Frink, speaking low to the driver as he closed the door, said, "To Greenville; and stir lively now, if ye want double pay for the job."

The horses were fresh and fleet, and, so stimulated, the driver put them to their work. But the noise of the rapid motion seemed to lull Bill, so that his neck became limber very soon after they started, and pointed his hat lower, lower, lower towards one window, when, with a loud snore, he recoiled and brought the hat to bear lower, lower, lower on the opposite port; then the discharge and rebound were such that he surged back and doubled into one corner of the carriage; where, for more than an hour, he kept up the fire seemingly without aim or object, other than to burn his powder. After a while, however, he appeared to be using smaller cartridges, or else his ammunition had become damp, — although no water was ever allowed near the magazine, — so that, at length, it merely fizzling out, he awoke. Yet it took him some time to call into order all his drunken and somnolent senses; but when he did, finally, arouse them, the remaining minutes of the ride were devoted to arrangements.

"I wish we had another man along," said Bill; "two is hardly help enough without we can ketch her nappin', for she'll use cold steel."

"You may keep out of her reach, if you have any fears, after you have pointed her out to me," replied the officer.

Arriving on the edge of the village, Bill checked the coach, when the driver drew up to the side of the road, a few rods from the corner of the street on which the cottage stood; and, as they were alighting, Frink said, "Don't leave your team, skipper; for we s'all be back in a few shakes with a woman and child, and p'r'aps we may be in a tearin' hurry."

When Elery parted from Jack he procured a barouche and pair, and took the reins and the road, at a round pace, for Greenville. But before he reached the place the horses became weary, and required so much urging as to make a dark prospect for a speedy return; yet he cheered himself with the thought that there was ample time, as Bill would not leave until nearly midnight. So thinking, he slowly turned the corner, and drove under a shed which was attached to a store that stood there; when, walking out and approaching the cottage, he saw Annie just coming through the gateway, and greeting her, said, "I am very glad to find you here, Miss McRae."

"And so late, too! I was just going home," she replied.

"But I wish you to return to Flora a moment, if it be late."

"Why, what has happened that can so change your voice?"

"Not much has, yet much may happen, and that soon — our friends must fly; for the hunters are once more on their trail, and are intending to take them from this house before morning."

"Is there no method of protecting them here?"

"No, neither she nor all who sympathize with her can openly face this foe with any hope of victory; for he comes in the name of the law."

"What a loyal people we are, to so respect enactments! Still, in that spirit, when reform shall come, lies the hope of duration."

"True. Yet how hard to forbear a blow, even when we know that what has its foundation on reason is wisest, surest, and most fatally overthrown by the same weapon. Will you come in with me and break the news to Flora?"

"Yes; in with you and away with you, any where you wish, if I can help to save or cheer them."

"We will see; yet *you* must not come near danger."

As they ascended the steps Flora came to the door, for she had recognized their voices; and, ushering them in, said, "I had given up the idea of seeing you before another night; yet I am very glad you have come, for we were sad; and it seemed as though the wind sought to make us more so — it has sounded, all the evening, as if it mourned for something, or strove to utter a warning."

"It was mourning over our separation," said Annie, when the tears started to her eyes and sorrow overspread her face.

Through this, the fugitive perceived it all; and, looking up to the captain, she inquired, "Must it be — has the hour come?"

"I fear that *this* is no longer a place of refuge. So the sooner we leave it the safer we may be. I will take Fred out to the carriage, and you — collecting only such things as are really necessary — come down to the store with Annie; when we will soon learn if the Muse can still afford you a secure shelter."

But a few minutes elapsed before they were all under the shed, when Annie said, "I must go with you, for I can do something; and I would rather meet what you meet, be it what it may, than remain here inactive to imagine the worst."

"I have strong arms, near the invader, which will strike home if the hour of need come," interposed Elery; "while you can do good service here, and we may gather force from the thought that you, at least, are safe. You shall learn something of the night by the morning's mail; and, if it be in my power, I will see you before nine o'clock in the evening. Hark!" And listening, he heard a carriage rapidly approaching, which, in a moment, drew up just beyond the store, when he added, in a whisper, "Go round on the other side of the carriage — quick!"

As they stood there, close and silent in the dense darkness, two men came up; and one of them, halting, said, "Here's a pair of horses; *he's* ahead of you; hold on while I cut the harnesses."

"Keep still — can't ye!" was the reply, in a voice that both the fugitive and Elery knew to be Frink's. "That's the house; don't ye see the glim through the winder? they haven't run, and if they're gittin' ready to, we'll sly back and give the leather a rippin'. Come on!"

The officer, in the mean time, had approached so near that he caught the faint outlines of female forms; but, on the instant, something cried through his heart that he was made to shield and cherish such: so his eyes grew dim; and, turning, he followed Frink. Yes, it was the quick impulse of an Anglo-Saxon soul; an instinct that may save the race from the fate of all which have gone before — for gentleness to woman is the undying glory of her knights, the grace of their deeds, the perfume of their memories.

In another minute Jack came stealthily after; but a low-spoken word from the captain arrested and turned him under the shed.

"This is close work," said Elery; "and we must make for your carriage, Jack: these horses have broken down."

"But my horses are no match for theirs; we had to run to keep way with their trot. And if we pass their carriage the driver will see us; so, as soon as he could make signal, we should be chased and overhauled. I don't mind that though, if you say the word, for we shall be two to two if they lay us alongside."

"Then there is nothing left for us but to seize their carriage; which I think can be done, if we go boldly to the work; and you must go with us a little way, Jack, so the coachman may see that there are two men."

"We can do it! and if the driver makes any fuss I'll straighten him and take the helm," said Jack.

"Come, Annie, let me help you into this barouche; and, when you hear us start, drive up by the cottage to your father's house, so that the sound of these wheels may prevent their hearing ours." Pressing her hand in the friendly darkness, Elery felt a tear fall upon his, which thrilled him with emotion as deep as that which shook Conrad, when he saw the single drop of blood on the forehead of Gulnare, and by it he was drawn to her as strongly as that repelled the corsair; yet he whispered, "Adieu; and, whatsoever happens, we can never forget you."

Flora and Annie exchanged a kiss in silence. So parting, the fugitives stole out by the store, and approached the carriage of Frink at a quick pace. But, as they were entering with all confidence, the driver inquired, "Where's the big man?"

"He will be following us soon," replied Elery; "there is another coach in waiting, just back, to bring up the rear; so now for the city. You drove well coming out, and you shall have ten dollars extra if you reach Trinity Church in an hour and a half."

On this the driver, mounting his box, drew rein without further question. And while he was turning his horses Elery softly opened the door, saying to Jack, "You must take your own carriage now and contrive some way to mislead or deceive them, if they undertake to pursue; and be sure to dog Frink, if he reach the city to-night, wherever he goes, and baffle him if possible."

Jack got out unobserved by the driver, and away whirled the fugitives; while, as he was passing to his own carriage, he heard the barouche rattling up the street.

When Bill and the officer went on, they entered the cottage yard and cautiously reconnoitred. But discovering no one through the lighted windows, they tried the front door; when, finding it unfastened, (for Annie had intended to return, for the purpose of putting out the lights and locking up,) they ventured in, and closed it after them. Yet before they had examined far, a carriage drove by, when Bill said, "There! somethin's on the move; you watch here and I'll see where it goes to."

And getting out as fast as he was able to do from a dim and strange place, he rushed up the street after the barouche, overtaking just as it reached Mr. McRae's house. Annie saw him, as she alighted, and, entering within the gate, said, "Do you wish for any thing of me, sir; or have you come to cut the harnesses of my horses, and so fulfil your threat?"

Frink saw at once that he had been overreached, and that there was no moment to lose; yet, wishing to turn away the apparent suspicion, he replied, "I was lookin' round for the hotel; will ye be good enough to show me whereabouts 'tis?"

But at that moment Mr. McRae (he having heard the carriage and voices) came to the door and said, "Annie, what is it?"

"A person inquiring for a public house, father."

"I can show it to him by going a few steps. Be still, Teaser!" he added, addressing a small Scotch terrier, that had followed him out, and was growling at the stranger through the fence.

Bill, however, beginning to fear that he might be entrapped, while, at best, it would take him from his purpose and his course, was on the point of leaving as Mr. McRae opened the gate to join him; so that, when Annie said, "Do not go, father, for he deserves to be in prison;" he broke into a run down the street; and the dog, diving between his master's legs through the partly open gate, darted away barking at his heels, and, as he reached the cottage, fastened to his ankle. On this, drawing a revolver, Bill dealt the dog a blow with the breech that sent him rolling into the gutter, and a bullet by his own ear through the rim of his hat; the report of which shot called a number of white-robed forms to the adjacent windows; but they saw nothing, for Frink had entered the house, where, seizing hold of the officer, he said, "They've cut; and we must run afore they raise the town, for it'll be hotter nor a hornet's nest; it will, by thunder!"

Thereupon Bill opened the back door very cautiously,—as the terrier had recovered his senses and was barking furiously at the front,—when, getting out, they retreated through the garden and across the field to the main road.

As they jumped over the fence into the street, half breathless, and looked up and down, and down and up, Bill said, huskily, "Where the devil's our carriage?"

"It must be that we've got on to the wrong street!" replied the officer.

Then they moved quickly down towards the corner, listening and looking in every direction. Having reached it, Bill said, "'Tis the right road, for here's the store which we turned round; there tu's the shed where we saw them hosses, and there's the cottage up there: don't ye hear that damned dog at the gate? Our cart has left, ye may bet your life on that; and it's more nor an even thing that *they*'re in it. That's my notion; 'tis, by thunder! But you hold on here and see if any thing's movin', while I go down to that are stable and git somethin' to chase 'em with—we'll give 'em a hot run yit, by thunder!" and going rapidly down to it, he knocked on the window two or three times, with emphasis.

The stable boy, rousing up, inquired, "What's broke?"

"My carriage and the hosses have run, so I want to hire."

"We hain't got none in."

"But you've got some saddle hosses."

"I guess not; 'cause we hain't got on'y one."

"Wal, let's look at him; and here's a handful o' change for ye." On this, the door was soon opened; when Bill, entering, gave him the silver, and said, "I must raise a hoss to go to York, right off."

"He's a tip-top one," replied the boy, pointing to a stall; "but ye'll have to ask Mr. McRy, what owns him, 'fore I can let him go."

"Where'bouts is he?"

"O, he lives more nor a quarter of a mild from this."

"Wal, you go and see him 'bout it, and here's a dollar for ye." While holding the note towards him, he inquired, "Ye don't know who lives in the cottage next to the store on the corner out here, du ye?"

"No, sir-ee! but I guess Captain Elery owns it, for he goes there several times frequently. I knows it, 'cause he puts his hoss up here, and gives me a shillin'."

He having taken the proffered money, and started on the expedition, Bill proceeded to bridle and saddle the horse, for he had no time to wait; and mounting, whip in hand, he rode up to the officer, and said, "Here's all I could raise, and I cribbed this; so you must go to the stable and settle for't, and come by the next train, for I'm on their tracks; they're takin' to water, but I s'all fetch 'em."

Then, drawing rein, he rode off towards the city at a killing pace, yet plying the whip whenever the horse slackened speed, or he grew impatient; for every thing had passed so rapidly that he thought there was still a chance of overtaking the fugitives. Thus, for an hour, he galloped, as the horse had remarkable strength and power of endurance. Seeing how fleetly he was borne on, Bill began to take more hope, so that he dared to look at the facts; and, at length, he said, between his teeth, "Then Elery's the chap! and I, like a bloody fool, let him worm the whole on't out on me! Yes, I outwitted him in a dog trade—p'r'aps he 'magines he's squared that are 'count now; but Bill Frink's arter him for another reck'nin', by thunder! If I on'y had some o' the right sort o' dogs, now, I'd feel sure on 'em — and we'll have a law to use sich, yit; yes, right here in York State, or any wheres we want to hunt 'em, 'cause it's one of our rights; and when we southerners set out for't they'll allow it — in course they will, them doughfaces! But what's that? a coach?"

True, it was a carriage; and Bill curbed his horse's speed that he might get his wind before the pursuit was discovered. But, absorbed by his pleasant meditations, he had approached so near that Jack, who was on the watch, caught the tramp of the advancing foeman, and, observing his manœuvre from the window, shouted to the coachman to drive on.

As Jack expected, the rider drew rein and rushed after; and when he came near, so he saw that it was Frink, the sailor thrust his head out of the window, and cried to the driver, "Keep ahead of that horseman, any how! Crack on, with all your might — I'll pay for spars and riggin'!"

But Bill's horse surged on at a tremendous pace. So, as he came up nearly abreast of the carriage, Jack drew his head in, and, throwing off his coat, sat down on the back seat in his shirt sleeves. Thereupon, tying a bright handkerchief around his head, he doubled up one of the cushions of the coach and held it in his arms, so that when Frink had reached a point where he could look in, as they dashed by one of the street lamps, he felt certain that he had seen a woman and a child; and, being satisfied that it was the party he sought, he slackened speed and fell behind, feeling that he had them where they could not escape.

The watchful driver favored his horses also; yet they still pressed on at a gallop, for nearly two miles, with exhausting force. But, as they neared the corner of Canal Street, Jack discovered that they were coming up with the fugitives; and Elery, hearing the rush, looked out; so that for an instant he and Frink were face to face. At the moment, Jack, having resumed his coat, thrust his body far out of the window, and shouted, "Down Canal to the North River!"—and round whirled the carriage, while Bill reined after it hotly, seeing nothing and hearing nothing besides.

Down that broad pavement they sped, for some minutes, at a dead run; but before they reached the river the horses were completely blown, so that they sank into a trot, and, at length, to a panting, weary walk, as they turned, by Jack's orders, towards the Battery. Then Bill, dismounting, led his horse, that he might the more quickly recover his wind, and be the better rested when the struggle should again commence. But the reason for flight pressed no further, as Jack felt satisfied that, ere this, the fugitives must have reached the Muse. Consequently, as they were passing St. John's Park, beneath the shadow of the bordering chestnuts, Jack checked the coach; when, with his coat on his arm, he jumped out, and, keeping in the shade, faced the horseman, saying, "You've chased me long enough, without showing your colors, to be a bloody pirate. So now train out your guns, or try to board, if you feel like it!"

Upon this, Bill looked at him, and then into the empty carriage, in utter amazement, but said no word.

Observing him, Jack declared further, "If it's the craft you're after, you may speak the man at the wheel, as my cruise is up. But if you want any thing of *me*, come and take it, or clear the coast."

Yet Bill looked once more into the carriage, and, raising the cushions, felt of the seats carefully. Having thus made sure that it was empty, he gazed at the driver, and then at Jack; upon which, putting his arm through the bridle rein, he walked up the street without speaking, but with his eye over his shoulder, until he felt at safe distance; when, mounting his horse, he turned a corner and disappeared.

Paying the coachman, Jack moved quickly away, and gaining a post of observation before Frink arrived at his hotel, as he had to find a stable for his horse, saw him approach and go in. A few minutes after Bill entered, Jack observed a man cautiously emerge from the same doorway, apparently disguised; for, although the night was warm, he was wrapped in a Spanish cloak so closely that but little of his face was visible; noting which, the sailor was not surprised to see him turn slyly round the first corner and peer frequently out, as though he was an impatient watcher.

When Bill entered the house, he passed immediately to the bar room, where, though it was after midnight, he found his friends awaiting his return, and extremely glad to see him. Calling them at once to the bar, he said, "I never was so bone dry in all my born days. I'm parched clean through and through; my tongue feels as how it had been salted, and hung up on a nail a month, if not more."

"I noticed that it was getting corned pretty fast before you left us," said one of his familiars.

"Wal, you ain't very mealy-mouthed about it, any how. But I'm ready for ye now; so let's take another horn. Now, one more. Now let's give 'em a bumper." Upon this Frink's face began to glow, while his spirits arose with the other spirits, (for he had been nearly in a state of collapse, so that, for some time, he had had a taste of his own dust on his tongue,) when he said, "I'm ripe for any thing now, boys. Come, let's go out and rile 'em." As there was no dissent from that proposition, but a cordial response, rather, they drank again, and sallied forth in quest of adventures — the true knights-errant of their order.

As they turned up the street, Jack took their course, just keeping them in view; while he saw that the man in the cloak was stealthily pursuing, also. This person was Featherstone; but why he had been seeking Frink for hours, and painfully watching to dog him now, he would have found difficult of explanation — only that he was restless and apprehensive, with a dread of to-morrow, which sleep refused to veil. He did not seek his pillow, for he knew that it had no charm sufficient for repose. Poppy and mandragora had suddenly ceased to lull his soul. Even Oblivion, in whose dark waters he had boastingly trusted, was so shrunken as to expose the ghastly shapes which lay in its bed; and some of the portentous shadows arose and stalked near: these, perhaps, he hoped to lay by making swift his judgment against the fugitives and delivering them over to woe. But whatever his thought, or hope, or purpose might be, we are left to conjecture; ascertaining this alone, that he could not resist the desire to watch and follow Frink. May it not have been an inevitable consequence — the mysterious and irresistible tie of Fate that only the tears of contrition and forgiveness can dissolve?

It was not long before Bill and his friends turned into a narrow, cross street, when, moving down a number of blocks, they halted before a weather-stained house, where, listening a moment, one said, "It's all right!" for he heard a fiddle sounding its merry invitation down through the open entry, while the heads of the gay dancers could be seen as they flitted past the dingy windows.

So Bill and his retinue, entering without ceremony, mounted up a long and steep flight of stairs, and, opening the hall door, strode through the dancers up to the bar in the further corner of the room. On reaching that barrier between flesh and spirit, Bill threw his hat to the floor and stamped upon it.

Then jerking the fiddler from the counter, on which he was perched, he tossed him in among the company, and said, "I want this here crowd o' rum-heads to stagger up and drink with me." When, taking out his pocket book, and slapping it down on the counter, he added, "And I guess there's rhino enough in there to buy ye all out; I du, by thunder!"

With this elegant and comprehensive call the company seemed to be delighted. So, breaking from the figures, they flocked around the new comers; and, while striving to make themselves particularly agreeable to Bill, they watched him with especial interest when he opened his pocket book, and did not fail to observe to what place he returned it.

In a few moments, after they had imbibed their many named and variously colored mixtures, Bill tossed the musician up to his old perch, and, while taking a partner, said, "Come on, boys! let's have an old-fashin fore and arter — a reg'lar break down! So, fiddler, I want ye to grease your elbow, and put it to us with all your might, and I'll fork over a dollar, slap; I will, by thunder!"

To it they went; and before the dance was over Jack entered the room and took a seat unobserved; for those who were not on the floor were watching the performers with lively interest, and uttering words of encouragement or warning whenever either of them appeared to falter or flag.

Theirs was no listless loitering to dreamy music, but a wildly exhausting dance, and long continued; for the fiddler had a nervous arm, and worked it to the utmost. Swiftly they wove the figures, all glowing with exertion, and the sweat flew in large, oily drops, as they had no time to mop it from their fiery faces. Yet still came the flying notes on ever swifter pinion, and on rushed the reel, until, at length, one after another, the Bacchantes broke away from the fascination of the fiddler, and sank into seats from sheer exhaustion.

Giving only a brief breathing time, Bill called the company once more to drink with him, and Jack came forward among the crowd, and filled a glass. But Bill, happening to observe him, — as his eye was sharp for such manœuvres, — saw that he slyly poured away what he pretended to drink. So he turned to the bar keeper and said, "Boss, you've got one customer here who's either a cold water squirt or a spy; and now he's got to drink a bumper, or I'll put him out; I will, by thunder!"

"Go it, captain," replied the bully; "I'll back ye; and if there's goin' to be a fight, I want to be counted in."

Thereupon Bill caught up a decanter, and, pouring out a tumbler full of some red liquid, imported spirit, probably, like his own, shoved the glass on the counter towards Jack, saying, "Now, give us a toast that'll tickle the ladies; and leave no heel-tap arter it, or I'll spile your mug!"

But, seeing that Jack did not incline to obey, he continued, "You'd better down with it cussed quick;" and, scrutinizing him a little more closely, Bill added, "Who in hell be ye? doggin' *me* — ha?"

On this Jack drew back a step, while his well-knit form dilated, his lips set, and his eyes flashed.

Seeing the signs of determined resistance, and feeling the disdain of the sailor, Bill knew him for a foe, and sprang for him. But, on the instant, he received a blow which staggered him, for Jack was master of the art, and lithe as a tiger. Yet while his left hand was flying in with a "finisher," it was caught by the bully, so as to break the blow. This gave Bill time to recover, and to fling his brawny arms around his antagonist. Yet, at the moment of closing, Jack took him by the throat, with his right hand, so as to make the machinery whistle under the pressure. On that there came a struggle which made the floor shake, while the women shrieked and sprang to keep clear of the vortex. But Frink, by his superior height and giant weight, could lift Jack off his footing; so that, through all the whirling, noise, and dust, he was slowly bearing him towards the stairway. Yet the sailor's strong fingers were feeling well nigh around Bill's windpipe, where the whistling had subsided, while his swollen face was turning from red to black. One eye, also, seemed about to leave the socket, and the scarred form of the other looked like the head of a mud-turtle half drawn under its shell. Bill felt it to be a desperate moment. Still, although he had gained nothing for a few seconds, he was already near the door; which seeing, he made a heavy surge as a last effort, wherein he succeeded in catching his shoulder against the edge of the door casing, and by it, as with a lever, he was slowly but surely twisting the sailor over the very brink of the stairs. The next instant they were wrapped in darkness; for either the great vibration or nefarious design had turned off the gas. On this Frink felt a hand in his pocket, and knew that his money and papers were gone, which was his last intellection, except the oppression of mortal fear; for the same murderous and determined hand clutched his ankle, (on the very spot where Teaser had imprinted a warning,) and pitched him backwards down the steep descent, whither he tumbled with a hurtle and a crash, while Jack was still fastened to his throat, and pressed to his broad and shielding chest.

As they struck at the bottom, Bill's arms burst apart; when Jack, bewildered and lost for a moment, found himself still clinging to the throat, which he let go with difficulty, as his fingers had stiffened into that form. Yet, feeling satisfied that his watching was at an end, at least for the remainder of the night, he rose up, went out and away, taking with him some severe bruises and a broken arm.

Following the party to the house, Featherstone had lingered

watching in the neighborhood until he heard the noise of the struggle; when, supposing that they were arresting the fugitives, (for it was in such a place that he believed they would be found, this being his idea of their life,) he rushed in and half way up the stairs, where he encountered the descending combatants to be thrown stunned and bleeding to the floor.

When the watchmen came in, as they did in a few minutes, to examine the wreck and make inquiry, they were informed by some of the inmates, that the men were fighting, and fell down stairs together.

So it seemed from appearances; and those were all they had to judge from, as Bill's friends had hid, to slip away slyly after the officers had gone. Indeed, they could have no suspicion of any other hand in the work, as the pair, where they lay, were a pictorial illustration of the narrative, for they were in close proximity, while both were bleeding and insensible. Thus Featherstone and Frink had met, at last, upon an appropriate and congenial field; from which they were borne off, in the same cart, to that receptacle whereto is nightly gathered the scum which darkness floats to light.

CHAPTER XLIII.

Deep, deep, are loving eyes,
Flowed with naphtha fiery sweet;
And the point is paradise,
Where their glances meet.
R. W. EMERSON.

THE fugitives were agitated, for the moment, when they heard the rush of the carriage and saw the horseman, though they soon perceived how Jack was misleading their pursuer, and opening them a safe path to the Muse. So they had no further immediate apprehension for themselves, but, on reaching the ship, they anxiously awaited the arrival of the sailor.

At length he came, with his arm in a sling, as he had stopped on the way and had the broken bone set. And, while he is telling them his story, let us return to those whom we have left, in more painful and fearful uncertainty, at Greenville.

When Bill broke away so suddenly from Mr. McRae's attentions, and ran down the street with the dog in chase, Annie communicated to her father, in few words, what had happened to her friends at the cottage.

"Why did you not fly to me at once?" he inquired with unwonted emphasis. "Had you done so, I would have gone with them through danger to safety or to death."

"I had no time to think of it. Mr. Elery scarcely told us what was threatening before they were gone. And even then it was a narrow chance, as the hunters stood close beside us, during nearly a minute, while we were under the store shed; where one of them, seeing these horses and suspecting flight, proposed to cut the harnesses; and, had the other assented to the act we should certainly have been discovered; on which there would have been bloody resistance, or Flora must have been taken. It was a thrilling moment."

"How came Mr. Elery to seize their horses?"

"For the reason that these had given out, and having learned from the sailor that they would certainly be overtaken if his were used. So there seemed to be no way but to deceive their driver; which they did, apparently with ease, as I heard the carriage turning in a minute after they left me."

"Then they have escaped for the time, certainly, and perhaps entirely; for the taking of those horses was a stroke of fortune which waits not on the doomed. Yet these men will make a struggle to overtake them; so I shall do what I can to thwart their purpose; and it may be of no small importance to drive down to the stable to prevent their getting any thing to follow with, there — at least these horses must go there for the night."

"I will go with you, father; and when we return we can stop at the cottage to close it up." But as they were passing out, Annie, startled by a suddenly awakening echo, cried, "Hark!" when listening an instant, she continued, "It is the tramp of a horse. He is galloping towards the city; they are certainly pursued, and we are too late!"

At that moment the stable boy came running up, and said, "Mr. McRy, there's a man down to the stable says as how he wants your hoss to go to York."

"Why do you come to me on that errand, when you know I don't lend him?"

"'Cause the gen'leman ask me to; but I'll go and tell him how he can't have him, no how. He's a reg'lar ole fireworks, he is!"

"I will see the man myself. So you may get into the carriage, Jerry, and drive us down to the stable."

As they passed by the cottage, Jerry, wishing to dispel the silence or make himself agreeable, said, "Ole Blazes asked me who lived here, and I said as how I didn't know; but I told him whose 'twas, 'cause I guess he wants to buy it—he's got lots o' money!"

"How idly, how unwittingly a great misfortune may be brought to fall! This is dreadful; for it is the clew! It comes, too, from where we least expected it—so falls a shaft of Fate." And turning to Jerry, she added, "*You!* how came you to know who owned it?"

"My eye! Jest as if I couldn't smell out that are! I knows Captain Elery jest like a mice."

"Drive on!" said Mr. McRae. "Something may yet be done."

In a few moments they reached the stable; when the officer, who stood in the doorway, stepped to one side for the carriage to pass in. But before Mr. McRae alighted, he caught sight of the vacant stall, and inquired, hastily, "Where is my horse?"

"He was right there where he belongs, when I went out o' here to go up to your house; that's sartain true!"

"Is this the person who sent you to me, Jerry?"

"No, sir, ee! he was enough sight bigger, and one of his eyes was bunged out, teau!"

"Then my horse has been stolen," said the owner, emphatically.

On this the stranger came forward, and stated, "I am authorized to pay for the ride to the city, or the horse, whichever you choose."

"Who are you?" inquired Mr. McRae, with increasing excitement.

"I belong in town, and am an officer of the law."

"Then it would have been better for you to have remained there, than come out here to connive at a robbery."

"Sir, I took no part in the transaction."

"Then how came you by your instructions to settle with me?"

"The person communicated to me what he had done, and what he wished me to do, as he rode past me, on the corner above."

"In that case, it was your duty to cry stop thief, immediately, or take the consequences of being an aiding and abetting party. Yet, criminal as that is, it sinks into utter insignificance when compared to the wickedness for which you came here — prowling in darkness to deprive a feeble mother and her tender child of their freedom, the most sacred right under heaven. You cannot know what it is to have a wife, a child, who, leaning upon you trustfully, look up to you for support in a way that opens the heart, and keeps alive a sense of God's infinite mercy in the soul."

"I looked upon it only in the light of business; I thought not of the wrong until I came near it," replied the officer, his eyes suffusing and his lip quivering as he continued, "Yes, I have a daughter who is dying, it may be, this very hour — and a wife watching over her wasted form. While it was my hope, out of this night's transactions, to bear home some things which are needful — some delicacy that might win a kindly smile to their loving eyes."

Before the officer had ceased speaking, Mr. McRae's indignation was gone; for his words, but above all his tone and accent, had the life of truth. And Annie was so roused by the light which not only softened but transfigured the picture, that she said, "What a conflict is life, and how many lie wounded! so that, rend the veil where we may, we are full likely to gaze on some tearful sorrow, or some aching heart. O, how dangerous it is to judge, seeing how little we can know of the motive or even the way of another! Indeed, most of our opinions, touching such things, are random arrows that may hurt the innocent."

"I was hasty, and you will forgive me the condemnation; for I see that you are a man," apologized Mr. McRae. "So I wish you to come home and pass the night at my house, and try to forget my words in my deeds."

"I feel your kindness, but I must be with *them* before morning," replied the officer, still more moved by their generous sentiments; "and I believe there is a 'train' passes near here at twelve o'clock which will take me to the city."

"There is one due at that hour," said Annie; "yet you will have time to go home with us and remain some minutes. Indeed, I desire you to do so very much."

Upon this, moving out together, they walked up to the cottage and closed it; and, while passing on, Annie inquired of the officer, "Do you think they will be overtaken?"

"If they are both travelling the same road it may depend on the power of your horse. Yet, after all, what can he do alone, except to follow and to watch? and in that, probably, he will be out-generalled, as he was here, for he is heavy and headstrong with liquor."

They soon after entered the house; and there, under the opening influence of pitying kindness, the officer told of long sickness and suffering, such as cry for redress in many a city room, although the gay and thoughtless passer by hears never the faintest whisper of woe. In consequence of this, Annie filled a basket with fruits and delicacies, and things more substantial than they, which she learned were needed; and when he was about to take leave, Mr. McRae laid some money in his hand.

But the officer shrank from it, saying, "That is something which I have never done, and I feel that I cannot now; yet your kindness to me and mine I shall never forget." And the tears glistened in his eyes as if to show that, however want might have stricken him, he had kept the gems of his nature.

"But," interposed Mr. McRae, "I wish to have you search for my horse, and that will help to repay you."

"I will take it upon me to find your horse, if you want me to do so, and charge whatever the service may be worth."

"Certainly, I desire you to attend to it as much as I respect your feelings," said Mr. McRae. And thus they separated — having become dear to each other by friendly offices, notwithstanding their singular and sinister meeting.

(On the next day but one — for he had some difficulty in finding him — the officer came with the horse. At which time Annie received touching thanks from the dying girl and the fond mother; and learning their residence, she went there, and helped to smooth a sufferer's pillow, and soothe the sorrow of the mourners.) When the officer had gone, Annie said, "Were I not so agitated with thoughts of *them*, I should be very happy now; for the oil and wine which we pour into the wounds of another, become light and gladness to the soul."

"True, true!" And walking the room, he at length added, "I have been thinking, my daughter, how fluently and thoughtlessly we denounce; for our friends had taken that man's horses in the same way in which he took mine, while you were equally aiding and abetting, after which I applauded the deed.

'O wad some power the giftie gie us
To see oursels as ithers see us!'

Indeed, *I* need such a mirror, whoever else can do without it.

And as for our friends, so many things have fallen in their favor that I trust they will escape; I think we may hope for the best."

Leaving her father, Annie retired to her chamber, to be alone rather than with any hope of sleep; for her thoughts and her heart were out on the road, now leading her into dark ambush, now on to the very edge of fierce encounter, where she saw the flying fugitives turn to bleed or fall, or be taken captive; and she could not choose between them, which to save.

But, at length, through the tumult of her hopes and fears, came love's morning star; and she prayed for him in whose arm, under God, Flora was hoping and trusting: so passing into her heart, he was shrined in holiest secrecy.

To allay the sweet trouble which now possessed her, she closed her eyes, and gentle Slumber came and led her towards the realm of Sleep; whither she glided, dreaming as Genius dreams, when before his inspired vision there passes some form, which, if wooed to his canvas in all its heavenly color and proportion, will range it in that regal line to whose sovereign sway we yield, joyfully, forevermore.

But not long was she so lapped in Elysium. Soon awakening, morning seemed to come loitering with slow steps up the steep east; and the mail train appeared to idle on its way. Yet, after long watching and listening, there was a whispering, a buzzing, a panting; when straight out of a gorge of the hills, like the swoop of an eagle, the locomotive came screaming down the ringing rail, bearing brief tidings of safety, over which father and daughter rejoiced and were exceeding glad.

Many times on that day did Annie look through the note alone, although she knew it by heart, and gaze upon it long; yet still returned it to lie within her bosom's snowy veil.

In the course of the morning Annie walked down to the cottage, and seeing no appearance of its having been further invaded, she opened the door and passed in — where she found all things as they had been left at the moment of flight. On this, she gradually moved out of the fearful and shadowy apprehensions which had so suddenly darkened the present and trailed down the future, so that she received Elery at the gate, in the evening, with a smile, and something of the brightness of hope playing on the surface of the flood of her feelings, as she said, "It is kind of you to come."

"It is what I ventured to promise," replied he, taking her hand; "and I hope that you have not been anxious for their safety to-day."

"Not since receiving your letter; that, indeed, was a great relief to us, although I saw there was peril which you did not mean to tell me. Was the danger so great as we feared?"

"We did not come to actual conflict; yet, at one moment, only a sword's length divided us. But your friend Jack thinks, though he avoids the confession, that the bolts fell thick where he gave battle; for he has a broken arm, and is so bruised as not to be able to get off ship, or even look aloft, to-day."

So, entering the house together, he told her the story as he had gathered it from the lips of the sailor.

On his finishing the relation, Annie said, "What a night he must have had! and what service he has rendered us! Truly, I so honor courage, that, sometimes, I can see no virtue in aught beside; for it is the spring of all high achievement, and has led the forlorn hope in all Freedom's advances. What power for change lies in a single resolute soul! And Jack is as generous as he is brave! O, how Flora has won you all to be her champions!"

"Has she not enlisted you also?" he inquired with a smile.

"Yes, I cheerfully confess it, for she has singular power. What self-control is hers, except when she sees a generous action! Then, we were friends by nature, and have so entirely confided in each other, from the first, that it will be painful to separate. Are there no means which we can take to shield and keep her here?"

"Not here, I think. Yet we shall watch the clouds for a few days; as they, in a great measure, will determine what course, and where."

"If it be not dangerous to her, we must meet before she takes flight again."

"You may, unless there should be some sudden alarm; but for a few days it would be safer for me to be your messenger."

"Will you come frequently, and let me know all?"

"If you wish me to do so, it will be my thought throughout the day, and the charm of the evening, unless some unfriendly stroke should fall to prevent my coming. Yet, if I dared to hope that you would welcome me for my own sake, I should think of it with a freer spirit. This is no new thought; but one that sprang to my lips almost at our first meeting; yet it has been awed back, until this moment, through fear of wounding where I adored. But now, seeing something before me which may divide us long, I cannot part from you, and take aught of peace along with me, without speaking of affection — of love, even." And pausing, like some high-swept wave ere it breaks, he tremblingly added, "Tell me, dear Annie, may I hope?"

On this, Annie's low-veiled eyes were slowly raised to his, as they stood together in the recess of the window, and, with quick-beating heart and heightened color, as though his deep-breathed tones had thrilled congenial chords, she replied, "Love is an infinite word; a flower so divine that it made me tremble when I saw it unfolding. Yet hope seeks no more than you ——"

At this point the sentence was interrupted by a sob, and finished with a kiss — love's first, soft, fearful, tearful kiss;

one that leaves melting eyes and "music vows" far behind, while it fills the heart with rapture to become a sainted emotion within the shrine and amid the incense of Memory. Then, speaking low, Elery said, "I can never hope, dear Annie, to mate you in amenity of manner, culture, or grace of utterance; and, in all things, I fear that I shall fall far below you; but I am thine, and thou art mine — a thought which runs the circle of the heavens."

On this he drew her nearer, that he might hear her reply; but it melted on her lips, —

"The moth's kiss first — the bee's kiss now!" ——

* * * * * * *

After this, they met nightly, and the dividing day seemed a long separation. But their conversation, deeply interesting as they found it, was too frequently broken to appear intelligible in consecutive record, without the tones, glances, and appliances which made it so to them. Hence, as there are so few whose memory or imagination cannot supply those, the interviews are passed over with the full conviction that not only the appropriate words, but all that can give them music and emotion, will be profusely furnished by every appreciating reader. And yet they gave utterance to feelings, on one evening, which, as they appear to have more thought than usually pertains to such scenes, may not be unworthy of note. On the occasion referred to, Elery said, "Tell me, dear Annie, when you first loved me."

"I do not know; for we love sooner and deeper than we are aware. Yet as I look back, by the light of such hours as these, I learn how Flora's story filled me with the hope of meeting you. And then, having met and parted, I had sad, sweet, half-formed thoughts while musing alone; and you were

39

so mingled with them, that soon I could not help desiring to see you oftener than you came."

"Yet I feared that you were treating me kindly on Flora's account; and even when I began to hope it were otherwise, I dared not speak; for I thought that, if there were any suddenness in declaring my feelings, you would look upon me as one who could have but narrow ideas of the infinite consequence."

"When we know one, as striking events and near observation have revealed your heart to mine, if we do not love soon, it seems to me that no after time can awaken the emotion."

"True; and, as I think of the circumstances which opened our acquaintance, I believe that Heaven, by its manifest leading, designed that we should meet to love, and take the watch of life together. So, through shine and gloom, we will keep the deck, for my heart asks only that and thee."

"So my heart replies; and we will shape our course by the stars, bearing on a flame as pure and lustrous as theirs."

"Yes; and as intense," Elery added. "I know not, indeed, how love may appear to others, but to me it opens out infinitely; so that I feel it to be that irresistible attraction which not only gave me form, but determines my orbit. It is the one cry of my nature, the one longing of my soul. Without it fame wears no attractive wreath, the saint no glory. Such was love's dream, traced with all gorgeous and tender colors, by fairy pencils, on the dissolving curtains of sleep. And *now* it is a dream no more, but real as lip to lip can impress it."

"The world floats by me as a little thing, and the heavens are near. Look thère!" said she, pointing up; "see how the stars smile on us! and the music of their first song is audible through all the passages of my heart. Do *you* hear it?"

"I cannot quite," replied he, kissing her; "and I shall not let you so turn away from me, even to gaze after the infinite."

"Do you think I can have such a wish? when to love and to be loved appear to me to be the hope and the crown of life? when it is my undying faith that two full according hearts make the charm and the music of existence, while memory lives, or aspiration continues?"

I may no more of bliss disclose,
Or paint the peace of their repose;
And o'er the deeper mystery
E'en Song itself must silent be.

CHAPTER XLIV.

I was the victim of circumstances. NAPOLEON.

FRINK and Featherstone being still unconscious, when, unloaded at the watch house, a member of the healing profession was called in. On examination, Featherstone was found to have a broken nose, with some severe contusions; while his front teeth were generally among the missing. Yet, on the whole, he was not so dangerously wounded but that, by administering the proper restoratives, he, in the course of an hour, so far recovered his senses as to be able to make out where he was, and, consequently, ask to be taken home.

On this, the one who had him in charge curtly replied, "The doctor advises that you hold on here."

"But I do not choose to remain," interposed Featherstone.

"Wal, ole Pill said you might wander a leetle; but you can't go out o' here; so your best way is not to git fractious about it, or I shall be under the painful necessity of ironin' you."

"I say, Smasheyes," hailed a rosy-looking covey, who had been picked up in the early part of the night for trying to quench his thirst in the gutter, or mop it dry with his clothes, "if ye let *him* do it, you'll be ironed by a flat."

"I should like to know for what I am detained?" inquired Featherstone.

"On'y to settle for the leetle amusement you had with the fancy last night. The fiddler says how you owe him a dollar, though he allows that it was ole One-eye who promised it;

yet he reckons as how it makes no difference which on ye called for the music, as you and he were tight friends; for the last he saw on ye you was a huggin' of each other."

At this point Featherstone had so far recovered that his wounds began to become painful. So he felt of his mouth and for his teeth, and then he touched his nose carefully, as well as many other protuberances of his face and head, when his hand visited the more remote parts of his frame that were complaining. After which he inquired, rather dismally, "How was all this done?"

"They du say you stared a leetle tu much for safety."

From this Featherstone thought it possible that he might have been observed, while watching the house, by some of the inmates, and was knocked down stairs for attempting to enter. So he inquired, "Have you the person who committed the assault in custody?"

"O, yes; he's hard and fast; and you shall have an early ticket to appear ag'in him; and I guess you'll win, for you look as how you'd had a prize fight, and they du say you got the best on't."

"But I do not wish to make complaint, or prosecute the matter in any form."

"O, now you're tu forgivin'; you must prosecute; the scales of justice 'll grow rusty if ye don't. Your proposition is liberal, I know, but you oughter be a leetle hard once in a while for the sake of keepin' our free institutions a workin', and to help grease the law machinery."

Perceiving that he must wait until he could speak with some higher official, Featherstone straightened partly up, and limped along to a small looking-glass which hung in the room, to *see* how he appeared, as he was not quite able to make out the new geography of his face by *feeling*. For both eyes had gone into full mourning, while his nose looked like a "long red," only more crooked, as the end of it was pointed round toward his left ear. And imparting additional novelty, and so heightening the effect of the whole phiz, his gashed upper lip had swelled out and turned up, as if surveying the recent alterations, or else fearing to fall into the cavity which was occasioned by the sudden departure of the teeth.

Having satisfied himself with looking, though it took him some time, Featherstone tied his handkerchief over the new and tender developments as well as he could, and, pulling his cloak around him, hobbled to a bench in the dimmest corner, where he waited in silence for the morning.

The examination of Frink disclosed such a condition that the surgeon ordered him to be immediately removed to the hospital. When there, he was found to have one shoulder badly broken, the scalp laid open across the back of the head, directly under which there was an indentation of the skull, although exhibiting no actual fracture. Yet he did not appear to be in immediate danger of dying, as he breathed with but little difficulty, notwithstanding his big throat was marked with a hand which might have been gauntleted with steel, for it left the blue wherever it had touched.

The surgeons proceeded to set the shoulder as well as they were able to do under the circumstances, and dressed the wound on the occiput. Yet they could say nothing definite as to the result, for they had no means of knowing the injury which the brain might have received, and time alone could determine it. Such, at least, was the information that James obtained, he having gone forth immediately on Jack's return and communicated to the fugitives.

When morning came, one of the officers, with whom Featherstone had some acquaintance, looked in. But seeing that he did not recognize him, the prisoner called him near, and made known his name, with his desire to leave immediately.

He also entered some complaint touching his unwarrantable detention, and finished with allusions to the great anxiety which it would cause his family. To which the officer politely replied, "I hold no authority to permit you to leave, yet I have no doubt but that you can easily establish your innocence. And as to the witnesses, of course the government will call the inmates of the house, as well as the watchmen who found you; and if you wish to have any others in court you may give me their names, and they shall be subpœnaed, if they can be found."

"But what am I charged with?" he inquired impatiently.

"I understand the allegation to be, that you quarrelled with a gentleman from the south, whom you seriously injured by throwing him down stairs."

"Did you learn the name of the person?"

"I heard it, but it has escaped me." And turning to the man who had Featherstone in charge, he said, "Do you remember the name of the southerner?"

"I don't think I edzactly got it; but it sounded sunthin' like Chink, or Shrink; at any rate it began with the same letter. But any how, they allowed he was a large man with on'y one eye, and looked as how he'd fit a number o' duels with broadswords, as one side of his face was all hacked up, and most of his fingers was chopped off."

The rumor of so bloody a battle soon passed from the purlieus to the Park, with the usual exaggerations; yet with quite as much truth, perhaps, as the facts came from the witnesses in the court of inquiry.

Before the examination took place, it was known to the southern men, who were tarrying at the hotel from which Bill sallied, that one of their influential fellow-citizens had been seriously if not fatally injured. The circumstance naturally drew them together; and, while thus standing, an officer came in, who, knowing at a glance from what quarter of the country they were, approached, and hearing some of their words, said, "As the gentleman of whom you are speaking is unable to appear in court, or give any account of himself, I wish to find some person who will go and identify him."

Thereupon one of the group inquired, "Whom have they rested for the act?"

"The man what did it was found in the same house, and made part of the same heap; he's a lawyer here by the name of Featherstone."

Rutledge, who was one of the number, hearing this, said, "I will go, if I can be of any service; and I may be, as I knew Frink."

Upon this, Carlo remarked, (for he has been to Paris since we last saw him,) "I might go if you could promise me any amusement; although Monsieur Frink was not one of our set."

The officer, however, replied, "I believe one will be sufficient."

Soon after, he and Rutledge went out together; and making the visit and returning to court, they took a seat beside the attorney to communicate the name and residence of the injured man, so that he might complete his papers.

On the case being called, Featherstone was conducted into court; and, when the complaint had been read and the plea entered, the attorney for the government put the woman on the stand who had officiated as Bill's partner in the fore and after.

That lady being sworn, and having stated her name, the attorney said to her, "Now, my good woman, I want you to go on and communicate to the honorable court what you know about the sad transaction at your house on last night."

"At the ball, do you mean?" inquired she.

"I wish, Fidelia, to have you begin at the beginning of the

quarrel between the prisoner now at the bar and Mr. Frink — giving all the melancholy circumstances up to the murderous end."

On this the counsel for the accused interposed, and, addressing the court, said, "I think my learned brother goes far, much farther, he himself must be aware, than the facts in the case will warrant, when he calls this misfortune a murder."

"I believe, may it please your honor, that the learned counsel is right; and, when he is, I can think of no rarer pleasure than to acknowledge it. Yet he will readily perceive that the exciting nature of the transaction is calculated to work upon the feelings; and that on such occasions we use words without being conscious of their full legal import; therefore, if the court please, I will restate my question in a form which I hope will be free of all objection. Now, Miss Fidelia — I believe that is your name."

"My name is Fidelia Constant."

"Well now, Miss Fidelia Constant, we wish you to make known to the honorable court what was done in your house by the prisoner at the bar, relative to the assault upon Mr. Frink." And turning to the counsel, that gentleman bowed graciously, seeming to say, "Your language, now, my learned brother, is within the rule;" while the highly intelligent and carefully cultivated spectators appeared to be astonished and delighted at such a display of legal acumen.

"Go on now, Fidelia," said the attorney.

"I can't, for I didn't understand what you asked me."

Here the court interposed, saying, "I will put the question. Witness, did you see the fight in your house last night?"

"Yes, I did; for it was so near I couldn't help it."

"Go on then and tell how it happened," said the judge; and thereupon he looked down on the voters, and they looked up to him, as though he had untied the gordian knot.

"I had been dancing with the big man from the south ——" commenced Fidelia.

"Does the witness, Mr. Attorney," inquired the court, interrupting, "refer to the party who is alleged to have been injured?"

"Yes, your honor."

"You may go on, now, witness," said the court.

"We had been dancin'," again commenced Fidelia, "and were restin', for it was so very warm, or hot, as you may say ——"

"I submit," said the counsel, interrupting, "that the thermometer would be the best evidence of the warmth of the weather."

"Miss Fidelia," said the attorney, "you need not state any thing concerning the temperature of the atmosphere."

"I should like to know how I can say any thing about refreshment if you won't let me tell why I took it."

"We do not wish to hear any thing concerning the refreshment," said the attorney, gently; "for that may be objectionable matter."

"You needn't be afeard of my tellin' any thing o' that kind."

"I mean that the inquiry is not material," explained the attorney, "and that it might lead to something irrelevant or impertinent."

"I should like to know what you say that for," sharpened up the witness. "I say I haven't said a word which looks like bein' irreverent or impertinent; so there!"

"O, no, Fidelia, certainly you have not," replied the attorney, soothingly. "You misapprehend me; I only mean to say that any thing relative to the refreshment could have no bearing on the case."

"Wal, then, I can't tell any thing about it; for it broke out at the refreshment."

"What broke out?" inquired the court, impatiently.

"Why, the rumpus," replied Fidelia.

"How did it break out?" the court followed up with.

"Wal, you see, it was very warm, and the southern planter and I, with a number of others, had been dancin'; so we was quite fatigued, as you may say, — and we *was* very much fatigued, — when he, very perlitely, as you may say, gin us an invite to take some refreshment."

At this point, the counsel interrupted with the inquiry, "Was the prisoner present while you were dancing?"

"To tell you the plain truth, I don't think he was; for I didn't see him — and I've got nothin' agin him but the rumpus he kicked up."

"Then, may it please your honor," delivered the counsel, with appropriate emphasis and gesticulation, "I submit that this testimony, so far as it has gone, is wholly and totally inadmissible."

"Certainly; no principle of evidence is more clear than that," decreed the judge. And turning, he said, "Witness, when did you first see the prisoner at the bar? or rather, at what stage of last night's performance did he come in?"

"I believe he slipped in while we was pertakin' of the refreshment, as you may say."

"What did he do then?" inquired the court.

"He wouldn't do nothin'; he wouldn't even taste no refreshment; and the southern gentleman urged him to give a sentiment for us, but he wouldn't do nothin' on'y fight, as you may say."

"Now, Miss Fidelia," said the attorney, wooingly, "tell us how it was."

"Wal, I will, if they'll let me. My partner in the dance, the gentleman planter from the south, that I spoke about afore, the one who asked us all to take refreshment, on account of the extreme heat, as you may say, — and I shouldn't have taken it if it hadn't been so warm and muggy, for I never does; so, as we were goin' up, or while we stood round the refreshment, I will not swear sartainly which, the man came up and —— "

"What man?" inquired the counsel, interrupting.

"Why, the man that rowed so, and scared us e'en a'most to pieces, as you may say."

"Well, go on," said the attorney, smiling at the counsel.

"I don't know whereabouts I was."

"You, testifying, with the oath of God upon you, against the life of a fellow-creature," exclaimed the counsel, with becoming vehemence, "say now that you do not know where you were!"

"I disremembered whereabouts I was in the story, as you may say; for you keep a tryin' to put me aout all the time."

"You had got where 'the man came up;' those are the words, as I have them among my minutes," suggested the court; "do they agree with yours, gentlemen?"

"Yes, your honor, they do with mine," replied the attorney.

"I have them," said the counsel, reading, "'the man came in'— a very material difference, I submit."

"Well, witness, how was it?" inquired the judge.

"I said *up;* for I didn't see him come in," replied she; "and you told me to tell on'y what I saw with my own eyes."

"What did he do when he came 'up'?" the attorney inquired.

"Is not that leading?" queried the counsel.

But Fidelia had got out of patience; so, reddening, she raised her voice, saying, "He wouldn't do nothin' till he drew back and struck my partner, the planter. Then he clinched him; and, my stars, how they twisted, and squirmed, and wriggled! and all the whole time the southerner was workin' towards the door, a tryin' to git away; and I pitied him so I didn't know what to do; and while I was a tryin' to think how to stop the squabble, the lights was dowst out by the jigglin', as you may say; and the next thing I heard —— "

"Witness," said the counsel, sharply, "you are not to relate what you heard."

"I will not press the inquiry further with Miss Fidelia," said the attorney, "as I have ample testimony with regard to the conclusion of the — affray." And turning to the counsel, he added, curtly, as beseems such irreconcilable foes, "She is your witness."

"You say," said the counsel, taking up the cross-examination, "that your name is Fidelia Constant — where were you born?"

"I can't remember; and you say you don't want hearsay evidence."

"Miss or Mrs. Fidelia Constant, are you a married woman?"

"It's none o' your business, you good-for-nothin'!"

"Witness! you must answer the questions of counsel," ruled the court, "unless, by so doing, you will criminate yourself."

"But you said, on'y a minute ago, how I mustn't tell a single word on'y about the fight; and I ain't agoin' to."

"If you address the court in that manner," threatened the judge, "I shall be under the necessity of punishing you for contempt."

"I haven't said how I felt any contempt for ye; and I guess I've got a right to think jest what I please, as much as other folks."

Seeing that the judge did not know, between his dignity and his popularity, what course to pursue, the adroit counsel said, "I pray the court to forbear; as I prefer to waive any further inquiry in that direction, rather than see this creature suffer for her ignorance of the reverence due to the bench."

"It is a matter of great doubt, with the court, whether it has a right to withhold its hand," the "bench" delivered, after due deliberation. "Yet it will so far yield to the prayer of counsel, as to stay proceedings pending the examination."

"Miss or Mrs. Fidelia," resumed the counsel, "what kind of refreshment were you taking when this fight, as you say, commenced?"

"Don't you believe the fight begun when I swore it did?"

"Woman," replied the counsel, "you are here to answer questions, not to ask them. What kind of refreshment was that? I repeat."

"What kind of refreshment?" she echoed.

"Yes, that was my question, *precisely!*" replied the counsel, standing sidewise to her, with his ear leaned towards her, while looking round very wisely on the spectators; "and I think it is pretty evident to all of us that you understood it at first."

On this she said, meekly, "There was a number o' kinds of refreshment."

"I've no doubt of that; but what kind did *you* take?"

"Me?"

"Yes, *you*."

"I took most a tumbler full o' water, with a leetle mite o' gin — not enough to hurt a muskeeter, as you may say."

"Was it what they call a gin sling, or a gin toddy, or a gin cocktail?"

"I don't know nothin' about it; and nobody but you would be mean enough to ask me; so there!"

"What did your partner in the fore and after take?"

"He took the same kind I did."

"How do you know that fact?" questioned the counsel.

" 'Cause he said he would, out o' compliment to me; and I turned it out myself from the same decanter; that's how."

"You took quite a fancy to your accomplished partner — didn't you?"

"Yes, I did; for he was a perlite man — a great sight more so than you be."

"You disliked the man that he pitched into?" queried the counsel.

"She has not said that he pitched into him," interposed the attorney. "She testified that the injured man was trying to get away."

"Miss or Mrs. Fidelia, do you know what Mr. Frink came to your house for, on last evening?"

"Come to our house for?" echoed Fidelia, while the spectators, and most of the attendant lawyers, leaned forward as if fearing to lose a single word.

"Yes," replied the counsel, while surveying the crowd, "that is what I asked, *precisely!*"

Thereupon, the attorney arose, and, addressing the court, said, "I feel it to be my duty, as an officer of the government, to interpose here; for I belive that there are some limits, even to a cross examination. And if law be instituted for the protection of society, as I hold it to be, then those who are called to the high places of its administration should see that its sanctuary is kept pure; in this view, if in no other, I apprehend that this honorable court will assert its power, and check the inquiry."

"I do not see the relevancy of the question," declared the court.

"May it please your honor," responded the counsel, rising, "suppose Frink told this woman that his bones were aching for a fight, and that he should hurt somebody if he wasn't held. Moreover, I propose to show your honor, by competent and unimpeachable testimony, that this same southern planter and gentleman went to her house ripe for a row with any body; and that he had one, too, of his own raising."

"Then you are not under the necessity of making the inquiry of this witness," the court remarked.

"I did it, your honor, because I thought that it would save time. But under the direction of the court I will not press it further. The witness may step down."

On this Fidelia smiled around as she moved towards her seat, when the counsel, looking up suddenly, said, "There is one question which I omitted — if the court will allow me." Receiving a nod from the quarter addressed, he turned to the witness, and added, "Miss Constant, will you step back once more? only for a moment."

She having taken the stand again, he inquired, "Do you see the man here with whom Mr. Frink had the quarrel?"

"No! I've been a lookin', every minute a'most, to see him come in."

"What made you expect that?"

"'Cause you said the prisoner was at the bar. So I looked round for it, and though I didn't see none, I knew by your appearance there must be one somewheres about; and I naterally s'posed he was in it."

"Then you say, on your oath," emphasized the counsel, "that the man there, with the cloak and bandage on, is not the one who 'rowed'?"

"I guess not; though he's so bundled up I won't say sartain; but if he'll take off his winter harness, and that are bloody dud, I can tell better."

"Mr. Featherstone," said his counsel, "will you have the goodness to lay aside your outer garment, and remove your handkerchief from your face a moment, only a moment?"

When the prisoner had slowly — from reluctance or pain —

done as was requested, Fidelia, looking at him closely, said, "It ain't *him* no more'n nothin' at all, for that man had brown hair and no whiskers, as you may say. But my sakes! he looks like a blue Monday!"

"We do not wish for any of your comparisons, witness," cried the counsel.

"Wal, I say he does; he looks as though he was an egg plant, and had been trod on by an elephant. O my! how he squelched him! He saw the elephant *some* where last night, I know he did. My sakes!"

As this testimony put a new face on the matter, Featherstone tied up his again. Thereupon the government placed other witnesses on the stand, who corroborated Fidelia in the fact of identity — that being the only point on which they were questioned.

Then the attorney called the officer who had Featherstone in charge through the night, and who was among the first on the field of action, and helped to gather up the wounded, to state what he knew of the matter in hearing. To which he replied, "I found Mr. Featherstone, the prisoner at the bar, at the bottom of the stairs with Frink, any way. How they got there I won't pretend to say; on'y they were piled clost, and 'peared as how they must have lost their understandin' nigh about the same place and time, while their mugs looked as if they had a whole hod of brick in their hats when they dove."

At this point the prisoner arose, and, removing his muffler, said, with very imperfect and seemingly painful articulation, "If the court will indulge me, I can explain the circumstance of which I am the victim."

After a few moments of deliberation the honorable court graciously assented to the proposition, although it was out of the approved course. For the experience of judges goes to show that, when the government has failed to prove the guilt charged, the prisoner does better to rest satisfied, even though he be entirely innocent of the particular offence, rather than take the stand himself, and thus expose the whole course of his life to unpleasant or curious questions.

Yet Featherstone, availing himself of the permission, said, "In the course of last evening I happened to be passing the house mentioned by the witnesses, and, hearing outcries, rushed in to see if I could render any assistance. But I had only ascended part way up a flight of stairs, when I suppose that I was struck with something, as I can remember nothing further. To which I will add, that I did not see Mr. Frink in that house last night, or any time, or quarrel with any person there, or elsewhere, to my knowledge."

On this, Mr. Rutledge, who had remained in the court room, drew his chair near to the attorney, and, talking with him in whispers a moment, that officer turning inquired, "Mr. Featherstone, have you any acquaintance with William Frink, Esq., of New Orleans?"

"I have met a person by that name."

"Yes, I am aware of that; as you have just told us that you suppose you met him on the stairs last night. But allow me to ask you, Mr. Featherstone, if you transacted any business with him yesterday?"

"I did."

"What was the nature of that business, if you will indulge me?"

"As I acted in the capacity of counsel, I am bound not to disclose it."

"Mr. Featherstone, are you a commissioner for the execution of the Fugitive Slave Act?"

"I hold an appointment which makes it my duty to enforce that statute if properly applied to."

"Have you taken any action, under that law, within the past twenty-four hours?"

"I have no right to answer such question."

"Under certain circumstances that is true, Mr. Commissioner. But I will now put you a question which I know Mr. *Featherstone* has a right, if he has the inclination, to answer, namely: does Mr. Frink claim any of your blood as his property?"

Thereupon Featherstone, turning to the judge, inquired fiercely, "Am I a witness or a prisoner? or by what warrant am I now held in this court?"

"As Mr. Featherstone volunteered to explain," said the attorney, addressing the bench, "we presumed that he might be anxious to clear up the whole mystery. Therefore I will ask the volunteer, Have you, or have you not, issued process which you knew at the time of issuing was intended to tear your own child from freedom, to consign him to bitter and life-long bondage?"

"You, Mr. Attorney, are the mere tool of another in these insinuations; therefore you are beneath my notice. But I am fully aware from whence the questions emanated, and they will not be answered on demand. I shall take my own time, and place, and manner of replying; yet they shall be responded to, to the entire satisfaction of one of us at least."

"If I am the one to whom this person addresses his threat," said Rutledge, rising, and in a tone and with a port that thrilled the court, "he may learn that I am not to be turned from my purpose by the menace of a miscreant. Consequently, if the attorney chooses to place me on the stand, I will relate this fiend's history until he shall crouch at my feet like a whipped cur, and howl there for mercy; unless it be that he is as insensible to honor as to justice, as reckless of reputation as of retribution."

Featherstone bent before this, as a snag bows to the wild sweep of the Mississippi's current, while the bitterest mortification and the direst hate entered into his heart to join all the other fell passions and emotions there, and so complete the hell of his bosom.

At length the court broke the silence by saying, "Gentlemen, however mystery may darken around another, in connection with the last night's, or any transactions, or wherever suspicion may attach, it is our office to see that it is legally presented to us before we proceed to the investigation; we cannot try two cases at once. So, Mr. Clerk, let Mr. Featherstone be discharged from custody; for it is plain that he is not guilty of the offence set forth in the complaint."

CHAPTER XLV.

> I' the world's volume
> Our Britain seems as of it, but not in it;
> In a great pool, a swan's nest.
>
> SHAKSPEARE.

BILL FRINK continued without mental restoration, though physically he was healing fast, for he seemed to have that vitality which enables the snake to move his body long after his head has been crushed, and sometimes even to so far restore it as to answer most of the purposes or wants of his crawling life.

On hearing of the catastrophe, the Rev. Mr. Frink hastened in to visit his brother, but by no effort could he rouse him to recognition or recollection, for he appeared to have very little notion of any thing. So the divine was obliged to seek elsewhere for the information that he most desired, and inquired for Bill's pocket book and papers of the attendants and of the superintendent, of the officers of the law, and of the landlord, saying to each on receiving their negative, "It is very strange that no one should know any thing of them, as I am certain that my brother had a large sum of money with him, for he was rich, and never travelled without it."

Finding no solution of the mystery elsewhere, the Rev. Joseph ventured to visit the house in which the unfortunate accident happened, for the purpose of making the same inquiry. On being shown in, he was very politely received by Fidelia, which attention, it must be stated for the sake of the clergyman's moral character, he returned with a contemptuous stare, and a rebukeful snuffing of the air, as it was redolent of that class of stimulants against which he had elected to point his cannon. The examination, however, was well nigh fruitless, as he found nothing except materials for a sermon, which he thought, and therefore we may think, was a "most lame and impotent conclusion."

Flora and Fred continued on board the Muse, where, although somewhat confined to her cabin for a few days, they were secure and happy; as Elery had frequent and sure intelligence of the condition of Frink, and the opinion was daily gaining confirmation that he would never entirely recover his senses.

Annie had been in the city and on board of the ship with her lover, where she passed a day and the night with Flora; at which time she gave her the outline of a story that delighted her exceedingly, and helped to make her more joyful than she had seemed for many a day.

They talked of impending changes, also, with Elery; as it was thought not to be safe for the fugitives to return to the cottage. But, before any thing was determined, Mr. McRae was taken into council, who, after weighing the doubts and considering the circumstances which would continue, for a time at least, to disturb them here, like all true men, still loving his fatherland, advised the United Kingdom. To this conclusion Annie was not averse, and talked to Elery of the prospect with a smile and with a hope.

After deep and anxious reflection Flora said, "Although I dearly love the land of my fathers, I see that I must leave it for a season, and it may be forever; because that, under existing circumstances, prejudices, and laws, my boy cannot rise up and be a man in the country of his birth; therefore I desire to pass within the protecting folds of the 'meteor flag' of England."

On hearing Flora so speak of her place of refuge, Elery was

sad; for he loved his country with the passion of a sailor who seeks to bear her barred ensign in peace or war in the van of nations. But, looking to the constellated stars which floated from his main, he saw and confessed the cloud, yet hopefully believed that it would pass away and leave them unsullied, for he thought that he beheld signs of a wind from the north-west. So he acquiesced in the necessity of a "flight into Egypt," (so he called it,) until that auspicious breeze should drive back the fogs of the gulf from the sky of the pilgrims.

Rutledge, also, was consulted; for Flora, having noticed his name among the arrivals at the hotels, told Elery how truly he had been her friend. So the sailor invited him on board his ship, where he and the daughter of Merton met, with mingled sadness and rejoicing; after which he became a frequent visitor while the Muse remained in port, seeing and admiring Annie; and at length he parted from them with kindly words and tokens, and bright assurances for the future.

Mr. McRae had many times talked of visiting the land of the Thistle, and Annie had fondly mused the while,—

By heather glade or hazel shade,
  In gloomy gorge or lonely dell,
With spots by raid or Genius made
  A glorious tale to tell.

The change which awaited their friends brought up the subject more earnestly and more frequently, until they were persuaded to leave their house in the care of Teaser and a faithful domestic, and take passage with the fugitives.

Out on the ocean Annie and Jack walked the Muse's deck many a night hour, while the larboard watch was on duty,—for he was mate and James was second,—where she listened to the story of his early days, followed by storm and peril on every sea; and he inhaled gentleness, grace, and enthusiasm from her speech; so each felt and feels the worth of the other. Fred stuck closely to James, and believed in him; and, mounting on to every spar and yard of the ship with him, held himself ready to shout "Land, ho!" whenever it should heave in sight; while Flora was the favorite of all, and rendered herself more dear, if possible, than ever.

There, too, by day and by night, a slender but active form was often seen beside the captain, walking or seated, and talking low, as if their world and wish were within whispering distance; while the father smiled upon it as though it were all his own, and turned back in fond memory to an earlier day.

At length Fred had found his opportunity to shout "Land, ho!" and the Muse was in port, and the party in Scotland. There, within sight of Stirling's towers, in an ancestral mansion of the McRae's, they had gathered among gentle kindred and friends, where Elery and Annie were wedded.

Saddened with excess of feeling, the lovers gave their hands and made their vows. Yet, after those thrilling and solemn moments, and the bright and touching congratulations, they could hardly be called the centre of attraction; for the sea voyage, or contentment of mind, had rounded the mustee's form to more than its maiden fulness, so that at twenty-seven she seemed more charming of outline than ever, while Thought had wrought her features into his own perfect expression. And as she stood amid the fair beauties of that land, infinite in her variety, her large, dark eyes now dim with emotion, now on fire with intelligence, revealing her to be Oriental in temperament as in hue, she so filled the imagination with a gorgeous vision of the dim East, as to evoke the clime of Ind, with its dusk gold, its tawny lions, and its atmosphere with the crimson tinge — those, as it were, the phantom pageant, and this the befitting canopy of a queen who won the enthusiastic admiration of all.

When the guests had departed, and the evening was drawing to a close, Flora took the hand of her deliverer, and, with smiles and tears, said, "I feel now that I have paid something of my immense debt, for without me you might never have met Annie, or meeting passed unknowing and unknown."

"Do you think so?" inquired he, with a playful smile; but he immediately added, with a thrill of emotion in his utterance, "Yes, my friend, you have paid and overpaid, for it was your fiery trial that exalted me to *this*. You, indeed, are free."

And Annie whispered, "I am sure, dear Flora, I could never have loved Frank so entirely and so admiringly if he had not done you such glorious service."

As they were standing near the open lattice, Elery, pointing to the stars, said, "Hush! *I* hear them singing *now*." But Annie touched him, and met his glance with eyes pleading for silence on that theme, for she thought it a reminiscence too sacred for even Flora's ears.

O Love! he who comes to thee with so leal a heart may well hear a strain of music from beyond the stars more sweetly entrancing than that which they chant when a new world joins their shining choir; for they, to the expanse of heaven, are but as glowworms amid a meadow's green.

A week, and Annie had gazed on the charming scenes through which the Wizard of the North evermore leads the Lady of the Lake. Yet though standing on the consecrated spot where

"His chain of gold the king unstrung,
The links o'er Malcolm's neck he flung,
Then gently drew the glittering band,
And laid the clasp on Ellen's hand,"

she felt no envy for the daughter of the Douglas! It is not for her to mourn that the glittering mail, the waving plumes, the rush of the barbed steeds athwart the ringing lists, the splintering lance, and clashing steel are dull and silent all, for she knows that generosity and valor still live, and are glowing in full knightly puissance in a heart devotedly her own.

Through many a green valley, by many a hoary summit, they travelled in that storied land, quickening their recollections and expanding their hearts by contact with the ruins which beauty, heroism, and love have consecrated; and

> "For which the palace of the present hour
> Must yield its pomp, and wait till ages are its dower."

Then, in one of the verdant vales of England, by the brink of bright water, wherein Fred sails the schooner which Jack has given him, in an ancient and picturesque cottage the party found repose.

There Flora will wait a more auspicious hour to return to her country. Strong in security, happy in rare friendship, happiest of all in the promise of her child, she looks back on the dangers which she has passed with silent and fervent thanksgiving, and forward with serene hope and trust.

As the friends sat together in the evening twilight, previous to the morning of their separation, talking of past hours and future prospects, Elery remarked, "I have seen care-worn and hunger-wasted faces here, such as never meet me in the States, where

> 'Plenty leaps
> To laughing life with her redundant horn.'

Yet, I confess, I shall feel more satisfaction in aiding the mind of Fred to unfold here, in a country where color cannot depress or close against him the gates of learning, or the field of war, where

> 'His spur may lance his courser's flank,
> Before proud chiefs of princely rank,'

or bar him from the great heights of her free debate; but rather is he invited to all; there to contend for the palm with the sons of kings and of genius."

"Yes," said Annie, "the moral sense of this people is such that to have been a slave is a title to consideration."

"But look to Ireland, to India," suggested Elery.

"That is the work of the government," said Mr. McRae; "and whatever of wrong is therein, the heart of England grieves over it, and will not always suffer it; for she has achieved a way to the throne, where she utters words of warning, or of menace, as freely and as fearlessly as did the prophets in the presence of the kings of Judah. Even emancipation was carried by a few brave lances, bearing down on serried ranks which were fortified with the appliances of the merchant, and armed with the remonstrances of the planter. So it will ever be with wrong, however embattled, before the Ithuriel spear of conscience."

Those were cheering thoughts to Flora, and she said, "Where freedom is the most sacredly guarded, there is my country. O, may the time soon come when that hope will lead me to my native land and to you;" and this was the earnest prayer of all.

So, on the morrow, they parted from the fugitives to embark

> "Once more upon the waters! yet once more!"

and sunny was their voyage, and soon they heard

> "The watch-dog's honest bark
> Bay deep-mouthed welcome as they drew near home."

CHAPTER XLVI.

But now 'tis past,
And the spell closes with its silent seal.
BYRON.

RUFUS MERTON'S sister has nearly accomplished the important work which she had laid out for herself, before visiting Europe; namely, the marriage of her daughters — for the eldest has espoused "Fed," and the other is affianced to Carlo; both men of such wealth as to be above any useful employment; and their tastes will lead them to bring up their children on the same course, so that they must, at length, strike the rocks of poverty; to go under, or awake to swim for their lives, and acquire new vigor in the struggle.

Bill Frink has been placed under guardianship, and put to board in a hospital for the insane. He has entirely recovered his bodily health, but of reason he has only just enough to be unreasonable, with so much of memory as to think that the institution wherein he is confined is a college, and such still-lingering aspiration that he pores, hour on hour, over a child's story book, as though he imagined it would conduct him into that armory where he had supposed that poets and orators found the shining panoply in which they took captive all human hearts, and conquered Time, and chained him to their triumphal chariots. He, indeed, never heard — and, if he had, it was not in his nature to comprehend — how the mother of Achilles ascended to the gods to obtain even the material armor for her son; how much more those polished and far-flaming arms which invest heroes with the power to overthrow and rebuild creeds and institutions!

Even Bill's reverend brother has been subdued, and consequently improved, as fear is a salutary potion for such natures. When forced to think, as he is, sometimes, that Park may hear of the circumstances which, probably, caused the fugitives to flee, he trembles. Still he can learn nothing that was done by his brother to molest them, although he has made many a cautious but palpitating inquiry; he only knows the coincidence, and gropes around in darkness and doubt.

Were it not that Bill's hand may yet appear in it, he would be glad that they were gone, let it be to what place soever; for he could not always bring himself to speak kindly of Flora, and of Fred he frequently said, "He was the sauciest boy I ever saw; and he will surely come to some untimely and terrible end." Yet we hope that the child may not suffer from his opinion; for he likes his school, and reverences his kind and skilful teacher, while he overflows with love for his mother and her friends. On such paths the hand of Heaven may lead him clear of this pious malediction — at least let us so trust; for it has been aforetime predicted, by similar prophets, of those on whom it came not to pass.

Mrs. Fardel peruses the dictionary frequently, yet she cannot quite satisfy herself which word, among a few, Park intended to apply to her; and this leads her to think of Aurelia; while both considerations have tended to abate something of her zeal in mercenary match-making.

The mansion of the Vernons appears to be fading back into the gloom in which we found it. The dress of the old gentleman has become worn and faded, his step short and unelastic, so that he leans more heavily on his staff as he comes out of the back passage, where, pausing on the sidewalk, and seeming to have no aim, or being unable to determine which way to move, he gazes now on vacancy, now upon the ground.

Mrs. Vernon has again retired to the gloomy region in the

rear — as only her economy and skill can maintain the household. There, industriously but silently, she meets the exigencies of the hour. Her form does not bend to the weight, neither does her pride; although the light of her life is paling, so that her atmosphere grows wintry, and hope sinks below the horizon, while night is steadily encroaching with clouds that leave no star.

Aurelia has obtained a divorce from Featherstone for cruelty, with alimony almost too meagre to spin therefrom the slender thread of subsistence; for if he had property, he managed to sequester it from her as effectually as from his creditors. So her insane dance is ended; and if she still linger in the dreary house, so haunted with sorrowful thoughts and recollections, it is some consolation to know that he who tempted her to the measure can no more drag her to the floor. If her beauty has faded with her woes, or her garments, the world cares not — indeed, observes not; for she dropped out of their memories when she fell from their sphere; and she knows not yet where to turn for repose, or hope, or consolation, but sits in the shadow and accuses Fate. A colony of spiders have taken possession of the deep recesses of the doorway, and stretched their gossamer nets across the entrance where she once passed so often and so gorgeous with the garniture of Fortune; for they have run a cord to her chamber window, and frequently look in upon her listlessness or her despair, to return to their spinning, their snaring, and their feasting, with an instinct of security for many a future day.

Featherstone, since his night adventure, which had such color of suspicion that it left a stain, has gradually lost what little practice he had of the better sort, and is sinking into a defender of drunkenness, rowdyism, and petty larceny, in the court where he last appeared. Yet he visits Mrs. Summers occasionally, for she still sees something in him to like, and discredits whatever is said against him ; so that even he is not without a friend.

Though Park is no longer young, he still dreams of love, and is worthy of the tenderest flame that ever filled the eye of beauty with divine light. In him are unsounded depths of affection. His sympathy with the weak, the wronged, and the suffering, is only the overflow of an inexhaustible fountain, which gathers volume as he advances in years. He keeps the course which he pointed out to the convention, alike regardless of sneers, ridicule, and denunciation; for great names cheer, a stout heart arms, and bright hopes lead him. He joyfully accepts every call to plead against human bondage before the sovereign people; and, in so doing, has taken the tribute of tears and admiration from many of the gifted and graceful of the land. His lofty spirit thirsted for these springs, and they are sweet to his soul. Thus animated, he is sowing the seeds of a glorious harvest; and though he may not be among the reapers, his name will kindle their enthusiasm and inspire their songs.

MRS. LESLIE'S JUVENILE SERIES.

During the last year, we published a uniform edition of a series of volumes on HOME LIFE by this popular author. They are noticed in the succeeding pages, and were designed for adults. Their popularity has greatly increased our confidence in our design, then announced, of publishing a series of volumes on subjects embraced in the same general title, but specially adapted to children and youth, and therefore styled MRS. LESLIE'S JUVENILE SERIES. Several volumes of this latter series were then ready for press. Two of them are now issued; and in the autumn we shall publish others.

VOL. I.

THE MOTHERLESS CHILDREN.

A thrilling story of orphanage, illustrating the trials and temptations of the young, and the happy results of Christian nurture.

VOL. II.

PLAY AND STUDY.

An interesting tale of school days, very suggestive of practical hints to parents and teachers, showing the manner in which they may aid their children and pupils in the invention of their own amusements for their relief and stimulus in study.

VOL. III.

HOWARD AND HIS TEACHER; with the Sister's Influence, and other Stories.

Illustrative of different modes of home government.

VOL. IV.

TRYING TO BE USEFUL.

The object of which is sufficiently indicated by its title. It exhibits the happy results of worthy resolution and endeavor.

VOL. V.

JACK THE CHIMNEY SWEEPER, and other Stories.

Illustrative of the Commandments and other precepts of the Bible.

VOL. VI.

NEVER GIVE UP; or, the Young Housekeeper.

Exhibiting the success and reward of perseverance in the acquisition of fortune and fame.

VOL. VII.

THE RICH POOR AND THE POOR RICH.

A story of unsurpassed interest, showing how the wise direction or the abuse of the love of acquisition may prove the salvation or the ruin of the young.

MRS. LESLIE'S SERIES FOR ADULTS.

VOL. I.

COURTESIES OF WEDDED LIFE.

This is a work of rare merit, designed for all who have been, are, or ever expect to be married. It is an able vindication of the divine institution of marriage, which lies at the foundation of social order and happiness. It is not didactic, but descriptive, most admirably adapted to control the judgment, to improve the heart, to multiply and perpetuate the amenities and joys of wedded life.

A simple, life-like tale. — *Boston Daily Journal.*

A series of graphic pictures portraying what married life should be. — *Boston Daily Bee.*

A book for thought and reflection, simple, easy, natural, and beautiful in style. — *Worcester Spy.*

The painting of life-scenes of thrilling interest. — *Boston Evening Transcript.*

Worthy to be read aloud in every family in the land. — *The City Item, Pa.*

Well calculated to increase the happiness of married life. — *Providence Daily Post.*

A graphic delineation of d[...]estic scenes. — *The Christian Mirror.*

A key to domestic happiness — *The Boston Atlas.*

The best book of the season. *New York Tribune.*

The genial, familiar, *home* [...]*le* of this book will secure it popularity and success. — *Chri*[...]*an Register.*

VO[...]. II.

CORA AND THE DOC[...]; or, Revelations of a Physici[...] Wife.

Few works that have issu[...] om the American press have excited more interest in thei[...] ontents, or more curiosity to know the author than this volume upon its first appearance — an interest and curiosity which the lapse of a few months have rather increased than diminished. The circumstances which originally produced the desire of its author to remain strictly *incognito* having ceased, her literary signature is affixed to this edition. It is distinguished for high-toned morality and ardent piety. In respect to literary merit and artistic finish, it is pronounced by Hon. J. T. Headley, "A remarkable illustration of the power of genius;" by Mrs. E. Hale, "Worthy to stand side by side with 'The Lamplighter,' and its influence even better than that;" by the Daily Advertiser, "Equal to Miss Bremer's 'Neighbors;'" by the American Index, "A mate for 'The Diary of a Physician;'" and by another Reviewer, "Superior to Mrs. Stowe's best;" and is spoken of by other Critics in similar terms.

VOL. III.

THE HOUSEHOLD ANGEL IN DISGUISE.

This volume, which has just issued from the press, is esteemed by most critics superior to either of the preceding in delineation of character, in graphic power and pathos, and in the unity, depth, and salutariness of the impression which it leaves on the reader. Its design is harmonious with them, being to encourage beneficence, and to secure a closer application of Christianity to domestic life. A glance at the notices of reviewers will confirm this opinion.

A sweet book, — pure, lovely, touching ! O that such books might be multiplied. — *Trumpet.*

A well-written story of high moral aim. — *Bangor Journal.*

A beautiful commingling of cultivated taste, exquisite sensibility, and elevated piety. — *Puritan Recorder.*

Judicious, interesting, instructive, and excellent. — *Evening Traveller.*

A natural and exciting story, simple in style, elevated in sentiment, and most happy in influence. — *New Bedford Mercury.*

Adapted to send an angel into every household. — *Evening Transcript.*

A charm to the reader. — *Daily Tribune.*

MRS. LESLIE'S HOME LIFE.

PUBLISHER'S NOTE.

THESE three 12mo. vols. of four or five hundred pages each, well printed, neatly bound, are admirably adapted, in the judgment of critics, the press, and the public, to promote the cause of popular and moral education. They are entitled "HOME LIFE," to indicate their object, which is the application of our common Christianity, free from all denominational bias, to the relations and duties, the joys and sorrows, of domestic life. They are not didactic treatises, but narratives of intense interest, a series of life-like pictures. They have their foundation in facts, but are embellished by an imagination controlled and chastened by religious sentiment.

They have already found their way into thousands of Family and Sabbath School Libraries, and their continued sale is an increasing indication of the public esteem of them. The FAMILY AND SABBATH SCHOOL SERIES are retailed for one dollar a volume, or three dollars a set, and sold at wholesale at a discount of one fourth from the above prices.

The volumes in "MRS. LESLIE'S JUVENILE SERIES," which retail at 75 cents per volume, are offered to the trade, to Sabbath Schools, and persons making remittance by mail or express at a corresponding discount. To any person enclosing two dollars and twenty-five cents current money, or post-office stamps in a letter addressed to the publishers, they will be immediately sent, neatly packed in a paper box.

Please write distinctly the post-office address, and the name of the express by which they are to be sent.

The name of their authoress, Mrs. Madeline Leslie, alias Mrs. Harriette Newell Woods Baker, wife of Rev. A. R. Baker, and daughter of the late Rev. Leonard Woods, D. D., of Andover, is a sufficient guarantee that their contents must be most suitable to your purpose. Multitudes of different Christian denominations, who have tried this series, pronounce it one of the best additions which they have made for many years to their libraries.

SHEPARD, CLARK & BROWN,
110 Washington Street, Boston.

VOLUME I.

THE COURTESIES OF WEDDED LIFE.

THIS is a work of rare merit, designed for all who have been, are, or ever expect to be married. It is an able vindication of the Divine Institution of marriage, which lies at the foundation of social order and happiness. It is not didactic, but descriptive, most admirably adapted to control the judgment, to improve the heart, to multiply and perpetuate the amenities and joys of wedded life.

"Seldom have we found a book so deeply interesting. The manner in which it is written, its life pictures, and the phases of human nature so finely portrayed, tend to inspire the reader with the fact that there is something pictured in the imagination so thoughtful, so life-like, that we are compelled to admire it. Mrs. Leslie has certainly done credit to herself, as she has to her subject. In treating of courtship and marriage, of the relation of husband and wife, their responsibilities to each other, their trials and rewards, we have seldom, if ever, found truer or more powerful delineation. Get this book and read it, and you will be convinced of the justness of our commendation." — *Evening Transcript.*

"A book for thought and reflection, simple, easy, natural, and beautiful in style, skilfully managed in its narrative, intensely interesting in its scenes, and highly moral in tone and tendency." — *Worcester Spy.*

"A series of life-like pictures woven into a story of great interest, simple and beautiful in style, natural in its scenes and characters that are drawn with the skill of an artist, pure and elevating in its moral tone, a great favorite with the public." — *The Critic.*

"A simple, life-like tale, more than outweighing all the sophistry and false philosophy of free love, by upholding the divine institution of marriage, and showing that piety in wedded companions conforms character to the loftiest standard, and adorns every day life with a continual succession of surpassing graces." — *Boston Daily Journal.*

"There is a mixture of humor and pathos in the narration, and altogether the book is just such as will suit the popular taste." — *Hingham Journal.*

"Its dedication is touching and significant — 'Affectionately inscribed to my beloved husband, on the twentieth anniversary of our marriage;' a series of graphic pictures portraying what married life should be, attractive and sensible, with much to guide, inspire, elevate, and refine whoever truly inhales its spirit; a fabric woven with such skill and beauty as to be appreciated and admired; excellent in style, and matched in interest only by the importance of its subject." — *Boston Daily Bee.*

"The perusal of this book will satisfy any one that it is a work of genius. Its style is beautiful, and a highly moral tone pervades it. To all wishing to read a really good book, or to present one to their friends, we give this advice: Purchase a copy of this work." — *Gloucester Advertiser.*

"The genial, familiar, *home* style of this book will secure a reading from beginning to end, and will carry all the force of good example. If this new and enterprising house publish books like this, they will deserve the patronage and thanks of the public." — *Christian Register.*

"It is a book so interesting as to deserve to be read with attention, and of such a character as to be worthy of such a reading." — *The Country Gentleman.*

"The story is essentially one of home. It deals with familiar scenes and incidents, and the characters are such as we daily meet. There is a pure morality in the book which enhances its beneficial influence, and commends it to the attention of those who believe in the uselessness of fiction. The authoress evidently regards the marriage tie as the most sacred of all earthly relations; and her composition will doubtless awaken many to a sense of the realities and responsibilities of wedded life, will cause them to pause and reflect ere they enter upon its duties, and will induce them to fulfil its purposes as a wise Power intended when he first joined man and woman in holy wedlock." — *Evening Gazette.*

"There can hardly be a nobler field of labor than that occupied by Mrs. Leslie in these pages, interesting and highly instructive." — *Daily Mail.*

"We have rarely read a work written in a style more interesting, with a feeling more sensitive to the right, and with a moral more direct. Every wife should read this aloud to her husband, and many, we doubt not, will feel conscious of their past remissness." — *Portsmouth Journal.*

"This is a tale of domestic life, simple, easy, and natural in style. Its characters are life-like, and its whole effect cannot be otherwise than salutary." — *Cleveland Herald.*

"It will be read with admiration by all who value lofty views and noble deeds." — *News.*

"It is natural and easy in style, and free from the eccentricities which disfigure many of the most popular works of the day." — *Daily Am. Citizen.*

"Graphic delineations of domestic scenes, where many a wife will find a picture of her own experience." — *Christian Mirror.*

"It answers well its purpose, and will be hailed by the thousands as the key to happiness. It will delight our readers, and shed new light on the time-honored institution of marriage." — *Boston Atlas.*

"The book is the best we have received this season." — *N. Y. Tribune.*

"It should be read by every husband and wife, and by all who expect to sustain that relation, to make them therein wiser, better, and happier." — *Bay State.*

"The design of this book is in a high degree praiseworthy. It is nothing less than to impress husbands and wives with their reciprocal obligations, and thus to facilitate the attainment of the ends of the marriage relation. The book is decidedly of a Christian tone, and though it takes the form of a tale, it is fruitful in lessons of a serious and practical nature. The story is ingeniously constructed." — *Puritan Recorder.*

"Christian decorum and courtesy are here exemplified in admirable style." — *Cleveland Herald.*

"It ought to be read by all." — *Syracuse Daily Journal.*

"Decidedly a family book, written with spirit and life, interesting and instructive." — *South Boston Mercury.*

"Full of deep and affecting lessons, tinged with high religious feeling, beautifully harmonious with the quiet, earnest flow of the narrative and the deeply interesting thread of the story." — *Gazette.*

"A well-written and interesting book." — *Saturday Evening Mail.*

"The author's wide popularity from her articles in 'The Happy Home,' and other magazines, and from her various contributions to the stock of family literature, cannot fail to be much increased and extended by this work." — *Salem Gazette.*

"Its design is to produce a more just appreciation of the marriage institution, and to increase the happiness of home. These are subjects of interest to every one, and presented, as they are here, in the form of a thrilling story, they will be found quite attractive to the reader." — *American Commercial Advertiser, Baltimore.*

"A wholesome and entertaining book, greatly superior in aim and tone to most of the novels of the day. The story of the first courtship and marriage, with its fluctuations of girlish feelings and womanly instincts, is an admirable picture of young love." — *The Eclectic.*

VOLUME II.

CORA AND THE DOCTOR;

OR, REVELATIONS OF A PHYSICIAN'S WIFE.

FEW works that have issued from the American press have excited more interest in their contents, or more curiosity to know the author, than this volume upon its first appearance — an interest and curiosity which the lapse of a few months have rather increased than diminished. The circumstances which originally produced the desire of its author to remain strictly *incognito* having ceased, her literary signature is affixed to this edition. It is distinguished for high-toned morality and ardent piety. In respect to literary merit and artistic finish, it is pronounced by Hon. J. T. Headley, "A remarkable illustration of the power of genius;" by Mrs. E. Hale, "Worthy to stand side by side with 'The Lamplighter,' and its influence even better than that;" by the Daily Advertiser, "Equal to Miss Bremer's 'Neighbors;'" by the American Index, "A mate for 'The Diary of a Physician;" and by another Reviewer, "Superior to Mrs. Stowe's best;" and is spoken of by other critics in similar terms. We subjoin a few extracts from other notices.

"It contains some of the most exquisite painting it has ever been our fortune to meet with." — *Puritan Recorder.*

"Unlike many of the romances of the day, this book may be read, not only without danger, but with decided profit. The devoted life of a skilful and conscientious physician is here truly and vividly portrayed. His many noble acts of benevolence and sympathy, while administering to the physical and mental sufferings of his patients, may naturally excite in them the most unbounded confidence, admiration, and love. Such an example is worthy of all imitation. The medical profession, though arduous, has its charms, when its duties are discharged, as in the case of Dr. Lenox, the hero of this story, with ability, and in an honest and Christian spirit. This book inculcates the purest morality, uncontaminated by sectarian influences. Its pages are replete with thrilling incidents, and the interest in the narrative is so ably sustained, that few persons would be willing to lay aside the volume after having commenced its perusal." — *W. D. Brincklie, M. D., Philadelphia.*

"Our heart has been made to throb with its dramatic incidents, and our eyes to well up with the pathos of its heart-revealings." — *M'Makin's Courier, Pa.*

"It has been read with a zest and interest seldom, if ever, experienced by a perusal of any similar or dissimilar production." — *Westfield News Letter.*

"It was rarely been our lot to peruse a more intensely interesting book than this. Its style is chaste and pure, and what strikes the mind of the reader more than any thing else is, the air of deep-toned piety by which it is characterized. None can read it without rising from its pages with the intention of aiming to be better and wiser." — *Wesleyan Journal.*

"This book, from first to last, is full of the most beautiful teaching, and yet conveyed in such a manner as to make the reader fall in love, not only with the instructions, but with the instructress. It is a remarkable illustration of the power of genius, to invest everyday life with far greater attractions that are gathered in the most highly wrought romance. One can hardly read a page without feeling his eyes filled with tears, either of sympathetic joy or of deep sorrow, over the touching scenes of exquisite sensibility that pervade the book. It is a work of enlivening interest, while its moral effect is above all praise. Read it and see." — *J. T. Headley.*

"Its aim is most excellent, its characters charmingly drawn, its incidents of lively interest, its religious influence sweet, and the fragrance it leaves behind pure and refreshing." — *Christian Mirror.*

"It is indeed a work of power, pathos, elegance, and Christian sentiment, one among thousands; sufficient to maintain the claim of its author to very unusual gifts." — *Evening Transcript.*

"Its style is very simple and winning, its moral lessons excellent, and its whole influence good." — *Congregationalist.*

"An earnest religious sentiment pervades the book, showing how much good a Christian physician may do." — *N. E. Farmer.*

"It represents the author's *beau ideal* of a Christian physician — a very attractive volume, teaching admirable lessons." — *Zion's Herald.*

"Its characters are religious in the best acceptation of the term — one of the most entertaining and edifying works of the day." — *Daily News, Pa.*

"Decidedly a book of mark and merit, and shows its authoress capable of achieving a future reputation equal in her own land to that of Miss Bremer among the people of her nativity. The plot is good, decidedly superior to Mrs. Stowe's best. An unusual fascination lingers upon every page, and makes one feel better for having read it — more disposed to be what he ought to be." — *Boston Bee.*

"It exhibits much literary refinement and moral culture, but more of the life of an upright and humane physician, earnest in doing good to all. It produces a great sensation in literary and religious circles." — *Barnstable Patriot.*

"It inculcates the purest religious sentiments and the highest moral duties." — *Godey's Lady's Book.*

"Those who have read it once will read it a second time; and it is worthy a place in every library." — *California Farmer.*

"A very devout and religions spirit runs through the book, and it deserves to be a favorite." — *Salem Observer.*

"It shows how much good may be done by a disciple, when his life is pervaded by the spirit of active humanity and vital Christianity." — *Cincinnati Columbian.*

"A mate for 'The Diary of a Physician,' a work of a peculiarly religious tone." — *Am. Index.*

"The joys and sorrows, the jealousies and confidences which mar or smooth the path of life, are here well introduced and dwelt upon. The book is very well written, and reminds one, in its structure and style, of Miss Bremer's 'Neighbors,' to which it bears no unfavorable resemblance. It is devoid of any of the coarse and harsh features of Miss Bremer's book, while it has much to remind the reader of her best passages. It displays great skill and good taste in the writer, a very devout and religious spirit, and it deserves to be a favorite." — *Boston Daily Advertiser.*

"The attention of the reader is captivated, almost from the first page, and thrilling incidents and charming scenes are freely interwoven throughout the story. An earnest religious sentiment pervades the book, and indeed it seems to have been the writer's design to show how much good a Christian physician may do. If our judgment is not greatly at fault, it will prove to be one of the most popular stories of the season." — *New England Farmer.*

"It is the product of a mind richly endowed and highly cultivated. Its style is pure and elevated, its moral tone of the highest order, its characters well sustained, and its interest increases from the first page to the last. It is nearly what 'The Diary of a Physician' would have been if the successive chapters of that book had formed one continuous and thrilling narrative. Its croup scene is enough to immortalize its author. No characters ever interested us more than those of Dr. Frank Lenox or his sister. It will be read and re-read wherever genius and taste have admirers." — *Maine Farmer.*

"This is a simple, but very charming tale of New England manners and opinions, written in the choicest of English, and apparently by a lady. It is very charmingly written, and will amply repay a perusal. Moreover, it is particularly well printed, and got up in the best Boston style." — *British Whig.*

"This is a book well calculated to take strong hold of the reader's mind, and to make there a permanent impression. There are numerous interesting passages and much variety of incidents. Warren's work, 'The Diary of a Physician,' though singularly able, is very monotonous, and the reader gets fatigued before he is half way through it, from its uniform darkness. It is almost invariably night with him, while we have cheerfulness in 'Cora and the Doctor.'" — *Chronicle.*

"There is much of literary refinement and moral culture exhibited in this book; but much of the life of an upright and humane physician, who was earnest in doing good to all. It is full of thrilling incidents, and has already produced a great sensation in literary and religious circles. No man, or woman, or child, can read it without being made better; and it illustrates the thousand opportunities to do good which are open to all, and which afford the highest happiness." — *Barnstable Patriot.*

"It is a book which must be seen and studied to be appreciated; and those who have read it once will read it a second time, as it is worthy a place in any library. The author is yet incognito, and much curiosity is evinced to learn her name. It is a deeply interesting book; and its great usefulness will secure it a large and rapid sale." — *California Farmer.*

VOLUME III.

THE HOUSEHOLD ANGEL IN DISGUISE.

THIS volume, which has just issued from the press, is esteemed by most critics superior to either of the preceding in delineation of character, in graphic power and pathos, and in the unity, depth, and salutariness of the impression which it leaves on the reader. Its design is harmonious with them, being to encourage beneficence, and to secure a closer application of Christianity to domestic life. A glance at the notices of reviewers will confirm this opinion.

"Mrs. Leslie is the daughter of Rev. Dr. Leonard Woods, of Andover, to whose memory this volume is affectionately dedicated. Her tale is one of domestic joys and sorrows, told with great tenderness and feeling. There is nothing forced in the book; the characters, the incidents, and the diction, are all traced naturally and by a master hand. Mrs. Leslie is a lady of refined culture, and a writer who understands well the emotions of the human heart. Our young and enterprising friends, the publishers, are to be congratulated upon the high character of the works they have issued." —*Old Colony Memorial.*

"Mrs. Leslie is a great scholar and eminent author, her style attractive and agreeable, her characters well conceived and presented with much force. Her work shows deep thought, patient and careful study." —*Dollar Newspaper.*

"Of the multitude of fictitious works which have recently issued from the press, we know of none from which we have enjoyed more pleasure. It is a most charming and interesting volume, a capital story of domestic life, written in chaste and glowing language, full of life, spirit, vivacity, and deep pathos. Its heroine is just such a character as we delight to contemplate — loving, lovable, and good. It is full of interest, and a deep religious sentiment pervades its pages, which adds greatly to its value, We have read it with but one regret, viz., that the living faith, the trustful hope, and active benevolence, which characterize several of the author's characters, are not more universally felt and practised." — *Bedford Sentinel.*

"It is consecrated to the promotion of Christian faith and virtue. In a well-written story of unflagging interest, it reveals the design of Providence in placing the Christian in trying relations, and shows the influence which a heart allied to Christ may have in moulding those with whom it is brought in contact." — *Guide to Holiness.*

"Sweet book! pure, lovely, touching! O that such books might be multiplied! We would that all children should read it, and all who are insensible of the value of pure religion. Mrs. Leslie is the daughter of Dr. Leonard Woods. In her dedication she bears a heartfelt testimony to the goodness of her father and the fervor of her love. Shepard, Clark & Co. are advancing among our Boston publishers to a front rank." — *Trumpet; also Portsmouth Journal.*

"A romantic story of great beauty, sound morals, and remarkable interest." — *Boston Herald.*

"A well-written story, pervaded with a high moral aim, and salutary in its influence upon the mind and heart." — *Bangor Daily Journal.*

"It is a beautiful commingling of cultivated taste, exquisite sensibility, and elevated piety — very worthy to be read for its artistic skill and literary grace, but still more for its fine illustration of a highly Christian domestic influence, and the warm, genial spirit which it is fitted to diffuse through the family circle." — *Puritan Recorder.*

"A good story, that cannot fail to exert a salutary, religious influence." — *Watchman and Reflector.*

"Nothing can come from this author's cultivated pen which is not judicious, interesting, instructive, and excellent." — *The Daily Evening Traveller.*

"The author comes of a good lineage, well reputed both for its mental and moral stamina. Her story of domestic life is natural and exciting, her style simple, her sentiments always elevated, and her influence upon young people happy." — *New Bedford Mercury.*

"The wide circulation of this story would send an angel into every household." — *The Evening Transcript.*

"A work of superior character, well planned, gracefully written, and conveying an excellent moral." — *Portfolio.*

"We have already given our opinion in favor of this novel, as a sober, staid work, interesting and instructive. It ought to please the readers of fiction." — *Hartford Daily Courant.*

"Its narrative is rational, its incidents impressive, its sentiments wholesome, and the entire volume attractive." — *Salem Register.*

"A most deeply interesting volume, a charm to the reader." — *Daily Tribune.*

"A wholesome, moral and religious tone is breathed through the book." — *Burlington Free Press.*

"It is written in a beautiful style, and cannot fail of a good impression." — *Advertiser.*

"'The Household Angel' justifies what might have been expected from the lady's antecedent. It is a gracefully written and spirited story. The characters are well discriminated, the plot ingenious, and a healthy vein of morality gives the work an additional charm." —*Evening Gazette.*

"It is a good book, and conveys a pure and Christian lesson. Its style and narrative are simple, and as attractive to the child as the adult." — *Springfield Republican.*

"From a perusal of 'The Household Angel,' we can truly say that it is written in a beautiful style, and contains wholesome truths, which cannot fail of leaving a good impression upon the mind of the reader. The beauty of Mrs. Leslie's style consists in her strict adherence to probabilities which render her writings truthful and natural. We advise any one who wishes to read good reading to purchase this work." — *Gloucester Advertiser.*

"It is well written, in an easy and engaging style, and carries through the story a healthful moral and religious impression." — *Congregational Journal.*

MRS. LESLIE'S JUVENILE SERIES.

We are happy to announce to our patrons, to the trade and the public, a new series of volumes, by the same popular author. They are of a similar character as the other series, and therefore presented under the same general title, but are much more simple and illustrative, being tastefully embellished with plates designed by Billings, and especially adapted to children and youth. We have just issued two volumes of this series, and other volumes are in progress.

"Mrs. Leslie has the freshness, the deep moral feeling, and the picturesque faculty that distinguished the English Mrs. Sherwood, and made her stories so universally popular."

THE MOTHERLESS CHILDREN.

"This book is a story of romance and great interest. The extremes of social life are portrayed in the experience of two orphans, shipwrecked, with their parents, on the New England coast, and adopted by the kindness of the humble residents on the seaboard. They are restored, after many years, to an aristocratic home in Old England, and are left in the enjoyment of wealth and titles, but retain the simplicity and goodness of heart to adorn prosperity." — *Contributor to the New York Express.*

"This is a well-written and deeply interesting story, and shows how good principles implanted in early life can resist the power of temptation in after years." — *Cin. Christian Herald.*

"Those who have read Mrs. Leslie's works will need no further inducement to peruse this one. Her stories are all illustrations of the benefits, in domestic life, of a well-regulated religious household — not the formal religion that checks the best impulses of joyous youth, but the unaffected piety that makes home the most blessed spot on earth." — *Ledger.*

"A very interesting and instructive work of its class, marked with great power and pathos, and showing artistic skill in working up the materials to a high effect. It has a good moral lesson running through it, and will be found a desirable addition to a juvenile or family library." — *Merry's Museum.*

"These books are by a lady well known as a popular writer. Their moral tone is excellent, and their literary merit commendable. Our young friends will find them pleasant and profitable reading." — *Boston Courier.*

"This book and the other volumes of the series are very neatly printed, and embellished with fine engravings. Mrs. Leslie is always a favorite with the juveniles, and her new set will no doubt sell well. All the children should have a copy of these valuable little books; in fact, their library will hardly be complete without." — *The News, Phila.*

"In this interesting story of orphans, the sorrows that sadden the young heart, and the temptations that lead multitudes of youth astray, are thrillingly portrayed; and the lesson, that nothing but Christian culture is a sufficient safeguard against the trials of early life, is well enforced. This pleasant volume has also the merit of being printed in beautiful style, on fine paper, with illustrations." — *Christian Review.*

"This is an interesting story, written in a pleasant style, and filled with wholesome truths." — *Providence Journal.*

"This and the other volumes of the Juvenile Series are from the easy and graceful pen of Mrs. Leslie. (This is her '*nom de plume.*') They are books to be read with much interest and profit by children ten years old and upwards, and also by mothers and teachers. In addition to good stories, she gives out many excellent suggestions, which evince much thought, and no small experience in training the young." — *Boston Recorder.*

"This is a moral tale, with plot, incident, and interest enough to make the reader who begins go through without a halt." — *Morning Chronicle.*

"This series of finely-written stories for children and youth are specially adapted to holiday presents. This volume is a story of orphanage, illustrating the trials and temptations of the young, and the happy results of Christian nurture." — *R. I. Schoolmaster.*

"This is a story of orphanage, illustrating the trials and temptations of the young, and the happy results of Christian nurture." — *Salem Register.*

"This and other volumes of the series, are beautifully got up and finely illustrated. Parents and others in search of an appropriate gift can do no better than to purchase these volumes." — *Gloucester Advertiser.*

"The books of this series are by Mrs. Leslie, whose works are so popular with readers of all classes. They are neatly printed, and will be warmly welcomed and highly prized by young people." — *Boston Evening Transcript.*

"The books cannot fail to interest young people, and indeed may be read by all with profit." — *The Myrtle.*

"This is one of a neat and attractive set of volumes, under the title of Mrs. Leslie's Juvenile Series. We have read it with much pleasure, and find it adapted to interest, instruct, and improve our youth. The whole series will be a most valuable addition to our juvenile literature."— *Maine Temperance Journal.*

"Mrs. Leslie is favorably known to the public as the author of many valuable works, and the editor of a religious magazine. This is the first volume of her Juvenile Series, beautifully got up in all respects, and destined to become very popular with the young people. She is evidently a warm lover of children, a nice observer of their character and taste." — *New Bedford Mercury.*

PLAY AND STUDY.

"This volume of Mrs. Leslie's Juvenile Series is an elegantly printed volume, showing, in an ingeniously wrought tale, the benefit of combining instruction with amusement in schools, and the method by which recreation may be made to stimulate a taste for study, as well as to relieve mental toil. The advantageous working of a judicious system is exemplified in the history of a school, and the characters of the excellent teachers are drawn to life." — *Cor. to N. Y. Express.*

"This is an interesting tale of school days, very suggestive of practical hints to parents and teachers, showing how they may aid their children and pupils in the invention of their own amusements for their relief and stimulus in study." — *R. I. Schoolmaster.*

"This, together with the other volumes of Mrs. Leslie's Juvenile Series, is a story such as a parent need not fear for a moment to put into the hands of his children. To the children themselves these books will prove most acceptable presents; and we predict for them a general popularity." — *Boston Gazette.*

"This is an account of the school life of some little boys and girls. It tells how they were interested in their studies by wise and kind teachers. It describes their sports and their progress in knowledge, and the development of their characters. It is a delightful book, and will be particularly charming and useful to school boys and girls. If the succeeding volumes are similar in style and spirit, the series will be an excellent one for holiday gifts." — *Cin. Christian Herald.*

"This and Mrs. Leslie's other books for children and youth are well written, interesting and instructive, of high moral aim, and cannot fail of becoming popular with young readers, especially as they are handsomely illustrated." — *Youth's Companion.*

"This volume is a tale of school days, showing how children should be managed, and inculcating in a pleasant way many valuable lessons for both young and old." — *N. E. Farmer.*

"This is an agreeable portraiture of school days, and imbodies practical and useful hints to teachers and parents. It shows how a wise system of management at home and at school may turn hours of recreation to account as an aid to study, instead of being the greatest hinderance to all improvement." — *Christian Review.*

"We have read this book with much satisfaction. The author is evidently familiar with excellent methods of school discipline, and shows that she understands human nature, can discover the latent qualities of different minds, and draw them out so as to give the most wise and efficient direction to the powers essential for success and usefulness." — *Christian Register.*

"The spirit that pervades this, and other books of this series, and the lessons they teach, will surely be of advantage to the little folks." — *N. Y. Chronicle.*

"This book is admirably adapted to its purpose of interesting and instructing the young. The lessons of moral conduct and behavior at school, at play, and in the household, are excellent; and the truthful description of scenes of real life is obvious on every page. It is rare to meet with a more perfect command of the language, way, humors, and caprice of childhood, while the methods of school and home education, here set forth, will be suggestive to the minds of more mature readers. The plates and typography are also excellent." — *N. Y. Evangelist.*

"Under the guise of an interesting story, some excellent lessons on the nature and necessity of both study and recreation are inculcated in this volume. It is a book deserving of extensive circulation — embellished with good engravings." — *Zion's Herald.*

"This forms one of Mrs. Leslie's Juvenile Series. It is a production of much merit, a pleasing story." —*Boston Traveller.*

"Mrs. Leslie's Juvenile Series will be welcomed by all the children." — *Springfield Republican.*

THE PARLOR LIBRARY.

TWELVE VOLUMES.

LIVES OF EMINENT MEN. Part I.
Containing Sketches of George Washington, Thomas Jefferson, John Adams, James Madison, James Monroe, Walter Scott, Mungo Park, Captain Cook, General Putnam, William Penn, General Joseph Warren, Daniel Boone, and others.......... 37½

LIVES OF EMINENT MEN. Part II.
Containing Sketches of Andrew Jackson, Duke of Wellington, Patrick Henry, John Hancock, Lafayette, and others......... 37½

THE HELPLESS ORPHANS,
AND OTHER TALES. Comprising Poor Little Lucy, New Flittertigibbet, Girls I have known, Dapple and his Friends, The Village Florist, etc.................................. 37½

TALES FOR THE TIMES,
Containing The Lame Pig, The Magic Spinning Wheel, Rill from the Town Pump, Too Handsome for anything, The Good-Natured Couple, etc., etc................................ 37½

HUMORIST'S TALES,
Containing The Bashful Man, Jim Doolivan, Mrs. Bullfrog, The Bold Eagle, The Haunted Quack, the Captain's Lady, Yellow Domino, etc.................................... 37½

THE FLOWER BASKET,
Containing The New Year's Day, Sketches beneath an Umbrella, The Legacy Hunter, The Haunted Maid, The Dream Fulfilled, The Love Match, The Man with a ———, etc................ 37½

WEALTH AND FASHION,
Containing The Two Coats, Passages in the Life of an Old Maid, My Friend Plum, The Broken Miniature, The Mysterious Correspondent, The Blind Boy, The Bank Note, etc............ 37½

FAIRY TALES,
Comprising The Storm Lights of Anzuska, The Iron Shroud, The Rotch of the Candle, The Sisters, The Comet, The Legend of Bethel Rock.. 37½

THE DROWNED FISHERMAN,
AND OTHER INTERESTING STORIES FOR THE YOUNG. 37½

THE OLD HALL,
Containing The Night Alarm, The Tapestried Chamber, The Land's End of Cornwall, The Necromancer, Bernard the Decore, The Piedmontese Courier, etc............................ 37½

THE ROSE BUD,
A Collection of Short Stories, among which are, The Young Minister and his Bride, The Parting Kiss, Love in the Olden Time, The Muffled Priest, Lover's Recompense, etc................. 37½

THE GARLAND,
Containing many short Sketches and Poems, designed as a Holiday and Birthday Present for Little Children.......... 37½

www.ingramcontent.com/pod-product-compliance
Lightning Source LLC
LaVergne TN
LVHW021317110826
845150LV00003B/600

* 9 7 8 1 4 2 5 5 5 7 4 6 1 *